COLLEGE OF
SHADOWS

CAMBRIDGE GOTHIC
STARTER LIBRARY

Get three exclusive short stories FOR FREE.

Sign up for the no-spam newsletter and get

COME OUT TO PLAY

A LATE ARRIVAL

A POISONED CHALICE

plus more exclusive content, all for free.

Details can be found at the end of COLLEGE OF
SHADOWS.

COLLEGE OF SHADOWS

CAMBRIDGE GOTHIC – BOOK 1

Mark Wells

A CAMBRIDGE TALES BOOK

First published in Great Britain in 2019 by Cambridge Tales Ltd
Copyright © Mark Wells 2019
Map of St John's College reproduced under licence from Jeremy
Bays
Copyright ©Jeremy Bays 2019, www.art-work-shop.co.uk

A catalogue record for this book is available from the British
Library.
ISBN 978-1-9160284-0-1
Formatting by Polgarus Studio

Cambridge Tales Ltd
115c Milton Road
Cambridge CB4 1XE
www.marknwells.com

To Karina, Michael, Thomas and Dad.
Thank you for your patience and support.

To St John's College for inspiring me to pursue my
dreams.

A note for readers

*An interactive map of St John's College with the locations
featured in this story is available to view on my website:*

www.marknwells.com

Prologue

Alfonso stepped out of the humid kitchen into the panelled wood corridor that linked the First and Second Courts of St John's College. He shivered as cold air whispered through the ancient passageway and ruffled his dark hair. Burying his chin into the thin leather jacket, Alfonso hunched his shoulders in an attempt to shield himself from the chill. Not for the first time, he regretted bringing little in the way of winter clothing for his summer in England.

"*Que frio!*" he said, his breath visible as it condensed in front of him.

"Not talking to yourself, Alfie, are you mate?" said the girl who followed him out of the kitchen. She was wrapped in a thick North Face parka and had a pink beanie pulled down tight over peroxide-blonde hair.

"No talk, Jane. Cold," said Alfonso.

"That's good, 'cos people will think you're funny if you go doing that sort of thing."

"Funny ha-ha, or funny crazy?"

"Well, I know you're crazy to come to rubbish old

England when you could be on a beach right now."

"Now? In Mallorca? Is after midnight," said Alfonso. "The people is in the street. Restaurants full."

"Not partying and drinking tequilas then?"

He shrugged. "*Sí*, maybe."

"Yeah, that's what I mean. Why come to dozy old Cambridge, when you could be somewhere warm having a great time!"

"I think also," said Alfonso. "But is good money here."

"Yeah, right," Jane snorted. "So, are you coming then or what? Only it's flipping freezing here."

Alfonso dug his hands in the pockets of his coat and nodded.

They filed out of the passageway and down the stone ramp into First Court, Jane's high heels clicking on the ancient paving stones like castanets. Ahead of them, Alfonso could make out the college's Great Gate, illuminated by the glow of lights from the Porter's Lodge.

Alfonso had enrolled at St John's as a waiter at the start of the summer, tipped off by his older sister that Cambridge colleges were always on the lookout for serving staff during the conference season. Alfonso remembered walking into the sixteenth-century dining hall on his first night and seeing the tables laid out in silver, candles flickering beneath the gilt-embossed ceiling as the throng of guests filed in. Since then he had barely had a night off.

"You should come clubbing with me," said Jane as they crossed the silent court. "My brothers work the doors at Vodka Revs, and they can get us in for free."

"Your brothers make doors?"

Jane looked at him. "No, Alfie. They are bouncers."

He had no idea what she meant by this.

"Guards," she said, trying again. "They guard the doors in case there's any trouble."

"Oh, they are strong then, your brothers?"

"They like to think so," said Jane, "but I'm their big sister, and they don't mess with me." She raised her mittened fists like a boxer. "I've been taking them to the gym for years. I used to go with my dad. We fought a lot, him and me."

"I am sorry," he said.

"Not like that, you idiot! Kickboxing, Alfie. Lots of girls do it now. Any boy gives me trouble, and I give him a good one between the legs. Sorted!" She twisted and faked a knee towards Alfonso, who instinctively dropped his hands to protect his vitals. Jane laughed.

"Don't worry, Alfie," she said. "You're all right. It's the English lads you've got to watch."

"The Spanish boys too, I think," said Alfonso, straightening up.

"I'll take your word for it," she said.

They continued walking towards the gatehouse on the far side of the court, Alfonso keeping a little more distance between them now. They stopped in the archway of the Great Gate, and Jane shielded herself from the entrance to the Porter's Lodge to reach inside her parka. From a pocket, she drew out a hip flask, unscrewed the top and offered it to him. Alfonso sniffed and smelt the rich aroma of college port. He shook his head. She shrugged, taking a swig before

3

producing a bunch of grapes from another pocket and offering him those instead. He recognised them from the silver fruit bowls laid out at the end of the feast. He looked towards the lodge before placing them inside his jacket, careful not to crush them. Jane stuffed the flask back into her parka pocket and winked.

The two conspirators entered the lodge and were greeted by a grey-haired night porter with a clipped military moustache who looked up from a copy of the *Cambridge News*.

"Evening, Jane. Finished for the night, have we?" he asked.

"Finished here, Bert, but the night is still young," she said.

"For the night shift, maybe," said Bert. "Not you, young lady. You should be getting home. You may have your looks right now, but too much partying and you'll end up like my Sue."

"I bet your Sue's lovely, Bert," said Jane. "If I ever meet her, I'll tell her you said that."

"She's said worse about me," said the porter before turning to Alfonso, who was rubbing his hands, enjoying the warmth of the lodge. "You're knocking off too, Mr Vidal?"

"No, sir, I go home."

Jane laughed. "That's what he means, silly."

Smiling, she turned to the porter.

"Yeah, we're the last ones, Bert. Me and Alfie here. So, open up the front gate, will you, 'cos you're keeping us from our night out."

"All right, young lady, just don't say I didn't warn you. Once those wrinkles start, no iron in the world's going to smooth them out."

"That'll be years from now," she said. "Besides, I'll have married some rich student by then."

The porter shook his head and reached for an enormous set of keys from somewhere under the counter. Checking the security cameras to make sure the street was clear, he led them out of the lodge and unlocked the wicket door in the Main Gate.

"Thank you, Bert," said Jane as she passed through.

"Thank you, sir," said Alfonso, ducking his head to follow her.

"Goodnight, Jane. And you, Mr Vidal," said Bert. "Mind how you go."

"His name's Alfie," said Jane, but her protest was lost in the squeal of hinges as the heavy door swung to with a thud. Alfonso heard the old iron lock rattle, followed by footsteps as the old porter retreated to the warmth of the lodge.

Jane pulled out a pack of cigarettes and offered him one.

At that moment he felt the phone in his trouser pocket vibrate and he shook his head as he removed it and stared at the Nokia's screen. It was a text from his sister in Catalan.

Call me. We have a problem.

He looked at the message, then at Jane, who had removed her gloves and was cupping her hands to light her cigarette. She inhaled deeply and blew out a long stream of smoke.

"Well, are you coming then or what?" she asked, jerking

5

a thumb towards the centre of town.

"I am good, Jane, thank you," said Alfonso.

Her eyes lingered on him for a moment through the plume of smoke. Then she shrugged.

"Well, be good, Alfie," she said, turning and clacking her way along Trinity Street towards King's Parade.

"Goodnight, Jane!" he called after her.

She raised a hand in acknowledgement, the cigarette glowing red in the dark, and headed off to meet her brothers.

Alfonso stood there and watched her go, reflecting on the fact he had just turned down the best offer he had had since coming to Cambridge. Jane had barely spoken to him before this evening, working her shifts without so much as a glance in his direction. He wasn't looking for a relationship, far from it, but he found her disinterest intriguing. Watching how she handled herself, it was clear she took no shit from anyone, least of all the chef, who had tried and failed on more than one occasion to intimidate her. She was also smart enough to do her job well, which meant that, like him, their names were always first on the roster for the lucrative conference dinners. Jane was an independent spirit, and that was something he could appreciate.

Alfonso's family were Catalan, and their parents had belonged to a Catalan nationalist organisation, which had been disbanded in the 1990s following a string of terrorist attacks that had led to their father being arrested on suspicion of being involved. The family moved to Mallorca, and Alfonso and his sister were there in 2017 to witness the brutal suppression of the Catalan independence elections by

6

the centrist government in Madrid.

It was during this period that the Catalan nationalists had reformed and, given their family's history, it was perhaps inevitable that the Vidal siblings would be recruited. Alfonso's sister, Raquel, had risen to a senior position in the newly formed cell and she had posted him to Cambridge, the cyber-tech capital of Europe, after he completed his master's in artificial intelligence. Here he had enrolled in a language course to improve his English, before applying for internships at some of the new AI start-ups operating in the cyber security sector. Which was why Raquel's text message had alarmed him and caused him to turn down Jane's offer. His cell leader needed to speak with him.

The wind ruffled the collar of his jacket as Alfonso scrolled through his phone for his sister's secure number and dialled. As he lifted the phone to his ear, he caught sight of movement in the little square opposite the entrance to St John's. Wondering if Jane was playing some sort of trick on him, Alfonso glanced down Trinity Street. In the distance, he could just make out her hunched profile, disappearing around the bend in the road.

"*Sí?*" his sister's voice broke the silence.

"It's me," he replied in Catalan, turning and scanning the square with its railings and assortment of trees for more movement. Nothing stirred.

"I thought you should know that we have had a problem with the fruit harvest." Raquel spoke slowly, but he could hear the tension in her voice.

"The fruit harvest?" he repeated, confirming she meant

7

the recruitment of new members to the cell.

"Yes. Sadly, some were affected by worms, and we had to remove them."

"Remove them?"

"They had burrowed deep, and we didn't want them to ruin the rest of the crop."

"How deep?"

"To the core in some cases."

Alfonso felt a chill that had nothing to do with the wind. He looked across the street to the little square and decided it was time to head home.

"Are you still there?" his sister asked.

"I'm moving," he said, turning away from town and heading past the college's chapel rising up on his left-hand side, its tall tower dwarfing the surrounding buildings. "It's probably time for me to move to new accommodation."

"That would be wise," said Raquel. "I think the weather may have turned."

Alfonso heard a noise behind him and looked over his shoulder. The scuff of a shoe, perhaps? He quickly scanned the row of shops in front of the college for movement. His senses told him that he was being watched, but he could not say from where.

"I think you may be right," he said into the phone. "I will have to call you in a few days when I have found somewhere new."

"Understood," she said. "Take care, brother."

"I will, sister. And *gracias*."

The line went dead.

Squaring his shoulders, Alfonso began to walk faster now, turning left into Bridge Street and crossing to the broad pavement on the far side of the road. He hurried past the row of restaurants and pubs, all closed, their tables empty. Up ahead he could just make out the turning into Portugal Place, the narrow lane that led down to Jesus Green. From there it was only a short walk to the footbridge that crossed the river and led to his lodgings on Chesterton Road. This was his usual route home, but when Alfonso reached the corner and peered into the alleyway, he hesitated.

The lane ran between St Clement's Church on the left and a row of terraced cottages opposite. The passageway was poorly lit with an old-fashioned streetlight that cast a dim glow on the meandering gap between the buildings. Alfonso had walked home this way many times, but tonight it looked darker and more forbidding than he remembered.

A gust of cold wind settled the matter. His ears were freezing, and the sooner he got back home, the better. Pulling his collar up around his neck, Alfonso headed into Portugal Place. The tightly packed buildings sheltered him from the wind, and he was glad of their protection.

"Is nothing to fear," he said.

"I'm not so sure about that," said a deep voice behind him.

Alfonso spun around and looked up as a shadow loomed over him. He began to scream.

"*Mare de Dieu!*"

But his voice was drowned in the shrieking of the wind

that swept through the narrow lane like a freight train. It rattled the bikes that were chained to the church railings and scattered discarded beer bottles across the paving stones.

After a few moments, the whistling of the wind subsided, replaced by the forlorn tinkling sound of an overturned bottle that rolled down the lane, bouncing over the cracks in the paving stones, before finally coming to rest with a clink in the gutter. Silence descended on Portugal Place, which remained empty and still. Throughout its meandering length, there was no trace of Alfonso Vidal. No indication whatsoever that he had walked that way. None save for an assortment of grapes, which lay crushed and discarded across the flagstones.

Chapter 1

"Nick! Get a move on!" yelled his father from the bottom of the stairs.

"Coming!" called back the tall, sandy-haired boy. But he remained motionless, staring out the window of his bedroom at the familiar rows of Victorian terraced houses with their soot-stained chimney pots and dark slate roofs for the last time. In the 18 years that Nick had lived in this house, this view had barely changed. The occasional Sky dish might have been added or set of curtains changed, but his hometown of Mansfield had stubbornly refused to transform itself and had settled into a sad, urban decline, surrounded by the slag heaps of its former glory. A decline he hoped to escape from today.

Nick turned from the window and stared at the suit he and his mum had bought from ASDA the day before. It lay on his bed next to a large kitbag filled with the rest of his clothes. He wasn't sure how to fold a suit, and after a couple of attempts he gave up and stuffed it on top of his sports kit.

"Have you got a tie?"

He looked up and saw his mum, tattooed arms folded,

watching him from the doorway. She was wearing her catering uniform from the local comprehensive school, where she worked preparing and serving food to the vast majority of pupils whose family income entitled them to free school meals. Pupils like him and his younger brother, Charlie.

"Not yet," he said and went over to the wardrobe. As far as ties were concerned, there weren't many choices. Ignoring his frayed and soiled school one, he picked his rugby club tie, which was, for the most part, clean despite the antics his teammates got up to after matches. Nick had played for Paviours RFC since he was seven years old, developing as a player and a person under coaches who were all ex-miners and knew a thing or two about managing young men. In the claustrophobic and dangerous world they had worked in, thousands of feet below the misty Nottinghamshire countryside, new starters did what they were told and did it correctly. Anyone who didn't listen was put through a fitness drill they wouldn't forget in a hurry. Those hardened veterans of the pits had taken the same no-nonsense approach to coaching the juniors at the club. At Paviours Nick had learned to play hard, uncompromising rugby, doing the basics well and never taking a step back. It wasn't always pretty, but they won more games than they lost. But after the game, win or lose, the coaches insisted they all wear a white shirt and tie for post-match tea and woe betide anyone who turned up without.

Nick fingered the cheap polyester material, worn shiny in places, and turned back to his kitbag, where he found his mother refolding the suit jacket and placing it carefully on top of his other clothes.

"Thanks, Mum," he said, offering her the tie.

The next thing he knew, her face was buried in his chest, and her strong arms were wrapped around him, squeezing him with surprising strength. Nick waited for her to say something, but she was silent. They merely stood like that for a while, his tall frame and her rotund figure filling the cramped bedroom, neither saying a word. Eventually, her grip eased, and she let him go. Nick looked down and saw her eyes were moist with tears.

"We are so proud of you," she said, her voice thick with emotion. "You know that, don't you?"

"Yeah, I suppose," he said, embarrassed but unable to look away from her fierce stare.

"Me, Charlie, your dad too. He's dead proud. Wouldn't ever say it, mind you, but I know it for a fact."

She was right. Nick's father wouldn't ever say it. Since the mine had closed, his dad said very little. As if expressing his thoughts would give people the opportunity to take something else away from him.

"You're the first, Nick," continued his mother, "first one in our family to go to university. You know that, don't you."

"You've told me, yeah," he replied, thinking, *Pretty much every day since the offer came through.*

"Charlie will be the next now. I can see it in him. Since you've done so well. You going to university is the best thing that could've happened to him."

"I suppose."

13

Nick thought of his brother. Charlie was three years younger than him and would be sitting his GCSEs this year. Physically, Charlie took more after his mother, being short and stocky with mousy brown hair. He was something of a joker at school, using humour to deflect jibes about his weight. But if a bully took his quick wit the wrong way, Charlie could also end up with a bloody lip, which Nick could do little about.

"Who did it, Charlie?" Nick would seethe on seeing him return home, his face bruised and his eyes red from crying.

"Nobody."

"What do you mean?"

"I don't want you getting involved, you'll only make things worse."

"So, this git is just going to get away with it, is he?"

"Just leave it. It's not important. I'll be more careful next time."

"How, exactly?"

"Next time he asks why I'm so fat, I won't tell him it's because his mum gives me a biscuit every time I kiss her."

Nick smiled at the memory but had known Charlie was right. Much as he would have loved to confront the bullies and settle a few scores on behalf of his brother, he knew the consequences for Charlie would have been dire. As he looked down at the shining eyes of his mother, he thought, not for the first time, that her admiration for his achievements was misplaced. It was his brother who was the real hero in this household. Charlie, the short, fat, spotty kid, who headed out the door each day to face another eight hours of torment in the cruel and unforgiving crucible of school. That was true courage.

And now, to make matters worse, Charlie would have to live in the shadow of an older brother who had done the unimaginable and was going off to take up his place at Cambridge to study law. That, Nick knew, was not going to make Charlie's life any easier. But he couldn't say that to his mother. She had invested so much of herself in his achievement. For her, it was like an acknowledgement of all that she had done to keep the family together after the closure of the pit and her husband's humiliating decline into anger and despondency. Her son's place at Cambridge, to her, was like a beacon of light in the darkness that had engulfed this whole community.

"Do us proud, Nick. Not just your family. Do it for all of us from around here."

"I will," he said. *No pressure, then.*

"You two coming or what!" yelled his father from downstairs.

"Just coming, love!" she called down.

"'Bout bloody time. Haven't got all day!"

Nick's mum smiled at him, wiping her damp cheeks with the back of her hands.

"Don't mind him. And don't you go using any of your dad's language. There's no need for that where you're going. Be polite and respectful. How you behave matters in this world, no matter where you come from."

"Will you two get a move on?" came his father's voice from downstairs.

"And will you stop shouting!" yelled back his mother, the colour rising in her cheeks. "He's on his bloody way!"

She looked up at Nick, her face flushed.

"I'll go and see to him," she said. "You know. To give you a moment."

As she clumped down the stairs, Nick slung his backpack over his shoulder and hefted the heavy kitbag. He looked around the room, the rugby posters on the walls and cheap plastic trophies on the shelves. The sagging bed and half-empty wardrobe. The desk.

How many hours had he spent at that desk? Its worn Formica top had been home to his toys, then comics, homework, textbooks and finally his A-level revision notes. Now it was empty. Save for the cards.

They had started arriving after his A-level results. No one in his school had got A*s before. Nor to his knowledge had anyone even applied for, let alone won, a place at Oxbridge. The thought of doing so had not crossed Nick's mind until last year, when a group of students from St John's College had visited his school as part of Cambridge University's outreach programme. He had gone along with his mates for a bit of a laugh, knowing his family wouldn't be able to afford him or his brother going to university anyway. But one of the Cambridge students, a girl from a South East London comprehensive, described how she had been awarded a full bursary by St John's, covering all her costs for the three years of her degree. Nick realised he wasn't going to get a better deal anywhere, so decided there was no harm in sending in an application. What did he have to lose, after all?

In October, when he had been invited for an interview, his first thought was that someone was playing a practical joke. But after his school confirmed the invitation was genuine, he was given permission to take a couple of days off in December to travel down to Cambridge for the interviews. Naturally, his friends gave him some stick, saying no one would understand his accent and he was only there to carry coal for the fires. But when he got there, the people he met turned out to be friendly enough. One of the professors, a good-natured old Scot with a splayed nose and twinkling green eyes, even used to play rugby, which got the conversation off to a good start.

Because Nick had decided to apply to read Law, something he hadn't studied at A-level, the questions at the interview were less about what he knew and more about how he would deal with different contractual situations involving a commuter trying to get to an important meeting in London. Nick didn't have a clue what the actual legal position was and just used common sense. When, after Christmas, the conditional offer arrived in the post, he couldn't quite believe it. Nor could his parents. His mother burst into tears, which was not unexpected. But even his father showed some appreciation for once: "Bugger me, son!", which for him was high praise indeed.

As for Charlie, he punched the air and ran around the kitchen table, his T-shirt over his head, muffling his excited yells, and his belly wobbling as he bumped into chairs and bounced off the cupboards.

At school, the staffroom went into overdrive, organising

extra tuition and revision classes, which Nick agreed to grudgingly, embarrassed by all the attention. These extra lessons often meant he was late for rugby practice, much to the annoyance of his coaches and the derision of his teammates, some of whom started speaking in posh accents during training.

"I say, Nick darling, pass me the ball, would you please?"

"Careful when you tackle, Nick dear, we don't want you damaging that enormous brain you have."

"Jolly good try Nick, old boy. Top show!"

Nick had tried to laugh it off, but he couldn't help noticing that his relationship with his friends had begun to change. They didn't hang out with him as much as before, and he found he was getting fewer texts or messages from them as the year went on. Not that he had any time to respond, given the amount of work his teachers were giving him. But it bothered him that his friends might think the offer from Cambridge had made him different somehow.

Any worries he had on that score all evaporated the day that A-level results were announced. It was like a dam had burst. His phone and Facebook accounts went mad with messages, emojis and GIFs. Then came the cards, from teachers, coaches, aunts and uncles, even people he barely knew. It was as if they had all been holding their breath for him.

Then the local papers got hold of the story, his picture making their front pages.

Star pupil wins place at Cambridge was one headline. *A star in the making* said another.

Needless to say, the name stuck. Even staff at the local chippy started calling him "Star Boy." Everyone, that is, except his dad, who called him just the same as he had always done.

"Son!" came his father's voice from downstairs, the warning clear.

"OK, Dad, I'm coming!"

Nick gave the room one last look and, heaving the bag up on his shoulder, headed for the stairs.

*****

Annabel stared out the window of the train at the flat landscape. The crops of wheat and barley had long been harvested. Now green tractors were ploughing up the soil, transforming the exhausted expanse of yellow stubble into fields of corrugated brown ridges, ready for a new cycle of planting, nurturing, growing and dying.

"A penny for your thoughts?"

Annabel turned and saw her gran sitting diagonally opposite her on the other side of the narrow table that separated the two sets of seats facing each other in the train compartment. The old woman was peering at her over a pair of reading glasses, her trusty Parker biro poised over the neatly folded copy of *The Times*, the crossword already half completed. Annabel knew that while those black button eyes might now struggle with the print of a newspaper, they didn't miss much when it came to observing people.

"Just looking at the harvest," she said, the smile coming from muscle memory as she searched for those elusive feelings of happiness to give it some meaning. They had withdrawn for the moment, and despite all the techniques her counsellor had taught her, it still took some effort of will to find them.

"I expect the farmers would be planting about now," said her gran, glancing out the window. "It's that time of year."

"Oh, yes, that's what I mean," said Annabel, following her gaze, relieved to break eye contact while she continued her search for those happy thoughts that she used to anchor herself in the here and now.

"As children, we loved harvest time," continued her gran. "We used to climb on top of the hay bales and watch the swallows flying overhead, twisting and turning this way and that. Beautiful little things, they were. I used to think it was remarkable they had travelled all the way back from South Africa and still had the energy to dance and pirouette above us."

Annabel remembered seeing the swallows too, over their home in Godalming, flitting in and out of the semi-circular nests tucked into the eaves of the tiled roof. Her smile spread as she finally located some happiness associated with that memory, recalling the sights and sounds of those fantastic creatures that had always fascinated her.

"They'll probably be on their way back there now," she said, thinking about the swallow's eye view of the Maasai Mara game reserve that she and her sister had enjoyed from the window of the small plane the summer before. It was the first time that her family had visited Africa, a reward for Serena's A-level results and her place at Balliol College, Oxford, to read English.

The two sisters had always dreamed of visiting Africa, Annabel because of the wildlife that had fascinated her since a child, while for her older sister it was the thought of walking in the epic landscapes of Hemingway and Conrad. Annabel remembered stepping out of the plane on the little airstrip near the lodge and grabbing her sister's arm in excitement as they were assaulted by the earthy smells and the fierce heat of a world that they had both longed to experience. It was one of the happiest moments of her life, the four of them together, sharing a magical holiday as a family. Their last holiday together, as it turned out.

Annabel looked out of the train's window at the sky, which was now empty of birds, the only movement visible coming from a bank of dark grey rainclouds that seemed to be tracking the train's progress as it sped along the line from London to Cambridge.

"Annabel?"

She turned and saw her grandmother looking at her.

"Sorry, Gran, I drifted off there for a moment."

"I was saying that perhaps you can learn more about them. Those swallows, I mean. How such tiny creatures can fly all the way to Africa and still find their way back to the same nesting location each year."

"I'm not sure it's something we cover in the first year, Gran," said Annabel, thinking about the details of her Natural Sciences Tripos, which the university had sent her after her place had been confirmed. "I think we might study animal behaviour at some point. Maybe there are some journals in the library I can look at."

"Well, only if you have time," said her Gran, turning back to her crossword. "I expect you will have more than enough to read without…" She paused and frowned.

"What is it, Gran?"

"Of course!" The old woman's face lit up as she leant forward, clicked the pen and began filling in a clue.

"Got another one?" asked Annabel.

"With your help, my dear. Quite a good one too. Five across, nine letters. *Russian fighter, limited food, looking for pastures new.*"

She stared at Annabel, eyebrows raised.

"Hmm," said Annabel, thinking. "Something to do with swallows?"

"Possibly."

Annabel ran through what they had just been talking about, trying to find an appropriate link.

"Flying, travelling, wandering…" she mumbled, then, a light bulb went on. "Migrating!"

"Almost. Think about *limited food*."

Annabel frowned, disappointed that her first attempt hadn't been right. She ran over her initial answer, playing with the letters in her head.

"Migration!" she said. "MIG is a Russian fighter plane. Ration, the limited food. Together you have 'migration' or finding pastures new."

"That's my girl!" Her grandmother sighed. "I don't know what I'm going to do while you're up here and I'm trying to do this on my own."

"If you get stuck, you can always text me."

The old woman peered over her glasses, doubtfully.

"Or call?" said Annabel.

"That I might do," she said, looking past Annabel out the window. "Looks like we are nearly there. Best get our things!"

Annabel turned and saw an assortment of buildings come into view. She felt the train begin to slow as the countryside receded to be replaced by functional-looking housing developments in pale yellow brick, and larger high-tech buildings, many still under construction.

"Looks like a lot of building work is going on," she said.

"That will be the new medical campus near the hospital, no doubt," said her grandmother, who, Annabel remembered, was a former nurse. "I've been reading about it. All sorts of high-tech companies have been set up here, apparently, attracted by the research possibilities."

"Makes sense, I suppose," said Annabel, standing up and staring out at the collection of cranes, gathered around the assortment of buildings. They looked like lopsided scarecrows, their red hazard lights blinking out a warning against the background of ominous dark clouds.

"We might need to organise a taxi, Gran," she said. "Looks like a storm's brewing."

*****

Thunder rolled over St John's College, rattling the leaded windows, lightning briefly illuminating their multifaceted panes. Heavy rain flushed torrents of water and early autumn leaves from the gargoyles guarding the rooftops and

23

towers. The buildings suffered this battering in silence, offering sanctuary to the latest infusion of new blood that poured into the college from all over the world.

Nick stood in the shelter of the covered passageway by the Cripps Porter's Lodge at the back of the college and watched as his father's white van edged out of the car park by the punt pool. He was not sure if his dad could see him through the rain, or whether he was even looking. When the red van lights had disappeared into the gloom, he looked around at the organised chaos of the car park.

Beneath umbrellas and waterproofs, mums were carrying lampshades and flower pots, dads were huffing and puffing with large suitcases and kitbags, and siblings were milling around, looking confused or getting in the way. And weaving amidst them all were the other freshers.

Nick considered them. Some were chatting and laughing with friends or siblings. Others were focused on the task at hand, diligently carrying their carefully assembled possessions off to their allotted rooms. There were the nervous ones, eyes darting around anxiously, and those who looked entirely at ease, as if they had grown up here. Nick stared at them all and wondered if any felt like him. An impostor.

His thoughts were disturbed by a hesitant voice behind him.

"Sorry, could I trouble you? Where is A Staircase, Cripps?"

Nick turned and saw a small, elderly woman with short grey hair, wrapped in a sturdy waterproof cape. She was holding an assortment of shopping bags, each bulging with

24

clothing and seemingly about to collapse.

"Here, let me help you with those," he said and reached forward to relieve the old lady of her burden.

"Thank you so much," she said, smiling her gratitude. "Annabel rushed off to get her room key and told me she was on A Staircase, Cripps."

"No problem," said Nick. "I'm on that staircase. I'll show you. It's just over there." He nodded towards a structure that looked like a three-storey shoe box on stilts overlooking the river. "I'm Nick, by the way."

"Nice to meet you, Nick. I'm Mrs Hamilton, Annabel's grandmother. Sorry to trouble you."

"No bother. I got here earlier. I'm all packed away."

He led her along the crowded walkway that ran beneath Cripps Court, the 1960s habitation block in which he and most of the freshers had their rooms. The squat, brutalist architecture had been a shock when he saw it for the first time. He had been expecting something more traditional, like the neighbouring New Court. But once he was inside his spacious room with its views over the river, his spirits picked up. It was twice the size of his bedroom at home, and rather than grimy rooftops, he looked out onto the grass-covered court with the Fisher Building in the distance.

"Coming through," warned Nick as he navigated past cases and boxes being unloaded with varying degrees of success by agitated, sweating owners. A Staircase was the furthest one from the Cripps car park, and by the time they reached its entrance, the two of them were on their own. Nick paused at the bottom of the steps and studied a room index set into the wall. On it, the numbers of each room had the name of the occupant and an "IN/OUT" indicator alongside.

"There you go, Mrs Hamilton," he said, indicating the sign with a nod of his head. "Which one are you?"

The old woman peered at the names. "There she is. A24, A. V. Hamilton. Oh!" She paused for a moment, a look of doubt on her face. "She appears to be OUT."

"Probably hasn't changed the sign." He switched it to IN. "Shall we?"

"Yes, let's!" said the elderly lady.

She set off up the stairs at a steady pace with Nick following a few feet behind. At the first landing, they met a black boy who observed them without a word. Mrs Hamilton said, "Good morning," before heading up the next flight.

"Excuse us," said Nick, to which the boy replied, "No problem," with an unmistakable Yorkshire accent.

They passed a family on the next landing who were arguing over where they should have lunch.

"We have a choice," said the mother. "The Copper Kettle or Fitzbillies."

"If it's a Chelsea bun you want, it HAS to be Fitzbillies," said the father authoritatively. He wore a faded college tie, Nick noticed.

When they reached the last staircase, Mrs Hamilton's steady progress was momentarily stopped by a yell from the top landing.

"Gran! There you are! I thought you must have got lost."

"Well, I probably would have got lost had it not been for Nick," said the old woman breathlessly as she put her head down and carried on up the final steps with newfound resolve.

"Gran, you didn't get a porter, did you? People will think I'm some sort of royalty."

"Nick is not a porter and you, my dear, are not OUT but IN."

"In what?" came the reply.

"Nick will explain. Now, where's your room? Ah, there!" Mrs Hamilton disappeared from view as Nick trudged up the stairs after her.

He reached the top and stopped when he caught sight of the girl waiting on the landing. She was small, with dark brown hair tied back in a ponytail, wearing a hoodie with the words *Leavers 2020* emblazoned across it. Dragging his eyes away from her chest, he found the girl staring back at him with a quizzical expression on her face.

"Hi, I'm Annabel. Can I help you with those?"

Her brown eyes never left his as she tucked a stray strand of hair behind her ear.

"Sorry?" he mumbled, trying to remember what she had just said.

She pointed down at the bags.

"I think those are mine. Unless you shop at Zara too, that is?"

He looked down, aware of how hot his face felt.

"Us porters don't tend to," he managed.

Totally lame, but it was all he could think of. He was

27

relieved to see Annabel wrinkle her nose in apology.

"Oh, sorry about that porter thing. Gran has a habit of embarrassing me in public."

Her nose had a small cluster of freckles, he noticed. Annabel cocked her head to one side, and he realised he needed to say or do something.

"She's great, by the way," he mumbled, "your gran, that is."

"Yeah," said Annabel, smiling, "she has that effect on all the men!"

"I'll be more careful next time."

Mrs Hamilton called from Annabel's room.

"Nick! Would you bring all that stuff in here? You and Annabel need to get the rest of her bags. I'm not going up and down those stairs again."

"Coming!" he called back.

Annabel mouthed "Sorry" as Nick headed through the doorway, thankful for the opportunity to gather his thoughts.

The scene inside the room was chaotic, with books and possessions sprawled across the bed and floor. On the desk was a large parcel neatly wrapped in birthday paper and a card addressed "To Annabel."

"Where do you want these?" he asked, wondering if that meant Annabel would be 18 or 19. She couldn't be younger, could she?

"Over by the window, please."

Nick stepped through the minefield of obstacles and deposited the bags by the window. At that moment a shaft of lightning broke through the dense clouds and lit up a Victorian manor house on the other side of the river. Much of the lawn was hidden from view by a mature plane tree, but as Nick stared out of the window, he could just make out the shape of a giant winged statue in the centre, its head bowed between hunched shoulders. An echoing rumble of thunder shook the glass before the clouds closed ranks once again and returned the garden to near darkness.

"Getting wild out there," he said.

"I'm sure it is, dear, but no time for that now," said Mrs Hamilton. "Will you and Annabel retrieve the other bags from the taxi? The driver's fare is still running."

"Sure, no problem," he said, turning around to find Mrs Hamilton sorting through Annabel's underwear. "I'll leave you to it, then," he mumbled and made a dash for the door.

"Oh, and Nick?"

He turned, trying to maintain eye contact as she folded something lacy into a drawer.

"Yes?"

"Make sure she's OUT, dear."

"Got it," he said and made his escape.

Annabel emerged from the communal kitchen on the landing.

"What was that all about?"

"Just tidying a few things away," he said. "Your gran said you had some other stuff?"

"Oh God, the taxi! We'd better hurry," she said and headed for the stairs.

He followed her, noticing how her ponytail bobbed up

and down as she skipped down the steps.

"So, when you're not a porter, what is it you do?" she asked.

"Law, first year."

"Poor you. Lots of heavy books with no pictures."

"Not thought of it that way," he said. "You?"

"Natural Sciences. Big books with lots of pictures."

"Right," he said.

"Still, it's not just about reading books here, is it?" she said, studying him as they reached the next landing. "Rower?"

"Rugby," he answered. "You?"

"Netball, but I thought I'd give rowing a go."

"OK," said Nick doubtfully as he looked at her diminutive frame. "Stroke side or bow side?"

"Cox, silly!" she laughed. "That way I get to stare at a boatload of super-fit blokes. What could be better?"

"A boatload of super-fit girls?" he suggested.

Annabel laughed.

When they reached the bottom of the stairwell, she stopped to look at the room index.

"Oh, I see now," she said, flicking her indicator to OUT. "So, which one are you?"

"A3," he said. "First Landing."

"N. A. Wood," she said slowly. "Middle name? Anything embarrassing?"

"Arsenal. Won the FA Cup the year I was born."

Her eyes bulged. "You're kidding!"

"Yes, I am," he said. "Andrew."

He was rewarded by another delighted laugh.

"Serves me right for asking," she said, smiling.

Nick decided it was time to quit while he was ahead.

"Come on," he said, "your taxi fare's running."

"Good point, well made!" said Annabel, who turned and headed for the car park. Nick followed and found that he was smiling.

Mrs Hamilton listened from the landing outside A24 and felt a pang of guilt at eavesdropping on her granddaughter's conversation. But, she reasoned, as the girl's guardian, she could be forgiven for doing so. It was a role that had been thrust upon her that dreadful day last Christmas, when her granddaughter had lost both her parents and sister in a car crash coming back from Oxford. Annabel had been home alone revising for her A-levels when the police had turned up. Mrs Hamilton would never forget the devastating phone call she had received that day and the interminable journey down from Yorkshire to join her distraught granddaughter. The Annabel she had found on arrival had been a broken child, her spirit crushed by the weight of grief. It was a sight the old woman hoped never to see again.

When the conditional offer from St John's arrived a few days later, it only seemed to deepen the grieving girl's sense of loss. The very people Annabel would have most wanted to share her news with were gone forever and would never know of her achievement. It was a grim time, and for a while, Mrs Hamilton didn't think there was any way her granddaughter would be able to sit her exams, let alone get the required grades.

But then the girl had rallied. Whether it was the existence

of the offer letter or the need to focus on something other than her lost family, Annabel knuckled down to her studies. Each night Mrs Hamilton saw her come home from school, pale and drawn but quietly determined. After a brief chat about the day's activities and a bite to eat, her granddaughter would head off to her room to revise. So, a few months later, when they had opened the letter from the examination board and seen the line of unbroken A*s down the page, Mrs Hamilton had felt it was a sign Annabel's fortunes had changed. The old woman wondered whether meeting Nick would be another such moment. A reminder to Annabel that after all that had happened to her, there were still good things in life to look forward to.

And, of course, Annabel would never know that her grandmother had been standing in the Cripps courtyard holding those bags for ten minutes, observing the young man before approaching him.

Mrs Hamilton returned to Annabel's bedroom and continued with the task of creating order from chaos. She headed for the bags Nick had left by the bed, only to be stopped by another flash of lightning outside. Mrs Hamilton glanced across at the Master's Lodge on the other side of the river as the answering rumble of thunder reverberated against the window pane. Peering through the rain-spattered glass, the old lady saw a swirl of autumn leaves rise up from the dark expanse of lawn. The fluttering form hovered for a moment before a violent squall sent it spiralling over the towering plane tree, whose branches shivered and swayed in alarm.

Instinctively, Mrs Hamilton's thoughts turned to Annabel and Nick, caught outside in the fury of the storm. She felt a brief and unexpected thrill of unease, before scolding herself and getting back to more pressing matters.

"Socks!"

Chapter 2

After the previous day's deluge, two of the city's early risers woke to find clear skies over the Cambridge skyline. The squirrel skipped over the puddles and leapt onto one of the trees that lined the damp and sandy path. It paused for a moment, alert, as a hunched figure, dressed in a crumpled dark suit and faded college scarf, ambled towards it at a steady pace. The squirrel kept still for a few seconds more, trying to determine if the approaching human was hostile. Then instinct took over, and it darted up the tree to safety.

"Cheeky," said the figure, continuing on the footpath that ran along the back of the colleges on the west side of the River Cam. It was before eight o'clock in the morning, and the path was empty, a temporary calm before the invasion of tourists who would descend on the city later that day, as they did throughout the year. Many of these visitors were drawn to the Backs, as this strip of land was known, by the prospect of having their photograph taken against the backdrop of King's College Chapel. However, the hunched figure had walked past that spot a few minutes earlier without so much as a glance towards the most photographed building in

Cambridge. Instead, he had made his way steadily north along the tree-covered path, past Clare College and Trinity, until he arrived at a set of dark wrought-iron gates nestled between a slow-moving stream on one side and Trinity's moat on the other.

The gate was tall, spiked and intimidating. Strangers could be forgiven for believing that it would be locked to outsiders. However, the small figure walked straight up to the barrier, pressed down on a simple latch and swung the heavy ironwork open on well-maintained hinges. He stepped over the threshold and closed the gate with deliberate care. Then he turned and straightened as if some burden had been lifted from his shoulders, breathing a deep sigh of satisfaction.

Professor Ravi Gupta, a university lecturer in Astronomy, tutor and Director of Studies at St John's, had entered his beloved college.

Ravi glanced up at the squirrel peering at him from a branch and watched as the startled creature scampered out of sight. He suppressed a grin and continued on his way along the heavily shadowed path. Coming to a bend in the track, he turned the corner and was presented with what he considered the most magnificent sight in Cambridge, whatever the tourist guides said about King's College Chapel. Before him stood St John's College New Court, with the morning sun reflecting off its gleaming sandstone surfaces.

Ravi paused in his walk, as he always did at this time of the morning, to take in the view. Known within the college as "The Wedding Cake" because of its impressive central tower that rose high above the spacious Gothic courtyard, New Court stood between the rambling Renaissance buildings to the east of the river and the cubist blocks of Cripps to the west. The latter was mercifully shielded from view by a tactfully planted spinney of trees that Ravi had managed to preserve when, as a much younger Fellow, he had sat on the Gardens Committee. English Heritage may have listed the Cripps building as Grade II*, but he wasn't going to let any modernist conservation experts spoil his morning view.

He straightened his shoulders as he took a deep, calming breath, enjoying the smell of the dew-covered lawns in front of him, shimmering in the early morning light. It was for moments like this that he had come to Cambridge almost fifty years ago as a young man from Nepal, funded by a generous scholarship. He had been smitten with the place then, and his love had only deepened with time.

The professor's reverie was broken by the sound of the old gate swinging open behind him, followed by the staccato rhythm of feet pounding up the path in his direction. He turned to see a young man and woman running towards him, both wearing tracksuits. Remembering that the freshers had arrived the day before, he stepped back to let the students jog by. As he did so, he recognised the flushed face of the girl leading the charge.

"Morning, Professor," she puffed as she passed him.

"Good morning... Annabel," he replied, remembering just in time the name of the sixth-former he had interviewed almost a year earlier. Hard to forget, given what had happened to her family.

Her running companion loped along behind her, tall, sandy-haired and muscular. Blowing a little harder, the youth managed a grunt. Ravi watched the pair head towards the college, Annabel sprinting the final stretch, the boy pumping his arms a little harder to match her pace before slowing to let her win.

Ravi felt a smile creep across his weathered face. Each year it was the same, the intake of freshers lifting his spirits and hopes for the year ahead. When they attended his rooms for supervisions, he enjoyed watching their eager minds wrestling with concepts that were now second nature to him. Sitting on the sofas in his office, discussing his assignments, they would often ask questions that were naive, but at times illuminating, expanding the boundaries of their own knowledge and, on occasion, challenging his own assumptions as well. He had long recognised that supervisions with his students were what kept him going.

A bell chimed eight times, waking him from his thoughts.

"Perchance it is I, for whom the bell tolls," he said, misquoting a passage from John Donne, before resuming his journey.

Rather than following the freshers' route towards New Court, Ravi took the right-hand path that ran parallel with the moat dividing the St John's lawns from those of Trinity. Halfway along, he passed a narrow iron bridge that linked the backs of the two colleges. There was a gate midway across the bridge, and this too was framed by a crown of intimidating spikes. Ravi smiled. The gate was owned by St John's College, and all requests from Trinity for a shared key had been politely but firmly declined by the college's governing body. He recalled with some collegiate pride the unanimous show of hands in the Fellows' Combination Room when the matter had last been put to the vote.

Some gates are best kept locked, he thought, prompting an image of another gate, far darker and more threatening, which he suppressed with a grimace, refusing to let that memory spoil his walk into college – not today, on such a beautiful morning. But his shoulders sagged a fraction as he continued on his way, crunching sandy gravel underfoot with a deliberate tread.

When the path met the river, it curved left in a gentle arc and disappeared beneath the drooping branches of a weeping willow. Dipping under the curtain of leaves, Ravi spotted ducks sleeping on the grassy slope that ran down to the water's edge. Unlike the squirrel, they showed no outward sign of alarm as he passed, their heads tucked comfortably between their folded wings.

Emerging into the sunlight, Ravi approached one of two bridges that straddled the river, linking the different halves of the college. This first was the Old Bridge, mistakenly referred to as the Wren Bridge by the punt guides who ferried tourists under its arched spans throughout the year. Like other members of the college, Ravi preferred to call it the Kitchen Bridge for the simple reason that, for centuries, produce from the college's estates had been brought across its well-worn surface to the fabled kitchens.

During the summer months, the broad span of the bridge also provided an excellent place to gather before supper and watch the punts weave their way downstream towards Magdalene College and Jesus Green. Pausing for a moment to lean on the Kitchen Bridge's stone balustrade, Ravi looked downstream at its better-known partner, the Bridge of Sighs, with its iconic roof and arched window frames. Ravi had often wondered why the addition of a roof to a bridge had held such a fascination for visitors. A similar mystique had evolved around its more venerated namesake in Venice. As a Professor of Astronomy, he far preferred a bridge that was open to the heavens. He remembered spending many an evening staring up at the stars from this very spot, fortified by a gin and tonic from the nearby College Bar, naturally.

As he looked up at the clear autumn sky, Ravi became aware that he was being watched. Two imposing horned antelopes stared down at him from the gateposts at the far end of the bridge. The yales, mythical horned creatures from the coat of arms of Lady Margaret Beaufort, the college's founder, were not alone in guarding the entrance to the eastern half of the college. Beyond them was another set of columns adorned by a pair of menacing stone eagles, Lady Margaret's other heraldic guardians, their wings spread in a challenge, poised to pounce on any who made it beyond the gates.

As he stared up into those blank stone eyes, that same dark memory rose again into Ravi's thoughts, and he felt a chill down his spine. Gripping the balustrade to steady himself, Ravi chided himself for his momentary weakness.

"Stop it! Superstitious old fool! That was a lifetime ago."

With an effort of will, Ravi dragged his gaze away from the creatures staring down at him and hurried between the gateposts, grateful to escape their unwavering scrutiny. Without looking up, he continued across a small paved courtyard towards an ugly low-rise building that occupied what remained of Kitchen Lane, the narrow passageway between the college's old courts and Trinity.

This squat structure housed the Buttery Dining Room, a large canteen built in the 1960s to cope with the surge in student numbers following the Second World War. Despite its lack of architectural merit, Ravi had to admit that the Buttery more than made up for it with the quality of its English breakfast, another of the great institutions of the British Empire that had become a much-valued part of his morning walk into the college.

Pushing through a set of heavy fire doors, the professor entered the long, narrow cafeteria and looked up and down the neat rows of tables. There were a few students already there, mainly graduates who had spent the summer working on their PhDs. Like him, most graduates lived in off-site accommodation, and were rarely seen except at meal times. He suspected these hostel-dwellers preferred someone else to cook for them first thing in the morning before going off to their academic faculties across the city. At John's you could get a cooked breakfast and a quick meal at lunchtime and be back for formal Hall in the evening with no need to worry about shopping, cooking or washing up.

The practicality of this arrangement was something that

Ravi had significantly admired when he had first arrived at Cambridge, and over the years, he had taken full advantage of it. The fridge in his terraced house in Newnham was empty apart from a net of lemons, Schweppes tonic water and a bottle of Cambridge Dry Gin, a gift from one of his former tutees. Since moving out of college almost a decade ago, he had needed little else in the way of provisions at home.

"Good morning, Professor," said a proud-looking Portuguese woman from behind the serving counter, with a look that could halt an undergraduate in his tracks. "The usual?"

"Thank you, Aurelia," he said. "A poached egg, mushrooms and tomatoes, please."

Aurelia had been serving Ravi for almost a quarter of a century, and whenever he found her standing there, spatula in hand, a flutter of excitement awoke in his chest. As he watched her ladle his food onto a plate, the hopeless romantic in him wondered if she had any idea of the affection that he had for her. Each day he watched her stern expression, hoping for the slightest sign that his feelings were reciprocated.

"Be careful, Professor, they are hot this morning," she said as she handed him his cooked breakfast.

"Excuse me?"

"The plates, they are hot."

"Oh, yes, of course," he said, admiring her beautiful cheekbones as he took the plate. An excruciating pain seared through his fingers and he dropped the plate onto the tray.

Aurelia, who had already moved onto the hot beverage counter, gave no indication that she had noticed.

"You want tea, Professor?"

"Yes, please, Aurelia," said Ravi, his eyes watering as he slid his tray along the counter.

The waitress took a small metal teapot, selected a bag of Twining's Earl Grey tea and added water.

"Earl Grey, no?" she said.

"Thank you, Aurelia."

"My pleasure, Professor," she said, with the briefest of smiles that held him mesmerised for a moment. Then his muse turned back to the queue forming behind him.

"OK, who's next?"

Their moment over, Ravi slid his tray around to the checkout and, as the glow in his chest and scorched hands faded a little, he reflected on their relationship. It was not a physical one, and he had to admit that their conversation, though familiar, lacked emotional depth. But every morning he drew solace from their brief encounter and the memory of her parting smile left him with a renewed sense of optimism for the day ahead.

By contrast, the greeting he received from the checkout operator had a more sobering effect. She was staring into the distance, deep in thought. The dark rings under the girl's eyes suggested she had been out too late for such an early shift.

"Good morning," he said.

She started as if woken from a dream.

"Morning," she said and, recovering quickly, ran the

items on his tray through the till. Ravi handed over his Buttery card, and she swiped it on the electronic payment sensor, automatically deducting the amount from his college account.

"Thank you…?" He raised his eyebrows.

"Jane," said the girl.

"Thank you, Jane," he said and picked up the tray, careful not to spill the tea as he adjusted the satchel on his shoulder.

"Do you want a hand with that?" asked Jane, showing a belated interest in her customer.

"No, thank you, I can manage," he said politely but firmly, as he tottered away from the checkout. He was old, but not that old.

Ravi made his way to the furthest table in the Buttery and sat in the corner, his back to the large window facing the Kitchen Bridge and its ominous statues. Pouring himself some tea, he made a start on his breakfast. More people drifted in, some on their own, others in clusters. At this time of the morning, Ravi did not feel inclined to make conversation, so he kept his head down and tucked into his egg. He had barely taken a few mouthfuls when he sensed rather than saw a shadow loom over him.

"Professor Gupta?" came the deep voice.

Ravi looked up and froze, his fork halfway to his mouth. A man-mountain stood in front of him, all shoulders and no neck. By his dark suit and waistcoat, the professor assumed the giant was a porter although he could not recall seeing him before.

"Yes?" Ravi raised his eyebrows, hoping the man would reveal his identity. His enquiry elicited no response from the square face with its cropped grey hair, the same colour as the eyes that stared at him without a trace of emotion.

"Forgive me. I can't remember your name?"

"Cummings, Professor Gupta," said the man. "The Dean would like a word with you."

"This minute?" asked Ravi, conscious that egg was running down his fork onto his fingers.

The broad shoulders moved in what Ravi realised must have been a shrug, although the effect was distracting given their size.

"The Dean was not specific as to when, Professor, but I dare say he didn't expect me to find you so quickly." The man glanced briefly at the state of Ravi's fingers. "I'm sure you have a moment or two to wash your hands."

"Thank you, Cummings," said Ravi, slightly irritated by the man's impertinence as he wiped his fingers with a napkin. "Did he say what it was about?"

The man considered him.

"There's been a disappearance, Professor."

Ravi could not help it. He flinched before making a clumsy attempt to cover his reaction by dabbing his mouth with his napkin.

"Really?" he said, feeling a tightening of his stomach that he was sure had nothing to do with the eggs.

"Yes, Professor," said Cummings.

Ravi looked up into that face and found its unblinking scrutiny deeply unsettling. To his relief Cummins gave the briefest of nods, and the colossal man left the Buttery as quietly as he had entered.

Ravi replaced his knife and fork and peered down at his unfinished breakfast. He had lost his appetite. Getting up from the table, Ravi slung the satchel over his shoulder and took his tray to the storage rack by the wash-up area. The crockery rattled, and when Ravi looked down at his hands, he noticed that they were shaking.

Chapter 3

The mobile phone vibrated on the bedside table, bumping up against the stainless-steel water bottle and causing it to rattle in unison. Their insistent chorus continued for several more seconds before a hand shot out from under the duvet and knocked the bottle to the floor. The spider-like fingers then began groping across the surface of the table until they located their buzzing quarry and silenced it with the downward stab of a thumb. Raising his head from the folds of his pillow, Giles Chamberlain peered at the display through his mop of blond hair.

"Oh, crap!"

The phone fell with a dull thud to the floor. Pulling the duvet off his naked body, he swung his legs out of bed. The heel of one foot connected with the water bottle, knocking it out of sight under the bedframe. For a moment, Giles thought about reaching for it, but his head was throbbing like a bass drum, and he decided that bending over right now wouldn't be a good idea. Instead, he eased himself to his feet and, leaning forward, started the gentle climb up the sloping floor of his seventeenth-century room towards one of two doors hidden in its oak-panelled walls.

Twisting a small brass handle, he swung it open to reveal a tiny kitchen cupboard complete with kettle, twin hobs and a fridge. Reaching down, he retrieved a bottle of milk from the latter, sniffed it and took a tentative mouthful. Eyes bulging, he lurched over to the other panelled door, yanked it open and vomited up the sour milk and the contents of his stomach into the sink. Fumbling for the tap, he ran the water to wash the worst of it away and remained there for a few minutes, his head bowed in penance before the porcelain shrine.

Slowly, he lifted his bloodshot eyes to peer in the mirror and saw the familiar face staring back at him, a milk-coloured moustache on his upper lip and other types of residue in the stubble of his chin.

"Morning, gorgeous," he said, splashing water onto his face before reaching for his toothbrush. As he began brushing his teeth, he surveyed the room's reflection in the mirror.

O3 Second Court was one of the oldest in the college, its two arched windows set high in the wall, either side of a large fireplace. At the far side of the room, at the bottom of the slope, was his bed, deliberately positioned so that if he made it back after a heavy night out, gravity would do the rest. A crack in one of the panels above his pillow was testimony to the success of this strategy, the result of him pitching into the wall after a late session with his student drama buddies at the Maypole pub.

Good to have left your mark on Cambridge, he reflected.

47

Elsewhere in the room, the only concessions to modern-day living were an Anglepoise lamp above the desk, a two-bar electric fire in the grate, a single light socket hanging from the ceiling rose, and the obligatory plug and internet points in the skirting board. With few other features of note, this relatively Spartan set figured low on the list in the annual room ballot. Instead, most third-years opted for the well-appointed en-suite rooms in New, North and Chapel Courts, which were not only more comfortable, but quieter too, which some considered important when preparing for final-year exams.

Giles, however, saw things differently. He preferred being at the centre of things and, in his view, Second Court was the beating heart of the college. In the north-west corner was the Old Library, guarded by a massive oak door that would have kept even Cromwell's thugs at bay. The Fellows' Combination Room ran along the north side of the court, its well-stocked table ensuring that the college's senior members assembled for lunch whatever their other commitments. The Junior Combination Room occupied the west side, with its sofas and Sky TV channel. This was conveniently located immediately adjacent to the College Bar, home to the some of the great late-night celebrations he had enjoyed at John's. And to the east, the leaded windows of the Hall shone like glittering jewels most nights of the week, where he and the other diners enjoyed a glass or two of wine with their evening meal.

His preference for dining in Hall mystified his closest friends, Ying and Trevor, both of whom preferred the practical convenience of the Buttery. Giles thought back to the grief they had given him towards the end of last term when the pressure of exams had precipitated a mini revolt.

"But Giles, we don't have time for Hall," Ying had complained.

"Ying, why on earth would anyone want to spend their evenings in a canteen when you can enjoy a three-course dinner in an Elizabethan banqueting room?"

"How about because the BDR is cheaper, quicker and you get to choose what you eat?"

"Well, yes," he conceded. "But you can do that anywhere. After all those years busting a gut to get into this place, don't you think we should make the most of it?"

"Giles, you never busted a gut to get in here," Trevor pointed out. "You're a bloody genius, mate."

"I'm not a genius."

"Your Master's Prize was just charm, was it?" Ying asked.

"He just liked my paper on Roman amphitheatres, that's all. Besides, don't you think dining in Hall is special?"

"By special, Giles, you mean Trevor and I having to listen to one of you scholars reading Grace in a dead language that no one understands?"

"Latin is not a dead language, it's just misunderstood," he retorted.

In the end, Ying had put her foot down and, naturally, Trevor had sided with her. So that night Giles had dined in Hall on his own. Apart from, that is, the twenty or so Fellows on High Table, who had stared down at the subdued figure eating by himself at the end of the lower table.

The Hall incident had been the first time Giles had felt a shift in his relationship with the others since meeting them at the Cambridge University Amateur Dramatic Club two years earlier when he'd known immediately he'd found two kindred spirits. Trevor, a lighting and sound specialist, had grown up in the Lake District with a rope in one hand and a carabiner in the other. Ying was a dancer and, when not gliding across the stage, had spent her evenings hanging off a climbing wall in Hong Kong, where her flawless technique and Lycra-clad figure had probably attracted as many admiring glances as they did in Cambridge. With rehearsals at the ADC taking up close to 20 hours a week during term, they didn't have much time to climb together once lectures started. But outside of term, the three of them had managed to climb together most holidays except for the summer just gone, when Giles had been on a four-week field trip to Egypt to study the ancient city of Armana.

On that occasion Giles had declined an invitation to join them in the last weeks before term started, claiming that after two years of idleness, it was finally time to knuckle down to his studies and write up the field notes for his dissertation. While partly true, Giles knew in his heart that the real reason for leaving them alone was far simpler. By the end of the Easter term, it had become obvious that his two best friends had fallen in love, leaving him as the gooseberry. The thought of joining them at the end of the holidays would only have rubbed in what he had been in denial about for some time. That they were the closest thing to family he had, and at the end of the year, they would be heading off to London to start a new life together, leaving Giles on his own once more.

As far as his family were concerned, there had never been any chance of him having brothers or sisters. Giles' parents both had successful careers in the City, where they met during the heady days of Big Bang, when "greed is good" had been the mantra. His unexpected arrival on the scene had come at the worst possible time in their careers and a nanny had been hired as soon as his mother returned from the hospital. Nanny Timmins, rather than his parents, had looked after Giles through his early years until a remote private school in Scotland could be found to take him on as a full boarder at the age of seven. Saying goodbye to her at the school gates was the last time he remembered crying in public.

After that, boarding school taught him it was best to keep his feelings to himself and not show weakness to anyone. To survive, he had filled his waking hours with sport, climbing and drama, something Giles discovered he excelled at. These pursuits gave him status among his peers and allowed Giles to cultivate the larger-than-life persona that he acted out each day to avoid having to think about the one thing he feared. Being truly alone.

"Get a grip, Chamberlain," he said to his reflection. "You're going all hormonal on me."

Closing his eyes, Giles splashed water onto his face. When he looked again, he saw that his haystack of blond hair needed a wash, but that would mean a detour to the single communal shower on O Staircase, almost certainly making him late for his first lecture. And despite his friends' flattering respect for his abilities, he knew he wasn't going to get the First he needed to stay on for a master's without putting in some serious hours of study this year.

A knock at the door brought him back to the present.

"Go away!" he called out.

"I'm not going anywhere," came the voice of Rose, his bedder. "Time you were up."

"I am up," said Giles, grabbing a pair of jeans and hopping on one leg as he struggled to pull the other one through.

"Come on, Giles, you're making me late for my rounds."

"Rose, I'm dressing," he yelled as he bounced down the slope, halting just before the bed.

"Can't a gentleman have a little privacy?" he complained as he slipped his feet into a pair of heavily scuffed trail shoes and pulled a base layer T-shirt over his head.

"Haven't you got your lectures to go to?" said Rose. "I thought you stay on here over the holidays so you could study?"

"I spent the holidays here so I could save you from all those lecherous conference suits," said Giles, grabbing a fleece and his backpack before heading for the door.

"They don't worry me," said Rose. "I've seen worse."

Giles opened the inner door of his rooms and reached for the latch of the outer door. All rooms in the old courts had two doors. Tradition had it that if you were prepared to accept visitors, the outer one was left open. He swung it open to reveal a well-proportioned woman wearing comfortable work clothes, embroidered with a college crest. Her mousy grey hair was tied back in a bun, revealing a pink, perspiring face, which reminded him once again of how prescient her parents had been in choosing their daughter's name.

"I thought you bedders had master keys."

"We do," said Rose, bustling past him and dragging a red vacuum cleaner behind her, "but experience has taught me to knock first. You never know what sights will greet you in a student's room. Or a Fellow's, for that matter," she said with a chuckle, which was cut short by a cry of alarm.

"Giles, what have you been up to!"

He followed her gaze and saw the jumble of climbing harnesses, carabiners and ropes piled high in his armchair.

"Oh… that," he said, evasively. "Don't worry, I'll sort it out later. Must dash. Lectures." He headed out the door.

"I hope you've not been doing anything you shouldn't," she called after him.

"Only in my dreams, Rose, only in my dreams."

Before she could reply, Giles disappeared down the twisting stairwell, eager to escape his bedder's inevitable questions, which he had absolutely no intention of answering.

*****

Rose deposited the vacuum cleaner on the floor by the tangle of ropes.

"I'll tackle you lot later," she said before casting a professional eye around the rest of the room. It was in its usual dishevelled state, most surfaces covered in climbing magazines, maps, hair-raising photographs and an assortment of ADC programmes perched on the mantelpiece. With a sigh, she began dragging the vacuum cleaner down the slope, and only then spotted his phone on the floor.

"Oh Lord!" she said, scooping it up and rushing out to the landing, where she opened the leaded window and peered down into Second Court. Giles had just emerged from the bottom of the staircase and was already scampering across the cobbles around the immaculate lawns.

"Giles, you forgot your phone!" she yelled.

The blond figure skidded to a halt and turned towards the window.

"Rose, what would I do without you?" he called up to her. "Be an angel and throw it down, would you?"

"Throw it?"

"I've not got time to come back up. Go on. I'll catch it!"

"I don't know about that."

Giles dropped to one knee and threw his arms out wide.

"But, soft! What light through yonder window breaks?" he began, his voice echoing around the court. "It is the east, and Juliet is the sun… Or was it bun, I can never remember?"

Rose lobbed the phone at him. Laughing, Giles reached up and caught it.

"Thanks, Juliet," he said, and blew her a kiss before dashing from the court.

Despite her 50 years, the bedder felt a faint flutter in her chest as she watched the dashing Romeo disappear. But then she noticed a couple of amused-looking freshers grinning in her direction and she pulled the window closed with a scowl.

"Riding for a fall, that one," she muttered under her breath and found herself staring at the Chapel Tower looming high above the court, its sharp pinnacles stabbing upwards into the clear blue sky. With a shudder, she turned her back to the window and, taking a deep breath, headed back along the landing to tackle Giles' room.

Chapter 4

At the same time as Rose knocked on Giles' door in Second Court, across the river in A24 Cripps, Annabel stuffed her jogging kit into the laundry bag and closed her wardrobe. She picked up her lilac Cambridge satchel, a birthday present from Gran, and checked she had everything. Notebook, pens, phone, compact umbrella, a map of Cambridge. She slid her college ID and key card into the pocket of her jeans. She cast a quick eye around the room that had become her new home.

"A place for everything and everything in its place," she said, reciting something her late mother used to say. What would her family think of her now, she wondered? Glancing up, she saw them smiling at her from their picture frame, alongside the birthday card she had received from Gran. In her heart, she knew that they would be proud of her being here. Perhaps even as proud as they had been of Serena.

The sob began rising from deep inside her, and she just managed to stifle it before it broke through her defences. Annabel leant against her desk for a second to steady herself. The sun streamed in through her window, and she closed her eyes, letting its rays warm her wet cheeks.

"The sun always rises," she said quietly. She had Gran to thank for that one.

Annabel wiped her cheeks with the palm of her hand and looked at herself in the mirror.

"Come on, girl. This is going to be great," she said firmly. With that, she swung the satchel over her shoulder, opened the door and headed off for her Natural Sciences induction day. First stop: the Museum of Zoology on Pembroke Street. She could not wait.

On the way down the stairs, Annabel found Nick closing the door to his room.

"All set?" she asked.

"Yep," said Nick.

"Is it just me or does it feel like the first day at school?"

"Yeah, only without the new uniform."

"And sandwich boxes."

"What? Oh, yeah, those too."

"Didn't you take sandwiches to school? Me, I couldn't bear the school food. At our place it was disgusting. What about yours?"

"I didn't mind it," he said, but she noticed him colouring up.

"What? You don't have to be embarrassed."

"No, it's just the adrenaline this morning. I'm pretty wired."

Something told her she had struck a nerve, so she decided to let it lie. They flicked their names to OUT and headed towards the passageway into New Court.

"What have you got first?" she said as they emerged into the sunshine briefly before turning left through the cloisters.

"Torts, followed by Contract, then Constitutional."

"Ouch!" said Annabel.

"And you?" asked Nick.

"Parasitology, Ecology and Conservation. This afternoon we're having an introduction to Statistical Analysis," she said, grimacing.

"Sounds heavy too," said Nick.

"We'll see. I've always been fascinated by parasites," said Annabel, as they approached the Bridge of Sighs. "Must be all those vampire movies."

Nick did not reply. She turned and found that he had stopped on the bridge and was standing there looking out through the iron bars that bisected each of the arched windows.

"What are you doing?" she asked, but Nick did not move. He was staring at something.

Annabel retraced her steps and followed his gaze across the river towards the walled garden. "Beautiful, isn't it," she said. "I love that little gate that opens out onto the river. Can you imagine turning up to a garden party by punt? How cool would that be?"

"Cool…" said Nick, frowning.

"Are you listening to me?" said Annabel.

"Sorry," he said, "I was distracted by something."

"Clearly," she said, looking around and noticing her tutor, Professor Gupta, heading towards them, his head bowed in concentration.

"Morning, Professor," she chirped.

"Oh… Morning," said the professor as he passed them.

Nick turned to face her.

"Annabel, when we moved in yesterday, there was a huge winged statue on the lawn. I saw it from your room. And now it's disappeared."

"Err, no. I don't think so," said Annabel. "Are you thinking about the eagle above New Court?"

"No, it was right there," he said, nodding towards the garden.

"Well," she said, "there are so many eagle statues around this place I'm amazed there isn't one in the Master's Garden."

Nick continued to stare through the bars.

"Come on," said Annabel, "we're causing a traffic jam."

A group of bedders edged past them in the opposite direction.

Still frowning, Nick left the window and followed her into Third Court. Annabel decided to change tack.

"I would not fancy being a bedder. Cleaning after students. I'm amazed they get all the rooms done by lunchtime," she said.

"Not much to do in my room," said Nick.

"You keep yours tidy, do you?" she asked.

"Try to."

"You're not one of those rugby players who hangs sweaty socks on the radiator, are you?" she asked.

He frowned but didn't answer.

"I knew it!" she said.

"Saves the environment," said Nick.

She bumped him with her shoulder.

"What?" he said.

They entered Second Court. Up ahead Annabel saw a student with tousled hair on one knee, blowing a kiss at an upstairs window.

"What do you think blondie's up to?" she asked, intrigued.

The student grabbed something out of the air, waved and ran off through the passageway into First Court.

"Good catch," said Nick.

Annabel spotted a rosy-cheeked face staring after him from the window.

"Now that's how to charm a bedder," she said.

They entered the passageway into First Court, passing the kitchens, where staff were already busy preparing food for lunch.

"Are you going tonight?" asked Nick. "To Hall, I mean."

"Yep! You?"

"Thought I'd try out the new gown," said Nick.

"I think mine's a bit on the long side," said Annabel, remembering seeing herself in the mirror. "I look like an extra from Harry Potter."

"Only without the owls," he said.

As they approached the Great Gate, Annabel saw a crush of students peering at the noticeboard opposite the Porter's Lodge. "What's all this?"

"Tutorial times," said Nick. "Who's your tutor?"

"Professor Gupta. You know, the one we passed earlier."

"What's he like?"

"We only met at the interview. He was playing good cop. Who's yours?"

"Mackenzie," said Nick, "the Dean."

"No! He was at my interview too," said Annabel. "Only he was playing bad cop. Grilling me on physics."

"That seems to be the pattern – the tutor softens you up while the supervisor goes for the kill."

"Yeah, well, Mackenzie asked a stinker," said Annabel.

"Which was?"

"How many times do you have to fold a piece of paper to reach the moon?" she said.

"You're kidding?"

"Yes, I am," she grinned.

Nick groaned. "Good one. Fifteen all."

They edged their way up to the noticeboard and checked their tutorial times. Annabel's was scheduled for Wednesday afternoon, Nick's on Thursday evening.

"That's late, isn't it?" she asked as they edged back through the throng.

"Rugby trials that afternoon. Mackenzie scheduled it for afterwards. Are you planning on doing any sport?"

Annabel thought for a minute. "Rowing, netball, hockey, tennis…"

"We have our studies as well, you know."

"I know, but I thought I'd try a few and then decide. You just doing rugby then?"

"I was thinking of something creative too. You know, to take my mind off the books."

"Such as?"

"Cheerleading crossed my mind."

Annabel laughed. "I'd like to see you try. They're serious gymnasts, you know. You don't want to go pulling anything."

"On the contrary, that was the idea," said Nick.

"Ooh, I'm referring that one to the umpire. That was definitely out."

"Fifteen-thirty, then." He conceded. "Listen, I've got to go. Had an email from the porters saying there's a parcel for me."

"Oh, right. Of course. In that case, I'll head off."

"You want to meet up before hall?"

"OK," she said, "I'll come by your room."

"Sure," he said. "Catch you later."

Nick disappeared into the Porter's Lodge, and Annabel turned towards the Great Gate.

That, my girl, is a date, Annabel thought as she stepped out into the street.

The hand that grabbed her jacket and hauled her back came out of nowhere. Before Annabel had time to cry out, something rushed past, inches from where she had been standing. A bell rang belatedly as the bike left the pavement and rejoined the peloton of bicycles heading down Trinity Street.

"Like the bulls in Pamplona," said a deep voice behind her.

Annabel turned and stared up into the grey eyes of a porter.

"Thank you," she said.

"No problem. Just some idiot in too much of a hurry."

62

At that moment, Annabel caught sight of the dashing Romeo from Second Court in the next wave of bikes. He was leaning back in the saddle, his blond hair streaming behind him, a pint of milk in one hand and a bacon roll in the other. Spotting Annabel, he gave her a cheerful wink, before speeding on.

"Like him, you mean?"

When the porter didn't respond, Annabel turned and found he was no longer there. She looked around, peering over the heads of the students streaming out of the college, and then up and down the street. There was no sign of him anywhere. Her guardian angel had just vanished.

Chapter 5

Ravi left the Buttery even more hunched than when he had entered. The brief conversation with Cummings about a disappearance had unsettled him and brought back unwelcome memories.

"It couldn't be happening again," he said to himself. As Dean, Robert probably just wanted to alert him to some prank his students might have been up to, like removing street signs or Fellows' bikes. He remembered one time when students had stolen a lecturer's Austin Seven and suspended it under the Bridge of Sighs. Something of that nature would be welcome, even if some of his tutees were at fault. Heaven knows, they had all done foolish things in their time. He and Robert included.

Barely noticing the people, Ravi made for the Dean's office, heading against the flow of students pouring over the Bridge of Sighs on their way to lectures. Their happy voices and nervous laughter washed over him, and he kept his body close to the wall to avoid contact.

"Morning, Professor!"

"Oh… Morning," he replied, belatedly recognising

Annabel and her friend after passing them on the bridge. Ravi turned and noticed the boy had stopped and was staring over towards the Master's Garden. He was pleased to see them taking in their surroundings. Too many students trudged through the college with their heads bent over mobile phones, oblivious to the views around them. He was about to leave them to it when he heard the boy talking about the disappearance of the winged statue.

Ravi paused, remembering what he had seen all those years ago. Something that had no right to be here. Not then, not now. An entity that he and Robert had done all in their power to prevent ever coming back again.

His thoughts returned to the boy and what he had seen, but when he looked up at the bridge, they were gone, replaced by a gaggle of bedders advancing on him.

"Morning, Professor," said the first.

Ravi ignored them, looking over their heads for any sign of the students. He was rewarded with a not-so-subtle aside from one of the bedders to her colleagues.

"Not on the same planet, that one."

"From a different world," said another.

Ravi stood there for a few moments, wondering at their description of him. The otherworldly references were unsettling. It was as if they were reading his thoughts, which of course he knew to be impossible. They probably knew he was a Professor of Astronomy. Yes, that must be it. Nothing more than that.

"You are reading too much into things, superstitious old fool!" he scolded himself, causing a couple of passing students to interrupt their conversation and stare at him. Scowling, he set off again, his head bowed, for his meeting with the Dean.

To the south of New Court was a covered walkway resembling a monastery's cloisters. Sun streamed through the arches, projecting a latticework of shadows on the paving stones and stretching onto the lush green grass of the enclosed court. He followed the walkway to the far side of the square and turned into the archway of I Staircase.

The names stencilled onto the room index were a mix of new and old. The new additions were bright and crisp, while the older names were much like their occupants, Ravi reflected: faded and hard to read. The faintest entry read "Prof. R. Mackenzie", and next to it the indicator was set to IN. Ravi smiled ruefully and began climbing the worn stone steps.

Built in the nineteenth century, New Court's stone staircases were much grander and more substantial than the twisted wooden ones that riddled the older parts of the college across the river. Even so, two centuries of Johnians had worn away the stone in the middle of each stair, leaving a smooth cavity that had been restored with a concrete filling. Gritting his own much-repaired teeth, Ravi stomped up the steps, past the well-appointed Bursary on the first floor, a large and airy hallway leading to Fellows' sets on the second floor, and finally, the more modest third-floor landing, where he paused for breath. Taking a few moments to compose himself, he approached Robert's room, which had the familiar line of stools outside for any students summoned before the Dean. At this time of the morning, these were empty, and the room's outer door stood invitingly ajar. Ravi knocked on the inner door.

"Enter!" came a familiar voice with its distinctive Scottish burr.

Ravi pushed the door open and was greeted by the morning sun streaming through a massive set of south-facing windows overlooking the Backs. He took in the deep-red sofas and armchairs arranged around a coffee table in front of a coal fireplace, before turning towards the business end of the room. There he saw a round-faced man with curly white hair sitting behind a large mahogany desk, studying a pile of papers.

"What is it, then?" said the man, raising his head. Ravi saw those piercing green eyes stare at him through a pair of thick, square glasses before the broad, ruddy face broke into a warm smile.

"Ravi!" said his old friend, rising from his chair and easing himself around the desk. Two new hip joints and a replacement knee were finally catching up with the former University Blue.

"Robert," Ravi said, crossing the room and extending his hand, which Robert grasped in a bone-crushing grip.

"Forgive me, I was just reading the Head Porter's report on last night's shenanigans and thought you might be one of my first miscreants of term!"

Ravi noted the neatly stacked reports on the desk next to a sgian-dubh, a traditional Scottish dagger that Robert used to open his mail. And to wag at badly behaved students when the occasion demanded it.

"No need to apologise," said Ravi, indicating the pile. "Any of my tutees?"

"Not so far, but I'll let you know if I come across one. Come and take a pew," said Robert and headed towards the sofas.

Ravi chose an armchair with its back to the window and settled into the soft upholstery.

"Can I get you a coffee?" said Robert, limping towards a small kitchen just off the main room. "I have one of these marvellous Nespresso machines. The Bursar said it would save me from breaking my neck going up and down the stairs to his set," said Robert. "Although I think the tight-fisted bugger was more concerned about me pinching his biscuits."

"I'd prefer tea," said Ravi.

"Of course! You'd have thought I'd know by now. Earl Grey?"

"Perfect."

"So good to see you again, Ravi. I trust you had a good trip," said Robert as he switched on the kettle and put a teabag in a teapot. "How was Nepal?"

"Interesting," said Ravi.

Robert gave him a look. "And what does that mean?"

"I visited the schools you obtained funding for, and they were in the process of fitting out the physics and chemistry classrooms with the new equipment."

"Excellent! They must have been delighted."

"Yes and no. Some of the schools had received an unexpected visit from the police, accompanied by a government official. He was investigating illegal arms shipments."

Ravi was interrupted by a noise that sounded like a rifle being loaded. He turned in time to see Robert ramming home a coffee cartridge into the polished chrome machine before slamming a lever down to prime the contraption.

"I'm sure that sort of thing is pretty standard in that part of the world," said Robert. "Can't be every day that the local schools get such a generous gift of equipment. It probably caused quite a stir."

His friend jabbed a button with his stubby finger, and the machine rumbled to life.

"It seems that was the case. The schools had to allow an inspection of the equipment, purchase orders, shipping documents, and bank records."

"And?" said Robert, who seemed preoccupied by his new toy, which was gurgling and steaming away.

"The official seemed very interested in where the equipment had come from and took copies of all the documentation away with him. Since then the schools have heard nothing more."

"Good, good. Glad to hear it," said Robert, extracting a cup from the machine and sniffing the steaming liquid.

"Where exactly did the funds come from, Robert? There's nothing we need to be concerned about, is there? Reputation-wise, I mean?"

"Not at all," said Robert. "It's from a benefactor who has been funding some research of mine. I've invited him to dinner this evening. He's been funding all sorts of scientific projects here in Cambridge. He was even interested in some of the early work we did together."

"Really?" asked Ravi, watching his friend closely, feeling a tightening of his stomach. "What, exactly?"

"Oh, this and that," said Robert evasively, "but when I mentioned the outreach stuff you do over in Nepal, he was only too delighted to help. I can imagine those children were pretty excited, weren't they?"

Ravi remembered the faces he had seen in the classrooms, poring over microscopes and circuit boards. He had to admit their enthusiasm had been infectious. It had been a proud moment.

"Yes, it's going to make quite a difference," he said, mellowing. "And you, Robert? Have you had a good break?"

"What, me? Oh, fine. Got some fishing in. Brora River, up near Dunrobin Castle on the east coast. Magnificent place. You should come with me sometime."

Ravi had visions of grey days and dense clouds and just smiled while his friend poured water into the teapot.

"Then I had to fly to Geneva to give a lecture at CERN. Same old stuff. Matter, antimatter, that sort of thing. They just can't get enough of it."

Ravi knew that Robert's research in the 1960s, which accelerated during the Cold War space race, continued to provide him and the university with significant amounts of funding from government and defence contractors. Much as he wished his friend well, it somewhat irked Ravi that Robert seemed happy to focus on fields of research that had the potential to deliver the world's ultimate destruction, whereas research in areas such as astronomy, which helped mankind understand the origins of its creation, were no longer of interest to him. That had not always been the case.

His thoughts were interrupted by Robert limping back into the living room, balancing a tray that Ravi noticed included a generous plate of shortbread biscuits.

"You know, the Bursar might have a point, about those stairs being the death of you," said Ravi.

"He'll have to catch me first!" laughed Robert as the rattling of the cups became more pronounced. "So, what brings you to Mackenzie Towers?"

"Your man Cummings sent me," said Ravi.

"Cummings?" said Robert.

"Yes, he said there had been a disappearance," said Ravi.

The crash made Ravi jump as the contents of the tray shattered on the coffee table, sending scalding hot liquid across its surface and onto the cream carpet. He sprang to his feet and reached inside his trouser pocket for a handkerchief, which he threw on the spreading puddle in a vain attempt to stem the flow.

"Quick, Robert! Do you have any napkins or tissues?" he said, looking up at his friend, who just stared at him.

"Robert, your carpet! Have you got a towel or something?"

But Robert slumped into one of the armchairs and stared into the fireplace.

Ravi ignored him and rushed to the bathroom. There he pulled a white hand towel off the rack and returned to mop up the rest of the tea and coffee. He looked over at his friend, who sat slumped in his chair, ashen-faced.

"Robert," said Ravi. "What is going on? Why did you ask me over here?"

"I didn't," he said.

"Then what's all this about a disappearance?" asked Ravi.

"I don't know, Ravi," said Robert. "I'd just been reading a letter about a missing waiter when you knocked on the door."

"Then it's a waiter who has disappeared?" asked Ravi, an uncomfortable feeling growing in the pit of his stomach. "Do you know how?"

"I've literally just opened the letter. It's from the waiter's sister. She says it was some weeks ago. About the time of…" Robert's voice trailed off, a faraway look on his face.

"What, Robert?"

His friend looked down at the floor and said nothing for a few moments. Then he seemed to gather himself. "Now look what I've done. I've gone and ruined a perfectly good carpet. The Bursar will kill me." He looked up and gave a half-hearted smile. "He'll probably send me to the Dean."

Ravi knew his friend well enough to know that he was covering up.

"Come on, Robert. You need to tell me. Why else would you send Cummings to find me?"

Robert looked blankly at Ravi, and now there was no lie in those green eyes.

"Ravi, I don't know who you are talking about. I know all the porters personally. Heavens, man, they're practically my personal police force. And I can tell you for a fact, not one of them is called Cummings."

Chapter 6

Jane stood near the entrance as the students filed into Hall. She wore a black skirt, white blouse, and college waistcoat. Her blonde hair was tied back in a bun, and she had gone easy on the lipstick, aware that Aurelia did not approve of her overdoing it. Neither, for that matter, did the Functions Manager, but Jane took more notice of Aurelia than her boss. Aurelia was a strong woman and had brought up three boys on a basic wage. Jane knew that this could not have been easy, and she respected Aurelia for it.

As the students passed the assembled serving staff, Jane observed them. All were wearing their college gowns as the rules of formal dining dictated. These were not full-length gowns like those of the Fellows. They were cut shorter, like a cape, with four lines of black velvet on the sleeves. Different, but not too fussy. She could relate to that.

Her focus switched to the students themselves. Some she had seen before, graduates mainly, who had spent the holidays working on their PhDs or other types of research. They tended to be older, and of course, all had brains the size of planets. Minds so full that some of them did not seem to have space for practical stuff like, well, how to dress. Two boys walked by whose clothing combination would have got them barred from the Regal. The taller one caught her eye and gave her a dazzling smile.

"Evening," he said.

"Evening," she replied, finding herself smiling in return.

Jane suddenly felt guilty for being so judgemental. In her experience it was not your ability or appearance that mattered – it was how you behaved. She glanced at Aurelia and saw she was smiling with genuine warmth at each of the guests coming into Hall. Following her lead, Jane started doing the same.

As she greeted the remaining diners, it was easy to spot the freshers. They were chatting excitedly, and she could understand why. If you had not experienced Hall before, it was like something out of *Harry Potter*. Minus the owls, of course.

She saw one of the regulars, a good-looking surfer dude, sweep into Hall accompanied by a Chinese girl and a heavy-set, bearded boy. Their blond leader gave her a wink, and she nodded back in acknowledgement.

"Shoulders, Jane," whispered Aurelia.

Jane straightened and waited for the last of the guests to enter, a tall boy and a girl who was half his size. They looked flushed, as if they had rushed to get there on time – or it could be that they were really into each other. Probably both, she decided. Aurelia motioned them towards two available places on a table by the far wall, before closing the panelled doors for Grace.

The guests stood to face each other along the three long tables that ran the length of the Hall. While they chatted, the Fellows entered at the far end of the Hall through an arched doorway leading from their Combination Room. That was where the Fellows' Steward stood and watched them find their places at High Table. Once they were all assembled, a bell was rung by the wine waiter, signalling to tonight's designated scholar that he or she should read out the College Grace from a wooden cardholder.

Jane saw the scholar step forward and turn to face the packed Hall. It was the surfer dude. He ignored the cardholder and smiled around at the Fellows and expectant students. Jane glanced at Aurelia, who was watching the boy intently.

He began in a deep, sombre voice.

"*Oculi omnium in te sperant, Domine, et tu das illis cibum in tempore, aperis manum tuam, et imples omne anima benedictione. Benedic, Domine, nos et dona tua, quae de tua largitate sumus sumpturi, et concede ut illis salubriter nutriti, tibi debitum obsequium praestare valeamus, per Jesum Christum Dominum nostrum.*"

There was a scraping of chairs, and the Fellows sat down, signalling to the rest of the Hall that it was time to do so. Conversations erupted as the guests settled into their places.

"He's got some balls," said Jane in awe.

"Jane!" said Aurelia.

"Well, he has. I'd never have done that without a script. Not with all the Fellows watching me."

"That may be so, but a young lady does not use such

words. The boy has courage, not…"

"Cojones?" suggested Jane with a look of innocence.

Aurelia scowled as she ushered Jane out towards the kitchen.

*****

"Well, that was impressive," said Ying as Giles rejoined them at the end of their table.

"Had to be done," he said, grinning.

"Pride comes before a fall, mate," said Trevor, wagging a soup spoon at him.

"So that's what you've been doing all summer holed up here," said Ying. "Reciting Latin to show off to the Fellows."

"Not entirely, although I have enjoyed brushing up on my Kennedy's *Latin Primer*. He was a Johnian, I might add." Giles stared wistfully at one of the old portraits. "Brought back memories of my first boarding school. The slipper, the cane. Happy days."

"The cane," said Ying. "They still do that sort of thing, do they?"

"Only on Tuesdays. And only if you have been particularly annoying. Like getting caught in the teachers' common room pouring salt in the sugar bowl."

"Nice," said Trevor.

"I thought so," said Giles.

A waitress appeared with steaming soup bowls, and he noticed it was the peroxide-blonde he had seen earlier.

"Thank you," he said.

"You're welcome," she said, meeting his eyes again.

"So apart from Latin, what else have you been doing over the summer?" asked Ying.

"Research," said Giles.

Trevor spluttered into his beard. "You? Research? Do you actually know where the University Library is?"

"It's that big ugly building off Grange Road, isn't it?" said Giles, waving his hand carelessly in the direction of New Court. "They were having an off day when they designed that one."

"Come on, Giles," persisted Ying, "you're not trying to tell me you were actually studying."

"I know you both find it hard to believe that I might enjoy opening a book or two, but it is true," he said, a look of pious innocence on his face. "Like the true Renaissance man that I aspire to be, I have been studying diligently over the summer."

"I'm speechless," said Ying.

"And that's something you don't hear often," said Trevor.

The waitress returned with bread rolls.

Trevor stared down at his empty bowl. "Ah. Bread rolls. I knew something was missing."

"Well, Giles, I'm impressed," said Ying. "I've known you now for what? Two years? I've yet to see you take this stuff seriously and you're nailed on for a First. If you're now going to study as well, you may end up being famous or something."

"Respect," mumbled Trevor, his mouth full of bread.

"Well, they weren't exactly academic books I was

reading," admitted Giles.

"Comics, then?" suggested Trevor.

"A bit more elevated than that," said Giles, pretending to be offended.

"Are you trying to tell me that you read poetry over the summer when you could have gone climbing?" demanded Ying, glancing over at the waitress. "Have you got a girlfriend or something? You seem very friendly with some of the staff."

"His bedder, you mean?" said Trevor, grimacing. "That's just not right. She could be my mum."

"Well, hard as it may seem, I did both," said Giles.

Trevor looked appalled. "Both bedders?"

"No, I read a book and did some climbing," said Giles.

The waitress returned and collected the plates. Ying gave her a suspicious look before turning on Giles.

"What book and what climbing?" she said. "Cambridge is as flat as a pancake."

He leant in closer and was delighted to see he now had their attention.

"There are plenty of good climbs if you know where to look for them," he said, tapping his nose, "hence the research."

Ying looked at him for a second and turned to Trevor.

"He's finally flipped," she said.

"Yep," said Trevor. "Tragic case. Boy genius gets lost on his way to Sainsbury's, stumbles into a library and his beautiful mind is overwhelmed by the discovery that people use them to read books."

"It wasn't a library, it was a bookshop," said Giles.

"You lost your mind in a bookshop?" said Trevor.

"No, I found a book in a bookshop."

"It is possible, I suppose," said Trevor.

"Which bookshop?" asked Ying.

"David's," said Giles.

"'G. David, Bookseller,' I'll think you'll find," corrected Trevor. "The one next to the Arts Theatre."

"The very same," said Giles.

The waitress returned and laid dinner plates in front of them. "Be careful, they're hot."

"Ow!" said Trevor, who had touched his plate despite the warning.

Ying gave him a look before turning back to Giles. "What on earth were you doing in David's bookshop?"

"Not exactly on earth, more under the earth," said Giles. "They have a basement."

"They do," agreed Trevor, dipping his finger into a glass of water.

"So, what's in this basement then?" asked Ying, doggedly persisting with her interrogation.

"A wonderful travel section," said Giles. "Not just Michael Palin and all the celebrity stuff you get in Heffers. But old titles too, many of them out of print. Quite a few were written by Cambridge climbers. Mallory and his pals. Those guys were awesome."

"OK," said Ying, but Giles was warming to the theme.

"You see, after the Great War, these chaps came back from the trenches to continue their education at Cambridge. Only now they wanted to live life to the full, which is hardly surprising given what they had just been through. Anyway, in those days the colleges were all male."

"Those were the days, mate," said Trevor.

"So?" said Ying, ignoring him.

"So, these frustrated young men couldn't bring girls back into college. If they were caught with them in their rooms, they could be sent down in disgrace. You see, in those days, the porters weren't there to keep tourists out. They were there to keep randy students in. Which, of course, was never going to happen, was it? You can imagine that our intrepid survivors from the trenches had faced far worse than a few old blokes in bowler hats guarding ancient college walls." He paused for effect. "And that's how it began."

"What began?" asked Ying.

Giles looked at them. "The night climbers of Cambridge."

"Balls?" asked the waitress.

Giles turned to see her looking at him, her face a mask of propriety.

"Meatballs?" she asked again, indicating the silver platter she carried.

He grinned. "My favourite! Though I believe Ying rather likes them too."

Ying rolled her eyes, but they sat there in silence until the waitress had finished serving.

"So, these night climbers?" asked Trevor after she had moved on.

Giles leant forward again. "I discovered an old book called *The Roof-Climber's Guide to St John's,* published in 1921 by Hartley, Grag and Darlington, three undergraduates who were students here. Top blokes," he said approvingly. "Climbing Cambridge college buildings had been going on for a while apparently, but because it was frowned on by college authorities, it had to be done at night. Anyway, our heroes had been scaling the various climbs of the college and very helpfully decided to publish a guide about their exploits."

"And you've got a copy," said Ying

"In my room," said Giles.

"There's a book in your room?" said Trevor, sounding impressed.

The waitress reappeared.

"Vegetables?"

"I've wondered that at times," said Giles, looking at his two friends, "but don't let appearances deceive you. They're not as thick as they look."

The waitress tried not to smile as she piled generous amounts of roast potatoes, beans and carrots on their plates.

When she had gone, Ying continued. "So, you've been reading a book?"

"I've been doing more than reading," said Giles.

"You've been writing notes as well?" said Trevor, spearing a roast potato with his fork.

Ying ignored him. "You've not gone and tried a climb, have you?"

"Might have…" said Giles, examining his wine glass.

Ying looked at him for a moment and then said, "OK. That's cool."

Trevor mumbled something with his mouth full of potato, which sounded like agreement. Giles leant forward again.

"So, are you guys interested in doing a spot of climbing this term?"

Ying and Trevor exchanged looks.

"What do you think?" she asked.

Trevor considered this for a moment. "Well, someone's got to make sure this idiot doesn't break his neck."

Giles needed to be sure. "Of course, this is still the sort of stuff you can get sent down for, so we're going to have to keep it pretty low-key."

"What do you mean?" said Ying.

"It's not a club I'm going to be advertising on the noticeboard."

"Just the three of us then," agreed Ying.

"I'm in," said Trevor loudly.

Giles was delighted. He'd have done it without them, but the idea of a secret society gave it a real edge.

"So, what are we going to call ourselves?" he asked.

"Call ourselves?"

"Well, we can't go around saying St John's Night Climbers, because that's a bit of a giveaway," he said.

"Good point, well made," said Trevor. "We need a name."

"That isn't a giveaway," said Giles.

"R&R. Rooftops and Ropes," said Ying. "Like, do you fancy a spot of R&R tonight?"

"Like it," said Giles, smiling.

"Has a certain ring to it," agreed Trevor.

"That's settled," said Giles, reaching for his glass. "A toast, ladies and gentlemen. To R&R."

Their glasses clinked between the silver candlesticks while, from the end of the table, the waitress looked on.

Chapter 7

"Evening, Ravi," said the Master as the Fellows filed into Hall from the Fellow's Combination Room. "Not with Robert tonight?"

Ravi turned to look at the short, round man in his early sixties who had glided alongside him without him noticing.

"Robert is bringing a guest with him this evening. He'll be along shortly, no doubt."

"Well, in that case, come and sit with me. I'd love to hear more about your trip to Nepal this summer. How are those schools doing?"

"Very well, thank you, Master. Each year we see steady progress."

"I am glad. Those schools are lucky to have such a conscientious mentor in yourself, Ravi. I look forward to hearing more over dinner."

The Master of St John's College, Dominic Lester, once again impressed Ravi with his remarkable knowledge of what each Fellow had been up to over the summer. A Professor of History, he had once had a career in the Foreign Office, and there were rumours that he had been working for MI5 during the later stages of the Cold War. Ravi had never spoken with the Master about it, and the man himself was a model of discretion.

As they moved to their seats on the High Table, Ravi saw Robert limp into Hall and sit further down the table from them, accompanied by a gaunt-looking man with jet-black hair slicked back from a widow's peak, wearing an expensive-looking suit. Ravi hadn't seen this person before, but the fact that he was without a gown suggested he was not an academic. Robert seemed deep in conversation, but Ravi noticed that the man's hawk-like eyes were scanning the other diners. When their eyes met, the man paused for a fraction of a second before turning to Robert and making a comment. Robert looked across at Ravi and smiled before whispering a few quiet words to his guest.

A bell sounded, and everyone rose for Grace, which was performed with some aplomb on this occasion by Chamberlain, a scholar whom Ravi knew was a regular in Hall. Once the amens were said, all took their seats and the Master immediately got down to the serious business of making small talk with the Fellows seated opposite.

"Good to see you, Jeremy, perhaps we could have a word after dinner about your sabbatical. I have some friends in Boston. Evening, Claire, how's that paper coming along? You must tell me about it tomorrow over lunch."

The Master's easy banter, refined in embassies throughout Europe and the Middle East, was one of his most significant assets. The fellowship of any college was a small community, and petty rivalries or perceived slights could cause all sorts of unpleasantness. Ravi had no doubt that the Master was well aware of the dangers and his management of the Fellows was, well, masterful.

The Master's people skills had also been used to good effect in persuading Johnians to make sizeable donations to the college, a vital part of any Master's job. St John's had one of the largest endowments in the university and made ·considerable contributions each year to the university's shared fund, which was redistributed to support the less well-funded colleges. Ravi had grown to respect and like the Master for the thoughtful way in which he dealt with his demanding role. He found himself looking forward to spending the evening catching up on their respective interests and hopes for the year ahead.

And catch up they did. The Master was good company, describing his recent visit to Yale to speak with their development team and some of the fascinating characters he had encountered from the various American embassies over the years. He also proved to be very knowledgeable about Nepal and showed a keen interest in the history of the Gurkhas, in particular the lives of their families while the menfolk served overseas. By the time dessert plates had been removed, Ravi had talked himself dry and could sit back and relax with a glass of wine while the Master spoke with the Senior Tutor about the prospects for the College Boat Club in the coming year.

Ravi looked down at the assembled students. The High Table was slightly raised and afforded him a good view of the three long tables that stretched back to the entrance leading to the kitchens. The candles flickered, casting a soft orange glow onto the lines of faces that talked animatedly between courses. The noise at the beginning of term was much louder and lighter in tone than later on in the academic year, when studies began to subdue the start-of-year enthusiasm. At this stage, the students still had plenty of energy and the pressure of assignment deadlines and reading lists was yet to have its deadening effect on decibel levels.

Ravi knew this from personal experience. Cambridge and Oxford were unusual in that they continued to operate small-group supervisions in the colleges to supplement the lectures provided by the university. Regular contact time with a leading professor in his field, surrounded by a small group of intelligent and motivated students, was an excellent formula for getting the most out of each individual. Ravi had seen it for himself.

When he thought back to how he had started, a naive boy from the Himalayas, he remembered that his first supervisions had been a daunting experience. He had felt entirely out of his depth at an academic level. He was awed by the legendary professor sitting in an armchair across a coffee table asking him for an opinion, and tongue-tied under the intense scrutiny of the British-born students around him. After a while, it had come as a surprise to him to realise that he understood what was being discussed, and as time progressed, understood it a lot better than his more sophisticated peers. Gradually his confidence had grown and so had his contributions in supervisions, to the point where he began to look forward to them with anticipation rather than dread.

These intimate gatherings were also where he learnt the value of listening carefully to people and picking up on their non-verbal cues, recognising the signs when they were unsure of what they were saying or, equally importantly, when they were holding back. He found the art of human interplay as fascinating as the scientific debates and by the time he had completed his degree with first-class honours, he knew that this was the type of study he was born for. For him, lecturing was a necessary evil, but his real fulfilment came from engaging with bright minds in a relaxed setting with a common interest in exploring his subject.

He had briefly entertained the idea of moving to Oxford to pursue his chosen career of becoming a Professor of Astronomy. He certainly had offers from Oxford colleges who had heard about this phenomenal talent from Nepal. But Cambridge still had so much to offer him. Its facilities were excellent, including the then recently opened Mullard Observatory to the west of the city. The prospect of operating the Half-Mile, One-Mile and Five-Kilometre Radio Telescopes and the Interplanetary Scintillation Array offered more than Oxford could at that time. His subsequent PhD had been a thrilling ride, fuelled by the excitement of his colleagues' discovery of the pulsar in 1971, one of the many astrological milestones achieved by the Cambridge team. His progression to Junior Research Fellow and then onto Teaching Fellow was rapid. Of course, he had made lifelong friends too.

Robert had been one of those sophisticated British students that had so impressed Ravi in his first Mathematics supervision at John's. It had been 1962, and Ravi remembered trekking up the stairs in Chapel Court, shivering in his thin cotton shirt, threadbare sweater and khaki twill trousers, trying to follow the enthusiastic banter of his fellow undergraduates. They had reached the door of Professor Dirac's rooms and knocked. Dirac had bellowed that they should enter and as the others filed in, Robert had noticed that Ravi was shivering. Mistaking this for fear, the kindly Robert had given him a reassuring wink and said, "Don't worry, I'm sure his bark is worse than his bite."

They had sat together on the sofa during the following hour, in which the brilliant and autistic Dirac had made little attempt to put them at ease and overwhelmed them with equations on his blackboard. When the bemused group of students had left the professor's room an hour later, Ravi had wondered if he was the only one who had failed to understand the concepts of cosmological models and large number hypotheses.

As they reached the bottom of the stairs, Robert said to him, "I know I said his bark would be far worse than his bite, but that was quite a bark! Was he speaking English or Martian?"

"I hope it was Martian," said Ravi, "because if it was English, I am in trouble."

"You and me both," said Robert, laughing and clapping Ravi on the back. "I'm Robert, by the way. Robert Mackenzie." He offered Ravi his hand.

"Ravi Gupta. Very nice to meet you, Robert," said Ravi, wincing at Robert's firm grip.

"Oh, sorry about that," said Robert. "Probably just relief at surviving that baptism by fire."

"It was indeed an ordeal," said Ravi.

"Heavens, man, you're shivering – are you all right?" said Robert, looking concerned at Ravi's quaking frame.

"I am cold, that's all. I am not yet used to the temperature here in England. It is warmer in Nepal," said Ravi apologetically.

"Here, take this," said Robert, unwinding his new college scarf from around his neck and wrapping it around Ravi's shoulders. Ravi was so cold he could not resist.

"Thank you, Robert, that is very kind of you. I will return it as soon as I get back to my room," said Ravi, amazed at the immediate effect it had on his body temperature.

"Don't mention it," said Robert warmly. "I've got my eye on another type of scarf, so you keep that one safely for me." He pulled the collar up on his tweed jacket and stuffed his hands into his pockets. "Fancy a cup of hot chocolate in my rooms? I'll stoke the fire, and we'll see if we can make sense of that diatribe of symbols Dirac's just given us."

"That would be most welcome," said Ravi, following his newfound friend for the first of their customary post-supervision socials.

Ravi smiled at the memory. He was not sure how he would have survived that first term without Robert. The Scot was not just an insightful mathematician, he was also an excellent study partner. Their good-natured discussions and arguments over mugs of tea in Robert's room accelerated their grasp of the concepts covered in the Cambridge Tripos up to the new standards expected of them by their demanding supervisors. He was also a thoughtful and selfless friend, who took it upon himself to introduce the young Ravi to the enthusiastic group of sportsmen for whom John's was famous, and to which Robert was a central figure. The scarf to which he referred in that chilly stairwell on their first meeting was the Cambridge Rugby Blue, which Robert duly acquired later that term, the first of three as an undergraduate. As a result, he had never asked for his original college scarf back, and when Ravi had suggested returning it at the end of their first year, Robert had insisted he keep it as a gift.

"Keep it as a reminder of our first mauling by Dirac," said Robert. "We survived, we happy few."

"Then I will wear it like a campaign medal," said Ravi. "From the field of battle."

And he had done. To this day Ravi wrapped himself in that scarf during the winter and spring terms. Worn and faded as it was, it had become his signature piece, a symbol of the longest friendship of his life.

"Eh, Ravi?" Robert's voice broke across his thoughts from the other side of the table.

"Sorry, Robert, I missed that," said Ravi, looking over at his friend.

"This is Julian Schiller, Ravi. The benefactor who got you the funding for those schools in Nepal. I was just saying how much those children appreciated the new classroom equipment."

"Indeed, they did," said Ravi, smiling and bowing his head towards the stranger, who returned the gesture, though his pale eyes never left Ravi's. "It was a most generous gift, Mr Schiller. The schools in that part of the world have to make do with insufficient resources, particularly for science. I cannot thank you enough."

"Julian, please," said Schiller, bowing his head. "And as for your schools initiative, I am only too happy to help. Robert has told me so much about your work together."

"Has he?" said Ravi, glancing towards his friend, who was reaching for his glass. "That was a long time ago. Our fields of interest have diverged somewhat since then."

"A shame," said Julian. "I thought your space-time theories sounded most interesting. Just the sort of innovative approach that I would consider funding."

"Indeed," said Ravi, glancing at his friend, who was sniffing the wine appreciatively. "What exactly is it you do, Julian?"

"I manage an environmental investment fund based in Switzerland. We are particularly interested in the exploration of space with a view to finding habitable planets for mankind and the means to get there."

"I see," said Ravi. "You think that is feasible, do you?"

"I think it is essential, don't you? Our stewardship of this planet has been so catastrophic, I fear that we have no choice but to look for opportunities beyond this world, however challenging that may be."

"You don't think that we might be better served by governments cooperating more effectively together?"

Schiller laughed, but there was no humour in it.

"A noble sentiment, Professor. But our governments seem incapable of working together to implement even the most modest climate goals. Take the latest UN Millennium Development Goals. Signing that agreement was one thing, getting people to change their behaviour has proven to be another. In the West, no one wants to implement unpopular but necessary measures for fear of being voted out of office at the next election. And in less democratic regimes, protecting the environment is low on their list of priorities compared to retaining their grip on power by any means necessary."

"You seem to have a pretty pessimistic view on the future of mankind, it would appear, Julian."

"On the contrary, I remain optimistic that a solution can be found, only not through the traditional approaches currently being employed. Education and research are the key. We need to find radical solutions that can explode the constraints of our current thinking. And then we need to fund them without waiting for governments to decide if it will or will not be a vote-winner at the ballot box."

Ravi had heard similar things before from his students at tutorials or during debates at the Cambridge Union. But he found the cold intensity of Julian's delivery unsettling. The man believed every word of his little speech and, from what Ravi understood, had the financial backing to implement it. His conviction would have been laudable, if the zeal with which he expressed it hadn't been so chilling. Ravi decided it was time to lighten the mood.

"Well, I am sure many of my colleagues will be delighted to approach you for funding of their research, university budgets being what they are. You will be a popular guest at many of the colleges, I have no doubt."

"You are indeed correct, Professor. Professor Mackenzie has been one such beneficiary already."

"I'm delighted to hear it, Julian," said Ravi, looking across at Robert, who had put his glass down and was watching Julian warily.

"And has your collaboration been fruitful?" asked Ravi politely.

"Very much so. Robert here has been remarkably helpful. We hope to make some exciting breakthroughs in the coming months."

A frown appeared across Robert's glistening forehead.

"Well, there's a lot more work to be done before we can take our findings to the next stage of development, Julian," said Robert.

"Come, Robert, you are too modest. Your discoveries are nothing short of stellar," said Julian.

"Well, yes, that's very kind," said Robert, who seemed flustered not by the flattery, Ravi thought, but by the direction the conversation was going. "But there are aspects that we have not yet had time to investigate. There are many more scenarios I'd like to run to confirm the viability of some of the practical applications."

"You have too little faith in your abilities," said Julian,

his eyes gleaming. "I have seen the evidence for myself and the possibilities for mankind are remarkable."

"I'm just saying we should be as rigorous in mitigating the risks as we are in pursuing the intended benefits," said Robert.

Ravi recognised the evident alarm in his friend's flushed face.

"You can't make an omelette without breaking a few eggs," said Julian. "Don't you agree, Professor Gupta?"

Ravi didn't like the way that this stranger was so dismissive of Robert's concerns. It smacked of arrogance, or bullying, or both.

"I've never been a fan of omelettes," said Ravi, holding the man's stare, something he found he could do as well as anyone after a lifetime of looking through telescopes. Julian must have noticed the edge in Ravi's response, because his face stiffened for a moment, before the smile returned. It was a smile that reminded Ravi of a shark.

"Forgive me, Professor, what exactly is it that you do now?"

"I observe the universe, looking for objects that might pose a threat to our world," said Ravi, not taking his eyes from Julian's.

"I see. An astrologer? Or is it astronomer? I always get them confused. One studies the stars, and the other is some sort of fairground fortune-teller? Which is it, exactly?"

Robert shifted uncomfortably in his chair.

"I think you'll find an astronomer sees things for what they are," said Ravi, "not what they appear to be."

"Is that so?" said Julian. "I would have thought that anyone who spends all that time looking down a long tunnel at faraway objects would lack a certain perspective."

"On the contrary," said Ravi. "One sees things with absolute clarity."

Julian's face flushed suddenly. "You fool!" he cried, lunging forward, and Ravi thought for an instant the man was going to leap at him. Instead, Julian grabbed a napkin and started dabbing furiously at his arm. Ravi glanced down and saw a large red stain spreading over the sleeve of his expensive jacket.

"Forgive me," said Aurelia, withdrawing the claret bottle that had splashed wine over his arm.

Julian turned on her, and without thinking Ravi found himself rising from his seat, all sense of protocol forgotten. The conversation around them died, and Fellows' heads turned along the table. Ravi and Julian stared at each other before Robert reached across and put a beefy hand on his guest's arm.

"Steady there, laddie. It was just an accident."

"An accident?" fumed Julian, glaring at Aurelia, who stood there unmoved.

The Fellows' Butler came hurrying over. "Let us get you something for that, sir. Some salt, perhaps?"

Julian continued to stare at Aurelia, a vein twitching on the side of his temple. She bowed an apology and resumed serving wine to the other diners. The conversation started up again, led by the Master, who asked the Fellow opposite him a question as Ravi resumed his seat. Julian shrugged off

Robert's hand and, balling up the napkin, stepped away from the table.

"I will be going now," he said.

It was strictly against protocol to leave before second Grace, but Robert wisely decided not to protest.

"If you must, Julian."

"I do. Thank you for dinner, Robert," said Julian, his voice strained.

"Let me escort you to the Porter's Lodge," said Robert, rising to his feet.

"That will not be necessary. I know my way, and I would not want to trouble you further tonight."

"No, I insist," said Robert.

Julian strode from the Hall and Ravi watched as Robert followed him, limping to keep up with his guest. The two men passed Aurelia, standing like a sentry at the door. Julian ignored her, and the waitress looked ahead, her face impassive. Then, to Ravi's surprise, Aurelia glanced across at him and her mouth twitched into a smile for the briefest of moments, before the mask returned.

Ravi's mouth dropped open and he stared in wonder at his muse as a warm glow spread throughout his body.

"I like that woman," said a quiet voice in his ear.

Ravi started and turned to find the Master surveying the waitress over his glass of wine.

"What?" he said, looking from the Master back to Aurelia again. "Oh, Aurelia, you mean?"

"You know her, do you, Ravi?"

Ravi felt the colour rising to his cheeks.

"Why, I believe she has been at the college for many years," he said with more formality than he had intended. "I have always found her to be a polite and attentive waitress."

"That may be," said the Master, studying him now, "but she is also an excellent judge of character, if I'm not mistaken."

Ravi smiled. "I'm sure you are right, Master."

The Master leant in close as the Fellows' Butler made his way towards the High Table carrying a small bell.

"Keep an eye on your friend Robert, won't you, Ravi?" he said in a hushed tone. "I wouldn't want him doing anything foolish, if it can be prevented."

Ravi didn't quite know how to respond to this and was saved from doing so by the aptly named Grace Bell, bringing the meal to a close, but leaving Ravi with much to ponder.

Chapter 8

Annabel and Nick left Hall and wandered into Second Court, along with the last of the other diners. Annabel would have stayed longer, but the waiters needed to clear the long tables.

"Fancy a drink?" Nick asked.

"OK, then," she said, not wanting the evening to end just yet.

They walked over the cobbles around the grass lawns, Annabel treading carefully in her heels. Nick opened the door to the College Bar. A roar of noise greeted them.

"Wow!" said Annabel. "Busy night!"

"What do you fancy?" yelled Nick above the din.

"A beer!" she yelled back.

"Find us a place, and I'll bring them over," he said before edging his way through the crowd towards the bar.

Annabel looked about her. The room stretched out either side of the doorway. High up along one side was a full-length, red-bladed oar, hanging above the bar itself, which was creaking under the scrum of students trying to get served. On the opposite side, large alcoves ran around the edge of the room, their red-cushioned seats occupied by noisy students and half-empty glasses covering the small tables in front of them. Dotted around the walls, Annabel spotted black-and-white photographs of college sporting teams, some so ancient that the colours had faded to dull sepia. Somehow, she felt comforted by the monochrome faces of former Johnians smiling back at her, welcoming the latest member of the college to their favourite drinking den.

Annabel heard the door open behind her and felt the cold rush of air as the last of the diners entered. She needed to find a place to sit. To her right, the space was rammed full of noisy students, so Annabel headed left and spotted an alcove that still had room left on the end of a bench. Clustered around the table was the blond Romeo she had seen this morning in Second Court. He was sitting there in deep conversation with two friends, a Chinese girl and bear-like boy, whose broad features and muscular forearms were covered in dark hair.

"Do you mind if I pinch these seats?" she asked.

The three looked up, and the boy stopped talking immediately. There was a pause before the Chinese girl said, "Be our guest," although it was clear from her tone that she did not welcome the interruption.

"Thanks," said Annabel.

"Excuse Ying," said the bear, indicating the girl, who turned on him.

"What do you mean by that?"

"That you were a bit harsh," said the bear.

"Me? What are you talking about?" She turned on

99

Annabel. "I wasn't, was I?"

"Not really," Annabel said.

"In other words: yes, Ying," said Blondie.

Ying opened her mouth as if to argue, then shrugged and turned to Annabel.

"OK, sorry. It's just that pretty-boy Giles here, after two years of constant schoolboy drivel, was finally saying something interesting." She held out her hand. "Ying."

"You'd better take it, she doesn't do that often," said the bear.

"I'm Annabel," she said, shaking Ying's hand.

"As for these two oafs, the beauty is Giles, and the beast is Trevor."

"Don't worry, she always gets that the wrong way around," said Trevor.

"We've met already," said Giles.

"How could I forget?" said Annabel.

"Really?" said Ying, her eyebrows raised. "You do seem to be showing far more interest in girls this term, Giles."

"Must be puberty," said Trevor, who made as if to check something under the table. "Yeah, looks like puberty all right. Or have you been stealing buns from Hall again?"

"Ha, ha. Very funny," said Giles. "You see, Annabel, under that apelike countenance, Trevor here thinks of himself as something of a wit."

"Don't mind them," said Ying. "So where did you two meet?"

"Giles nearly ran me down on his bike this morning," said Annabel.

"That's harsh," said Giles. "I was in perfect control."

"With a carton of milk in one hand and a bacon sandwich in the other," continued Annabel.

"That's how he always rides," said Trevor. "Lucky he wasn't reading his lecture notes as well."

"While playing games on his phone," added Ying.

"Life is too short," said Giles, leaning back against the chair, waving his glass of beer in the air. "So much to do, so much to see."

"Speaking of which," said Ying, a noticeable huskiness to her voice, "things are looking up."

Annabel turned and saw Nick approaching the table with a bottle of beer in each hand.

"Here you go," he said, handing a bottle to Annabel.

"Come and join us," said Ying, leaning forward with a broad smile. Behind her, Trevor rolled his eyes as Annabel made room and Nick perched on the seat next to her.

"This is Nick, by the way," said Annabel.

He nodded at the others.

"I take it that you two are together," said Giles, looking pointedly at Ying, who ignored him and continued to gaze at Nick.

"Just friends," said Nick, taking a swig from his bottle.

"Good friends," said Annabel, putting her hand on his thigh.

Nick convulsed and spilt beer onto his gown. Annabel withdrew her hand and felt her face flush with embarrassment as Giles studied her with interest over his glass.

"Right," he said. "Well, I'm Giles. This brute is Trevor.

And the vampire homing in on Nick here is Ying. She preys on freshers, so watch yourself!"

"I'm just friendly," said Ying. "Besides, it's nice to keep Trevor on his toes." She pouted at Trevor. "Don't worry, Annabel. Believe it or not, I'm more into big hairy brutes than tall, brooding types. No offence, gorgeous," she added to Nick.

"None taken," he said.

"So," said Trevor, "are you saying Bella got it wrong with Edward, and she should have gone with Jacob?"

"No," said Ying, "that was different."

"How, exactly?"

While Trevor and Ying embarked upon a protracted discussion of alternative outcomes to the *Twilight* saga, Giles turned to Annabel.

"This could go on for a while. I suggest we leave them to it. So, what are you studying?"

"Natural Sciences, though I'm hoping to focus on zoology," said Annabel.

"What about you, Nick?"

"Law," said Nick.

"Ouch!" said Giles.

"Why does everyone say that?" asked Nick.

Giles shrugged. "Say 'Law' to a Cambridge student and most people flinch. You've heard about Pavlov's dogs? It's like that."

"Is it really that bad?" said Nick.

"Nah, it's never as bad as people make out. The hours in the library. The huge number of cases to read. The brutal supervisions with argumentative dons, who resent the fact that their thicker contemporaries are now earning millions in the city. Piece of cake, really."

"You certainly know how to sell it, Giles," said Annabel, looking at Nick sympathetically.

"Ah, but there is, as always, a silver lining, Nick," said Giles, tapping his nose. "Six years of hard labour and you'll be earning more money than you can shake a stick at. No time to spend it, mind you. But that means you can pay off your student loan and be free as a bird by 30 with a CV to die for."

Annabel could tell from the frown on Nick's face that he wasn't particularly sold on this idea, so she decided to change tack.

"So, what about you, Giles? What are you studying?"

"Mummies and tombs."

"Sorry?"

"Archaeology, my dear. Digging up dead people. Can't beat it."

"What's it like?" said Annabel.

"Best field trips in town," he said, "though Geography runs it close."

"Do you get any field trips for Law?" Annabel asked.

"Wormwood Scrubs was last year's highlight, I think," said Giles.

"That's not making me feel any better," said Nick.

Giles grinned and held up his bottle. Nick sighed and clinked it with his own.

"Listen, I'm going to give you a tip," said the older

student, tapping the side of his nose. "It's not something I share with everyone, but it's worked for me."

He leant forward, and Annabel found herself doing the same.

"It doesn't matter what subject you read, if you set out intending to enjoy it, you probably will. But if you expect it to be tough, it will break your balls. Seriously, Nick," he said, "even with Law, there'll be loads of great stuff to discover. Like an intrepid archaeologist, you just need to go dig it up. Lord Denning, for instance. I've read some of his judgements. Brilliant stuff. He made the law work for him, you see. You just need to have the right mindset."

"Like envisioning the ball sailing between the uprights, you mean," said Nick.

"Something like that," said Giles, frowning momentarily. "Whatever." He tapped his chest for emphasis. "For me it's all about digging up some mysterious treasure. You know. Indiana Jones and all that. Whereas for you, Annabel, it's probably all about discovering some strange, exotic animal?"

"Hopefully."

"And you, Nick," Giles continued, turning to him. "It's all about winning. Am I right?"

"Sort of," said Nick.

"There you go!" said Giles enthusiastically. "Trust me, if you believe it hard enough, it will happen."

"What are you droning on about now, Giles?" asked Ying.

She and Trevor had apparently resolved their *Twilight* plot debate.

"Mind games," said Giles. "Speaking of games, either of you two any good at ultimate frisbee? John's just missed out on Cuppers last year," he said, indicating a sepia photograph on the wall by the window.

Annabel noticed that despite the apparent age of the picture, it was dated 2020. On closer inspection, the blazer-clad men and women lounging on the lawns, looking dreamily into the distance, included a dapper-looking Giles, champagne glass in one hand and a circular disc in the other.

"Not really," said Annabel, "I was thinking more about giving rowing a try. Cox, obviously."

"Sound plan," Giles nodded. "Get others to do the hard work. You, Nick?"

"Rugby, if they'll have me," said Nick.

"Well, Trevor should help you there," said Giles, turning to the huge bear in the corner. "He's vice-captain this year, or is it the captain of vice? I can never remember. Either way, he'll be watching you run out at training." He turned to Trevor. "Got any questions for a prospective Redboy here?"

Trevor looked at Nick. "Forward or back?"

"Winger," said Nick.

"Fast?"

"Eleven point five," said Nick.

"That'll do," said Trevor. He reached over and shook Nick's hand. "You're in."

"Now, don't go getting your nose broken, Nick," said Ying. "Or Trevor here will have some genuine competition."

"I thought you said you liked the way it bent to the left?" said Trevor, trying to focus on his nose, which sat slightly off-centre between his crossed eyes.

Annabel laughed and was pleased to see a grin finally appear on Nick's face.

"Listen, I'm thinking of heading off," she said, placing her empty bottle on the table. "Busy day tomorrow."

"Hate to break it to you, girl, but busy it ain't," said Ying. "Wait till week five. Then you'll be thinking back to today and wondering how it all went wrong."

"What's so bad about week five?" asked Annabel.

"Freshers' burnout week," said Ying. "Too much work, not enough time and no more parties."

"That's when you'll find out who your real friends are," said Trevor. "They'll be the ones dragging you in here for stress-relief sessions."

"And here you will find us," said Giles, holding his arms out wide. "Your experienced stress-relievers. Always ready to pass on advice after you buy the next round."

"Yes, well, I'll know where to come then," said Annabel as she and Nick rose to go.

"See you around," said Nick. "See you at training, Trevor."

Trevor nodded. Ying blew Nick a kiss and winked at Annabel.

Annabel gave Nick a gentle nudge towards the door and followed him as he edged his way through the boisterous crowd.

Once outside, the chill air hit them, and Annabel stared up at the night sky, enjoying the relative peace and quiet after the din inside. They began walking across the cobbles, heading for Third Court.

"Friendly bunch," said Nick.

"They were, weren't they?"

Then, with mounting horror, Annabel remembered the moment she had grabbed Nick's knee and felt the colour rising to her cheeks.

Did I really do that? she thought. *What was I thinking? More to the point, what is Nick thinking? That I'm some sort of stalker. Oh shit! Pull yourself together, girl!*

Both of them were quiet as they crossed Third Court and the silence became painful as they began climbing the Bridge of Sighs. Annabel felt she had to say something.

"It's good to meet some of the older students," she blurted out.

"Yeah," he said.

Annabel remembered the way Ying's eyes had crawled all over Nick and wondered if he was thinking about her.

"I liked Giles," she said.

"I think he'd had one or two," Nick replied.

"Still, I liked his stuff about a positive mindset."

"I suppose so," he said and fell silent again.

Annabel remembered Nick's comment about them being "just friends". What did he mean by that? Were they just starting out as friends? Would they only ever be friends? Would he like to be more than just friends?

"I might ask them about the statue," he said, interrupting her thoughts.

"What?" said Annabel, wondering why he was bringing that up. What was it with him and this so-called statue? What was so important about it, anyway? "Yeah. Good idea."

They turned right at the cloisters and headed through the passageway under the Wedding Cake towards Cripps. As they came out on the other side, Annabel could see A Staircase up ahead. Realising time was running out, she tried again.

"So, what have you got on tomorrow?"

"Lectures, then rugby trials and a tutorial with Mackenzie in the evening," he said.

"Me too," said Annabel. "I mean, me and the other NatScis are meeting our tutor too."

"Gupta?" he asked. "Where's he?"

"Second Court, above the Old Library. What about Mackenzie?"

"New Court. Had my interview there."

They reached the staircase and started climbing.

"Still, it'll be good to meet the other lawyers," she suggested.

"Suppose so."

"Well, if not, you can always switch to…" Annabel almost said her own subject but saved herself.

"Mummies," he said.

"What?"

They had reached Nick's landing, and when she looked up at him, the glow of the light framed his neat, sandy hair. Annabel felt something warm stir inside.

"Egyptian mummies," he said, "with Indiana Giles."

"Oh yes," she said with a laugh.

They stood there for a moment, a few feet apart, and she looked into his eyes. He didn't move or say anything. His stillness only made her thoughts spin even faster. Would he say anything? If he were going to, this would be the time.

"Bugger!"

"Sorry?" said Annabel.

"I forgot to switch my room to IN," he explained, turning.

"Oh," she said, deflating. "Me too."

The moment had passed.

*****

Nick looked down at her.

"I'll switch them over," he said.

He headed for the stairs and grimaced. For a moment back there on the landing, he had thought Annabel was going to kiss him. Indeed, he had been thinking about nothing else ever since she had touched his knee in the bar. When that had happened, he had nearly dropped his beer.

Then there was the walk back over the Bridge of Sighs. Just the two of them. That had been torture. He had not known what to say. And all she wanted to talk about was bloody Giles. He had hoped mentioning the statue would have got her attention, but that hadn't worked. Compared to a pretty-boy scholar with his mind games bullshit, a Midlands rugby player must be a real let-down.

Her voice from the top of the stairs broke into his thoughts.

"So, I'll see you in the morning?"

"Sure," he replied.

He heard her climbing up the next flight of stairs, and his heart sank further.

"Sleep well," she called down.

Nick thought about setting off after her but decided that would freak her out. Instead, he stood at the foot of the stairs and glowered at the room index. Nick was about to jab their room switches to IN when something made the hairs on the back of his neck stand up. Trusting his athlete's instincts, Nick flung himself flat, grunting as his body hit the paving stones. A cold wind swept over him, and he lay there for a moment, adrenaline pulsing through his body, gown flapping over his head. Peering up through its folds, he imagined he saw a massive pair of wings gliding across the river before the darkness enveloped them.

*****

At the top of the stairwell, Annabel heard the howling sound as she inserted her key in the lock and her door blew open with a bang. The wind whistled around the landing, and she spun around, her heart in her mouth. Almost as soon as it began, the noise died away, leaving her standing alone, her heart thumping.

She ran to the stairwell and looked down.

"Nick, are you all right?"

When he didn't reply, Annabel's heart beat even faster, and she was about to start down the stairs when Nick answered.

"Yeah, yeah, I'm fine," he called up.

"What was that?"

"Just the wind," he answered, and after a brief pause, "See you in the morning."

She waited a few moments longer until she heard him coming up the stairs.

"OK. Sleep well."

"You too."

Annabel waited until she heard him begin to unlock his door, then turned and headed for her room, unsettled in so many ways.

*****

On the landing below, Nick locked both doors behind him. He walked over to the sink and splashed water on his face before looking up into the mirror. His hair was dishevelled and his skin pale. He looked like he had seen a ghost.

"First the statue and now this," he said to his reflection. "You better not be losing it, mate. You've only just got here."

Nick picked up his toothbrush and began brushing his teeth, finding some level of calm from the simple action. Turning from the mirror, he scanned his room and saw rugby socks and his lucky SpongeBob briefs hanging on the radiator. At least his failure to invite Annabel in had saved her from seeing those. Retrieving them from the heater, he noted they were stiff but dry and stuffed them into the bottom of his wardrobe. Taking a hanger from the rail, Nick removed his gown from his shoulders and was about to hang it up when he froze.

The back of his new gown lay in tatters, lines of ragged rents running from shoulder to hem. Nick stared at it in shock, and for the first time that week, forgot the promise he had made to his mum.

"What the…!"

111

Chapter 9

The next morning Ravi made his way along the Backs towards St John's. The events of the previous day had disturbed him and last night's walk home to Newnham had failed to provide the respite it usually did. The gin and tonic, with more gin than tonic, had helped induce a fitful sleep, but when he woke, he did not feel rested. So, he set off to college, hoping that the walk would allow him to replay the day's events again and put them in some sort of perspective.

The missing waiter, the phantom statue and Robert's behaviour stirred memories of events he had tried to bury long ago. Add to that the appearance of a man like Julian in their midst and Ravi sensed darkness growing in the heart of the college, the same one that had threatened St John's before, almost half a century ago.

*****

The tunnel shifted and swayed like the body of a snake and Ravi had to reach out to the wall to steady himself. It was smooth to the touch, like glass almost, and he could see his own reflection staring back at him from the shimmering surface. His wide and disbelieving eyes were partly obscured by the thick glossy hair that fell across his young, clean-shaven face, his tall, thin body strangely shortened by the curve of the tunnel.

With his hands resting against the tunnel wall, he felt a tingle of energy transmit itself through his fingertips, growing in strength as it ran up his arms. Unsettled, Ravi pushed himself away from the wall and stood there swaying, fighting the wave of nausea that rose up inside him. Holding his arms out for balance, he looked around for something to focus on. In the far distance, he caught sight of a thin sliver of white light, its horizontal slit unwavering in the darkness. Ravi used it to block out the unsettling sensations around him.

It took some minutes for his body to adjust to the tunnel's pulsating movement, but when it did, Ravi took a steadying breath and risked a look back the way he had come. Behind him, he saw the dim yellow glow of the doorway he had come through and beyond that the rows of books lining the walls of the room. That was when Ravi knew this was not a dream.

This was real. Unbelievable, but real nonetheless. Here he was, a Junior Research Fellow, standing in a passageway he had reasoned – no, hoped – would be here. If it hadn't been for Robert, he would have given up trying a long time ago. But his friend had never doubted him.

"It's there, Ravi. We know it is. We just have to find it. If it were easy, someone else would have done it. Besides…" Ravi remembered his friend's green eyes twinkling with excitement. "Can you imagine what they are going to say when we do!"

Ravi smiled at the memory, but his growing sense of elation was dampened by guilt that Robert wasn't with him. He wondered whether he should head back and wait for his friend, so they could share this moment together. But then there was that thin sliver of white light in the distance. Ravi resumed his journey, taking deep breaths to calm his nerves. Moving faster now, he became ever more aware that the light ahead was growing sharper and as it did so, tiny diamond-like crystals twinkled within the surface of the tunnel wall. Something about the pinpricks of light struck Ravi as odd, and he paused for a moment to look more closely.

Ravi's mouth fell open, his eyes widened, and he gasped in shock. He staggered for a moment as comprehension hit him like a blow to his stomach. He understood what he was seeing, and the enormity of it sucked all the breath from his body.

These crystals were not on the surface of the tunnel. Indeed, they weren't in the shaft at all. They were way beyond the confines of the dimension in which Ravi was travelling. These lights came from a long, long way away. Millions of light-years away. These were stars. And Ravi was standing amongst them.

*****

Ravi looked up and found he was gripping the wrought-iron gates at the back of St John's. His bony hands felt hot and sweaty against the cold metal. The Backs lay behind him, unnoticed and unimportant. Reaching down, he unhooked the latch and pushed the gate open. St John's silently welcomed its troubled son, who barely heard the clang of the gate closing behind him. As his footsteps crunched across the familiar path, he looked across at its magnificent tower, standing there in the morning sunlight, and his resolve began to return. This was his home. This was his purpose in life. If forces were gathering that could damage it in any way, he was not going to stand by and let them walk through its gates unopposed. He was going to fight. Alone, if he had to.

By the time he strode across the Kitchen Bridge he felt a sense of purpose he had not had for years. He thrust open the door to the Buttery and stepped inside, pausing only when he saw Aurelia standing behind the serving counter. She looked up in surprise, and when their eyes met, he remembered his battle of wills with Julian. Not alone, perhaps!

And that was when the spring-loaded door swung back on its hinges and smacked him in the face.

Ravi was pitched backwards, his briefcase flying from his grasp and spilling papers into the air. The world seemed to turn upside down, his feet appearing above him before he landed with a thump that knocked the wind out of him and cracked his head against the floor. Lying there, dazed, Ravi stared up through the confetti of paper at the exit sign above the doorway and wondered if anyone had noticed that the light bulb needed replacing. Then Aurelia's concerned face appeared above him, staring down at him. What beautiful eyes she had, dark but fiery, like coal. Her lips, full and red, were whispering words to him. What was she was saying? What words did she have for him?

"Hey! Professor? Can you hear me? What are you doing down there?"

"Beautiful…" croaked Ravi.

"Sorry, what did you say, Professor?" said Aurelia, leaning closer to him.

"You," he whispered, his voice deep and husky as he reached for her. But at that moment he felt someone grab his hand and place it firmly by his side.

"There you go, Professor. That was quite an entrance," said a perky voice.

A face surrounded by peroxide-blonde hair interposed itself between him and Aurelia.

"You don't want to go doing anything silly now, do you? Not when you've just gone and banged your head."

Her face looked familiar, but he couldn't quite place it.

"Grab his other arm, Aurelia," she said.

The two women reached under his arms and pulled him up to a sitting position.

"Gave us quite a fright, you did, Professor," continued the waitress, adjusting Ravi's jacket and taking his other hand from Aurelia. "Now look into my eyes, Professor," she said as she squared up in front of him. "We do this all the time in kickboxing. You know, just to make sure there's no concussion."

Ravi looked up into her face.

"Which day is it, Professor?" she asked, speaking clearly and slowly.

"It's Wednesday," he replied.

"Very good. And, seeing as your subject is Astronomy, what is the closest planet to Earth?" she said.

"Venus," he said, and his eyes drifted towards Aurelia again.

"Focus!" said the waitress firmly, raising a finger. She held it in front of him and moved it from right to left. His eyes tracked the finger steadily. As they did so, something like clarity returned. And with it the shocking realisation of what had just happened.

"There you go," said the waitress, apparently satisfied. "You'll live. Let's get you on your feet."

Then the two women reached under his arms and heaved him upright. Ravi stood there, a little unsteady, aware of the heat rising in his cheeks as he watched the others gather up his things.

"Now you go and sit down in your usual place, Professor, and we will go and bring you your breakfast," said the waitress, ushering Ravi towards the table by the window.

"But does Aurelia know what I want?" said Ravi as he sat down gingerly in the chair.

Jane smiled.

"Professor, Aurelia knows exactly what you want."

Ravi looked towards Aurelia and felt his pulse quicken that she should know him so well.

"She does?"

"Poached egg, mushrooms and tomato. Followed by toast, butter, marmalade and Earl Grey tea," said the waitress. "We all know Professor Gupta. You're as reliable as Big Ben."

117

"Oh," he said. "Of course."

A thought occurred to him.

"How did you know I was an Astronomy professor?" he asked.

"Well, it was pretty obvious from the contents of your briefcase, Professor," said the waitress, stuffing a pile of journals into his bag, before handing it back to him. "There you go. No harm done."

"Indeed," he said. "Thank you, Jane."

The girl stared at him, clearly impressed that he remembered her name.

"My, we are full of surprises this morning, aren't we? Well then, you just sit here, and your breakfast will be along shortly."

Jane gave him a smile and headed back to the checkout, where her other early-morning regulars were waiting to pay.

Twenty minutes later Ravi left the Buttery, mortified at the scene he had caused. Aurelia and Jane had been very kind, but his face burned with the thought of what they must think of him.

"You utter fool!" he said to himself.

The fresh air that greeted him outside in Second Court was a welcome relief, and he leant against the stone doorway to gather himself. The gaggle of students heading towards the Buttery gave him a queer look and Ravi pushed himself away from the wall. Ignoring their stares, he headed for his rooms. He needed to compose himself before confronting Robert. Fortunately, he met no one else as he crossed the courtyard. If he had, the frown on his face would have deterred even the most cheerful of souls.

Ravi's rooms were situated at the top of E Staircase in the north-west corner of Second Court. This staircase was unusual in that it was far broader than any other in the college, at least until the first-floor landing – the reason being that this was the former entrance to the Old Library.

For almost five centuries, members of the college had used these steps to access one of the most extensive libraries in Cambridge. Now the old entrance was no longer used, and access to the library was only possible through the new atrium in Chapel Court.

The new library was an impressive structure, artfully integrating modern study spaces into the 1930s architecture of the court. Not only did it offer a wide range of core reference materials for each subject, but it also provided students with super-fast broadband, excellent soundproofing, and climate control without the need for wasteful air-conditioning. The new library had won a clutch of awards, a major selling point of St John's to potential scholars and popular with the students. For all that, Ravi hated it.

For him, there was only one library at St John's, and that was the original one accessed from his stairwell. He had first entered the Old Library as a young man and had been overwhelmed by the sense of history and learning that permeated every dark enclave. It was like stepping into a religious sanctum, packed with tomes of sacred texts, scrolls and parchments, penned by scholars over centuries and presided over by a busy but silent ministry of librarians and researchers. Each time he had entered its cavernous depths, he felt like he was stepping back in history, and the wonder of the place had never left him.

For this reason, Ravi had spent over two decades waiting for a set of rooms to become available on that staircase. When the Fellows' Rooms Committee finally confirmed his request, he remembered punching his fist in the air in triumph, prompting some disapproving looks from his colleagues in the Combination Room.

For a few happy years after taking residence on E Staircase, he would walk out of his door on the top floor, descend a rickety wooden stairwell to the first-floor landing and be inside the ancient place of learning in less than a minute. It gave him enormous joy and comfort to be within a few steps of what he felt to be the academic heart of the college. Only now, that heart had a ghastly modern pacemaker attached to it. Admittedly one that had breathed new life into the place, but at an emotional cost to him personally.

When the new library had opened in 1994, the oak-panelled door of the Old Library had been locked to all. Ravi had petitioned the then Master for clemency against this trespass and had even enlisted Robert's support to lobby for Ravi to be given access through the original entrance. However, the Old Library housed an archive of priceless manuscripts and it had been decided that the security of those treasures was of paramount importance. Indeed, the installation of a labyrinthine set of security measures was a necessary condition of the College's unrelenting insurers. As a consequence, Ravi's passionate protests had fallen on deaf ears.

This had been one of his most painful and frustrating experiences at St John's, and he had spent weeks brooding over the injustice that had been done to him. Having failed to negotiate a right of access, Ravi had conducted a stubborn but ineffective demonstration over the following two decades. Each day he made a point of entering the new library, turning left at reception and heading through the exhibition space that led to the archive section. There he would greet the two college archivists and sign the visitors' book, before proceeding through the fireproof glass partition into the vaults. A short walk between the corridor of bookcases stacked with manuscripts led him to the leaded Oriel Window. There he ascended the wrought-iron circular staircase that climbed up into the musty stillness of the Old Library itself.

It was a pilgrimage he had made every weekday since the new library opened, whatever the weather and however onerous his other commitments. Few people noticed this protest, save for the archivists, who had grown accustomed to his daily ritual. The entire journey took just under four minutes. Not very long in the scheme of things, but Ravi begrudged every second of it.

Once in the Old Library, how much time he would spend there depended on his mood. If he was still vexed, he would walk to the old entrance and stare accusingly at the old barred door before returning the way he had come. On those occasions, the archivists would keep their heads down while he stomped out of the library to exorcise his demons with a brisk walk around the courts.

On other occasions, when the magic of the place had lifted his spirits, he would stop to peruse the collection of papers from the legendary astronomer Fred Hoyle, whose old brass telescope was stored as an exhibit on the upper floor. Sometimes he would point the device at the old coat of arms mounted at the far end of the library and examine the knots and fissures in the ancient carving. Some years ago, one of the archivists had discovered him making his observation and had mumbled an apology for disturbing him. Ravi had enjoyed the moment, aware that this would only reinforce his reputation amongst the library staff for being odd, which of course suited him perfectly. In his experience, strange people tended to be left alone, and that was how he liked it.

Ravi found himself standing alone once again, this time at the bottom of E Staircase. How long he had paused there, he had no idea. Looking around Second Court, Ravi noticed a few bedders staring at him as they pushed the linen cart across the cobbles. A grumpy scowl made them look away and, with a grunt of grim satisfaction, he switched his nameplate to IN before stomping up the creaky stairs to his rooms.

When Ravi reached the top landing, he patted his pockets for his keys. For a terrible moment, he feared he had dropped them during his calamitous fall in the Buttery. But then he felt the reassuring lump in his jacket pocket and with a sigh unlocked the outer door of his rooms. His attention was immediately drawn to a white paper envelope resting against the foot of the inner door. It must have been stuffed underneath late last night or early this morning. He picked it up and recognised Robert's handwriting.

"Hmm," he said, pushing the door open and heading for his desk. This involved navigating round an old brown leather sofa and a matching pair of armchairs. Books and periodicals lined the walls in sagging bookcases that reached up to high leaded windows. More volumes, either too big or just too numerous to be accommodated on shelves, were piled up on wooden chairs. Ravi did not care. He liked to think he could put his hand on anything he needed, provided his bedder had not attempted to tidy the place, which she was now either too lazy or too frightened to do.

If the room was obscured mainly by academic clutter, Ravi's desk was not much better. It was an old oak unit with two sets of side drawers that flanked the sitter's legs. It had a green writing top, which could barely be seen beneath the voluminous journals and assortment of brass instruments that lay scattered around its surface. There was no computer to be seen.

Ravi thought desktop PCs were ugly and took up too much room on his desk. Instead, discreetly hidden in a drawer was a laptop which he only used out of necessity, preferring handwritten notes whenever possible. It amused him that many of his students thought him a Luddite for having a computer-free office when down at the Cavendish, he had an array of state-of-the-art devices for processing vast quantities of data from the cosmos. "Speak softly and carry a big stick," Theodore Roosevelt had once said. A sentiment that Ravi fully endorsed.

Behind the desk stood a brown leather swivel chair, the armrests worn down at the corners. The desk lamp was made of brass, as were the matching pair of lamp stands at either side of the sofa, which provided ample light for supervisions in winter months.

Ravi set his briefcase on the floor by the desk and eased himself into his leather chair. Its familiar contours greeted him like an old friend, though groaning a little under his weight.

A bit creaky, he thought, *but there again, aren't we all.*

Ravi reached for an old metal ruler, a relic of his schooldays in Nepal, its worn edge thin and tapered with use, making it an excellent letter opener. He inserted the sharp edge under the lip of Robert's envelope and tore the paper open with a satisfying rip. Inside was a plain white card, headed with the formal title and address of the Dean. Underneath in his friend's flowing script was a simple message.

Ravi, must talk. Come when you can. Robert.

Ravi checked the battered academic diary that sat on a pile of correspondence in his in-tray. There was nothing listed until this afternoon, when his tutees would be arriving for their first tutorial social.

Ravi looked around his room. There would be over twenty of them, and he would have to clear some of the chairs to accommodate them all. Something to attend to after lunch, he decided. Outside, a clock chimed nine o'clock. Taking out a piece of memo paper, he scrawled a note to the catering department, ordering enough tea, sandwiches and cake to feed a flotilla of rowing crews. Standing up from his desk, sharp pain from his bruised back provided an unwelcome reminder of his fall in the Buttery. He reached for the kitchen docket and added another item.

Nurofen.

Chapter 10

Nick walked down St John's Street surrounded by hungover freshers. A morning of Law lectures beckoned, but first, he had a more pressing matter to attend to. In his backpack, rolled carefully into a plastic bag, was the gown his parents had bought him, its dark fabric now in tatters. He knew he had to get it mended urgently. The thought of turning up to a formal Hall with his gown in this state did not bear thinking about. How could he explain what happened without Annabel thinking he was some sort of attention-seeking psycho? He shuddered at the thought.

Things had been going so well, too. After she had put her hand on his knee in the bar, he thought he had a chance with her at least. And when they had said goodbye on the landing, she had not used the dreaded words, "I'd just like us to be friends." He knew, like everyone else, what that meant.

That was why he had kept quiet on their run this morning. To see if Annabel would say anything about it. Not a peep. They had padded along, and by the end, he was relieved when they made it back to New Court, though he could not help but overtake her on the final sprint. He hoped that had not upset her. She had looked a bit flustered at the end. Bugger. Maybe that was it. She did not like losing.

"Idiot," he said, and drew a couple of looks from some girls around him.

The ranks of students had grown as they passed Trinity College, its entrance guarded by porters in bowler hats, nodding and smiling to their departing students. Then Nick noticed Heffers, the largest bookshop in Cambridge, its windows packed with textbooks from a vast range of subjects. Its Law section would be making a significant dent in his student loan in the coming weeks, and he was glad to be swept past by the flow of bodies.

More students joined the throng, filing out of a nondescript archway that was the front gate of Gonville and Caius College, so different from the grand entrance of Trinity. The street then narrowed until it opened out onto a square in front of the Senate House, the place where, fingers crossed, he would be awarded his final degree in three years' time.

King's Parade stretched out in front of him with King's College Chapel rising up on his right, but his first destination was hidden somewhere to the left. Weaving through the gaps that now opened up around him, Nick navigated out of the main flow of student traffic towards a shop on the corner, just beyond Great St Mary's Church.

Ryder and Amies was one of the oldest outfitters in Cambridge and from their website he knew they had been supplying university robes, scarves and ties for more than a century. It was their label inside his college gown, so if there was anywhere that could fix it, this would be the place.

When he opened the front door, a little brass bell rang above his head, announcing his arrival and making Nick feel like he was stepping back in time. Wooden cabinets and drawers lined the walls, filled with layers of scarves, ties and hoodies, their vibrant college designs creating a kaleidoscope of colour at odds with the traditional surroundings. Headless mannequins were stationed around the floor decked out in long, academic robes representing different faculties or colleges.

As he stared around at the displays, one in the far corner caught Nick's eye, its duck egg colour incongruous against the dark robes surrounding it. Crossing the room for a closer look, Nick felt a buzz of excitement when he read the motif *CURUFC* stitched on the chest pocket in gold thread. A Cambridge Blue, the legendary blazer awarded to the elite sportsmen and women of the university who played in the annual varsity match against Oxford. Nick thought about some of rugby's all-time greats who had worn that blazer, Rob Andrew, Gavin Hastings, Mike Gibson, all of whom had gone on to play for their country and the British Lions. No doubt, they would have come here, to Ryder and Amies, for a fitting before setting off to Twickenham and their path to glory that followed. Reaching forward, his fingers brushed the crest of the rampant red lion with something approaching awe.

"May I help you with that?"

Nick pulled his hand back and turned to find a smartly

dressed woman with a Ryder and Amies badge on her lapel.

"No, just looking," he said.

"Something to aim for, perhaps?"

"Perhaps."

"We have to dream before our dreams can come true," she said.

Nick didn't quite know how to respond to that, but was saved from doing so when her face broke into a smile.

"Don't mind me. I'm Ruth. How can I help you?"

"Oh, right," he said, removing his backpack and extracting the torn gown, still smelling of stale beer. "I had an accident and I wondered if you could repair it."

The shop assistant reached for the gown and, taking it by her fingertips, held it up in front of her.

"I see," she said. "An accident, you say?"

"I fell over on the way back from the bar."

"Hmm," she said, examining the long rends in the fabric. "Well, we'll see what we can do. If we can salvage it, we will. Otherwise, you'll need to get a new one."

"I'd prefer a repair," he said, knowing he didn't have the money for a new one.

The woman studied him. "We will see what we can do. Can you come back next week?"

"No problem."

"Name?"

"Wood," he said.

"St John's, isn't it?" she said, checking the bands of velvet on the sleeves.

"That's right."

She filled out a ticket with his name and college and attached it to the gown with a safety pin.

"I look forward to seeing you next week then, Mr Wood."

"Right. Thanks," he said and headed for the door, risking one more glance at the blazer as he did so.

"Forty-two."

Nick turned to see the shop assistant looking at him.

"Sorry?"

"You'll need it in a forty-two."

He smiled. "One day, perhaps."

"I'll have your gown ready next week, Mr Wood."

"Thanks, Ruth."

The little bell rang again as Nick stepped outside and breathed in the cold air, which felt fresh and invigorating after the mustiness of the old shop. Turning, he found a crowd of students peering down at a collection of small wooden noticeboards inside the Ryder and Amies window. An older student with a goatee beard was explaining their purpose to the others as he leant against the window, tapping ash from a rollup.

"Varsity squads. Sports captains pin their team sheet up in the window of Ryder and Amies before the annual fixture against The Other Place."

"A bit public school, isn't it?"

"Too right. Rugby team's packed with them. Especially John's. Toffs, the lot."

Nick felt a prickle of annoyance at this and was about to say something when he was interrupted.

"That'll be me then," said a soft Welsh accent.

Nick turned and saw a ginger-haired giant, a Blues scarf wrapped around his bull-like neck, standing just behind the group of startled students. The youth with the rollup pushed himself away from the window.

"Sorry, didn't see you there, mate," said Goatee.

"Easily done," said the giant, his face impassive. "Don't let me interrupt you. You were saying something."

The youth took a long drag on the cigarette and exhaled slowly while maintaining eye contact with the giant. The group of students shifted uneasily between the two figures.

"Come on, let's go," said one of the others.

Goatee waited a moment longer before flicking his cigarette onto the pavement. "Yeah. Who needs a scarf anyway?" he said, leading his friends away down King's Parade, casting a dark look over his shoulder at the Welshman.

The giant shook his head and smiled at Nick, "Power to the people, eh?"

Nick smiled and stepped on the still smoking rollup.

"Takes all sorts," he said and looked in the window at the boards. On a faded piece of paper, he saw the following announcement:

CAMBRIDGE UNIVERSITY RUGBY UNION FOOTBALL CLUB

TEAM TO PLAY OXFORD UNIVERSITY

TWICKENHAM 2.00PM, 10TH DECEMBER 2020

Below were printed the names of the players who had represented the university in last year's Varsity match.

Against each was also the name of their college.

"So, which one are you?" he asked.

"That's me. G.P. Evans – St John's."

"I'm from there too," Nick said offering his hand, "Nick."

The big man took it. "Gareth. Nice to meet you."

"So, what position do you play, Gareth?"

"Scrum-half," said the giant, evidently enjoying the look of surprise on Nick's face. "Only kidding, I'm a number eight. Although I started as scrum-half many years ago. Just kept growing."

"I started out as a prop."

"And now?" asked Gareth, raising an eyebrow.

"Winger," said Nick.

"A flyer," said Gareth.

"I don't know about that."

"Well, it's always good to have pace. And Grange Road has plenty of space out wide. You should come along to trials on Thursday."

"I'll think about it," said Nick, not sure if he fancied making a fool of himself.

"So where are you off to now?" Gareth asked.

"Law. Sidgwick Site."

"I'm heading that way. Land Economy," said Gareth.

They set off together down King's Parade.

"So where are you from originally, Nick?"

"Nottingham. You?"

"Cardigan Bay," said Gareth.

"Sounds lovely. Is it?" said Nick.

"When the sun shines," said Gareth. "Which isn't that often, mind you. Still, there's some great countryside. It's why I'm here. Doing research on sustainable development. What about you – a lawyer, you say?"

"Mum's idea. A good living," he replied. "We'll see."

They passed King's College Chapel on the right and continued along the row of shops opposite until they reached the corner of Benet Street. There they found a crowd of students clustered around a large glass window. Inside, a locust-shaped automaton swayed back and forth astride an impressive golden timepiece.

"Seems like someone has tried to steal the locust," said Gareth.

Nick looked. Sure enough, the window in front of the metallic insect had been shattered into a spider's web of small contusions, although the clock itself appeared unharmed. The bizarre-looking locust continued to rock back and forth on its spindly legs, oblivious to the commotion outside its damaged cage.

"Some idiot wanting a trophy?" suggested Gareth.

Nick said nothing. He was studying the impact high up on the glass.

"What could have done that, do you think? A brick?" asked Gareth.

"Or a bird strike," said Nick.

Gareth looked up at the window again, his expression thoughtful.

"Well, it would have to be quite a big bird. We had a golden eagle on Llanllwni Mountain a couple of years ago.

They're pretty powerful. They'll take down a sheep no problem."

"Not a student then," said Nick, thinking about the other night.

"What do you mean?"

"Some bird buzzed me the other night. Damaged my gown. That's what I was dropping off in Ryder and Amies."

"Could be an owl, I suppose. You don't get too many eagles around here on account of the lack of mountains," said Gareth, smiling.

Embarrassed, Nick looked down at the Latin inscription under the clock. "Any idea what that means?"

"*The world passeth away, and the lust thereof,*" said a voice behind them.

They turned to see a porter dressed in a dark coat standing a few feet away. He was almost as tall as Gareth, though his hair was grey and cropped.

"A Latin scholar?" said Gareth, impressed.

"The Bible, First Epistle of St John. This world will eventually fade, but the man who truly believes in God will endure beyond time."

"I see," said Gareth.

"Hey, it winked," said Nick.

"Yes, it's supposed to do that. Only now and again, mind you," said the porter, speaking very slowly and clearly. "Encourages you to keep looking."

They stared at the creature's eyes, but they didn't move again.

Something about the way the porter had said "keep

looking" bothered Nick, and he was about to ask him what he meant when he realised that the man was no longer there. Nick turned around and looked over the heads of the crowd, but there was no sign of him.

"We'd better go," said Gareth, "I have a library to go to."

"I suppose so," said Nick, still thinking about the porter.

They left the locust to continue its millennial meal and continued down Trumpington Street.

"That's Catz," said Gareth, interrupting his thoughts and pointing to a big courtyard behind a set of large gates. "They have a good rugby squad this year, apparently."

"How do you know that?" said Nick.

"The Tab, the university blog site," said Gareth. "Everyone is hoping they're going to beat us this season."

"The Redboys, you mean?" asked Nick, referring to the name given to John's rugby team.

Gareth nodded. "Well, I say this season. Pretty much every college wants to beat us every season."

"Why is that?"

"Well, we're big, red and good at rugby. As a Welshman, I can't see what the problem is," he said, smiling.

"Are you playing for the college as well?" asked Nick.

"If they'll have me."

"We have to dream before our dreams come true," said Nick.

"That's good," said Gareth, "Wordsworth?"

"Ruth at Ryder and Amies," said Nick.

Gareth laughed. They reached the corner of Silver Street.

"So, I'll see you at trials on Thursday then, Nick?"

"Yeah, right. See you there."

Gareth nodded and headed off down Trumpington Street, head bowed, oblivious to the awestruck glances from those around him.

Nick smiled and checked his watch.

"Holy…!"

Only five minutes to go before lectures! If he legged it, he might just about make it in time. Breaking into a run, he swerved around pedestrians on the narrow pavement, his backpack banging against his shoulders. Had he looked behind him, he might have seen the grey-haired porter watching him from the entrance of an alleyway, a Ryder and Amies bag in his hand.

Chapter 11

After dropping off his order at the Catering Manager's office in the college kitchen, Ravi headed off to see Robert. There were more people about now as students and Fellows emerged from their rooms and studies for another day of term. Ravi's shoes beat a steady rhythm as he passed them in the New Court cloisters and made for Robert's stairwell.

The sign read "Prof. R. Mackenzie – IN" and Ravi began his ascent, passing the Bursar's office with its enormous display of flowers in the reception area. He wondered if anyone would notice if he took one or two for his afternoon's tutorial. Something to brighten the place up, perhaps.

Ravi reached the top floor and headed for Robert's room. The outer door was open, so he knocked on the inner.

"Who is it?" came Robert's voice.

"Ravi."

"Come in."

Ravi opened the door and stepped into the room. He looked over to the desk and saw Robert seated, facing a dark-haired young woman. "Oh, I'm sorry. Am I disturbing you?"

"Not at all. Quite the contrary, Ravi, thank you for

coming over at such short notice."

Robert rose and came over to shake his hand. Ravi noted that they were not sitting on the armchairs or sofa, meaning this must be a formal meeting.

"Let me introduce you to Miss Vidal. She has come to England to look for her brother. Miss Vidal, this is Professor Gupta."

The woman rose to meet him. She was wearing a simple pale-blue dress and a navy cardigan over which her long hair cascaded in gentle waves. Her dark eyes studied him as they shook hands.

"Nice to meet you, Professor," she said.

"Nice to meet you too, Miss Vidal," said Ravi. "I am sorry to hear about your brother."

"Thank you, Professor," she said. "My family is very concerned."

Her English was accented, but she took the time to pronounce her words carefully.

"Please join us, Ravi," said Robert.

Ravi waited for the woman to sit before taking the chair next to her.

"Miss Vidal's brother had been working for St John's College for some months before his disappearance," explained Robert. "She has been speaking with some of the staff who were on duty the night he disappeared."

"Very sensible. I'm sure our staff will cooperate fully. Have you considered speaking with the police?"

"I don't think that will be necessary at this stage," said Robert. Ravi detected a hint of irritation in his voice, although he was doing his best to hide it. No college liked the police sniffing around its courts. Apart from disturbing the Fellowship, the aspiring journalists in the student press were always on the lookout for the merest whiff of scandal, especially at a venerable old college like St John's.

"I have written to the Master to advise him of the situation," said Robert, "and have promised Miss Vidal that we will provide her with whatever assistance we can."

"Of course." Ravi looked at the woman listening carefully to Robert's summary, which sounded to Ravi like a standard response.

"Is there anything that *I* can do, Miss Vidal? I would be happy to help in any way I can," he found himself saying, moved by the sight of her hanging on his friend's every word. She turned and stared intently at him as if looking for some sort of flaw or lack of sincerity. After what seemed an age she nodded.

"Thank you, Professor Gupta."

"Excellent!" said Robert, sounding relieved and rising from his chair. It was clear the meeting was over. The woman waited for a moment then rose as well. *On her terms*, Ravi thought.

"How long are you planning to stay in Cambridge, Miss Vidal?" he asked, getting to his feet.

"Until I find my brother." It was a statement of intent.

"In that case," he said, "might I suggest that we meet each week to review progress?"

"That would be good."

"Saturday morning, perhaps? In my office?"

"Thank you, Professor." She shook his hand, her grip cool and firm, her eyes not leaving his own. *Making sure I don't forget.*

She then turned to Robert. "Thank you, Professor Mackenzie. I am happy to have met you."

"The pleasure is all mine."

Ravi didn't sense a great deal of conviction in the statement, which irked him.

"Forgive me, Miss Vidal," said Ravi. "I'm afraid I don't know your brother's name."

"Alfonso," she said, and Ravi noticed the first flicker of emotion in those dark eyes.

"Of course. Then I look forward to seeing you again on Saturday."

"*Sí*, Saturday," she said before turning to follow Robert as he limped over to the door.

"Sorry about that," said Robert after the young woman had left and indicated they should head for the sofas. "The porters told me when I arrived that this girl was asking for me and there was no one else I could think of who could help at this time in the morning."

Ravi found this odd. Robert usually dealt with such matters without the need for assistance. Clearly, something had unsettled him.

"Well, if you think I can be of help."

"No one better. Tea?" he said, heading for the kitchen. "Ah, I don't seem to have a teapot, I'm afraid. Will coffee do?"

"That will be fine."

Ravi watched as his friend grabbed a couple of mugs from the cupboard.

"So there has been no news about Alfonso?"

"What? Her brother, you mean? No, not a word," said Robert. "How do you like your coffee?"

"Black," said Ravi, still annoyed that his friend didn't seem to be taking the matter of the missing waiter that seriously. "Who exactly have you spoken to about Alfonso, Robert?"

"Well, I spoke to the Domestic Bursar about it, naturally. He's responsible for catering around here. Apparently, kitchen staff come and go all the time. The DB assumed this chap had been pinched by Trinity or one of the other colleges. Probably pay more than us. There you go!" he said as he found a black-and-gold capsule and slotted it into the machine.

"Does anyone remember what time he left college on the day he disappeared?" asked Ravi.

"I don't know, Ravi," said Robert. "You'll need to speak to the porters about that. Late, probably."

"Well, we need to get our facts straight in case the police become involved," said Ravi.

"Why, yes, but let's hope it doesn't come to that. We don't want any bad publicity coming back to St John's."

"You don't think someone, or something, could be behind this, do you, Robert?" He took the offered mug. "It won't be the first time things have disappeared that no one could explain."

Ravi could see his friend hesitate for a moment before

141

retreating to the coffee machine.

"That was a long time ago, Ravi. What makes you think that this is in any way related?"

"You, Robert," said Ravi.

"Me?"

"There's something you are not telling me."

"You are imagining things, Ravi. A waiter has gone missing on his way home. It has nothing to do with us."

Robert brought his mug over to the coffee table, his easy-going manner replaced by a frostiness that Ravi hadn't seen before. Surprised by his friend's behaviour, Ravi decided it was time to take the offensive.

"A creature has been sighted in the college, Robert."

His friend froze. There was no mistaking the panic in those green eyes.

"What are you talking about? I'd have heard about something like that. Someone would have reported it."

"A first-year saw it, Robert. Near the library."

"That's not possible. The student must have been mistaken. Probably drunk. The porters have had to deal with half a dozen already. Come on, Ravi. You know what they are like in Freshers' Week."

"I overheard him telling a girl the other morning. He was quite sober, I assure you."

"The boy was probably trying to impress her, Ravi. You know how it goes. When people are infatuated with someone, they do the stupidest things."

"Like Mary, you mean."

Robert shot him a hurt look. "Why are you bringing that

up again after all this time, Ravi? I thought we had put that behind us?"

Even now, half a century later, Ravi was surprised how much it still hurt to think of the one girl who had come between them. *Now is not the time*, he chided himself. There were more pressing matters to resolve.

"Tell me about the research, Robert."

Robert flinched. "Research?"

"Yesterday, when we first talked about this, you mentioned some research you were doing," said Ravi.

"What? Oh, that," said Robert. "Just some research papers to finish, that's all."

"With Schiller," said Ravi.

"Oh, that? Julian, you mean. Well, yes. He's funding some theoretical research."

"What exactly, Robert?"

"Just some of our early stuff. You know. With Hawking's last book, people seem more interested in it nowadays."

"What we worked on in 1969?"

"Some of it," said Robert, the colour draining from his face.

"Einstein's parallel universe theory?" said Ravi.

Robert studied the carpet.

"Well, related to that, yes," he said.

"The work we swore we would never pursue again."

"It was Julian who dug up the old papers from somewhere. He simply wanted me to verify some of the concepts."

"Verify? How, exactly?"

Robert said nothing. He just sat there, looking miserable, staring into his coffee for what seemed like an age. When he spoke, his voice was quiet.

"Rock samples."

"You went back! How could you?"

"I was desperate, Ravi. The light-speed research wasn't yielding the results Julian wanted. Despite all the advances, the achievements, the breakthroughs on so many fronts, we still couldn't prove that we could create the means for interstellar travel through conventional means. Julian was becoming increasingly angry and frustrated. It looked like he was going to pull my funding. I had to give him something!" Robert looked at Ravi, his expression like that of a child with his hand caught in the sweetie jar. "It was just a few rocks. Nothing more, Ravi. Honest."

Ravi stared at him, scarcely able to believe what he said. He had suspected something like this but had hoped it could not be the case. Because that would mean Robert had betrayed his trust. A trust he thought was unbreakable.

Ravi felt an overwhelming sense of sadness weigh down on him as the two friends sat across from each other in uncomfortable silence. He stared into the swirling blackness of his coffee, and his thoughts circled back to another time.

*****

Ravi was falling. Sharp rocks tore at the backs of his trousers as his body accelerated down the slope. Pain blossomed with each bounce over its uneven surface, his heels shuddering as he tried in vain to get some sort of purchase. He tried to cry out, but all he could manage was a spluttering cough as clouds of red dust clogged his mouth and throat.

Ravi managed to squint through flailing legs, and his eyes widened in alarm. The edge of the slope was rushing towards him and beyond that was a vertical drop to the deep red of the valley floor. In desperation, he reached out with his hands, and his palms burned as the rock face skinned them like sandpaper. Ravi screamed. "No!"

A searing pain erupted across his chest and tore into his armpits. Ravi's scream was cut short as all the air was forced from his lungs by the massive pressure on his ribs. He lay there unable to breathe or speak or, for that matter, comprehend why he was no longer moving. Was he dead? Was that it? Was this darkness above him merely death, come to claim him from his fall?

Then he felt something begin to grow inside him. Something so profound and powerful that it couldn't be resisted any longer. The need to breathe.

He coughed. A dry, hacking cough. It doubled him up, and he felt spasms of pain shoot through his chest as he coughed again, this time exploring the welcome relief of dusty air finding a passage to his lungs. Gasping, he sucked it in, feeling his heart hammer its life-affirming drum roll against his bruised and battered chest. Ravi lay curled like that for a few moments longer before rolling onto his back and staring into the violet sky.

Sweat stung his eyes, and he blinked it away. When he looked again, Ravi found himself peering up into the tanned face of a god grinning down at him. The sunlight cast a pale halo around a face from which piercing green eyes looked at him with a mix of concern and amusement.

"How are you doing there, laddie? For a moment there, I thought you were going to beat me to the bottom."

Robert stood above him, a leather backpack hanging from broad, muscular shoulders. In his calloused hands, he held a climbing rope that snaked down and looped under Ravi's arms and around his heaving chest.

"Robert," said Ravi, disbelieving. "What are you doing here?"

His friend laughed. "You know what, I was going to ask you the same question."

"I thought you were playing rugby today!"

"Cancelled. Frozen pitch. So, I thought I'd go back to our workspace."

"Why didn't you wait for me?"

"I tried, but you weren't around, Ravi. The porters said they had seen you with a young lady. Is there someone you haven't told me about?"

Ravi felt embarrassed and decided to change the subject. He didn't want Robert knowing about Mary just yet.

"You could have waited, Robert. I thought we agreed we were going to do this together."

"Well, we are here now, aren't we?" said his friend, extending his hand. "Come on, there's something you have to see."

Ravi sat up and groaned as pain spread down his battered back. He took Robert's hand, wincing as it hoisted him upright. Ravi stood there unsteadily for a moment, getting his balance and his bearings. A few yards further on was the jagged edge of the slope and then the sheer drop, but here the surface was relatively flat. Robert, like him, was roped up, the ends secured to a rocky outcrop further up the slope.

"How are you doing? Steady enough?" Robert asked.

Ravi was sore all over, but the rock face that had caused him so much pain now felt reassuringly solid underfoot.

"I'm fine. Thank you."

"Good, because I don't want you falling over when I show you this next thing."

"What, exactly?"

"Over there," said Robert, smiling as he pointed over Ravi's shoulder.

Ravi turned and had to shield his eyes against the intensity of the light. As they adjusted, his mouth fell open as he understood why. Two suns stared back down at him, their sharp white light boring through the alien atmosphere, casting almost no shadow on the blood-coloured valley beyond.

*****

Ravi closed his eyes to blot out the memory of that moment of discovery that he and Robert had shared all those years before. When he opened them again, he saw his friend sitting across from him. The man who once had represented everything that Ravi valued in this world – courage, honesty and integrity - but who had then betrayed Ravi's trust, not once, but twice. For that, he could find no room in his heart for forgiveness.

"Robert. How long have you been working with Julian?" he asked.

Robert stared into his coffee, avoiding eye contact.

"A couple of years, perhaps."

"I want you to stop."

"Is that really necessary?"

"You have allowed someone to manipulate you."

"That's not what happened…"

"You have done something you promised you would never do."

"It wasn't like that."

"You have put people's lives at risk, and for what?"

"It was my research…"

"For your own ego."

"Ravi," said Robert, his voice pleading now, "what you and I did back then. What we achieved. Julian said it was incredible."

Ravi stared at the man sitting opposite him.

"Robert," he said, "you disappoint me."

Robert flinched at those words as if he had been struck. He gaped at Ravi in shocked silence, unable to respond. Ravi stared back at him, his eyes as cold and pitiless as his heart. At last, Robert bowed his head and spoke, his voice barely audible.

"I'm sorry, Ravi."

"So am I, Robert."

"What must I do?"

"You must put a stop to this before more harm is done," said Ravi. "You must tell Julian that you withdraw your support. Without you, he would be a fool to continue, and from what I saw of the man, he doesn't strike me as one of those."

Robert did not argue. They both knew what he said was true. Ravi rose stiffly to his feet and, ignoring the bruises from his fall in the Buttery, limped towards the door.

"Julian is not going to be happy," said Robert.

Ravi turned at the entranceway.

"You seem to be under the mistaken belief that I give a damn what Julian might think."

With that, Ravi stepped into the hallway and closed the door on his friend.

Chapter 12

Annabel returned from lectures and sat down at her desk. She looked at her bulging satchel and let out a long sigh. The volume of reading they were expected to do was piling up, and she was wondering whether her plan of joining a range of college societies was feasible. Maybe Nick had been right to focus on just one and keep on top of his studies.

Nick.

She had not really expected to meet someone like him just yet. The thrill of coming up to Cambridge had been enough. Maybe that was why she had been caught off-guard.

It was not a "lust at first sight" sort of thing. When Annabel had first met Nick, she had thought he was OK-looking. Tall and sporty, but no model. It was not his dress sense either, which was understated to the point of being scruffy. No, it was his eyes. There was an intensity to them. When he looked at you, he really did just that. Look. Dead straight. How disarming was that? He did not take himself too seriously either, which she liked. She had expected people here to be full of themselves, but he was, well, normal.

"Normal," she said aloud. "You're going for normal now, are you girl? Hi Nick, I like you because you're normal."

Annabel thought back to this morning's jog. Nick had been friendly enough. But there was something different from the previous night. He had seemed a bit preoccupied and even out-sprinted her on the final leg. Was it something she had said? She did not think so. Perhaps she should ask him. Scratch that. Being a bloke, he probably wouldn't want to talk about it.

"Come on girl, don't go frightening him off just yet," she admonished herself. "If it's meant to be…"

She looked at the photo of her mum and dad. They had met at Stirling University. Her dad had been a marine biologist and keen diver. Mum, a county junior at golf, had come from Surrey and had chosen Stirling because it had a nine-hole course in the grounds. After marrying, Annabel's father had worked for an oil company. His work had taken them all around the world, with spells in South America, the Middle East and South East Asia. She had been born in Hong Kong and could still remember birthday parties in the swimming pool and messing around on boats with her dad.

Dad and boats. Now there was a lifelong love affair. She remembered how excited he used to get at the shipping forecast. Wherever they were in the world, he would check the clock to make sure they didn't miss it. Annabel looked at her own watch. It was already past two o'clock, and she had a tutorial with Professor Gupta and the other Natural Scientists!

Annabel rushed to the bathroom and just had time to brush

her teeth and check herself in the mirror before heading over to Second Court. She arrived at E Staircase a few minutes later and was pleased to find she was not the only student converging on the same corner of Second Court.

A couple of pale-faced geeks who looked like they had walked out of *The Big Bang Theory* came from the passageway to Chapel Court and approached her. Both wore black T-shirts, one under a long trench coat and the other under a hoodie.

"Hi. Are you here to see Professor Gupta?" she asked.

The hoodie introduced himself. "Hi, I'm Ashley, but you can call me Ash. All my friends do."

"Hi, Ash. I'm Annabel." She held out her hand. Ash looked at it in surprise, then shook it vigorously. Annabel wondered if this was meant as a joke, but by the earnest expression on Ash's face, she decided it was not.

"And you are?" Annabel asked the trench coat.

"Brian." The boy didn't look up, his face half hidden beneath lank brown hair. Unlike his friend Ash, he kept his hands deep in the pockets of his jeans.

"So, are you two studying Natural Sciences?" she asked.

"You bet," said Ash, beaming. "I'm here for the quantum physics mainly. But I like all the other stuff too. You?"

"I'm more of a biologist," said Annabel. "I'm interested in animal behaviour." She turned to Brian. "You?"

"I like all science," he said.

Annabel waited for him to say more. But Brian just stared at the cobblestones, and she realised that was all they were going to get by way of explanation.

"Right," she said, "nice." She looked up at Ash, who was still beaming at her. "So, now we've introduced ourselves, shall we head on up to see the professor?"

"Great!" said Ash and bounded past her on lanky legs towards the wooden stairwell. Brian followed him, his trainers moving in short strides below his coat with surprising speed. Annabel was left to follow in their wake, passing the sign that indicated Professor Gupta's room was E7 and he was IN.

When they reached the first-floor landing, Annabel noticed the wooden entrance to the Old Library with its brightly painted coat of arms in red, blue and gold above the oak-panelled door.

"That's impressive," she said, but the others did not hear her. They had continued their ascent up the twisting flight of stairs leading to the second landing. *Like a couple of mountain goats*, she thought.

"It certainly is," came a deep voice from below. Annabel turned. Climbing the stairs towards her, his bright white teeth shining in the dark corridor, was an Adonis from myth and legend made real.

The deity had dark, curly hair, blue eyes and a deep mahogany tan. He towered over her, with shoulders that seemed to fill the stairwell. His well-cut blazer and tie were straight out of a Ralph Lauren advert, which helped her identify the accent as American. She stared at him for a moment until she realised he was holding out a hand the size of a baseball glove.

"Hi, I'm Brett. Nice to meet you."

"Hi, I'm Annabel," was all she could manage as he took her hand in a confident, firm grip. It was surprisingly dry and calloused, she noticed, like the hand of a labourer.

"So where are we heading, Annabel?" he asked, dazzling her again by the brightness of his teeth in the dark of the landing.

"Professor Gupta's tutorial is that way," she said, pointing vaguely to the stairs.

"That's the one. After you."

The stairs were extremely narrow, and Annabel felt very self-conscious knowing that his massive frame was just behind her. When she reached the top landing, she turned and was not surprised to see Brett had to angle his shoulders to avoid rubbing the sleeves of his blazer against the old plasterwork.

"Quite a squeeze," said Brett. "Neat, though, don't you think?"

"Cosy, yes," she agreed. "Mind you, I seem to spend my whole time gawking at this place."

"Gawking?" said Brett.

"Sorry, staring," said Annabel, giggling for no reason. *Oh, get a grip, girl*, she pleaded with herself, feeling the colour rising up her neck. She was saved by the sound of voices coming from the door at the end of the landing.

"Sounds like the others have already arrived. Shall we enter the lion's den?" she asked.

"I'm ready if you are," Brett replied.

Annabel turned to hide her pink face and knocked on the door to E7. They waited a few seconds, and she was about to try again when it was opened by Professor Gupta, wearing his familiar crumpled suit. The old man's face broke into a smile, revealing crooked teeth.

"Ah, Annabel," he said. "Good to see you again. And I see you have brought Brett with you."

"We met on the stairs," she explained, shaking his hand.

"Excellent. Come in, come in," said Ravi, waving them into the room, which was already filling up with other tutees, holding cups of tea and plates of cake. Annabel edged past a sofa and found some space by a bookcase sagging under the weight of books piled on top of its shelves.

"So, Brett, how are you settling in?" asked the professor.

"Very well, thank you, sir. The coaches have been keeping me busy."

"Ah, yes. Well, at least the river's relatively quiet at this time of year. Mind your head on some of these beams. These rooms weren't built for Olympians."

"I'll bear that in mind, Professor," said Brett.

"Can I get you both a cup of tea and some cake?"

"Ooh, yes please," said Annabel.

"I have Earl Grey, Assam or Darjeeling," he said. "How do you take it?"

"Earl Grey, please, Professor. White, without," said Annabel.

He looked up at Brett.

"I'll have what she's having," he said.

"Excellent, bear with me."

As Professor Gupta made off to fetch their tea, Annabel turned to Brett.

"Olympian?"

"Trials only," said Brett. "No medals, I'm afraid."

"I take it you're not a cox then?"

He laughed, and she noticed that those teeth really were perfect.

"I think we'd sit low in the stern if that were the case. I normally row at stroke."

"I see," said Annabel, nodding and trying to look like she knew what he was talking about.

"You row, then?" asked Brett.

"Haven't a clue," admitted Annabel. "Though I might give coxing a go. Try for one of the college boats."

"Great idea, I'm sure you'll love it!" said Brett, his eyes shining. "There's no better feeling than being out on the water. It's magical."

Those blue eyes, she thought. "Magical."

She was saved by Professor Gupta, who returned bearing cups.

"Your tea," he said as he handed them over. "Come and choose your cake. We have Victoria sponge, carrot, and a delicious Belgian chocolate cake."

There was a knock at the door

"Excuse me," he said and left them to greet more new arrivals.

"Victoria sponge?" said Brett to Annabel.

"Are you worried about calories at all?" asked Annabel.

"Damn right I am. I need close to 8000 a day," said Brett.

"Then you're going to love Victoria sponge," said Annabel, leading him towards the coffee table in the centre of the room. The cakes had been cut into generous portions, and she put a thick slab on his plate before taking a slice of chocolate cake for herself.

"You don't like Victoria sponge?" he asked.

"Girls and chocolate." she said. "We have a special relationship."

She watched Brett take a bite of the cake and laughed when some of the sugar powder ended up on the tip of his nose. "Besides, it's a nightmare for retaining your dignity."

"Thanks," mumbled Brett, smiling as he went in search of a napkin.

Annabel saw Brian and Ash standing self-consciously in the corner, looking at the noisy gathering from a safe distance. She decided that in the interests of self-preservation, it was time to introduce the American to the only other people she knew in the room.

"Brett, can I introduce you to Brian and Ash?" she said as she waved them to come over. Ash started towards her, with Brian following him like a shadow. Brett turned around, wiping his face with a napkin, and broke into a warm smile.

"Hi, fellas!" he said, reaching out with his hand. Ash grabbed it enthusiastically, and Brett's smile broadened as he pumped their fists up and down. When Ash had finished, Brett offered his hand to Brian, who merely stared at the ground.

"Are you a first-year too, Brett?" asked Ash as the American graciously withdrew his hand.

"Nope. Came over here to do my master's," said Brett, "and some rowing."

"Where are you from originally?" asked Annabel.

"Memphis, Tennessee," said Brett, exaggerating his southern drawl.

"Isn't that where Elvis came from?" asked Ash.

"Uh huh-huh," said Brett in a deep voice.

Annabel laughed.

"And the Memphis Belle," said Brian quietly.

They turned to look at him and, as if on cue, he began to speak in a flat monotone voice.

"The Memphis Belle was a B-17F flying fortress from the Ninety-First Bomb Group, stationed at Bassingbourn near Cambridge in 1942. It was the first bomber to complete a tour of twenty-five missions. They made a film about it and the crew used to drink at The Eagle pub on Bene't Street. They signed their names on the ceiling there with their cigarette lighters. There's a plaque on the wall with a photo of the original crew and the actors from the 1990 movie."

As suddenly as he had started, Brian stopped. Annabel just stared at him. She was pretty sure he had not taken a breath during his pronouncement.

"Brian knows a lot about the American military," explained Ash. "He studied it when researching the Manhattan Project."

"So, you're saying that the Memphis Belle crew was based near here," said Brett, "and they used to drink in a bar downtown?"

"A pub," corrected Brian. "The Eagle."

"I've got to see that," said Brett.

"Then you should also see the graves," said Brian.

"The what?"

"The graves," said Brian, "at the American Cemetery in Madingley. It's the largest American cemetery in Britain. There are three thousand, eight hundred and twelve graves there and a memorial to another five thousand, one hundred and twenty-seven aircrew and sailors who died while stationed in Britain during the war." He paused for a moment before continuing. "It's rather beautiful. But sad at the same time."

Annabel looked at Brian and then at Brett, who had a thoughtful expression on his face.

"I'd like it if you showed me that sometime, Brian."

Brian glanced up at the enormous American and nodded before returning to stare at an incongruously large flower display on the table.

Annabel found herself fascinated by her companions. She could not imagine two more different people than Brett and Brian, and here they were chatting over tea and cake. Had Gupta put something in the water? She took another sip from her cup and caught sight of Ash beaming at her as if thinking the same, before his face contorted into an outrageous wink. Annabel found herself grinning back.

A bell tinkled, and they all turned to see Professor Gupta standing in the middle of the room. The chatter subsided, and he replaced the little brass bell on the table, smiling.

"Welcome, everyone. I'm not one for speeches, you will be glad to know. But I hope you will forgive me if I say a few words. I promise it will be no more than a minute."

Annabel noticed Brian reach for his digital watch and set the timer.

"As your tutor, I am here to help you with your pastoral needs." He paused. "By that I mean you can come to me with anything that is troubling you."

Annabel caught him looking directly at her for a fraction of a second before continuing.

"Just to be clear, I am not here to help you with your assignments." There was laughter around the room. "If you have any academic issues, please take them up with your Director of Studies. Contrary to rumour, your professors are here to help, not catch you out. Though they do expect you to take your studies seriously, as I'm sure you will too."

A few smiles were exchanged around the room.

"St John's College is blessed with some of the finest academic minds for Natural Sciences in the university, if not the world, so you will be in good hands. The very best."

He spoke with a confidence that gave Annabel a stir of pride.

"My job as your tutor is to ensure that if things go wrong, or if you are struggling to balance the academic with your other pursuits at Cambridge –" his eyes lingered for a moment on Brett – "you have someone to whom you can talk. Someone who knows what you are going through and can offer words of counsel, comfort, and the occasional cup of tea."

Again, a chuckle from around the room that was interrupted by the digital beeping of Brian's alarm.

"Thank you," said the professor, smiling. "Now, I see that there is some cake left. Please eat up, or it will only go to waste."

People started chatting again, and Brett turned to the others.

"Such a great guy. What does he teach?"

"Astronomy," said Ash. "He's a legend, apparently."

"He won the Gold Medal from the Royal Astronomical Society a few years ago for his work on black holes," said Brian. "He's currently involved as a consultant to the Euclid space mission's investigation into dark energy."

Annabel decided that this might develop into another of Brian's long monologues.

"More tea, anyone?" she said.

"Good idea!" said Brett. They broke away from the others, leaving Brian to continue his career summary of Professor Gupta to the ever-attentive Ash.

"I might just help myself to that last piece of carrot cake," said Brett.

"Excellent choice," said Annabel. "Packed with calories and it's also one of your five a day."

"You had me at calories," he said and headed for the coffee table. Annabel moved over to the tray of teapots in the corner of the room. She was just pouring herself another cup of Earl Grey when Professor Gupta joined her.

"Earl Grey, my favourite. Would you top me up, please, Annabel?" he said, holding out his cup and saucer.

"Of course," she said. "It's very good of you to host us today, Professor."

"Well, it's a simple formula. Plenty of cake and lashings of tea, but I find it does the trick."

Together they observed the rest of the room. Students

were talking in small groups, some laughing, some in earnest conversation, others examining the professor's full bookshelves. She noticed that Brett had managed to grab a slice of carrot cake and was negotiating his way back through the crowd.

"I was hoping to ask you a favour, Annabel," said Professor Gupta, whose voice had taken on a more serious tone.

"A favour?" said Annabel.

"Yes. I couldn't help but notice you with a young man on the Bridge of Sighs the other day."

"Oh," said Annabel, wondered where this was going. "Nick, you mean?"

"Nick?"

"Nick Wood. He's a lawyer."

Annabel noticed that Brett was now standing behind the professor, who continued, unaware they had an audience.

"Please forgive me – I didn't mean to eavesdrop on a private conversation, but he mentioned that a statue had disappeared."

"Oh, that," she said, relieved. "Yes, Nick said he had seen something from my bedroom window." Annabel glanced at Brett. "When he was helping me unpack my things. He wasn't staying there or anything."

"No, you misunderstand me, Annabel," said the professor. "I'd like to speak to Nick about what he saw. From the window, I mean."

"Right, so it's about the missing statue."

"That's right. We had something that went missing, and

I'd like to find out if this is related."

"OK. So Nick's not in any trouble then?"

"Not with me," said Professor Gupta. "Do you think he might be in trouble with someone else?"

Annabel glanced at Brett. "I hope not," she said.

"So, would you let him know I'd like to see him?" asked the professor. "Perhaps when you see him in the morning?"

"When we go jogging, you mean," said Annabel, just to clarify that statement.

"Or I could leave him a note. Do you happen to know his room number?"

"A7 Cripps," she said automatically. "Not that I've ever been there, of course. It's just that he's on my staircase. You know." She saw Brett backing out of earshot to join Ash and Brian.

"Of course," said Professor Gupta, who followed her gaze and saw the retreating American. "Ah. I see," he said and nodded before taking a sip of tea. "Life here in Cambridge can be quite complicated, can't it, Annabel?"

"True, Professor."

"So many opportunities. It's hard to know which ones to pursue."

Annabel looked at the crumpled old professor standing next to her, peering around the room at his students.

"I can see why they chose you to be a tutor, Professor Gupta," she said.

"Why, thank you, Annabel," he said, inclining his head towards her before taking another sip. "One thing you learn when you have been around young people for as long as I have: no matter how complicated life gets most things look a lot better after a good cup of tea."

"You should meet my gran, Professor. I think you'd get on really well."

"She's a believer in its restorative powers, then?" he asked.

"Believer?" said Annabel. "Gran's one of the tea disciples."

"In that case, I look forward to you introducing us one day."

Annabel peered once more around the room and decided that she needed to clear her head.

"You know, Professor, if you don't mind, I think I'm going to head back now."

"Well, you can always pop by for a chat some time. My door is always open and the kettle hot. I'll drop Nick a note about meeting up."

"Thank you, Professor. I'll tell him it's nothing serious, so he doesn't go worrying about it."

"I didn't say it wasn't serious, Annabel," he said, and something about his tone of voice made her stop. "I just don't think he's in trouble."

"In that case, Professor, I'll make sure he comes around when he gets your note."

"Thank you, Annabel, I would appreciate that very much."

He smiled and headed back to join the others.

Annabel was halfway to the door when she heard Brett call after her.

"Annabel!"

She saw him edging through the crowd towards her, holding a plate stacked with chocolate cake.

"I was wondering if you fancied coming down to the boathouse some time. I could see if we can get out on the river and give you an introduction to coxing."

"That would be great," she said, delighted. "Are you sure you don't mind?"

"Not at all, it would be my pleasure. When would suit you?"

Annabel thought for a moment and said, "How about tomorrow morning, say six-thirty a.m.?"

"Don't you have another commitment then?"

Annabel smiled.

"Nick has rugby trials tomorrow, so he'll need to conserve his energy."

"Rugby, right," he said.

"So, six-thirty a.m. at the main Porter's Lodge?"

"Six-thirty a.m. it is."

"See you then."

When Annabel emerged into Second Court, she saw Giles on the far side of the courtyard with a backpack slung over his shoulder. He blew her an exaggerated kiss before disappearing into Chapel Court. Annabel smiled and glanced up towards the heavens.

"So many opportunities, Mum. So many opportunities."

Chapter 13

Giles strode into Chapel Court. *You're a lucky boy, Nick*, he thought. That Annabel was seriously good-looking. But who was he to stand in the way of young love? And didn't all these freshers look young! He'd felt old when he'd first arrived at John's, and now he felt positively ancient. Besides, Nick didn't look like the sort of chap you would want to mess with. No, best leave the young lovers to it and focus on more lofty ambitions. Which was why he was now heading for the library.

Giles had decided that tonight it was time for some R&R with the new members of the club. And what better induction than an ascent that was featured on the cover of *The Roof-Climber's Guide to St John's*. The clock tower in New Court, no less. Start with a flourish and all that.

This was not a climb he had attempted yet, so it was time for a spot of reconnaissance while it was still light – and where better than the new library, which overlooked New Court from the east side of the river. Giles leant against the library's revolving wooden door and sauntered into cavernous foyer, nodding at the two librarians policing the front desk.

"Afternoon, ladies."

They glanced up from their screens, the look of surprise on their faces gratifying. Before either of them could recover, Giles had turned right and disappeared up the central staircase. This was a modern, spiral affair that wound clockwise up from the lobby. This early in the term, the library was practically deserted. Most of its regulars were not into their rhythm yet, and the freshers were busy having too much fun.

Giles sprang up the stairs two at a time, and on reaching the third floor, he headed into the John Hall Law Library. This sat at the top of the garden wing, so named because it jutted out into the Master's Garden. The Law section was built under the eaves of the roof and was the highest point in the building. Around its walls were large windows with desks allowing students a magnificent view of the Master's Lodge and the river. By Giles' reckoning, this would be the closest location from which to observe New Court. However, as soon as he reached the furthest window, he realised he had made a miscalculation. The two massive trees at the southern end of the Master's Garden, both laden with a dense covering of autumn leaves, all but obscured the New Court building.

"Bugger," he muttered.

Undaunted, Giles retreated from the Law Library and, turning right through a set of glass doors, entered the Computer Room instead. This ran south towards Second Court and was filled with rows of large monitors running down both sides of the room. Giles ignored these and went from desk to desk, checking if each new vantage point provided him with an unencumbered view across the river. To his relief, he was rewarded with the sight of the Wedding Cake pinnacle rising majestically above New Court's roof.

"Excellent," he said.

"Shush," came a reply from behind him.

Giles turned and was alarmed to see the bald head of Mr Weston, the senior librarian, peering round from behind one of the computer screens. Mr Weston had a permanent frown, which was accentuated by the half-moon glasses that perched on his nose.

"Sorry," Giles whispered.

Mr Weston gave him a frosty stare before returning to study the screen in front of him. Giles breathed out slowly and sat down at the desk nearest the window. With some care, he angled the computer screen so that he would be out of sight of the librarian's hawk-like eyes. Giles opened his backpack and retrieved a large textbook from his Archaeology reading list, into which was inserted the much smaller *Roof-Climber's Guide* by Hartley, Grag and Darlington. The next twenty minutes was spent comparing the description in the guide with the profile of the tower he could see from his secret vantage point. There was a moment of alarm when Mr Weston clicked off his screen and rose to leave the room. Giles had been so engrossed in his observations that he slammed the textbook shut to hide its insertion. Mr Weston froze, and Giles pivoted in his chair to face him.

"Gosh, Mr Weston, you startled me!" he said truthfully.

The librarian looked at him, then at the book, then at the blank computer screen.

"So, you prefer paper to digital research, do you, Mr Chamberlain?"

"Oh yes, Mr Weston," said Giles, looking at the blank screen in front of him. "Paper's my thing, most definitely. Can't stand all this high-tech nonsense."

"And yet you choose to sit in the Computer Room to read your book." He looked down through his half-moon glasses at the tome in front of Giles. "Ah yes, *Religion and Empire: The Dynamics of Aztec and Inca Expansionism.* A fine book indeed."

"Riveting," nodded Giles, patting the closed book affectionately. "It's why I like to read up here, Mr Weston. Less chance of being disturbed."

Mr Weston cast a brief glance towards New Court, before looking down at him over the top of his glasses.

"In that case, Mr Chamberlain, I shall leave you in peace. To finish your studies," he said and, with a brief nod, left the room. Giles had the uncomfortable feeling that the librarian was not entirely convinced by his explanation. Worried that Weston might return to check out his story, Giles completed his study of the roofline, buttresses and location of the lightning conductor referred to in the guide and committed them to memory. He planned to do another survey from the lawns in front of New Court with Ying and Trevor before supper, so he felt he had enough for now.

The others had not wanted to join him in the library because it would have attracted too much attention, and now he was pleased they had not. On the other hand, three friends enjoying the view of St John's from the Backs would go unnoticed by anyone. His job here done, he returned the books to his backpack and headed down to the lobby.

On reaching the ground floor, Giles was about to make for the entrance when a voice called out to him.

"Mr Chamberlain!"

He turned and saw the senior librarian peering at him from across the lobby.

"Yes, Mr Weston."

"That book," said the librarian.

"Book?"

"The one in your bag, Mr Chamberlain."

"Oh, that, you mean? Very useful, it was."

"I'm sure it was, Mr Chamberlain," said the librarian.

"Well, nice to speak to you again, Mr Weston. Must dash," interrupted Giles. "So many things to do before supper."

"Mr Chamberlain," repeated Weston, raising his tone. Giles hesitated.

"Mr Weston?"

"Is it signed out for removal from the library? I would not want you to add to the list of fines you have incurred these past two years," said Weston. "The Dean keeps a wary eye on miscreants to whom I have drawn his attention."

"Well, I'm sure this one's signed out," said Giles. "I'm a stickler for that sort of thing. We archaeologists, we love records and archives. I did a module on it in my first term, I think."

"Then the British Library can rest easy at night, knowing that your future research materials will be a model of order and diligence," said Weston, continuing to survey the screen in front of him.

"Well, naturally," said Giles. "Safe as houses, me."

"Then I'm sure we will find that item listed in your extensive record of authorised withdrawals on the library's register," said Weston.

"Take my word for it," said Giles.

"Well, you see, I take it as a matter of personal pride to double-check every entry, Mr Chamberlain," he said. "It's one of the characteristics of a librarian. Thoroughness." Weston peered at Giles above his glasses. "Shall we?"

Giles approached the desk, opened his backpack and handed over the book.

"Ah yes, Conrad and Demarest. Let me just check on the digital archive." The librarian placed emphasis on the word *digital.* "Clever, these computers. So easy to find things."

As he scrolled down the screen, he asked, "Did you enjoy the book, Mr Chamberlain?"

"Definitely," said Giles. "Amazing what those fellas got up to. Must have been the coca leaves."

Weston glanced up at Giles.

"So, you are researching the origins of cocaine, are you, Mr Chamberlain?"

"Scholastic necessity, Mr Weston," said Giles, his face a picture of sincerity.

Weston returned to the screen and peered through his glasses.

"Well, hard as it may be to believe, Mr Chamberlain, this one has yet to be signed out. So why don't I just complete the process for you? Start this term as we mean to go on."

"Sounds like an excellent plan," said Giles. "There again, what was it that General Patton once said?"

"'No plan survives contact with the enemy?'" completed Weston.

Giles stared at the librarian.

"He did indeed, Mr Weston. Are you a historian, by any chance?"

"I read, Mr Chamberlain," said Weston. "It…"

"…goes with the job?" suggested Giles.

"Indeed," said Weston and, for a moment, Giles could have sworn there was a hint of amusement in those furrowed brows. Weston handed him back the book.

"Glad we sorted that out then," said Giles, turning to go.

"Mr Chamberlain," came the librarian's monotone voice. "The other book."

Giles turned back to the desk and was about to ask, "What book?", when he saw the expression on Weston's face. They both knew there was another book in his bag.

"It's not a library book, Mr Weston. It's one of my own."

"A collector of books," said Weston. "A man after my own heart. May I see it, please?"

Giles knew he was not going to be able to leave the library without showing the guide to the librarian. He reached inside and handed over the much thinner publication. Weston studied it through his glasses and read the title aloud.

"*The Roof-Climber's Guide to St John's*. Nineteen twenty-one, Metcalfe & Co., Cambridge, England."

The librarian checked inside the front cover and examined the stamp.

"G. David Bookseller, Sixteen St Edward's Passage, Cambridge." He gave the briefest of grunts and shut the cover. "A favourite of mine."

Giles was not sure if Weston was referring to the bookshop or the book.

"Great, isn't it?" he said doubtfully.

Weston studied Giles above his glasses as if contemplating what course of action to take. Then he held out the book. Giles reached for it. Weston held it for a moment longer, and Giles looked at him. The librarian dropped his voice.

"If you're planning to climb the Wedding Cake, watch out for the lightning conductor cable," said Weston. "It has a tendency to come loose."

He released the book and Giles gaped at him in astonishment.

"How…?"

The bald-headed man sighed. "I read, Mr Chamberlain. You should try it sometime."

Chapter 14

Giles left the library foyer, a bemused grin on his face. He swung open the revolving door and felt a dull thump from the other side. Peering around the heavy timber frame, he saw a young woman sprawled on the floor, holding her face.

"Oh lord," he said, squatting down beside her, "I am so sorry."

The woman was holding her nose, and he saw blood on her hands. Giles pulled a dirty handkerchief from his jeans, took one look at it and stuffed it back in his pocket. Instead, he whipped off the buff that he wore around his wrist and offered it to her.

"Here," he said. "Use this."

Peering at him through watery eyes, she took the buff and applied it to her nose to stem the bleeding.

"*Collons de Dieu!*" she muttered.

"Let's get you sitting up, so you don't swallow any blood," said Giles, who had plenty of experience of nosebleeds from playing hockey. "Put your head between your legs."

She stared at him and uttered the word "*Bandarra!*"

"So that will be a no then."

The woman started getting to her feet, and he reached forward to help her. She shook him off.

"*Au va!*"

"So sorry," he said, stepping back.

She got to her feet and bent forward to avoid dripping more blood on her dress. There was a splattering of blood down the light-blue material. She glared at Giles, who held up his hands.

"Listen. I didn't realise you were outside the door. You can't really see from the other side."

She rolled her eyes and checked the buff to see if the bleeding had stopped. Giles thought it might have slowed, but there were still red stringy blobs dripping from the end of her nose.

"Shit," she said, applying the buff again to her face.

At least she speaks some English, he thought.

"I am so sorry. Really, I am. Can I at least help you get cleaned up? My room's in the next courtyard. Honest."

Her watery eyes scrutinised him from above the buff. He was not sure whether she was going to answer or take a swing at him. When she spoke, her voice was muffled by the buff.

"Your room is where?"

"Just over there," he said, pointing to the passageway. "In Second Court. I'd take you to the College Nurse, but I think she's finished now."

The woman considered this for a moment. Then nodded.

"OK, show me."

"Right, no problem. I'll lead, shall I?"

She picked up her handbag while maintaining the pressure on her nose with the other and followed him through the passageway.

"It's just over there in that turret," he said, pointing over to O Staircase.

She looked across and followed him.

"I am so sorry, you know," he said as they crossed the courtyard.

"I know, you tell me already," she said.

Giles decided that actions spoke louder than words and started up the steps, the woman following. The staircase was ancient, and the oak steps creaked underfoot. Giles kept looking back to ensure she was all right. When they finally arrived at his landing, he prayed that Rose had tidied up the mess he had left her that morning. Stepping into his room, he was relieved to see that the room was neat and clean, with no clothes, bottles or shoes lying on the floor. Even his climbing gear was neatly stowed in the far corner of the room.

"Come in and make yourself at home."

The woman stepped across the threshold and peered around the room.

"Here, let me get you something to replace that," he said, indicating the blood-soaked buff.

Giles rummaged through his drawers and found a red spotted handkerchief from a pirate punting party.

"There you go," he said. "Here, let me take that from you."

He exchanged the handkerchief for the buff and, opening his bathroom panel, put it in the wash basket under the sink.

"Why don't you clean yourself up here, while I go and get you a fresh towel?"

Giles found a microfibre towel in his climbing gear, which he handed to the woman. She washed the dried blood from her nose and gently dabbed her face, careful not to start the bleeding again.

"That seems to have done the trick," he said.

She looked up at him, and Giles saw her face clearly for the first time. Despite some redness around her nose, her elegant features were flawless.

"Lord," he said out loud.

"Is bad?" she said.

"What? No. I mean… Not really. In fact, not at all."

"You sure?" she asked.

"Yes, definitely."

She offered him the towel. "Thank you."

"The least I could do."

They stood there for a moment, her by the sink, him in the middle of the sloping floor.

"Can I get you a cup of tea, or coffee, or something else?"

"Tea is good, thank you. No milk."

That's good, thought Giles, remembering his last encounter with a milk bottle. He went over to the kitchen cupboard and flicked on the kettle. When he returned, he saw that the woman was sitting on the edge of his armchair, examining the blood-spattered dress.

"*Quin merder*," she said.

"Ah, right, yes. Let's see if I've got anything to cover that up."

At the back of his wardrobe, he found a dress shirt from the May Ball. Thankfully it was clean and ironed, and he offered it to her.

"You sure?" she said.

"No problem. Go on, I'd feel better if you did."

She put it on and rolled up the sleeves, which hung down over her hands. Then she removed the belt from around her dress and tied it again around the shirt. She looked quizzical.

"Is good?"

"Works for me," said Giles.

The kettle started whistling.

"I'll be right back," he said and returned to the kitchen. Giles looked through his collection of mugs, found a dark one that hid the tannin stains and popped a teabag inside before filling it with steaming water. Remembering that she wanted it black, he fished it out with a fork after a couple of seconds and deposited it on the drying rack next to a collection of others. He returned with the steaming cup, making sure to close the kitchen door to hide the mess behind him.

"I hope it's not too strong," he said.

She reached for the cup and gently held it under her nose. "Is no problem, I cannot smell."

"Ah yes," he said. "I'm…"

"Sorry. *Sí*, I know," she said, smiling.

He found himself smiling back.

"You climb," she said, indicating the photographs around the room.

"What? Oh, well, yes," said Giles. "Whenever I can. Bit of a hobby of mine."

The woman walked to a picture on the mantlepiece and studied it.

"Formentor," she said.

"Good spot!" said Giles, walking over to join her. "My friends and I did El Fumat and La Crevata last Easter. We had a brilliant time."

"*Sí*," she said. "Good climbs."

"So, you're a climber too?" he asked.

"Is a hobby, like you," she said as she looked around the room at his equipment and magazines.

"Listen, what with knocking you over and you bleeding all over the college, I completely forgot my manners," he said. "I'm Giles. Giles Chamberlain." He held out his hand.

"Raquel Vidal," she said and took it. Her skin was cold.

"Nice to meet you, Raquel." *Even if I had to knock you out to do so.*

"It was unusual," she said and sipped her tea.

"Are you studying here?" he asked.

"No," she said. "I am here to find my brother."

"Your brother?" he said.

"Yes, he worked in your college. He is a waiter. But he is missing," she said. "So, I came to find him."

"I'm sorry, I had no idea."

"I have spoken with Dean Mackenzie. He is helping."

"Professor Mackenzie," said Giles.

"And Professor Gupta. He is a good man."

"Professor Gupta?" said Giles, surprised.

"You not like the professor?"

"No, no. Gupta's a great bloke. I'm just surprised that

he's involved, that's all."

Raquel shrugged. "The Dean asked him to help. I think he will. He is strong."

"The Dean?"

"No, Professor Gupta is strong. Like a bull."

"I'd not thought about him that way, but now that you say it, I can see what you mean."

"He said he would help. I think he will."

"Well, if there's anything I can do, please let me know."

She looked at him. "Thank you, Giles. I will."

For once in his life, Giles could think of nothing else to say. Then the sound of footsteps on the stairwell brought him back to the present. He checked his watch.

"Oh crap. That'll be my friends."

"No problem, I have to go," she said, getting up from the chair.

"Get your kit on, Giles, we're coming in," called Trevor.

The door swung open, and Trevor entered the room closely followed by Ying. They stopped short when they saw Raquel.

"Oh, hello?" said Ying.

"Sorry, we didn't expect…" began Trevor.

Ying noticed the swelling around Raquel's nose and the blood stains on her skirt.

"What happened to you?" asked Ying.

"Is OK. Was an accident," said Raquel, glancing at Giles.

"Raquel banged her nose on the library door," he explained. "My fault, really."

"Giles, you idiot. Have you put any ice on it yet?" asked Ying.

"Not yet," he said, realising that would have been the sensible thing to do.

"Giles, you are hopeless. Why don't you go down to the kitchen and get some? Trevor, you go with him. See if they've got some ibuprofen to reduce the inflammation."

Giles looked at Trevor and then at Raquel.

"Well, what are you waiting for?" demanded Ying.

They headed off down the stairwell, two steps at a time.

"New tactics?" asked Trevor as they reached the courtyard.

"What do you mean?"

"I've heard of sweeping a girl off her feet," said Trevor, "but knocking them out is a new one."

"Ha, ha, very funny," said Giles as they turned into the passageway and entered the college kitchens. A big man in his chef's whites looked up, a cleaver in one hand and a red cabbage in the other.

"Sorry to disturb you, Chef," said Giles. "Bit of an emergency. Someone needs some ice for some bruising."

The chef stared at them, weighing up whether this was some sort of prank.

Then he slammed the cleaver into the cabbage, splitting it like a skull.

"Jane! See to these gentlemen."

A waitress came out from behind a rack of glasses.

"What do you want?" she said. "Got lost or something?"

"Sorry, but I've got a girl with a bruised nose, and I need some ice to stop the swelling."

"Not been fighting, have you?" she said, frowning.

"No, it was an accident, she was hit by a door."

"That's what they all say," said Jane. "OK, wait there a moment. And don't touch nothing or Chef will have your fingers off!"

She headed over to some freezers in the Wine Steward's section. Trevor turned to Giles.

"So, who is the poor victim?"

"Raquel Vidal. I literally just bumped into her outside the library."

"Clearly."

"It was that library door. You know how lethal it is. Didn't even know the girl was there."

"She a student then?"

"No, looking for her missing brother, apparently."

"Alfie's sister?" asked Jane, who had just returned with a bag of ice.

"Who is Alfie?" asked Trevor.

"Alfonso, he was a mate of mine. Worked here as a waiter," she said, handing him the ice.

"No idea," said Giles. "You don't have any painkillers, do you?"

"Who do you think we are? The bloody NHS or something?" She gave Giles a look and then relented. "OK, wait there a moment."

Giles turned to Trevor. "Best take the ice upstairs, I'll be along in a minute."

Trevor headed off, and Giles waited for the waitress. When she came back, she was carrying a packet of ibuprofen and a folded piece of paper.

"Here you go. And I've written you some instructions." She handed him the pills and a note.

"Thanks very much," said Giles, a little surprised.

The girl turned and walked back into the kitchen. The chef gave Giles a look as if to say, *so what are you still doing here?* Giles left and turned into Second Court. As he began climbing the stairs, he opened the folded piece of paper.

We need to talk. Jane.

Chapter 15

An hour later Ying had left with Raquel, having spent most of the time in Giles' room applying a cold compress to the latter's nose and talking about their climbing experiences in Mallorca. The two women seemed to get on well together, mainly as Ying's Spanish was fluent enough to share a few discreet confidences about Giles, much to the amusement of Raquel. When they finally departed, Ying mouthed to him, "You owe me big-time."

Giles and Trevor had then spent half an hour assessing the climb they had planned for later that night. While *The Roof-Climber's Guide* had recommended accessing New Court's roof from one of its top-floor rooms, Giles had pointed out that this would involve persuading some of the second-years to allow them access to their bedrooms, and this would probably draw too much attention to their activities. Instead, he proposed using a route that had been described in another publication he had found in David's Bookshop: *The Night Climbers of Cambridge* by Whipplesnaith. The author advocated the use of the sturdy lead drainpipes that ran from the ground floor of New Court to the top ramparts.

There were several such drainpipes located around the court, some more exposed than others. In the end, they had decided on a pair of drainpipes by B Staircase. These were tucked behind a buttress that not only offered some degree of protection from any late-night walkers through the court, but also a useful corner section for a chimney technique towards the top of the climb. Trevor had tested the pipes, both of which were well secured to the wall. The larger pipe also had the advantage of a small gap, which allowed a climber to get their fingers behind it to lever themselves up. There were also some steel bands that secured the pipes to the wall, which would provide convenient footholds at regular intervals.

Having completed their reconnaissance, Giles and Trevor headed off to Hall to meet up with Ying. Over supper, Giles had to endure Ying's not-so-subtle attempts to point out Raquel's many qualities, including the fact that she was currently unattached. Eventually, they returned to that evening's plan of action. They would meet in E Staircase, New Court, which was directly below the central clock tower.

It was just before midnight when Giles left his room again, this time with his backpack over one shoulder as he headed down the spiral staircase for tonight's inaugural outing of the R&R club. The pack was filled with an assortment of carabiners, cams, hexes, nuts, extenders, a harness and a 10.5 mm single rope. Giles wore a soft-shell top and bottoms, base layer and rock shoes. He missed his buff, but he zipped up his fleece against the chill.

He was not expecting many people to be about at this hour, but he adopted his usual "not a care in the world" attitude as he set off through the college. In his experience, the more confident you looked, the less likely it was that any of the porters would question you for being out and about after dark with a bag on your shoulder.

He looked up at the sky as he walked through Third Court. It was a clear night, dry with a slight breeze. Perfect conditions for climbing. The breeze would muffle any sounds they made on the ascent. He crossed the Bridge of Sighs and entered New Court. The lights lit up the cloisters in front of him, but there was no one to be seen. As he walked along, he looked up at the windows around the court. A couple of rooms had their lights on, but apart from that, there was no activity.

As he approached E Staircase, the broad outline of Trevor and the smaller figure of Ying could just be made out in the shadows of the passageway. They were kissing. *Must be the adrenaline*, he thought.

"Good cover," he whispered and saw Ying jump.

"Where've you been?" she said, prising herself from Trevor's arms.

"Checking my gear. You guys set?"

Trevor patted the backpack he had on his shoulder. "All set."

"Good. I brought my phone to see if we can record the moment."

"Like it," said Ying.

"OK, let's harness up."

They filed out of the passageway and followed the path that ran along the inside of the courtyard to B Staircase. The fire escape sign cast a dim light, and the climbers moved behind the buttress to shield themselves from the cloisters. With practised ease, each harnessed up and checked the others' knots. When they had finished, Giles assigned roles.

"So, Ying, lead climber?"

"No, you're the founding member, Giles. You get the honour. Besides, you've studied the route."

"OK, I'll take the lead, you next and then Trevor can bring up the rear. When we get to the tower, Trevor will belay for me, while you record the moment for the archives."

The others nodded.

"OK, let's do this."

Giles attached a rope to his harness and Trevor, and Ying kept a watchful eye for any late-night wanderers. He looked up at the drainpipes, which disappeared up the side of the building to the rampart three storeys above them. After waiting for his eyes to adjust to the darkness, he slipped his hands behind the nearest pipe and began to climb.

Despite the darkness, Giles felt relaxed and confident, using his fingers and toes to feel his way. His rubberised rock shoes found secure purchase on the sandstone crevices, and there were plenty of handholds offered by a ledge or window sill where he paused to look up. His only concern was that some of the old sandstone would crumble, so he made sure of his footing before going for the next hold.

The rooms behind the glass were dark and the windows closed. The occupants were sleeping or catching up on some late-night studies, but he was careful to move slowly to minimise any noise. Within a few minutes, he was at the roof parapet. Reaching up with his arms, he pulled himself over onto the leaded roof space. There he paused for a moment, breathing deeply, but enjoying the adrenaline surge through his body. Time for the others.

Giles moved over to a nearby chimney stack and, removing a sling from a carabiner on his belt, made it fast. After fixing the safety rope to the sling, he went back to the parapet and gave it a jerk to signal Ying to follow. Then he braced himself and maintained the tension on the rope as she began to climb.

Ying moved effortlessly up the same route he had taken, and it was not long before her head and shoulders appeared over the parapet wall. Her smile shone white in the darkness as she levered herself up and over before landing softly on the roof beside him. Giles untied the rope from her harness and was about to feed it back to Trevor when he heard a low whistle. Someone was approaching!

Giles peered over the parapet and saw shadows walking through the cloisters from the Bridge of Sighs. He could not quite make out their voices, but one of them was raised. He waited to see if they would continue along the cloisters or turn right and head for the E Staircase archway. If they did so, it was possible they might see Trevor in the corner behind the rampart. He could feel Ying tense next to him. Holding a finger to his lips, he watched as the shadows reached the central span of the cloisters before continuing on, away from the tower.

Ying exhaled a sigh, but Giles kept watching the shadows

until two figures appeared at the far end of the cloisters. One was tall, the other thick-set and walking with a limp. When they turned into the entrance of I Staircase, Giles recognised the shorter of the two as the Dean before they disappeared through the fire doors.

"Come on, Giles!" whispered Ying.

Giles looked down and could just make out the shape of Trevor in the courtyard. He fed the rope down to him and, while Trevor made himself fast, watched the entrance to I Staircase for a sign of movement. A sharp pull on the line signalled that Trevor was making his ascent and Giles took up the slack, focusing on the task at hand. Trevor was not as quick as Ying, but he was sure-footed and steady. He was soon hoisting himself above the parapet, puffing slightly.

"That was interesting," he said quietly.

"Who were they?" asked Ying.

"Not sure," said Trevor, "I was too busy keeping out of sight."

"One was Mackenzie," said Giles, who had had plenty of run-ins with the Dean in his time.

"Are you sure?" said Ying.

"I saw him when they entered the stairwell," said Giles. "Not sure who the other one was."

He looked at the others and then broke into a big grin. "Is this fun or what?"

"Super cool," said Ying.

"Beats YouTube," said Trevor.

"Come on, it gets better," said Giles.

They moved along the roof, carefully stepping over the

leaded ridges until they came to the rampart. Scrambling over this, they made their way around to the southern aspect of the tower to take in the view. They were high above the cloisters now, and Giles could see the college lawns stretching below them towards Trinity's Wren Library. Moonlight flickered off the river, and in the distance, the spires and towers of the city cast a dark profile against the night sky.

"Not bad, eh?" he said, turning to Ying, who was staring towards King's College Chapel.

"Softly I am leaving," she began to recite.

"Just as softly as I came;

I softly wave goodbye

To the clouds in the western sky."

Trevor stared at her. "Where did that come from?"

"Xu Zhi Mo. My mum used to read it to me when I was a child."

"It's also on a memorial stone at the back of King's College," said Giles.

Ying turned towards him, raising an eyebrow. "And there was me thinking you walked around with your head in the clouds."

"Speaking of which," he said, grinning. "Ready for the tower?"

"Lead on, Macduff," said Trevor.

They headed across the roof, careful not to disturb any of the tiles. When they reached the side of the clock tower, Giles stared up at the structure. It had a pair of buttresses on each corner, rising up above the blank clock face and the leaded windows of the canopy above. There an octagonal crown tapered up into a sharp point, on top of which stood a wind vane that pivoted gently in the breeze, moonlight reflecting off its gold surface.

"OK," said Giles, "when I get to the crown, I'll secure the sling to one of those ramparts. Trevor can belay me for the last stretch to the pinnacle."

"Got it," said Trevor.

Giles looked around to see where the moon was coming from and dug in his trouser pocket for his phone, which he gave to Ying. "If you try over by the wall, you should have enough light to get a decent shot."

Ying looked at where he was pointing.

"Right. I'll give it a go," she said and headed over to the edge of the roof.

Giles made the rope fast to his harness, and Trevor checked it.

"All good?"

Trevor nodded. Giles reached for the buttress ridge and began to climb.

One of the unique features about the tower above New Court was that the four faces cut into the sandstone panels had never been fitted with working clocks. Giles had no idea why, but the good news for a climber was that these provided excellent hand and footholds by which to reach the leaded window sill above. Taking full advantage of this architectural folly, he climbed up alongside the glass panes and steadied himself against the flying buttress. Giles then began to chimney his way up between the flying buttress and the primary structure, using his feet and back to lever himself up in stages until he could get a handhold on the crown above him.

Giles was high above New Court now, its lawn hundreds of feet below him, and he made sure he climbed patiently, one move at a time. It was a few minutes before he reached the low rampart of the crown and, taking a firm handhold, he pivoted and swung himself up. Breathing hard, Giles removed a sling from his belt and attached it to the rampart. Then he ran the safety rope through an extension to the sling to prevent it snagging and, taking a deep breath, stood up.

The breeze ruffled his hair and fanned his face, cooling the sweat on his forehead. Around the crown's rampart were eight mini spires and Giles rested his hand against one of them, posing so that Ying could get a good shot with the phone.

At that moment something screeched behind him, and he instinctively ducked, gripping the spire with both hands. Turning, he looked up towards the sloping cone of the roof and saw the wind vane weaving from side to side in the breeze a few feet above his head, the cockerel's rusty hinges squeaking with the gust. Heart hammering in his chest, Giles balanced there for a while to calm himself as a passage from *Hamlet* floated into his head.

It was about to speak when the cock crew,
And then it started like a guilty thing,
Upon a fearful summons.

Taking steadying breaths, he looked up at the ridges of the conical roof, which were adorned with ornamental stone decorations. These would provide him with perfect hand and footholds for the last section. He reached up and felt something cold and metallic under his fingers. It was the lightning conductor that the librarian had warned him about earlier that evening.

"I may not read, Mr Weston, but I do listen," he said to himself.

Smiling, Giles moved his hand to one side to get a firmer purchase on the stonework before easing himself up to stand just below the weather vane itself. Giles unclipped another sling, which he wrapped around the spire, securing his rope to it with a carabiner. Using the base of the weather vane as a foothold, he grasped the steel rod in both hands and pulled himself upright so that his chest lay pressed against the vane's direction panel and his face adjacent to the golden cockerel itself.

Giles found his chest was pumping with adrenaline now and it was hard to remain calm as he surveyed the college laid out beneath him, its roofs and towers bathed in moonlight.

"Wow!" he breathed. He had never felt so alive in Cambridge.

A flash of light caught his eye, and he looked down to see Ying's dark profile against the edge of the roof below.

Good girl, he thought to himself. Then an idea came to him. *No point in doing things by halves, Giles.*

Making sure he had a firm grip on the pole in his right hand and his right foot squarely planted against the base, Giles pushed himself away from the steel post and reached out into space. He held this star shape for a few seconds, willing Ying to take the photo as he stared up into the heavens. And that was when he saw it. And jumped.

*****

The wind howled, and Ying screamed. She could not help herself. One moment Giles was in the image screen of the phone and the next he was gone. She heard Trevor grunt as he took up the slack on the belay and a sickening thump as something banged against the tower above her.

"Trevor?" she yelled. "What happened? Have you got him?"

There was an agonising pause before Trevor responded.

"Yeah, I've got him." She saw him leaning back, bracing himself against the pull of the rope. "He must have slipped."

She looked up to see if she could make out where Giles was. But it was impossible to see him against the night sky.

"I'm going up there to see if he's hurt," she said and took a step towards the tower.

"Wait!" said Trevor. "I won't be able to hold two of you. See if he can hear us."

"Giles!" called Ying, "Giles, are you OK?"

There was a pause.

"Giles!"

"Yes, I'm OK," said a voice in a hushed tone. "Keep it quiet, will you? You'll wake the whole college. I'll be down in a moment."

Ying sagged with relief and looked at Trevor. He stood there, immobile, as dependable as ever, his face a study in concentration. God but she loved him. He glanced over at her and smiled.

"He's supporting his own weight. Feels like he's OK."

Ying saw Giles' face appear above the crown of the tower. He had removed the slings from the parapet and spire and was carefully working his way back down the flying buttress. To her experienced eye, he looked awkward as he edged down the clock face. When he dropped the last few feet to land on the roof, he stumbled.

"Giles!" Ying ran forwards and grabbed him. She felt him wince, but she didn't let go for a while, hugging him tightly.

"You're hurt," she said when she finally released him.

"Bruised, that's all," said Giles.

"What happened?" asked Trevor, coming over to join them. "Did you slip?"

"Not exactly," said Giles, who leant against him for support. "Thanks for the belay. I thought I was going to roll off the tower."

"Yeah, well, good you roped up."

"Too bloody right," said Ying. She was getting over her initial shock and was feeling sick now. "So, if you didn't slip, what happened?"

"I jumped."

"You did what!"

"I jumped," he said, looking up at the sky.

"Are you mad! What did you do that for?"

"Did you bang your head as well?" asked Trevor.

"Probably," admitted Giles, "but that's not it."

"I don't understand," said Ying, "what in hell's name made you jump?"

He looked at them both, his face shadowy in the moonlight.

"I saw the angel of death."

Chapter 16

Giles saw the look on their faces when they realised how serious he was.

"Giles, you're freaking me out," said Ying.

"That was quite a bump to the head," said Trevor. "I think we need to get you back down."

But Giles just stood there on the roof of New Court, looking up at the moon. He was not really sure what he had seen on the tower. But it had scared him. Wings and talons. And eyes. Yellow against the night sky.

"Giles!" said Ying. Her sharp tone cut through his thoughts, and he saw that Trevor had already collected their gear and was waiting for him. Together they made their way back over the rooftops to the drainpipe where they had first made their ascent. Trevor checked that the rope was securely attached to Giles' harness.

"I'm fine, Trevor, really."

"I'll be the judge of that."

"Are you climbing down, or do you want us to lower you?" Ying asked.

"Climbing," said Giles, annoyed at the way they were

mothering him. As if to prove it, he swung himself over the wall to make his descent and almost missed his footing, grabbing the drainpipe to regain his balance. Ignoring the look of alarm on Ying's face, he began to edge his way down, being careful to avoid giving her more reason to be concerned.

Giles had reached the first floor when he heard a door bang somewhere in the courtyard. He wedged his feet against the window ledge and looked around. At the far side of the court, the man he had seen with the Dean earlier stepped out from I Staircase and paused to light a cigarette. The orange glow of the flame lit up his face, reflecting off pale features and dark, glossy hair. The red dot of the smoke flared brightly for a moment as he took a deep drag and looked up at the buildings around him. Giles crouched motionless, not daring to breathe, expecting to be spotted at any moment. The dot flared again, but no cry or shout rang out. Then it was spinning through the air before falling on a dark patch of lawn, where it glowed for a few seconds before going out.

Giles scanned the far side of the courtyard for signs of the man, but he was nowhere to be seen. Then the unmistakable sound of footsteps could be heard approaching through the cloisters. They kept coming, loud and purposeful, and Giles was sure he had been spotted. His mind raced as he wondered what explanation he could give for hanging off a college wall at this time of night. Lost his keys? Girlfriend threw him out? College Bat Society?

But then the footsteps took on an echo and began to fade

as Giles let out a long breath. Their owner had walked beneath him, out of New Court and over the Bridge of Sighs. Sagging with relief, he flexed his hands, which ached from gripping the drainpipe all this time, and continued his descent until he felt the welcome sensation of cobbles under his feet. Giles untied the rope and yanked it a couple of times to signal he was clear. It disappeared upwards, and it was not long before Ying swung over the parapet and made an uninterrupted descent.

"Giles, are you OK?" she asked. "I thought he'd spotted you."

"Well, if he did, he didn't want to hang around."

"Like you, you mean."

"Ha, ha, very funny," said Giles, but was pleased that she was able to joke again after the incident on the clock tower.

"OK, Trevor needs us to belay for him while he comes down."

Ying untied the rope, fed it through her harness and readied herself. When she was set, she took up the slack and tugged the line twice. Giles watched it pay out slowly as Trevor made his way down.

"Well, that was eventful," Trevor said on reaching the bottom.

"No shit, Sherlock," said Ying.

Giles looked at their grinning faces. They were buzzing.

"Sorry I freaked out on the clock tower."

"No problem," said Trevor, "the evening needed livening up. I was finding climbing college buildings at night rather dull."

"Yeah, swinging around on a rope above the Dean was so last year," said Ying.

Giles smiled.

"Still, I just wanted to say, you were great."

Ying came over, grabbing him by his arms.

"You are bloody mad, you know that, don't you?"

He nodded.

"That's why we love you," she said. "So, don't go killing yourself, because R&R would be a bit crap if there were only two of us."

Giles did not really know what else to say.

"Time for bed," said Trevor.

They stowed everything in their backpacks and headed back over the Bridge of Sighs. At this time of night, they were not surprised to find the courts deserted.

"I'll see you two tomorrow," Giles said when they got to Second Court.

"Here," said Ying, handing him his phone. "We'll take a look at the photos tomorrow."

"Thanks. Just send me a text to make sure I'm up."

"Will do," said Ying, squeezing Trevor's arm. "Though we might not be up too early ourselves."

"Till tomorrow, then," said Giles.

The others waved as they headed off for Chapel Court, Trevor's arm wrapped around Ying's shoulder.

Giles walked over to O Staircase and climbed up the creaking spiral steps. Outside the door of his room, he was just reaching for his keys when a floorboard creaked behind him. Spinning around, he saw a hooded figure standing on the next flight of steps.

"What the hell?" he yelled, backing up against his door.

"Shush!" hissed the voice. "Or you'll wake the whole staircase!"

Giles stood there frozen, trying to work out where he had heard that voice before. The figure remained motionless for a few moments longer before a pink-mittened hand reached up and pulled back the hood of what he now realised was a parka coat. Giles found himself staring at a pale face framed by peroxide-blonde hair.

"Holy crap," he said. "It's you! I thought you were a ghost!"

"Bit jumpy, ain't you?" said Jane, smiling. "You've not been up to no good or nothing?"

"What? Me?" said Giles, conscious of the bag full of climbing gear digging into his back. "I've just been out and about with friends. More to the point, what are *you* doing here?"

"I left you a note, remember?" said Jane. "*We need to talk?*"

Giles did remember her scribbled note from the kitchen.

"Well, yes. But I didn't think that meant you'd be stalking me in my staircase at this time of night."

"Yeah, well, I came around after me shift, and your sign said IN. So, I came up here and knocked on your door. When you didn't reply, I figured I'd wait on the step for you."

"So, you've just been sitting here all that time? What have you been doing?"

She held up her smartphone. "Facebook."

Giles wasn't sure he believed her, but he suddenly felt exhausted and didn't feel like arguing the point.

"Listen, Jane, I'm knackered. If it can't wait till morning, can we at least do this over a coffee?"

"Yeah, as long as it's just coffee."

"Don't worry, I've had quite enough excitement for one night. Coffee is all I'm interested in." Giles opened his door and switched on the lights as he entered the room.

"Nice place," said Jane, admiring the panelled walls.

"I like it," said Giles, dumping his backpack by the wardrobe and heading for the kitchen cupboard. Jane wandered over to the mantlepiece and looked at his photos.

"You took these?"

"Yep," said Giles. "How do you take your coffee?" Then he remembered he was out of milk. "Oh, sorry, I've run out of milk."

"Not to worry," said Jane, producing a handful of UHT milk portions from her coat pocket. "Brought me own."

He put the kettle on and rinsed out some cups in the sink.

"You a climber then?" she asked.

"Now and then," said Giles, wiping out the cups with a tea towel.

"Was that what you were doing tonight?"

"What makes you think that?" he said.

Jane sat down in the armchair. "Oh, I dunno. You're wearing climbing shoes, the knees of your trousers are scraped, and one of your nails is bleeding. That and the fact your backpack looks like it has ropes and carabiners inside it."

She removed her mittens and grinned at him from the chair.

"So, you're a climber too then," he said.

"There's a climbing wall at the gym. I've had a go. If I'm honest, I prefer having me feet planted firmly on the ground. Not a great fan of heights, me."

The kettle boiled, and he spooned out some instant coffee into mugs.

"But as for you, Giles, you look like one of them adrenaline junkies. You know, the types who love jumping off mountains and stuff," she continued. "Am I right or what?"

"Junkie is harsh," he said as he brought the mugs over.

"I knew it!" she said as she took her mug. "Blond, brainy and bonkers."

He pulled up his desk chair and sat down. Reaching forward, he took one of the milk portions.

"May I?"

"Be my guest," she said, adding two to her coffee. "Don't worry, I got those from the bin today. It's criminal what the kitchens throw out. I recycle, me. Saves landfill."

She gave him an innocent look.

"Yeah, right. So, what about this mysterious message, then? What's that all about?"

He watched her as he took a sip of coffee and noticed a shadow cross her face.

"Yeah, well, it's about Alfie," she said.

"Raquel's brother?"

"Yeah, we used to work the same shift."

"Do you know what happened to him? If you do, you need to tell his sister, she's worried sick."

Jane stared into her milky coffee. "That's just it. I don't really know what happened."

For the first time, she seemed unsure of herself, and her voice lost its edge as she continued.

"Me and him used to do the late shift. That's the last time I saw him. A few weeks ago. We was clearing up after a feast. He went off home, and I never saw him again."

"So, what do you think happened?"

"Nuffin' good," she said. Her lips pursed beneath the pink lip gloss.

"Come on, Jane," said Giles, "what is it?"

"You'll think I'm some sort of stupid bimbo or something."

Giles got up from his chair and knelt down in front of her.

"Come on, Jane," he said again. "It's obvious you're not just some dumb waitress."

She gave him a sharp look.

"The way you nailed me as a night climber."

"Well, it is a bit bloody obvious, isn't it?" she said.

"To you, maybe, but most people around here don't have a clue. Trust me, I'd have been sent down if they had."

She frowned.

"I haven't told anyone, not even my brothers. So, I don't want you telling no one."

"Listen, Jane, you keep quiet about my night climbing,

and I'll keep your secret safe. Deal?"

"Deal," she said and offered him a fist. Giles made one too, and they touched knuckles.

"So, what's the story?" he asked.

"Well, it was the day after I'd said goodnight to Alfie," she began. "I'd turned up for me shift as usual and Kevin, the Fellow's butler, was mardy as hell because Alfie hadn't turned up and we was short-staffed."

"Go on."

"Anyway, I was cross because I had to do wash-up on me own at the end of the shift, which meant I finished later than usual. It wasn't until well after midnight that I left college, and I was planning on going clubbing at me brothers' place. So, I was in a right hurry when I set off, rushing down Trinity Street like Usain Bolt in heels. Got to Great St Mary's and I was about to turn into the Market Square when I saw this hang glider thing swoop over King's with a big whoosh. Blimey, I thought, I must be seeing things. Then I hears a massive thump further down King's Parade, and I think, bloody hell, it's gone and crashed."

She looked straight ahead, reliving the moment.

"So, I legs it down King's Parade because I've got me first aid certificate and I'm thinking I can help or something. And when I gets to the Copper Kettle, I can see this hang glider smashing into the Corpus Clock. Only there's this terrible banging noise because this thing is still hammering away at the clock. And then I realised it isn't a hang glider at all. It's…"

"A fallen angel," Giles said.

"What did you just say?"

"Hold on," said Giles, reaching inside his jacket pocket and pulling out his phone. He unlocked the passcode and tapped the camera icon.

"Ere, you're not recording this, are you?" demanded Jane, alarmed.

"No, just wait a moment. I just want to see…" He stopped and stared at the last photo Ying had taken that night on top of the New Court tower.

"What? What is it?" asked Jane.

Giles turned the screen around and showed her. Jane's eyes widened, and her mouth dropped open.

"Fuck me!" she said. "That's the one! That's the clock killer!"

Giles held the phone away from them, and they both looked at the screen. In the middle of the image was the weather vane, its golden cockerel glinting in the moonlight. Giles was nowhere to be seen. But where he had been standing moments before was the ghostly outline of pale wings spread wide across the night sky.

Chapter 17

Annabel opened her eyes and stared at the ceiling of her room. It was still dark, and her alarm had yet to ring. This was what her subconscious always did when she did not want to be late for something, like a flight, or a train, or an exam. Before going to bed, she would tell herself to get up at a particular time and then, on cue, her conscious self would kick in just before the signal. Lying there, she tried to remember what was so crucial about this morning. Then a grin spread across her lips.

A date. With the tall, dark, handsome Brett from Yale.

"Gorgeous," she said, dreamily.

She closed her eyes and tried to imagine the scene. Out on the water, the sun rising behind him, casting a deep yellow glow on his muscular, tanned arms as he reached forward with his hands. Then his long legs driving against the footplate, the tendons in his thighs taut with the effort. His eyes locked onto hers, watching her call out the rhythm as he propelled them powerfully through the water.

The alarm began beeping and the delicious image dissolved as she opened her eyes to reveal her bedroom ceiling again. Annabel hit the clock forcefully and sat up in bed.

"Don't get ahead of yourself, girl. It's just a training run."

But she could not suppress her excitement as she swung out of bed and padded across the wood floor to her en-suite bathroom. Turning on the light, she looked in the mirror and yelped in horror at the sight that greeted her.

There, on her forehead, the most enormous spot had appeared, red and swollen with the beginnings of a peak to it.

"You have got to be kidding me!" she moaned.

Images of the chocolate cake she had eaten the previous day at Professor Gupta's jumped to mind.

"You idiot! Now, look what you've done."

Checking the time, she ran through the options.

A: Grin and bear it. Annabel grimaced. The thought of meeting up with Brett only for him to focus on the white-capped volcano growing on her forehead was the stuff of nightmares. No, that was *not* going to happen.

B: Stand him up. Claim to be ill, or to have pulled a muscle or something, and wait until the spot subsides before resurfacing into college life. No, that wouldn't work. He would think she had wimped out. Or was lazy. Or did not really like him! And then he would be fair game for all those long-legged athletic girls at the rowing club, falling over themselves to swap places with her. No way was she going to let that happen.

Or C: Cover it up. Wear a cap, or a beanie, or a bandana, anything that would hide this mark of shame until the eruption was over. Not great, but a lot better than options A or B. Annabel looked gloomily at her forehead, a sinking feeling in her stomach. It was going to be a monster, all right.

"I'm never eating chocolate again," she promised herself, not for the first time.

Rummaging around in her wash bag, she found some witch hazel and dabbed it on the tight red skin, wincing at the stinging sensation. Then she hurried back to her bedroom and rifled through the set of drawers until she found the red bandana she usually wore for hockey. Returning to the mirror, she carefully placed the rolled-up material over the spot and tied the ends behind her head, wincing as the material pressed on her sensitive skin. She looked at herself, and her spirits rose a little.

A bit Pirates of the Caribbean, she thought, *but better than the Elephant Man*.

Annabel glanced at her clock and was appalled to see it was already almost six a.m.

She slipped on her jogging kit and trainers, yanked open the door to her room and dashed down the stairs to meet her date.

*****

It was still dark as Annabel ran over the Bridge of Sighs and entered the old courts. When she came pounding into First Court, she was relieved to see a tall, athletic figure wearing a hoodie and jogging bottoms, waiting under the archway of the Main Gate.

"Hi there," she said, slowing as she approached. "Sorry I'm late."

The figure turned, and even though his features were still

in shadow, somehow Annabel knew it was not Brett. She stopped short a few yards from the stranger, who stared at her from under his dark hood. His silence frightened her, and she found herself backing away.

"Hey, Annabel!" came a shout from the other side of the court. Annabel spun around and saw a YALE top jogging towards her from the passageway to Second Court. Without looking back, she ran towards Brett's reassuringly familiar frame and practically threw herself into his arms.

"Whoa, there," he said as she clung to him. "Good morning to you too."

She looked up at his bemused but smiling face.

"Am I glad to see you," she said. "That man just freaked me out!"

"Which man?" asked Brett.

Annabel looked back at the archway. It was deserted.

"A man was standing there. He was really creepy," she said, peering around the court for any sign of the stranger. "I thought he was you."

"I see – so you think I'm creepy, is that it?"

She looked up at him. "No, I didn't mean that. I… I just got spooked, that's all."

Brett smiled. "Just messing with you." He looked around. "Well, the creep seems to have gone now, so shall we make a start?"

Annabel realised that she was still hugging him. "What? Oh, yes, of course. Sorry," she said, letting go.

"No problem," he said, smiling. "Shall I lead, or do you know the way?"

"You lead," said Annabel, who had never been to the college boathouse and was happy to be guided by him.

"Sure. Let's go then," said Brett, breaking into a jog. "Let me know if I'm going too slow for you. I tend to take it easy first thing."

"Likewise," she said, hoping that his "easy" would be something she could cope with.

Annabel followed Brett as he ducked through the wicket gate and turned left towards Bridge Street and the river. She risked a glance around for any sign of the stranger, but there was no one else to be seen. Brett's long legs were already eating up the yards with no apparent effort, and Annabel put on a burst of speed to catch up with him. Still a little shaken by her earlier encounter, she was keen to stay close to the American.

Brett headed straight across Bridge Street past the Round Church and turned left around the ugly, concrete car park onto Park Street. Together they jogged along the empty road that fronted onto the pretty terraced cottages and followed these, past the Maypole pub into Lower Park Street, and onto Jesus Green.

Brett was as good as his word, setting a comfortable pace, and as Annabel got into her rhythm, she began to relax and look around at the early morning scene. On the other side of a brook, lights shone through the trees from the Tudor brickwork of Jesus College, while on her left Jesus Green lay covered in a dusting of dawn's early dew.

Brett made no attempt to talk, content to jog along in silence. Annabel didn't mind. This was his training run, and she was happy the Olympian wanted to share it with her. They continued on the path, crossing a boulevard of large lime trees until they came to the pedestrian crossing on Victoria Avenue. There was no traffic, and they turned left to follow the road leading to the iron bridge over the Cam.

"There's Maggie," said Brett, pointing to a building on the far side of the river just to the right of the bridge.

"Sorry?" said Annabel.

"Lady Margaret Boat Club," said Brett, smiling, "or Maggie."

Annabel looked and could just make out the bright red doors of the timber-framed building in the glow of the street lights. As they jogged over the bridge, she peered down and could see an elegant little boat already floating on the river. Then Brett turned right into a driveway and trotted around the back of the boathouse and down onto the slipway. Annabel's breath was misting in the crisp morning air as Brett hailed a person carrying a pair of red-bladed oars down to the boat.

"Hey there, Blades."

"Morning, Brett," said the middle-aged man, wrapped in a red fleece top. "Just about got her ready for you."

"That's great. Much appreciated. I hope it wasn't too much trouble for you."

"Not at all. It's quiet at this time, and these old tubs aren't too difficult to handle."

He placed the oars carefully on the slipway before coming back over to see his first crew of the morning. Brett stepped forward and shook his hand before doing the introductions.

"Blades. This is the lady I mentioned on the phone," said the American. "Annabel Hamilton, this is Blades, Maggie's boatman."

Annabel and Blades shook hands.

"Nice to meet you, Annabel," said the boatman. "Brett here was telling me you fancy doing a bit of coxing this year."

"Well, I'm a complete novice, but yes, that would be great."

"Don't you worry. Everyone has to start somewhere. Lady Margaret has a good reputation for bringing on novices. Some even went on to row in the Boat Race, so you never know."

"I'd be happy just to make it into a St John's crew."

Blades winced. "Now, don't you go saying nothing about St John's Boat Club down here. It's Lady Margaret Boat Club you're rowing for."

"Sorry," said Annabel, "like I said, I'm new to all this."

"Not to worry. It's an oddity for sure, but we haven't been called St John's Boat Club for more than a century," said Blades.

"Why's that then?" asked Annabel.

"A dark secret," said Blades, winking. "I'll leave Brett to fill you in on the details when you're out on the river. Here put this on." He handed her a compact orange life jacket. "All coxes have to wear one of these."

Annabel slipped it over her head and clipped the strap around her midriff. She looked at Brett, who nodded. "We'll take her out now before the other crews arrive."

"I'm expecting a lot more next week," said Blades,

heading off to the boathouse. "More flaming blazers."

"I'll have to remember that one," said Brett grinning as Blades disappeared inside.

"Sorry, did I miss something?" asked Annabel.

"An in-joke," said Brett, smiling. "Lady Margaret's colours are a fiery red. And if you row for a college boat you get a jacket in that same colour. In fact, the name 'blazer' has its origin here. When Lady Margaret crews used to turn up for regattas wearing their bright red jackets, the other crews used to call them 'blazers' and the name stuck."

"Cool," said Annabel. "That's something I'm going to love telling Gran."

"OK, let's have a look at the boat we're taking out this morning."

They walked to the edge of the water and Annabel looked down at the old wooden boat. It was facing upstream towards town and looked like something from *The Wind in the Willows*.

"This is what's known as tub. She's not fast, but she is stable, which is great for novices getting to know the ropes."

"I'm all for that," said Annabel, looking at the dark, murky water of the river.

Annabel watched the American go about setting up with practised ease. After locking the oars into place, he stepped into the middle of the boat, settling himself into the seat. Slipping his stockinged feet into the training shoes that were screwed to the footplate, Brett slid back and forth, checking that the wheels moved smoothly over the runners. Satisfied, he looked up at her.

"Now it's your turn. I'll hold the bank while you step in. Take it steady and put your first foot in the middle of the boat and then bring your next foot in before sitting down in the stern."

Annabel did as instructed and was pleased that she did not wobble too much as she sat down on the varnished wooden seat.

"A natural," said Brett, smiling.

"We haven't got going yet," she said. "What next?"

"You see those two bits of cord either side of your seat? Those are attached to the rudder. If you pull the right one forward, you turn the boat to the right or bow side. The left turns you to the left or stroke side."

"So, right is bow side, left is stroke side?" said Annabel.

"That's it," said Brett. "It's easier to remember in an eight because the person closest to you is called stroke and their blade is on the left side of the boat. Bow's blade is on the opposite side. You'll get used to it. Let's push off and see how we get on."

"Go for it."

Brett shifted his weight to lift the land-side oar off the concrete and gave the slipway a gentle shove to edge them out into the flow. When they were clear of the bank, he balanced the boat with both oars.

"Right, Annabel, we're going to head upriver for a few minutes, so you can get the hang of steering. Boats keep to the right hand side of the river."

"Bowside," said Annabel.

"You've got it! As cox, you are in charge of the boat, so

this is where you would normally assert your authority on the crew. That'll be me."

"I like it already," said Annabel.

"I'm going to call out the commands that a cox will normally use, and I want you to repeat them after me. Are you good with that?"

"All good," said Annabel.

"So, come forward."

"Come forward," repeated Annabel. Brett immediately pushed his hands away from his body and slid towards her on his seat. His broad shoulders arched under his Yale hoodie, his knees pressed up against his chest, and Annabel found his face within inches of hers. He held that position, his breath misting the gap between them. Annabel could sense the power of his muscles, coiled in front of her. She felt a tingle go down her spine and held her breath.

"OK, look at my blades," he said.

"Sorry?" said Annabel.

"The ends of the oars."

"Oh, I thought you meant the boatman for a minute."

"Of course," he said, smiling. "Yeah, it's what we all call him. Sort of goes with the job."

She stared into his eyes a few inches from hers.

"Anyway," he said, "back to these blades?"

"Oh, right, yes, of course," she said, looking over at the oars.

"You can see that they are lying face up on the water," he continued. "That is when they are feathered."

"Feathered," she said.

"Good. What I'm going to do now is square blades, which is what we do when we are ready for the start."

"Square blades," she repeated.

He twisted his wrists, turning the red blades vertical, and they dipped into the water.

"Right, I'm going to go off light, and we can increase the pressure later to half, three-quarters and maybe even full."

"Light," said Annabel.

"As you command," said Brett, straightening his legs and driving himself smoothly away from Annabel, his arms pulling the oars with him. The boat eased forwards through the water, and she heard waves lap against its varnished wooden hull.

Brett was already moving back towards her, arms stretched out in front of him, before driving himself away from her again. Annabel felt the pressure from the back of her seat as the boat began to accelerate. Brett continued with this steady rhythm, and they picked up speed. Annabel checked ahead to make sure they were not heading into the bank or one of the houseboats moored at the edge of the water. She gently pulled forward the cord in her right hand and was rewarded with the bow of the boat edging to starboard. She then did the same with her left, and they turned to port. Meanwhile, Brett was moving back and forth smoothly, propelling them along with surprising speed.

"Getting the hang of it?" he asked.

"I think so."

"Good. Before we increase the rate, you need to know how to slow the boat. That way you can stop us from hitting something. The command is 'easy there.'"

"Easy there," she repeated.

Brett finished his stroke and stopped sliding, resting his hands in front of him, his blades feathered above the water. The boat glided forward under her current momentum.

Brett nodded. "Now hold it up."

"Hold it up," she repeated.

Brett immediately squared his blades in the water and Annabel lurched forwards, almost falling into his lap as the boat came to a standstill.

"Wow, that works," she said, settling herself back in her seat again, her face flushed.

He smiled. "How was it for you?"

"Good," she said. "I think I've got it."

"OK, so we'll head up to the weir, turn there and put some speed on coming back. Sound good?"

"Sounds great," said Annabel, smiling. "So, come forward."

Brett slid forward and paused in front of her. She waited a few seconds, enjoying the moment.

"Square blades."

He twisted his wrists inches from her chest.

"Light pressure. Go!" she said.

Brett pushed himself away from her, and the tub began to move through the water as he eased into a steady rhythm. Annabel watched him as he slid back and forth. This was fun, she decided as they glided along. Then she asked the question that had been on her mind since they got in the boat.

"So, what's this dark secret of the Lady Margaret Boat Club?"

"Ah, that," said Brett. "Allegedly it involved the death of a cox of another college."

"Really?" said Annabel, all ears.

"You may have heard about the Cambridge Bumps. They're these crazy races only you Brits would be mad enough to do. Basically, you line up all the different college boats on the river, a boat length and a half apart. Then, get this. Someone fires a cannon. Yep, a cannon, and all the boats go hell for leather trying to 'bump' the boat in front of them. Like I said, it's crazy."

"Sounds brilliant," said Annabel, her eyes gleaming.

"That's not all. If you bump the boat ahead of you, both boats move to the side of the river, and the next day they start again, only this time they have switched places, which means that the faster boat is now ahead of the slower boat. The race is run over four days, and if a crew manages to get four bumps in succession, each of the crew is awarded their own oar."

"What? A mini oar, surely?" said Annabel.

"No, a full-size oar, with the names of each member of the crew painted on the blade. Plus, the names of the four colleges that they bumped," said Brett.

"That's fantastic," said Annabel, remembering the oar hanging over St John's Bar. "But what has this got to do with Lady Margaret?"

"Well, you can imagine how much momentum there is behind a boat with eight athletes pulling hard, trying to chase down a slower boat. All these boats have pointed bows to cleave through the water, and they can be pretty sharp. And who is in the stern of the slower boat?"

"The cox," said Annabel, her eyes widening. "You don't mean that a John's boat rammed a cox from another club?"

"Rammed and killed him, so the legend goes," said Brett.

"No!" said Annabel, suddenly conscious of her lower back resting against the seat in the stern.

"And for that reason, St John's College Boat Club was banned from the river for a hundred years. Which is how the Lady Margaret Boat Club was formed."

"To avoid the ban and allow members of the college to continue to row," said Annabel.

"You got it," said Brett. "Anyway, that's the reason that all college boats have a 'bow ball' on the front, to prevent anyone from getting injured in a collision."

Annabel looked over his shoulder and saw a small rubber ball attached to the bow of their tub.

"So, when does the ban on St John's Boat Club get lifted?" she asked.

"Apparently it expired some years ago. Needless to say, there was a unanimous decision to remain as Lady Margaret Boat Club. You Brits like your traditions."

"What a story!" said Annabel.

"A legend," corrected Brett, "and like most legends, it's not strictly speaking true. Blades says it was another boat club, not Lady Margaret."

Annabel was about to ask which boat club when she heard the sound of rushing water. Looking past Brett, she saw the weir looming ahead of them.

"Brett, stop!"

He smiled and kept rowing.

"I mean… Easy there!"

Brett finished his stroke and stopped rowing. The boat continued towards the rushing water.

"Hold it up!"

Brett dropped the blades in the water, and the boat came to a stop. He looked over his shoulder and back at Annabel.

"I'd have thought a weir was hard to miss, don't you think?"

"Sorry," she said. "I wasn't paying attention."

"No problem, but as a cox, never forget that you are the only one who can see ahead. Your crew is relying on you."

"Got it." She felt a little embarrassed, but he just smiled.

"OK, so now we need to turn around. Give the command 'spin turn,' and I'll show you how it works."

"Spin turn," said Annabel.

Brett pushed forward with one oar and pulled back with the other. He repeated this a couple of times, and the tub gently spun on the spot until it was facing the opposite direction.

"Nice," said Annabel, marvelling at how simple he made it seem.

"I think that's probably enough for now," said Brett. "Hopefully that will give you a head start when you come down for novice trials."

"It's been super, Brett," said Annabel. "Thank you so much."

"No problem," he said. "And as I'm nicely warmed up now, how about putting me through my paces on the return leg? Then we can get the boat out and be back in time for breakfast."

"Sounds great," said Annabel. The thought of seeing Brett in action again gave her stomach a flutter of excitement.

"OK then, cox. I'm all yours," he said.

I wish, thought Annabel. But she settled herself in her seat and gripped the two cords.

"Come forward!"

Brett slid towards her and paused, ready.

"Square blades!"

He twisted the blades, so they were vertical in the water.

"Ready. Go!"

Brett exploded backwards, the boat immediately lurching forwards, pushing Annabel back in her seat. Before she knew it, Brett had finished the stroke and was sliding towards her. Again, he drove away, and again, and again. Each time Annabel found her back arching as the seat drove into her, the boat picking up speed with each stroke. Brett's eyes were calm and focused on the weir behind her, keeping his head level. The veins bulged in his neck and forearms as the sound of the oars striking the water dropped from an urgent tempo to a high but steady rhythm. While the old tub was not designed for speed, Annabel was impressed at the pace Brett had generated in so short a space of time. She adjusted the rudder to ensure they maintained position in the middle of the river as they sped back towards the boathouse.

"Last ten," said Brett, as he swung back and forth. "Call it on the catch."

"What?" asked Annabel, confused.

"One!" he grunted as his blades bit into the water.

"Two!" he said, repeating the action as she grasped his meaning.

"Three!" they said together.

"Four!" she said as Brett, silent now, drove his knees down.

"Five!" She looked ahead and could see they were nearing the iron bridge.

"Six!" She adjusted the rudder as they sped around the curve of the river towards the boathouse.

"Seven!" Blades looked up to see them powering their way back towards him.

"Eight!" Something caught her eye up on the bridge ahead.

"Nine!" It was someone standing there, his outline silhouetted against the early morning sky.

"Ten!" She stared up at the figure as the boat sped under the bridge, and with a thrill of fear, Annabel realised it was the man in the hoodie looking down at her, his face hidden in shadow.

It all happened so fast. Annabel heard Blades yell from the bank. A large object rose up from the inky water in front of the boat. Annabel yanked the starboard rudder cord, and the tub began to slew around. Brett's port blade hit the object and buried itself deep in the river. The forward momentum of the boat was transmitted up the oar, through the rigger and into the handle, which whipped up into Brett's face and hit him in the temple with a tremendous crack. The blade continued on its trajectory, pulling the rigger down into the river as the tub tipped on its side. Brett's body fell sideways over the edge of the boat, and his deadweight pushed it under the water.

Annabel was still gripping the useless rudder cords as the tub capsized, its heavy wooden shell thrusting her deep into the icy river. Screaming as she went under, her mouth and throat filled with water. She gagged and found herself tumbling upside down in the icy cold darkness. The poppers on the life jacket burst open and she heard the sharp hiss of gas as it inflated. Her body lurched upwards, but she was still under the boat and her head collided with the rigger. Gasping in pain, more water flooded into her lungs as something snagged onto the strap of her life jacket and dragged her down, pulling her deeper beneath the surface.

Annabel reached out with her hands but found nothing to hold onto, her fingers gripping only cold water. She tried waving her arms, but her clothes felt heavy, and her legs thrashed ineffectually. As her struggles became feebler, she kicked out one more time, but her shoes were deadweights. Her vision began to blur as she sank deeper towards the riverbed. For a moment she thought she saw a light in the distance, but it dimmed and drifted further away.

"Mum!" she thought before the darkness took her.

Chapter 18

The Buttery was already busy when Nick arrived on his way to morning lectures. With rugby trials later that afternoon, he planned on having his main meal now and a light lunch later. It was what Nick did most match days at home, so he opted for a full English breakfast, cereal and a stack of toast. His tray was laden when he approached the checkout.

"Good morning. How are you this morning?" said the woman standing there. Nick noticed she had the same sort of outfit his mother wore to work.

"Good, thanks."

"You want coffee or tea with that?"

"Coffee, please," said Nick.

"It's OK, I can bring it over," she said.

"You don't need to, I can come back," he said, thinking of his mother.

"Is no problem. You go sit."

"Thanks. It's Nick, by the way."

Nick fished his Buttery card from the back pocket of his jeans and swiped it on the reader.

"Enjoy your breakfast, Nick," she said, smiling.

Taking his tray, he walked between the tables, looking for an empty one. Most of them were already full. There was one towards the back that had only one occupant. It was Annabel's tutor. The old professor sat there quietly in his crumpled suit, a faded college scarf draped over his shoulders and a cup of tea poised in front of his face, staring into space.

"May I join you?" asked Nick.

The professor started and looked up. His face brightened in recognition.

"Ah, Mr Wood, isn't it?"

Nick was surprised he knew his name.

"Yes, it is. Nick Wood."

He put his tray down and took his backpack from his shoulders.

"Professor Ravi Gupta. Nice to meet you," said the old man, offering his hand.

Nick took it as he sat down opposite him. "Nice to meet you, Professor."

"Thank you for coming to see me so soon," said the professor.

"Sorry?" asked Nick, confused.

The professor frowned. "Ah, I see now that Annabel didn't pass on my message."

"No. This was the only table free."

"A coincidence, then," said the professor. "How interesting."

"Your coffee, Nick," came a voice behind him.

Nick turned and saw the waitress standing there with his coffee.

"Good morning, Professor," she said.

At this, the old man's face lit up.

"Good morning, Aurelia. I see you have already met Mr Wood."

"Yes, we have already met. A very polite young man," she said, setting the cup and saucer down on the table.

"Can I get you any more tea, Professor?"

"No thank you, Aurelia," said the professor, still smiling broadly.

"Well, good day, gentlemen."

Aurelia turned and headed back between the tables. Nick noticed the professor's eyes following her progress, the smile fading as she left them. *You old dog*, Nick thought as he started on his muesli.

"Aurelia seems to have a high opinion of you, Nick," said the professor, studying him over his tea.

Nick shrugged. "Just being polite."

The professor nodded and put his tea down.

"So, Nick, tell me about the missing statue."

Nick almost choked on his mouthful of cereal. *Thanks, Annabel*, he thought. He swallowed painfully as the professor watched him.

"It was nothing really. It was when I was helping Annabel move into her room. I just looked across the river and saw this statue in the Master's Garden. But the next day it wasn't there. I dunno really."

Saying it out loud to a Fellow of the college made it sound even more ridiculous. He reached for his coffee and took a sip, to hide his embarrassment as much as anything.

The old man studied him, not saying a word, and Nick wished there had been somewhere else to sit.

"Nick, do you play sport at all?" asked the professor.

"What?"

"I saw you running with Annabel the other morning, and I wondered if you played sport at all?"

"Well, yes, rugby."

"Ah, a rugby player," said the professor. "Robert, your tutor, was an outstanding rugby player. Did you know that?"

"Yes, he mentioned it at interview."

"He played both for the college and the university."

"He's a Blue?" asked Nick.

"Three years running," said the professor, absently fingering his scarf. "I, on the other hand, am a Professor of Astronomy. The most exercise I get is walking to and from the observatory."

Nick refilled his cup, not sure where this conversation was going.

"I used to love watching Robert play. He was a winger, you know. Very fast."

"I'm on the wing too," said Nick.

"Indeed," said the professor, raising an eyebrow. "Anyway, on one occasion after watching him play, Robert said that he would enjoy looking through one of the telescopes down at the observatory. I think he was conscious that I always supported him in his activities, but he had never shown any interest in mine."

Nick sipped his coffee politely.

"Anyway, I took Robert down to the Institute of

Astronomy on Madingley Road and showed him the telescopes we used. He particularly liked a wonderful old instrument, known as the Thorrowgood Telescope, which is housed in a wooden shed in the grounds to this day."

The old professor leant forward, his eyes gleaming with enthusiasm. "I don't know whether you are aware, but to use the main telescope, one must first use the finder scope to identify the star or planet that one wishes to observe. It is quite tricky to do, particularly because the optical finder on an antique instrument like the Thorrowgood will invert the image."

"Oh, right," said Nick.

"I remember that night like it was yesterday. Robert and I sitting there in that shed, gazing up at the stars, wrapped in thick coats and scarves trying to keep warm."

The professor stared up at the ceiling of the Buttery and Nick thought, *Oh no, this guy's bonkers!*

It was as if Gupta had heard him, because he dropped his gaze and stared straight at Nick. There was nothing misty in his look now.

"Nick, what struck me that night was that Robert was able to see stars through the finder scope that I was unable to see. His eyesight was that good."

He paused as if waiting for Nick to grasp the point of the story. He couldn't.

"My point, Nick," said the professor, speaking with deliberate care, "is that if you are anything like the sportsman that Robert was, you too will have excellent eyesight. And as a lawyer, you don't strike me as the type of person who jumps to hasty conclusions. I don't believe for a minute that you made a mistake in your observation from Annabel's room. Which is why I would like you to tell me exactly what this statue looked like."

"You believe me, then?" said Nick, amazed.

"I do, Nick. What exactly did you see?" said the professor. "Describe it to me in as much detail as you can."

Nick thought back to that image through the rain-splattered window.

"OK, well, the statue was a dark colour. Grey, I think. Like granite."

"The shape of the statue?" asked the professor.

"It was some sort of bird. It had its back to me, so I couldn't be sure exactly what it was. But I assumed it was an eagle."

"What made you think that?"

Nick thought for a moment.

"Well, I knew that the college symbol was an eagle, and it was a statue in the Master's Garden, so I imagined it was an eagle."

"You imagined," said the professor.

"Because of its wings, they were hunched. Like that!" Nick said, pointing past the professor through the windows at the end of the Buttery. The old man turned in his chair and stared at the two giant stone eagles perched on top of the pillars standing sentinel over the bridge.

"Those eagles, you mean?"

"Yes," said Nick. "Only bigger."

"How big, exactly?" said the professor, but Nick noticed

a wariness in his voice now.

Nick tried to picture the scene on the Master's lawn as the lightning flashed through the break in the clouds.

"Twice my size. Must have weighed a tonne. But the next day, there were no marks on the grass, nothing. It had just disappeared. Statues don't do that."

Then the professor said something bizarre.

"Not in our world, perhaps."

Nick just stared at him, but Gupta seemed deadly serious as he continued.

"It is not unusual to come across things that have no rational explanation, but that doesn't mean they didn't happen. In this of all places, we seek to understand the incomprehensible. To challenge the boundaries of what is known. To dare to believe in something beyond our limited human understanding. To suspend disbelief and remain curious."

Nick remembered his torn gown and the broken clock window. He wondered if he should mention these as well, but decided he had probably said too much already. Gupta was Annabel's tutor after all, and he didn't want any of this getting back to her.

"Listen, I'm sorry, Professor," he said, standing up. "I have to go to lectures."

The old man looked disappointed. "Ah yes. I understand."

There was something in the way he said it that made Nick feel the strange little man really did understand. Way more than he was telling.

"It was nice meeting you, Professor."

"And you, Nick. Good luck with the rugby this afternoon."

"Cheers."

Nick picked up his tray and took it to the collection rack. As he left the Buttery, he saw the old man standing by the window, holding the old scarf in his hands and staring up at the statues. In a different world.

*****

Ravi looked across at the column of red stone. Its sheer sides rose from the valley floor below and protruded like a blunt and bloody needle hundreds of feet into the violet sky. The irregular surface was lacerated by vertical scars where whole sections of stone had fallen away and now lay like broken splinters at its base. There was something otherworldly about the way it looked, and it took Ravi a few moments to realise what it was. The column cast no shadow. The binary suns high in the sky above them illuminated the rock's entire surface. The result was that the column seemed to glow like a bar from the electric fireplace back in his college room.

"I wouldn't fancy climbing that, would you?" asked Robert at his shoulder.

"No, certainly," Ravi agreed. "But you have to say it is magnificent."

"Certainly is. Mind you, the others are too."

Ravi looked down the broad valley that wound its way between the surrounding cliffs. It was littered with more of these red columns, sprouting from the valley floor like stone saplings fed by the wine-coloured river that meandered between their roots. Some were taller than the specimen in front of them, while others were jagged stumps, their shattered superstructures lying forlornly at their sides like felled trunks of stone.

"So many," said Ravi, finding it hard to take in the alien landscape that lay before him. "What do you think causes them? It's as if they've erupted from the ground."

"Well, it's hard to imagine they are formed by erosion, given their height," mused Robert.

Ravi looked up and shaded his eyes to peer at the top of the massive column in front of them. A shape caught his eye.

"Robert, what's that up there? Your eyes are better than mine."

"What are you looking at?"

"The top of the column. Is that a tree?"

Robert squinted, holding a hand up to blot out the glare.

"It could be, I suppose. But if so, it's the only one we've seen so far. Hard to imagine anything growing up there in this infernal sunshine. Without any shade, it must be baking on top."

"I wish I'd brought binoculars," said Ravi, reproaching himself. "There's definitely something."

He removed his glasses and wiped them with his handkerchief before looking again.

"I don't think it's a tree," said Robert, "but it's got branches or something similar sticking out." He winced and shook his head, wiping sweat from his eyes. "Christ, but it's hot, Ravi. Shall we see if we can find some shade? I'm roasting here."

Ravi squinted, but try as he might, he couldn't make out what the shape was. Bowing his head in defeat, he turned to face his friend.

"Of course. Next time I'll come prepared. I should have thought about it before. Shall we head down into the valley itself?"

"Good plan. If the water in that river isn't drinkable, at least we'll be able to cool off a bit."

Ravi cast one more look at the shape at the top of the column before following his friend, ignoring the uncomfortable feeling tingling down his spine that they were being watched.

Chapter 19

Later that afternoon, Nick tasted the sweat on his lips as he limped wearily down the avenue of trees between the Scholars' and Fellows' Gardens. Shambling alongside him was Gareth, a muddy kitbag over one broad shoulder. Neither of them said a word as they made their way back into college.

The walk back from Grange Road had been a slow and painful affair for Nick, physically and emotionally. Although his body was bruised, it was nothing compared to the damage his ego had taken. The step up to university level had come as a humiliating shock, the size and speed of the other players frightening.

The afternoon had begun with a punishing set of drills, which had gone well enough, and Nick was pleased to be selected for the final practice session alongside some of the existing Blues. But when it came to the game itself, he had been left for dead by his opposite number, a New Zealander, who had run rings around him. When Nick had managed to get close enough to tackle his man, he had been flattened by a brutal forearm that left him lying dazed on the turf.

It hadn't been much better when he had the ball in hand. Nick had made the mistake of trying to cut inside the winger, and though he wrong-footed his man, he was then cut down by a covering tackle and spilt the ball, which allowed the opposition to counter-attack and score. He had managed to salvage some self-esteem in the last quarter, when the genuine Blues contenders upped their intensity to impress the watching selectors and allowed him to put in some solid defensive tackles. But by the end, he was relieved when the final whistle blew and he could limp from the pitch and gather his things for the walk back to college.

By contrast, Gareth had fared much better. Nick had seen first-hand what a class act the big Welshman was. Gareth's physical size had been an asset, but it was his speed and awareness that impressed Nick – and the selectors too, no doubt. Gareth had been in the thick of the action, knocking people over, harrying the opposition and stealing turnover ball at the breakdown. That was not to say he had emerged unscathed.

"What did you do to your hand?" asked Nick. "I saw you go off for treatment?"

Gareth examined his taped fingers. "Dislocated a finger. The physio pulled it back in and then taped it up. It's happened before. It'll be fine, just a bit tender at the moment." He gave Nick a quizzical look. "When did you get that one?"

Nick reached up and gently probed the swelling over his right eye.

"That New Zealander. Almost took my head off."

"Ah yes, you were unlucky there," said Gareth. "Kiwi played for Auckland last season. Decided to come over here to do an MPhil and experience playing at Twickenham."

"Yeah, well, that's not an experience I'm going to have."

"You're a bit harsh on yourself," said Gareth.

"Harsh but fair," said Nick in a tone that brooked no argument, and Gareth wisely decided not to pursue the matter. They reached the Eagle Gate in New Court, and Gareth gave his eye an appraising look.

"You might want to get some ice on that if you want to see out of it tomorrow."

"That good, eh?"

"A beauty," said Gareth. "If we go now, I'll introduce you to the college nurse. A good person to know around here. Saves on having to buy tape and painkillers yourself. I just need to collect a parcel from the Great Gate Lodge."

Nick didn't mind. If he was honest, he was glad of the company. They might not be in the same league as players, but he appreciated Gareth taking him under his wing. There was something about running out on a pitch together that created a brotherhood of sorts, and at the moment he could do with all the support he could get.

"Afternoon, gents," said the porter as they entered the lodge.

"Afternoon, Bert," said Gareth.

"Been in the wars, have we?" asked the porter, looking at the pair of them.

"Rugby trials," said Gareth.

"You might want to get some ice on that one, young

man," said Bert, looking at the swelling around Nick's eye.

"Thanks," said Nick.

"I'm taking him to see the College nurse.'

"Good idea. Anyway, what can we do for you?"

"Parcel, Bert," said Gareth. "My mum's been writing to me."

"Right you are. G. Evans, isn't it?" said the porter, heading over to a pile of parcels. "Always loved getting a parcel, me. Wherever I was in the world, me missus would send me something."

"You were a globetrotter then, Bert?" asked Gareth.

"Royal Marine. Sent us all over the place. But no matter where we were, the Royal Mail found us. Priceless, they were." He retrieved a parcel and put it on the counter. "And you, sir?" he asked, turning to Nick.

"Nick Wood. Though I'm not sure I've got anything."

"Ah yes, Mr Wood. We wondered when you were coming in," said Bert. "I have a note here from Professor Gupta."

"Yeah, I've seen him already," said Nick.

"Well, he left this for you only an hour ago. Gave it to me before he ordered a taxi."

Nick frowned, and Bert retrieved a cream envelope from below the counter. It was addressed in a spidery scrawl.

To Nick Wood. By hand.

"Did he say what it was about?" Nick asked, tearing it open.

"Just said it was important you got it."

Nick unfolded the letter and read.

E7 Second Court
3rd October, 10.30am
Dear Nick,

I've just heard that Annabel has been in an accident and has been taken to Addenbrooke's Hospital. I'm on my way to see her now. I thought you would like to know.

Yours sincerely,
Professor Ravi Gupta

"Shit!" said Nick. He looked up at the porter. "How do I get to the hospital?"

"I can get you a taxi," said Bert.

"Please!" said Nick.

"Trouble?" asked Gareth.

"A friend of mine has had an accident."

"Serious?"

"It doesn't say." His mind was racing. What sort of accident?

"If you wait in the Forecourt, the taxi will be along in a minute," said Bert, putting down the phone.

"Right, thanks," said Nick, then groaned. "Oh, I don't have any money. On me, I mean."

"I'll give you a docket," said the porter. "Just give it to the driver. Hospital visits are on the college account."

Nick took the piece of paper. "Thanks. Can I leave this with you?" he said, turning to Gareth and holding out his kitbag.

"No problem. I'll keep hold of it until you get back."

"OK. Thanks!" he said, heading for the door.

"And get that eye seen to!" called Gareth after him as Nick broke into a run, his aches and pains forgotten.

*****

"Thanks," said Nick, as the taxi pulled away from the drop-off zone in front of Addenbrooke's Hospital, an ugly structure of glass and concrete that sat in the middle of a sprawling medical campus on the outskirts of the city.

People were entering and leaving the building through a set of oversized revolving doors, which turned slowly to accommodate the old or infirm using crutches or wheelchairs. Nick joined the hesitant, shuffling flow of visitors and followed them inside. As soon as he stepped into the foyer, the smell of disinfectant hit him, as did the noise from all the people milling around the entrance. Ahead of him, he saw a circular desk curving out from a wall emblazoned with the words WELCOME TO ADDENBROOKE'S HOSPITAL.

The receptionist, a well-dressed black man, looked up and surveyed the swelling around Nick's eye.

"If you're looking for A and E, it's the entrance around the corner. Go out through the main door again and turn right. You can't miss it."

"No, it's not that," said Nick, approaching the desk. "I'm here to visit a friend of mine. Annabel Hamilton. She was brought in earlier today."

"Do you know which ward she's on?"

"No, I'm afraid not."

"What was she brought in for?"

"I don't know."

"You don't know?"

"No, she's been in some sort of accident."

The receptionist turned to the computer in front of him and said, "What's the name again?"

"Annabel Hamilton."

"Middle name?"

"Not sure," he said.

The receptionist looked at him again. Nick remembered the sign at the bottom of A Staircase.

"But it begins with a V."

"It begins with a V?"

"Yes." He took a guess: "Victoria." He said it with more confidence than he felt, but the tapping began again.

"When was she admitted?"

"This morning."

"And it was an accident, you say?"

"Yes."

The tapping continued then stopped.

"Right, I need to know her date of birth."

"Sorry?" said Nick.

"I can't let anyone onto the ward unless they know the patient's full name and date of birth."

Nick noticed a CCTV camera on the wall behind the reception desk pointing directly at him above a sign saying ZERO TOLERANCE OF VIOLENCE AGAINST OUR STAFF.

Come on, think!

Then he remembered the birthday present he'd seen on Annabel's desk the day they'd arrived.

"Fifth of October, 1997."

The receptionist grunted.

"1996?" said Nick.

"No, you guessed right the first time. Miss Hamilton is on Ward B4. Go through the food court, turn left and take the lift to the second floor. Visiting hours finish at eight p.m."

"Thanks."

The receptionist nodded. "And you might ask them for some ice for that eye."

Nick headed for the food court, where the smell of disinfectant lost its battle with the aroma from the Costa Coffee concession and followed the signs for the lifts. The doors opened, and a man wearing a hoodie stepped out as Nick stepped in. He pressed the button for the second floor, and as the door closed, he noticed a puddle in the corner.

What hospital staff have to put up with.

Nick held his breath until the doors opened again and stepped out onto an empty corridor. Following the signs for Ward B4, he made his way to a small waiting area outside a set of electronic doors. These were shut, but through the glass panel, he could see a nurse sitting at a desk, playing with her ponytail as she looked at her computer screen. He tapped on the window. The nurse looked up and peered at him over her black-framed glasses, before reaching for something under her desk. There was a click. Nick pulled open the door and approached the counter.

"I've come to see Annabel Hamilton?" he said.

The nurse gave him a long, hard look before checking the schedule in front of her.

"At the end on the right," she said.

"Thanks," Nick said and headed off down the ward.

It was long and wide with large windows at the far end. On either side of the central aisle, there were curtained partitions providing each patient with a rudimentary level of privacy. Nick moved quietly along, and as he neared the curtain, he heard murmured voices. The familiar figure of Professor Gupta came into view. He sat hunched in a chair beside the bed, looking very old.

Annabel was propped up against the pillows, a livid red mark in the centre of her forehead and dark rings under her eyes. Dressed in a lightweight hospital gown, she looked pale and listless, a shadow of the girl who had lit up his world these last few days.

"Ah, I see you have a visitor, my dear," said Professor Gupta.

Annabel looked first at the professor and, following his gaze, spotted Nick.

"Nick!" she said, covering her mouth, her eyes filling with tears.

"Hi Annabel," he said.

She held out a hand and he moved around to the side of the bed to take it. It felt cold and clammy.

"What are you doing here?" she asked, blinking away tears.

"The professor left me a note."

"The professor?"

Annabel loosened her grip, and they both turned to see the professor looking out of the window at the darkening sky.

"Professor," said Annabel. "Thank you so much."

The professor started as if surprised there was someone still there, before smiling back at her.

"Don't mention it, my dear. I thought a friendly face would be welcome."

Nick sat down on the edge of the bed, Annabel still gripping his hand.

"Annabel," said the professor, "now that Nick is here, I was going to get a cup of tea and perhaps visit Brett. Can I get you anything at all?"

A shadow crossed her face.

"No thank you, Professor. I'm fine for the moment." Then she continued in an anxious voice, "You will tell me how he is, won't you?"

"Of course. And don't you worry, Brett's in good hands."

Annabel's grip tightened.

"And you, Nick – something for that eye, perhaps?"

"No, it's fine. I can hardly feel it," Nick lied. Now that he was here, he realised how much it was throbbing.

"By the way, I'm expecting your grandmother shortly, Annabel. Her train is due about now."

"Thanks, Professor."

Professor Gupta smiled at them both and left. Annabel turned back to Nick and examined his face. "Nick, what have you done?"

"It's nothing," he said, ignoring the pain. "I'm more concerned about you. What happened?"

Annabel leant back onto her pillow and tears welled up again.

"Oh, Nick. It was awful."

She began to relate the story of her early morning outing with Brett.

"Brett trialled for the US Olympic squad and said I was a natural."

Nick felt something stir inside him. *Just great.*

"Anyway, we'd nearly finished and were heading back, and that's when it happened."

Tears welled up in her eyes as she stared down at her polyester hospital gown.

"We hit something in the water. It might have been a swan or a log or something washed down from the weir. I couldn't see it in the dark under the bridge."

She closed her eyes as she relived the moment.

"Brett's oar swung up and hit him in the face. The boat capsized, and we both fell in the river."

Her voice became desperate.

"I tried to get out, but I couldn't. The water was so cold and got in my throat, and I couldn't breathe and…"

Annabel let go of his hand and covered her eyes as she began to cry, her shoulders shaking. Nick wanted to hug her, but he'd been on the Good Lad training at school and knew she was vulnerable right now. Instead, he just sat on the bed, looking down at the floor until her sobbing eased, and her breathing became more regular. Finally, she wiped her eyes and looked at him once more.

"Brett and I could have died today, and it was all my fault."

"But you didn't," he said. "You both made it."

"That's only because someone pulled me from the water and gave me CPR."

"What?"

"A stranger saved my life Nick. And then he went back into the river and saved Brett too. Only Brett hasn't recovered consciousness yet," her voice began to tremble again. "That's why he's still in intensive care."

"He's going to be OK, though?" said Nick, feeling the first pang of sympathy for the American.

"He's got a fractured skull," she said miserably, "though the doctors say that might have saved him."

"Sorry?" asked Nick.

"Brett was unconscious when he went under. Even though he was in the river longer than me, he didn't swallow as much water."

Annabel held out her hand and he took it.

"So, you have no idea who this stranger was?" he said.

"No, it all happened so fast. Blades, the college boatman, said it was hard to make out his features under the hoodie."

"Hoodie?" Nick remembered the figure leaving the lift and the puddle on the floor. He was about to ask Annabel about her rescuer when he was interrupted by an anguished cry from across the ward.

"Annabel!"

Nick spun around. There was Mrs Hamilton, red-cheeked and breathing hard, rushing towards them.

"Gran!" cried Annabel, letting go of his hand and throwing her arms open.

Nick moved out of the way as grandmother and granddaughter hugged each other. Annabel began sobbing again. Getting up from the bed, he started backing away. Things were getting way too emotional for him right now. *Time to leave.*

"Nick! Where are you off to?"

The old lady had spotted him.

"Hello, Mrs Hamilton," he said, hesitating at the edge of the cubicle.

Getting up from the bed she advanced on him, a steely look in her eye, and he wondered for a moment if he was in trouble. Then, to his amazement, the old lady reached up, took his head in her bony hands and kissed him on both cheeks.

"Thank you for being here!" she said, releasing him.

Nick caught sight of Annabel over Mrs Hamilton's shoulder, staring at her grandmother. She looked as surprised as he was, but he was pleased to see her face had recovered some of the colour that had been missing earlier. He heard footsteps behind him and turned to see Professor Gupta appear around the screen. He looked tired but happy.

"Brett has recovered consciousness," he announced. "He's going to be all right."

Annabel burst into tears. Mrs Hamilton left Nick and returned to her granddaughter.

"It seems that Mr Davis has been fortunate. He has a

fractured skull, but the scans suggest there is no internal bleeding. Severe concussion and a bad headache. Nothing life-threatening. There is every chance he will make a full recovery. Though I don't think he will be rowing for a good while."

"Poor Brett," said Annabel and Nick felt his stomach tighten a notch.

"Anyway, they are keeping him in the hospital for observation. His mother is flying over from the United States. She should be here tomorrow to speak with the consultant."

"Well, that sounds very encouraging," said Mrs Hamilton, patting Annabel's hand.

There came the sound of more people approaching down the ward. Nick saw two odd-looking individuals peering in each of the cubicles. One was tall and gangly and the other short and skinny with long hair. When they saw Nick, they hurried towards him, the taller one leading, the other following like a misshapen shadow.

"I know you. You're from John's," said the taller one. It wasn't a question, it was a statement.

"Err, yes," said Nick. "And you are?"

"I'm Ashley, but my friends call me Ash," he said, offering his hand. Nick took it and found his hand being shaken vigorously.

"And this is Brian," said Ash, indicating his companion.

Brian made no effort to shake hands and stared instead at the linoleum floor.

"Ash! Brian!" cried Annabel.

Ash dodged past Nick and went over to Annabel's bedside. "Hello, Annabel," he said, Brian following close behind.

"It is so good to see you," said Annabel, smiling at the odd-looking pair. "Thank you so much for coming."

"Professor Gupta left us a note," said Ash. "We came as soon as we could."

"After *The Simpsons*," added Brian.

"Oh, right," said Annabel, not quite sure how to respond to that.

"So, what happened?" asked Ash. "Professor Gupta said you had an accident and were in the hospital. What sort of accident was it? Was it a car accident, a bike accident? Or did someone hit you or something? You've got a nasty mark on your head."

"What? Oh, no," said Annabel, colouring slightly. "I fell in the river."

"Did you bang your head? Can't you swim? Did you swallow the water? It's probably got algae, you know."

"Did you drown?" asked Brian.

Before Annabel could answer these questions, Professor Gupta cut in.

"I'm sure that Annabel doesn't want to go through all that just now, gentlemen," he said. "On the other hand, as she couldn't go to lectures today, would you like to fill her in on what she missed?"

Ash looked delighted.

"No problem, Professor. We only had four today. It won't take long."

Nick looked on as Annabel settled back against her

pillows. She was listening with a tired smile as her strange friends began giving her a blow-by-blow account of the day's topics. He decided it was time to go. His head was throbbing, and he could barely see out of his right eye.

"Annabel, I'm heading back," he said.

"Oh, Nick," she said, looking up. "Thank you so much for coming."

He would have liked to say more, but he didn't feel comfortable doing that in front of an audience.

"See you," he said.

Annabel mouthed *Thank you*, before turning back to the others.

"Here, Nick, take this." Professor Gupta handed him a £5 note. "For the bus home."

"Thanks, Professor."

"Will we be seeing you tomorrow, Nick?" asked Mrs Hamilton who had come over to say goodbye. "I'll be staying at the college. The professor has kindly arranged for me to have a guest room."

"I'll see what I can do," he said.

"Good. And before you go, there's something I need you to do for me."

"Sure," he said.

"I want you to get yourself down to A and E and have someone check you for concussion. That knock looks really nasty."

"Oh, that," he said, "no, it's nothing, really."

"Nick, I used to be a nurse. If you don't do it, I'll take you there myself. I mean it."

He could see she did too.

"OK, Mrs Hamilton."

"Good. Now if you'll forgive me, I need to rescue Annabel from her friends Ash and Brian," she said, giving him a wink. "Wish me luck."

With that, she turned and headed back towards the cubicle.

*****

An hour later, Nick was finally seen by an exhausted junior doctor, who confirmed no signs of a concussion. After being issued with an ice pack for his eye and strapping for a bruised shoulder, he managed to get away as the first of the night's drunks was escorted through the door by a police minder.

It was after eleven p.m. when he stepped off the bus in the city centre. By now, Nick's whole body seemed to be aching, and all he wanted was to get back to his room, have a shower and go to bed. Walking up Sidney Street past Sainsbury's, he passed groups of students heading in the opposite direction, going clubbing. None of them paid him any attention, but as he neared the Round Church all that started to change.

The first indication that there was trouble ahead was the sound of whooping and laughing from a rowdy bunch on the corner of St John's Street. There were half a dozen of them meandering past the Forecourt entrance, and Nick could tell by the way they were staggering about that they were drunk. Coming the opposite way was a dark-haired girl, heading in the direction of Bridge Street. She saw the group ahead of her and, keeping her head down, tried to walk past them. She had almost made it when one stepped in front of her, his arms spread.

"Whoa, there, gorgeous! Why so shy?" He reached up and removed a cigarette from his lips and exhaled into the air. With a jolt, Nick recognised the student with the goatee beard he and Gareth had seen outside Ryder and Amies. "You're kidding me," he said under his breath.

"Please, I just want to go to my hotel," the girl protested.

This was followed by laughter as the group paused and gathered around her.

"You don't want to do that," said Goatee. "Come with us. We're heading back to my place, aren't we, boys?" More laughter.

"No. Thank you," said the girl.

Nick felt his heart begin to beat faster and he took his hands out of his pockets as he approached the group.

"You don't mean that, do you?" continued Goatee, moving closer to the girl. He was right in her face now.

Nick was hungry, sore and fed up, but he could feel the blood beginning to pump through his temples as the red mist began to descend over his one good eye.

"Leave her alone," he said.

The laughter faltered, and a couple of faces turned to look in his direction.

"Fuck off, mate. What's your problem?" said Goatee, not moving.

"You are," Nick growled and charged.

They must have been drinking for some time because it

took the group a moment to realise what was going on. That was all Nick needed.

His shoulder hit Goatee just below the sternum with a satisfying thump. Wrapping his arms around the legs of his target, Nick hoisted him off his feet like a tackle bag in training. Pumping his legs, Nick ploughed through the stunned group until his feet hit the low wall at the far side of the pavement and he stumbled, pitching himself and his opponent over onto the lawn beyond. Goatee landed on his back with Nick's full body weight on top of him.

"Ooof!"

As his opponent lay winded on the ground, Nick scrambled to his feet and turned to face the others. Some were standing there in shock, but others were clambering onto the wall. One lunged at him, and Nick swung an uppercut that hit him in his midriff, causing the student to jackknife as they fell back onto the ground. The attacker groaned and rolled onto his side as Nick started to pick himself up. But someone grabbed him by his training top and brought a knee up into his ribcage. Pain erupted in Nick's chest as the air was driven from his body. His attacker grabbed him by the hair and raised his face up in time for Nick to see a fist pulled back, ready to strike.

"Not so fast, dipshit!"

A foot swung through the air and connected with his attacker's jaw. There was a crunch, and the man fell like a sack of potatoes. Nick dropped to his knees, gasping for breath, and saw a pair of stockinged feet planted in the grass between the sprawled bodies. As he gasped for breath, he looked up and saw a small figure in a North Face parka and pink beanie standing above him.

"I wouldn't if I were you, fellas," said the girl, interposing herself between the remaining students and Nick.

They looked at her, but none showed any inclination to join their fallen comrades. There came the sound of footsteps and Bert, the porter, appeared from the Forecourt Lodge. In his hand, he had a torch the size of a policeman's baton. He shone it on Nick and the other prone bodies.

"What's been going on here?" he said, shining the torch at the figure standing sentinel over Nick. "Now then, Jane. What have you been up to?"

"Just teaching these lads some manners."

Bert scanned the beam over the bodies of the students on the ground. One got unsteadily to his feet, wiping the blood from his mouth, and pointed an accusing finger at Jane. "I'm bleeding, you bitch!"

Jane took a step forward, and he flinched.

"That's enough of that sort of language," said Bert, shining the torch directly in his face. "Now, unless you all want to spend the evening sleeping things off in a cell, I suggest you pack yourselves off before the police arrive."

Goatee was crouched on his hands and knees on the grass, holding his stomach. He looked across accusingly at Nick. "That psycho assaulted us. I'm going to press charges."

"That's not how it looked on the CCTV," said Bert, indicating a set of cameras over the Forecourt entrance. "From what I could see, this gentleman prevented you and your friends from committing a sexual assault."

"Sexual assault!" spluttered Goatee, but he did not sound so sure of himself now.

"That's what it will look like on the footage. Five lads surrounding a woman who was walking home alone. You can imagine how that will go down in court. And when the police breathalyse you, well, your college will take a dim view of that sort of publicity. Might have to send you down rather than be seen condoning that sort of behaviour." He paused to let his words sink in. "Do you really want that on your CVs?"

In the distance, the sound of a police siren could be heard.

"Come on, Jezz," said one of the group. "We don't need that sort of hassle."

Jezz looked daggers at Nick as he got to his feet.

"You'd better watch your fucking back, psycho."

"I shouldn't bother, mate," said Jane, "as I'll be doing that for him."

"And don't forget," said Bert, shining his light in each of their faces, "we now have a nice clear image of each of you chaps on the cameras, should it ever be needed."

Jezz stood glowering at them for a moment, before spitting on the pavement.

"Fucking hate John's," he said and limped over to join his friends. They gathered around him and began heading off down Trinity Street. Nick watched them go through his one good eye.

"So, taking on five guys, eh?" said Jane, smiling at him. "I reckon psycho's about right?"

He looked at the diminutive figure who had saved him from a beating.

"Thanks. You know… for…"

"Nah, don't worry about it. We look after our own, don't we, Bert?"

"Try to," agreed the porter.

Nick stared around and saw the dark-haired woman standing a few feet away. She had been watching him. Now she approached him until her face was inches from his.

"Thank you," she said.

"No problem," he mumbled. Then he noticed the bruising around her nose. "Are you all right? Your nose?"

She smiled. "Is not now. Is before. An accident."

"Hey, you're… You're not Alfie's sister, are you?" asked Jane, staring at her.

"Alfonso?" said the woman. "Yes, yes I am. Raquel Vidal."

"I'm Jane," said the waitress. "I used to work with your brother. We must talk, you and me."

"*Sí*, we must," said Raquel. She turned back to Nick. "But first I must know your name."

"Nick," he said.

"Thank you, Nick." She kissed him on both cheeks. "You are a good man."

Turning, she went over to join Jane.

"I'll see you around, psycho," said Jane, waving one of her pink mittens as the two women headed off down Bridge Street.

Nick watched them go until the image began to sway and

pinpricks of light popped in front of his eyes. He reached out to steady himself, and a firm hand gripped his arm.

"Steady there, Mr Wood," said Bert. "I think we've had quite enough excitement for one day, don't you?"

"You're not wrong," said Nick, leaning on the porter as they headed back into college.

Chapter 20

As Bert escorted Nick back to his room, Ravi sat behind his desk in Second Court. The study was dark but for the single desk lamp that illuminated a pile of envelopes in front of him. He had been out of his office most of the day, and he had not had time to check his mail until now.

Earlier that evening, he and Mrs Hamilton had said goodnight to Annabel. The girl was tired but in better spirits after her stream of visitors. Ravi had been pleased that Nick, Ashley and Brian had responded so quickly to his note and thought well of them for doing so.

It was clear to Ravi that Nick cared deeply about Annabel, and in their own dysfunctional way, so did Ashley and Brian. The latter two had also wanted to visit Brett after Ravi told them the American was still in the intensive care ward. He was not entirely sure whether this was down to concern about Brett's condition or Ashley's enthusiasm for seeing an intensive care unit in action. Either way, he had refused to allow it, believing a visit from this duo would be too much for Brett at that time.

But before leaving the hospital, Ravi had checked on the

American. Since he had regained consciousness, Brett's bedside had been surrounded by a collection of nurses who had promised to keep an eye on the handsome Olympian overnight. He had felt sure his tutee would be well looked after.

"He's in good hands," one tanned male nurse had said, fussing around Brett's pillow. "He'll sleep like a baby, this one."

Ravi had remembered Brett's bright blue eyes shining back at the nurse from under his heavily bandaged forehead. The look between the two men had been unmistakable, and sitting now in his study, Ravi thought about Annabel. He wondered if she knew he was gay.

Then there was Mrs Hamilton, who, despite his protests, had insisted on doing her own carrying of a small overnight bag from the ward to the waiting taxi. She had proved good company, showing a keen interest in him and his work.

"How often do you go back to Nepal, Professor?"

"Every summer. As part of our outreach programme. St. John's runs a very generous bursary scheme for students from disadvantaged backgrounds. It's the reason I came here all those years ago."

"Well, I'm delighted you did. You have been extremely kind to Annabel. I am sure she is very grateful, Professor Gupta, as am I."

For once, Ravi didn't know quite what to say.

On arrival at the Forecourt Lodge, they had been greeted by Bert, who had taken Mrs Hamilton to the junior guest rooms just behind the Divinity School off All Saints Passage.

He had also reserved another room for Brett's mother, for the following day.

Ravi looked at his watch. It was eleven-thirty p.m. Robert would have left by now. Ravi wanted to hear how his conversation with Julian had gone, but that would have to wait for the morning. Rising to his feet, he felt a wave of weariness wash over him. His bed in Newnham seemed a long way away. The leather sofa was calling to him, and he removed his jacket before making his way over to it. Easing himself down into its worn and cracked cushions, he rolled onto his side and lay there for a moment. His eyes fell on the armillary sphere whose brass curves glinted like gold in the light from his desk lamp.

"Suns and stars, birds and beasts, blood and stone," he breathed before sleep took him.

*****

Ravi sprang from rock to rock, following Robert's lead as they descended down the narrow ravine towards the valley below. His breathing was fast, not just from the effort of keeping up with his friend, but also from the excitement he felt at the enormity of what they were doing. Scrambling over rocks that no human had ever climbed, under a sky that none had ever seen and on a world that… well, as far as he could make out, must be light-years away from the one he had inhabited.

Up ahead, Robert sprang from a rocky outcrop and landed with a grunt on the sandy red earth of the valley floor. A couple of seconds later, Ravi joined him, panting slightly and leaning against his friend as they looked out across this alien landscape. The valley floor was half a mile across, littered by boulders and slabs of red rock that had sheared off and fallen from the cliffs around them. There was a gentle slope that led down to the dark line of the river, which snaked its way around the tall red columns rising up from the centre of the valley into the violet sky.

Robert turned to him and grinned.

"That was fun!" he said, using the back of his hand to wipe sweat from his forehead. His shirt, like Ravi's, was soaked, the buttons undone and his sleeves rolled up, exposing muscular forearms that glistened with perspiration.

"It will be warm work heading back," said Ravi, looking back up the ravine.

"That's for sure!" agreed Robert. "Still, now that we're here, shall we take a look at that river? A splash of water wouldn't go amiss. What do you say?"

Ravi nodded. "Good idea."

They headed out towards the river, their heavily scuffed shoes kicking up clouds of dust that clung to their trousers, staining them a rusty red colour. Up ahead, bright sunlight reflected off the surface of the water, casting silvery lines on the base of the nearby pillar. Ravi noticed Robert pulling a handkerchief from his pocket as he approached the river's edge.

"Be careful, Robert," warned Ravi. "We don't know what is in it."

His friend reached the water's edge and stared down into the stream.

"Looks clear enough to me," he said, kneeling down and

dipping his handkerchief into the water. Robert held the cloth over his outstretched hand, allowing droplets to pool in his palm. He leant forward and sniffed it.

"It's water, all right," he said, splashing the water on his face and pressing the damp handkerchief to his brow.

"Oh," he sighed, "lovely!" Dipping it in the stream again, he used the wet cloth to wipe the back of his neck.

"We probably shouldn't drink it until we have boiled it first," said Ravi.

Robert considered this. "True, but it's certainly refreshing. Here, try it."

He dipped the handkerchief in the river again and offered it to Ravi, who took it and wiped his face and neck. Cooling liquid ran down his skin.

"It is indeed," he said and knelt down next to his friend, dipping the cloth in the stream and using it to clean the dirt and dust away from his torn fingers.

Robert reached both hands in the river and splashed water over his face and head, before shaking his hair like a dog, showering Ravi with droplets. They both laughed, their spirits as high as the suns overhead.

"So, what do you make of this place?" asked Robert, looking around.

Ravi straightened up and stared about him. The walls of the valley were made of the same distinctive red stone as the columns, their sheer faces scored by deep ravines like the one they had used as a route down from the upper slopes. There were also ripples along the base of the cliffs running parallel to the valley floor.

"Those look like signs of erosion," said Ravi, indicating the curves. "That suggests the river has covered the entire valley at times. Perhaps it's a seasonal thing."

"Not much vegetation, is there?" noted Robert.

Ravi could see he was right. There seemed almost nothing organic across the entire valley, save for pale grey lichen that clustered in clumps around crevices and depressions in the rock face.

"Perhaps the daylight is too harsh for plants to expose themselves," he suggested, shielding his eyes from the glare. "We may see more life emerge at night."

"Like in the deserts back home, you mean?"

"It's possible," said Ravi. "There is water here, so I see no reason why life shouldn't be viable."

Robert squinted up at the sky.

"So how long before it becomes dark, do you think?"

"There is no way to tell, just yet," said Ravi. "In a binary star system, it could be some time before anywhere gets truly dark, and then it might only be for a relatively short time before one of the suns emerges again. We shall have to wait and see."

"And what about that sky? Have you ever seen such a colour?"

"The closest I have seen was at the *aurora borealis*, but nothing on this scale."

"Extraordinary," said Robert, before turning to Ravi, ginning. "You must be feeling pretty excited!"

Ravi looked at his friend. He smiled back, but the enormity of what he was experiencing was stirring such deep emotions within him that he almost felt like weeping.

"Words cannot describe it."

His friend clapped him on the back and Ravi winced as pain flared from the scrapes and bruises of his earlier tumble down the slope.

"Not sure about you, but I could do with getting out of the sun. Mind if we find some shade?" said Robert, standing up and looking around. "How about over there?"

He pointed to a fissure in the cliff wall near the ravine they had used to enter the valley. The base had been eroded to such an extent that there was a clear overhang casting a dark shadow into the gap.

"Looks good to me," said Ravi. He bent down to dip the handkerchief one more time in the stream. He swirled it around and was about to pull it out when it seemed to snag on one of the boulders beneath the surface. Ravi gave it a tug and then the handkerchief was ripped from his fingers. He cried out and leapt backwards, falling on his backside. Kicking with his feet, he pushed himself away from the stream. Robert turned and stared down at him.

"What are you playing at?"

"There's – there's something in the river!"

"What?"

"The handkerchief! Something snatched it out of my fingers!"

Robert dashed forward and squatted down at the water's edge.

"Robert! Be careful!"

His friend stared into the water as Ravi got to his feet and joined him, standing slightly back.

"Can't see anything, Ravi. Are you sure you didn't just drop it?"

"Something definitely tugged it from my fingers," he insisted, remembering the sharp yank of the cloth against the raw skin of his fingers. He stared into the water, which was crystal-clear but for particles of red sand drifting with the current. He could make out the mahogany brown of the river bed, broken up by the irregular shapes of boulders worn smooth by the flow of water over time. Nothing stirred.

"Well, I still don't see anything, old man," said Robert, getting to his feet. "Not to worry, I have plenty more back in college. What about that shade?"

Ravi thought he saw concern in Robert's face as he studied him, as if Robert was worried the heat was starting to affect Ravi's senses.

"Well, what do you say?" asked Robert.

Sweat dripped down Ravi's nose, and he wiped it away with the back of his hand.

"I suppose it might be good to get out of the sun for a while," he admitted.

"Good man. Come on then," said Robert, turning and heading off towards the shelter of the cliff wall.

After giving the stream one last look, Ravi followed, his mind a whirl. Part of him felt a thrill of excitement that there might indeed be something living in the river. If that was the case, then one of the great questions he had had as a boy might now be answered. Ever since he had first stared at the stars above the mountains over Nepal, he had asked himself, *is there anyone else out there*? But that emotion was now mixed with another that at this, the most incredible moment of his life, he wanted to ignore, but couldn't. Because somewhere deep inside, a feeling stirred that was as old and instinctive as when man first emerged from the safety of his cave and into the unknown world beyond.

It was fear.

*****

Ravi woke with a start and stared up at the ancient timbers in the ceiling above him. Confused, he looked around and saw the walls lined with bookcases and chairs piled high with papers. This wasn't his bedroom, but it was reassuringly familiar nonetheless. Then he saw the coffee table with the scientific journals and his gold-rimmed glasses lying where he had left them the night before. He breathed out slowly, and settled back into the leather of the sofa, the memories of the previous day's trip to the hospital beginning to displace the vivid recollections of that other time and that other place, half a century earlier.

With an effort, he pushed himself up from the cushions and groaned as pain rang down his back, not from the reimagined bumps and bruises of his dream, but from the present reality of old age. Ravi reached for his glasses and, after settling them on his nose, eased himself to his feet, exhaling slowly as he did so. It had been a long time since he last slept in his study, and as comfy as the old sofa was, it was a poor substitute for his own bed.

"You're getting too old for this sort of thing," he chided

himself, as he shuffled over to the cupboard sink to wash and shave.

After a restorative breakfast in the Buttery, where he received a raised eyebrow from Aurelia at the unusually crumpled state of his suit, Ravi set off for Robert's room. He pushed through the Buttery doors and headed for the Kitchen Bridge, between the pillars where the St John's eagles and yales maintained their eternal vigil over the Backs.

Ravi's thoughts drifted back to his conversation with Robert earlier in the week and the uncompromising way he had treated his friend. Deeply unpleasant as it had been, it had also been necessary to ensure Robert stopped this nonsense with Julian. But still, he felt guilty and wanted to check that all was well between them. The last thing he wanted was for an outsider to drive a wedge between them, not after all they had been through together. Looking up to Robert's rooms in the western wing of New Court, Ravi was pleased to see that a window was open, and the curtains were drawn back.

"Excellent!" he said to himself. "Nothing that a cup of tea and a good chat can't mend."

He set off along the sandy path that curved around the lawns and ran along the herbaceous border in front of New Court. Nestling against the wall, the south-facing flower beds had lost much of their summer colour and vibrancy. Ahead he could see two of the college gardeners with their wheelbarrows loaded with forks and hedge trimmers, about to start work.

Ravi admired the St John's gardeners. Steady,

unflappable types. Only a few months earlier the grass lawns in Third Court had been turned into muddy quagmires by May Ball revellers, dancing barefoot on the hallowed turf as party music played into the early hours. Now, thanks to the gardeners' patience and horticultural skills, those same lawns were a deep green, ready for the start of the new academic year.

These thoughts were interrupted by a sudden movement from up ahead. Ravi saw the gardeners rush into the flower beds adjacent to the western wing of New Court and disappear behind the thick bushes. Then one of the gardeners reappeared, took a few steps towards the path and retched onto the ground. The other gardener emerged wide-eyed, looked up and saw Ravi.

"Professor!" he yelled, the anguish evident in his voice.

The gardener waved for him to come over, before turning and looking back at the hedge, his hand covering his mouth.

Ravi started to run, a sense of dread rising from his stomach. By the time he reached them, he felt sick.

"What is it?" he asked, panting.

"It's the Dean," said Peter, his face pale.

"What? The Dean…?" said Ravi, glancing up at Robert's rooms forty feet above them, where the window lay open. "What about him?"

"No, Professor," said Peter. "In the bushes."

Ravi looked down at the foot of the wall and gasped.

Robert lay on his back, one arm stretched out under the bush, the other folded across his thick chest. He looked so peaceful that, for a moment, Ravi thought he was asleep.

"Robert, are you…?"

And that was when he saw the unnatural angle of the neck, and he realised his friend was not sleeping.

"Robert!" Ravi fell to his knees next to the body.

Robert's bright green eyes stared sightlessly towards the heavens. His mouth lay open, but no breath misted the morning air, no sound came from his lips. Ravi just stared at his face, willing it to move or twitch or do anything to deny what his eyes were showing him. But it did nothing. Robert's body lay there rigid in front of him, its silence speaking its own terrible truth, with a finality that could not be challenged.

Ravi reached forward and clasped Robert's cold, outstretched fingers in his shaking hands. Thoughts of their last conversation flooded his mind: Robert's look of hurt and shame as Ravi had angrily accused him of betraying his confidence before storming from his room without so much as a goodbye.

As he knelt there in the soil, the tears flowing down his cheeks, Ravi tried to say something to the man who had always been there for him, but he found he could only manage two words.

"My friend…"

Chapter 21

Gargoyles howled, and fiendish maws opened wide as Giles fell, the night air whistling through his hair as he rushed towards them. He twisted and turned in a vain attempt to avoid these wicked outcrops before jagged teeth ripped into his flesh, and he screamed in pain. Then he was falling once more, tossed from one stony demon to another, and with each impact, he felt bones shatter, again and again.

Bang, bang!

"No, please!"

Bang, bang!

"Please!"

"Giles?"

"Please…!"

"Giles! It's me, Rose!"

The shout startled him awake, and the scream died in his throat. Blinking, he found himself staring not up at the night sky, but at the faded ceiling of his room. The knocking on his study door had stopped, and for a while, Giles lay on his bed in silence, the twisted sheets beneath him damp with sweat and the duvet lying discarded on the floor. At the memory of the dream, a shiver ran down his naked body, and he felt his skin crawl. It had been so vivid. So real.

His thoughts were interrupted by the sound of a key scraping in the lock. Hinges creaked, and the door began to swing open.

"Rose!" he yelled. "I'm not dressed!"

Giles flung out an arm and managed to grab the duvet from the floor, dragging it over himself moments before Rose's curious face peered around the door.

"You told me I should use my key next time," she said.

"Yes, well, that's because I didn't think you would!" he retorted, adjusting the duvet as he swung his legs out of bed.

"I thought you'd have gone to lectures by now. It's past nine o'clock."

Giles reached for his phone.

"Oh, crap!"

"Giles!"

"Sorry," he said, springing out of bed with the duvet wrapped around him like a makeshift toga. His clothes were scattered across the floor, and Giles wasn't sure how he was going to be able to dress without revealing more than he intended. "Err, Rose? Do you mind popping out for a moment?"

"Don't worry. I'll be back in ten minutes, mind. I don't want you making me late as well."

"I'll be long gone by then," he promised.

True to his word, by the time Rose peeked around his door ten minutes later, Giles was already pedalling down King's Parade at breakneck speed, his legs spinning like

Bradley Wiggins. Even so, he arrived late for his first lecture and tried unsuccessfully to sneak in at the back of the auditorium unnoticed. Unfortunately, a squeaky door meant that most of the audience turned around, including the lecturer, who made a point of staring at Giles and then up at the clock above the whiteboard.

"Sorry!" Giles announced. "I'll be reporting that to maintenance. Shoddy work. Carry on, Professor."

The snorts of laughter only deepened the scowl he received from the lecturer, but Giles made sure he slipped out quickly at the end before the professor could catch up with him. He spent the rest of the afternoon in the Museum of Archaeology and Anthropology on Pembroke Street, preparing for a supervision on Egyptian monumental architecture, which was scheduled for early the following week. He usually loved this sort of work, but today he found it impossible to concentrate.

Each time he saw a symbol of a bird or other mythical winged monster, he had flashbacks to the creature that had swooped on him above New Court. He trawled the archive, and by late afternoon he was surrounded by a studio's worth of material, none of which really matched up to the image he retained in his mind's eye.

Frustrated at his lack of progress, Giles resigned himself to returning over the weekend to complete his work. Having missed breakfast, he decided to treat himself to a Chelsea bun from Fitzbillies on the way back to college. But wheeling his bike around the corner into Trumpington Street, he was dismayed to discover a large group of tourists, each kitted out in distinctive yellow waterproof tops and baseball caps, had descended on the tea shop like a plague of locusts.

"Oh lord!" he said, peering over their heads as the leader began taking orders for buns.

"Time for a royal visit," he said to himself and strode out into the middle of the pavement, where he made a great show of pointing at the roof of the Pitt Building on the opposite side of the road. This impressive-looking structure had a high tower with a masthead from which a university flag fluttered proudly in the breeze.

"Will you look at that!" he exclaimed loudly, pointing excitedly at the flag. "The Duke and Duchess must be in!"

Some of the tourists in the queue turned from peering in the shop window and followed his gaze up at the flag. Before long he had managed to get more of the party out on the street and staring up at the tower, their cameras out and snapping away at the Gothic but relatively unremarkable building. Some of the party had even started crossing the street to peer inside what Giles knew was a conference centre. A gap opened up in the crowd and he took the opportunity to edge his way inside the shop.

"The Duke and Duchess of Cambridge!" he kept repeating to the yellow jackets inside the shop, gesticulating enthusiastically towards the street, and before long he had manoeuvred himself to the front of the rapidly thinning queue. When he reached the counter, the girl in the white apron looked at him quizzically.

"Are William and Kate really out there?"

"There or thereabouts," he said.

"What, in Cambridge?"

"I was thinking more like Sandringham."

She laughed.

"A Chelsea bun to go, please?"

Giles paid for the bun and jumped on his bike as the throng of camera-wielding tourists poured into the Pitt Building to the bemusement of the wide-eyed reception staff. Some even waved to Giles as he cycled off.

"Enjoy your visit," he called out to them. "Give the Duke my best!"

Giles was still in good spirits hours later, when Ying and Trevor arrived at his room before supper. He decided this would be an excellent time to suggest another night climb.

"Hi, how goes it?" he asked as Ying stuck her head around the door.

"Good," she said. "Shall we go eat? We are starving. There again, Trevor, you're always starving, aren't you, babe?"

"A healthy appetite, that's all," said Trevor, following her into the room, gown in hand. "Hi, Giles."

"Hi, Trev. Listen, I've been thinking about tonight. How do you fancy a bit of R&R?"

He saw them exchange looks.

"Are you sure you want to, so soon after last time?" asked Ying. "Only, you gave us quite a scare."

"Don't worry, a moment of madness. I'm fine now. Honest!" Giles said, smiling brightly. "Besides, I've been thinking about a change of venue tonight."

"Go on," said Ying, not sounding particularly enthusiastic.

"Look, I thought it would be cool to get a photograph of somewhere iconic, as we didn't get a good one at the top of New Court in the end."

Giles hadn't shown them the image of the winged figure, as he was sure they would think he had Photoshopped it after the event.

"I thought we should try somewhere less exposed."

"Meaning?" asked Ying.

"Meaning, somewhere where we are less likely to break our necks?" suggested Trevor.

Giles gave him a look but decided not to argue. He needed them on board if the plan was to work.

"So where are you suggesting?" asked Ying.

"The Bridge of Sighs," said Giles.

"The Bridge of Sighs?" repeated Ying.

"Yes, it's in *The Roof-Climber's Guide*. Not as high as the Wedding Cake, and if any of us slipped, we'd land in the river," he added helpfully.

Ying looked at Trevor, who raised his eyebrows but didn't protest.

"And you'd like to get a photo of one of us climbing on it?" she asked.

"Why not? We could take one from the Kitchen Bridge looking back. We could take our cameras. You've got that good one, Trevor. The one with the tripod."

"It could be a good shot, I suppose," agreed Trevor.

"So, what do you say?" said Giles, looking at Ying, who was studying him suspiciously.

"OK, but no funny business this time. We do the climb, get the photos and head back."

"Absolutely!" said Giles. "Scout's honour!"

This seemed to satisfy Ying, who gave him a reluctant smile.

"Excellent!" Giles beamed, relieved she hadn't thought to ask him if he had ever been a Scout, which he hadn't, of course. "So, R&R it is!"

The three of them reassembled back in his room at eleven p.m. to pore over the route in his well-thumbed *Roof-Climber's Guide*. After checking their kit and Trevor's camera, Giles made tea while they waited for the College Bar to empty. Just after eleven-thirty, he came back into the room from the landing window and made an announcement in his best Bomber Command voice.

"OK, chaps. It's on."

His crew gathered their gear, filed out of the room and crept down the creaky turret staircase. After navigating their way across a deserted Second Court, they headed for the north-east corner of Third Court, where they hid in a passageway adjacent to the Old Library. In this corner of the old square was an architectural oddity, often missed by the casual observer, known as the Furnace Hole. The Old Library, which pre-dated Third Court, had windows reaching up to its roof on the south side. These were essential to allow sunlight to illuminate the scholars' reading desks within. So, when later designing Third Court, its seventeenth-century architect had left space between the new accommodation block and the library, allowing light to shine down through the window. This gap became known as the Furnace Hole and provided the original night climbers with a relatively easy access point to the Bridge of Sighs.

"OK, who's leading tonight?" whispered Giles.

"Ladies first," said Ying, who seemed keen to keep a grip on things this time.

"Be my guest," said Giles.

Ying led the others up the single-storey climb into the Furnace Hole and then across onto the balustrade facing the river. The breeze blew back through the aperture as they looked across the water towards New Court and Cripps. After a brief pause to admire the view, they edged around a buttress and Ying led them along a narrow sloping roof to the Bridge of Sighs itself. Once there, she used a drainpipe to pull herself up the first ten feet of the bridge wall, before working her way along a narrow ledge around the buttress and out above the river.

Giles admired the ease with which she moved, planting her right foot on the ridge that curved around the top of the bridge's north-facing window, straightening herself up and, gripping the top of the rampart, swinging herself up and over onto its roof. *Poetry in motion*, he thought.

He turned and nodded to Trevor. Despite having the tripod slung over his shoulder, Trevor had no difficulty following Ying's lead and was soon standing alongside her on the Bridge's roof, giving Giles the thumbs-up that it was OK to follow.

As climbs went, it did not have the same heart-thumping buzz of New Court's clock tower, but the setting was glorious, and Giles found himself grinning madly as he traversed over the gently flowing river. When he reached the rampart and clambered over, he saw the others were smiling too, all of them caught up in the exhilaration of the moment.

They headed to the far side of the bridge by New Court. The plan was for Trevor to continue down the south face of the bridge and edge along the river wall to the Backs. From there he could make his way on foot to the Kitchen Bridge and set up the camera. This was quite a tricky section, and Ying decided to lead with Trevor to follow carrying his tripod. Giles agreed to remain on the bridge and belay them to avoid anyone falling in the river and damaging the expensive camera equipment.

"Are you OK with that?" Trevor asked, aware that Giles was usually the one who tackled the most difficult aspects of any climb.

"No problem," said Giles. "This way I get more time to pose in front of the camera."

"As long as that is all you do," said Ying, harnessing up.

"Really, Ying," he said in mock surprise. "Would I do anything daft?"

In the darkness, it was hard to make out her expression, but the snort of derision was unmistakable.

"Here, take this." He unclipped his GoPro camera from his helmet and handed it to her. "You'll get a better shot from over there. Make sure you get my best profile, mind you!"

She took it and gave him a suspicious look.

"So, what is that exactly?"

Giles looked to one side and pointed with both his hands towards the heavens in a pose like Usain Bolt. Ying grinned and stuffed the camera into her fleece pocket, zipping it up.

"Yeah, well, OK then."

It took Ying and Trevor twenty minutes to descend from the bridge roof and edge along the ledge that ran around the base of the New Court wall, a few feet above the dark and murky water. As he paid out the rope, Giles felt a pang of disappointment that it wasn't him leading the way, but this was masked by the thrill of excitement that he was now the only person left on top of the bridge.

"It's all going according to plan," he said under his breath.

Eventually, he saw Ying and Trevor make it to the low river wall that ran along the edge of the paddock. Ying turned and gave him a thumbs-up. He waved an acknowledgement and waited while they undid their harnesses beneath the branches of the old yew tree that marked the edge of the Backs.

When the rope went slack, Giles reeled it in quickly to avoid it trailing in the water, before winding it into a neat coil. Then, as the others made their way around to the Kitchen Bridge to set up the cameras, Giles headed back to the middle of the bridge and squatted down behind the rampart. He opened his backpack and stuffed the rope inside before removing the items he had stowed in the pack without telling the others: a pair of ice axes he used for winter mountaineering in the Cairngorms.

Giles turned the gently curving axes over in his grip, and

the moonlight flashed off the hardened steel pick edges. Squatting here now, he was glad he had them with him.

Giles knew he hadn't just imagined the winged apparition the other night above New Court. The blurred image from his phone and Jane's story of the creature attacking the Corpus Clock had convinced him there was indeed something lurking over the night skies of Cambridge. But convincing other people was a different matter. When he had first told his friends about what he had seen on the New Court roof, Ying and Trevor had reacted as if Giles had lost it, and he couldn't blame them. His story was so incredible that he would have found it hard to accept too. Giles knew hard evidence would be needed to convince them that what he had seen was real. And that was what he planned to give them tonight.

Giles glanced over the parapet and out towards the Kitchen Bridge. He could just about make out Ying and Trevor standing behind the balustrade, hunched over what he assumed must be the camera on its tripod. He waited until he saw the smaller figure of Ying step away and wave a hand towards him. They were ready.

Giles peered down into the river between the two bridges, seeing in its rippled surface the reflection of moon and stars high above his head. The night was clear and visibility excellent. Looking out across the Backs, the city skyline looked peaceful and serene. Giles squatted there for a minute or two longer, enjoying the moment, before checking his watch. Well past midnight. It was time.

"OK, my feathered friend," he said, standing up and spreading his arms out wide, with an ice axe in each hand. "Supper's ready!"

Chapter 22

Ravi sat in his dark study, staring at the faded scarf neatly folded on his desk, framed in the beam of the single lamp. The shock of Robert's death had hit him hard, and he had struggled through the rest of the day on autopilot, cancelling all his appointments.

The police had been to question him and the two gardeners who had found the body. They had conducted a thorough search of the Dean's room, but from what he understood had found no note to explain why his friend should have taken his life. Nor had there been any evidence of something amiss. The police had removed Robert's body later that afternoon and expected to confirm the cause of death within a few days, but from their initial examination, it appeared to be a broken neck from the fall.

As Ravi came to terms with the reality of Robert's death, the same nagging doubt kept coming back. Had he been the one to drive his friend to suicide? His demand that Robert should cease work on his most significant discovery? His cruel words when he had left Robert the other morning? Had he pushed him too far? The more the day wore on, the more that dreadful thought had grown in his mind and with it the memory of that moment all those years ago that had come to define their friendship. A memory that he had tried to bury, to consign to an archive that his mind would not, could not, reference. But now, as the evening shadows crept across the floor of his unlit study and enveloped him in darkness, he found himself unable to deny it any longer.

*****

The climb back up the scree slope of the ravine was exhausting. Ravi sucked in the hot air over parched lips. They were as dry as sandpaper. His throat was raw, but he barely had enough saliva to swallow. Ravi paused, breathing hard and resting his hands on his knees. His khaki trousers were now covered in a patina of red dust. He looked back down the slope and saw Robert struggling up behind him, sweat glistening off his ruddy face and dripping onto his open shirt.

Ravi didn't remember the ravine being anywhere as high as this, but there again, in the excitement of their earlier descent, he had been preoccupied with the sight of the foreign landscape around them and the alien sky above their heads. The sky had changed from the violet of earlier in the day, to a deep purple as one of the two suns dipped beyond the horizon. As the transformation unfurled before his eyes, Ravi had stood there in wonder, marvelling at the spectacle in silence, unable to express his feelings as he witnessed something he had never dared believe.

By the time the first sun had disappeared, many hours

had passed, and both of them realised how hungry and thirsty they were. Robert had suggested they head back, and Ravi had felt he had no choice but to agree, frustrated at himself that he hadn't thought to bring something with him. Neither of them dared trust the alien water from the river. He remembered the feeling of the handkerchief being tugged from his fingers and could not shake his sense of unease that there was something else inhabiting those waters, lurking in the shadows of the stream.

"Hard going, eh?" Robert panted, reaching out and laying a scuffed and bleeding hand on Ravi's shoulder, patting it wearily.

Ravi knew his friend was fit, but Robert's powerful frame was built for speed, not endurance, and he was struggling to match Ravi, who was more used to this type of terrain from his childhood in Nepal.

"We are almost there," said Ravi, turning to stare up the slope, shielding his eyes from the remaining sun, which glared down the ravine at them. He could see the sharp edge of the ridge a few hundred feet ahead of them where they had first emerged. "When we reach the top, it levels out, and the going will be easier as we make our way along to the entrance of the cave."

"A bit of shade would be good," said Robert, wiping his forehead with the back of his forearm, leaving a rusty red stain of dust on his shirtsleeve.

Ravi thought about the location of the cave. It was set in a fissure in the cliff face at the top of the scree slope that he had slipped down earlier that day. Given the angle of the remaining sun, there was a good chance the cliff face would now be in shadow.

"If we head up the ravine a bit further and come out at the base of the cliff, we should find some shade there. What do you think?"

"Sounds good to me," said Robert, panting like a dog in the sun. "You lead the way, old boy."

They set off again, Ravi taking it steady, mindful of his friend's laboured breathing behind him and not wanting to discourage him by opening up too large a gap. Within half an hour they had clambered out of the ravine at the base of the cliff and paused, his chest rising and falling as sweat ran down his nose and dripped onto the red soil between his scuffed shoes. Turning, he saw Robert grunting as he levered himself up over the last few rocks to join him. When his friend finally stopped next to him, Robert just stood there, hands on hips, sucking in air, his soiled white shirt transparent with perspiration, unable to speak for a while.

Ravi looked around and was pleased to see they were indeed standing in the shade as he had predicted, and he looked up gratefully at the cliff that towered above them. And that was when he saw them.

At first, he thought his eyes were playing tricks on him as if struggling to adjust from the glare of the sunshine to the relative darkness of the shadows. He had fumbled with his glasses, removing them and wiping the lenses on the damp cotton of his shirt, before hooking them back on his nose and peering up again. Fifty or so feet above him, something clinging to the cliff wall stirred.

"Well, I don't fancy doing that again in a hurry," said Robert.

Ravi didn't respond. He was staring at the shape that lay flattened against the cliff face, protruding from its surface like a grey blister on the red rock. From across the valley, he had seen more of these, looking like clumps of lichen, but now he realised they were much more substantial than that, their bulk disguised by the scale of the cliffs. They must have been twenty feet across and half as deep. What Ravi had thought were flat, leaf-like structures of flakes now rippled with movement as the shapes flexed and shifted.

"What is it?" asked Robert, looking up the cliff face. "Seen some more stars, have you?"

"No, Robert. Something else."

He heard his friend gasp.

"Lord! Ravi, what the hell are they?"

Ravi scanned the cliff and saw more shapes, some in shadow, some still catching the last rays of sunlight. These were motionless, but those that the shadow touched seemed to be stirring.

"I don't know, Robert, but unless I'm mistaken, they appear to be waking up."

"What do you mean?"

"The shadow. Robert. Look at the shadow! It's reviving them."

They looked around at the surrounding cliffs. As darkness spread across their tall sides, the grey blemishes began to quiver and shift as if touched by an invisible hand.

"So many, Ravi," breathed Robert. "They are everywhere!"

There came the sound of a creaking noise above them. Ravi looked up.

"Robert! Look!"

One of the shapes was bulging out from the cliff face, and as it did so, Ravi saw it clearly for the first time. The flakes of grey lichen flexed and ruffled before sweeping outwards and settling back into two smooth, round humps either side of a long, curved back. This began as a broad V at its top and tapered down into a narrow point at its base. The back arched and as it did so, Ravi realised that what he had first thought were flakes had a pattern and symmetry to them that could only have one purpose.

"Feathers…" he breathed, observing the interlocking ridges and curves that wrapped themselves around the shape.

"What was that?" asked Robert, his voice hushed.

"Feathers, Robert," whispered Ravi. "I think those things are wings."

"Well, if they are, they are some of the biggest I have ever seen."

As if in response, the shape above them shook itself and then stretched out wings that extended more than twenty feet across and a set of tail feathers that uncoiled into a full fan. As it did so, the other shapes above it began to stir, similarly shaking their bodies as if waking from a long sleep. Each one bore the same unmistakeable profile of winged shoulders and tail. Then a head appeared above the nearest creature, and it swivelled to look out across the valley so that its face became visible for the first time. Ravi had expected a bill or a beak of some description, but what he saw made him cry out in shock. A cry that the creature heard, turning its head towards him.

Ravi found himself staring into a humanoid face whose feathered forehead and cheekbones tapered towards a hooked nose, tight-lipped mouth and pointed chin. But what held his gaze and froze him to the spot were the eyes. Two yellow orbs, each bisected by cat-like irises, which stared at him with an intensity that made him feel weak at the knees.

"Ravi?" said Robert.

"Yes?" he replied, unable to tear his eyes away to look at his friend.

"How far is it to the cave's mouth, do you think?"

"A hundred yards or so," said Ravi, speaking as calmly as he could under that stare.

"What say you to the idea of heading that way, nice and gently?"

"Sounds like an excellent idea, Robert."

"Good. In that case…"

Ravi heard his friend take a step, his foot crunching on the sandy surface of the slope. Immediately the creature's head shifted its gaze to Robert, who stopped moving and held his breath. By contrast, Ravi felt as if he had been released from the hypnotic grip of those eyes and he relaxed his neck muscles, which were stiff from staring up at the creature. He risked a glance over to Robert and beyond him along the cliff face to the fissure in the distance that housed the cave entrance. It looked a lot more than a hundred yards right now, but here at the top of the slope, the ground seemed reasonably level and mercifully free of obstacles.

"Robert, I'm going to start walking towards you, and I'd like you to tell me what the creature does when I move."

"Got it. Off you go, laddie. I'll just keep an eye on our friend here."

Ravi rested his hand against the cliff face for balance, noting how sweaty his palm was despite the shade. He took a step.

"Oh, that's caught its attention," said Robert. "It's watching you now. Easy does it."

Ravi wasn't sure if Robert meant him or the creature, so he paused within touching distance of his friend and turned to look up. The eyes were indeed staring at him, but the head was cocked to one side as if curious.

"What do you think?" he said. "Should we go on?"

"That's the general idea," said Robert. "Let's see how it responds to that."

Robert began backing along the slope and Ravi followed, both of them looking up at the creature as they edged along.

"There we go," said Robert, talking to the creature. "Nice and easy, no need to get alarmed. Just a gentle evening stroll."

The creature's head twisted, its yellow eyes remaining fixed on them as they moved step by cautious step along the top of the slope. They had gone perhaps a dozen paces when they heard a rustling noise above them. Ravi looked up and saw one of the other creatures had begun to test its wings.

"Looks like more of them are waking up now," whispered Ravi.

"Well, as long as they don't spot us, we should…" But Robert never finished the sentence. His foot dislodged a rock, and he tottered backwards, crying out as his arms cartwheeled in a vain effort to retain his balance. Ravi reached out just in time to grab Robert's flailing hand, heaving and hauling him back against the side of the cliff. Robert pressed himself against it as they both listened to the thud, thud, thud of the rock, tumbling down the slope and over the edge of the valley wall.

"Oh, bugger," said his friend.

A spine-tingling screech rang out, its harsh tone making Ravi flinch and cover his ears. This was followed by a cacophony of flapping noises from all around them, as creature after creature launched itself into the air. Instinctively Ravi turned back to look at the place where the nearest creature had been moments before, but that part of the cliff face was now deserted. Twisting around, he looked over the valley and saw a massive pair of wings gliding out to the edge of the cliff's shadow, banking in a tight turn seconds before reaching the sunlight and heading back towards them. Though it was still some distance away, Ravi could see, quite distinctly, two yellow eyes staring straight at him.

A hand gripped his arm and yanked him along the slope.

"Time to go, laddie! I'm not sure he's here to make friends!" yelled Robert, all pretence at stealth now abandoned. Slipping and sliding, Ravi stumbled after him, breaking eye contact with the creature as he checked where he was placing his feet to avoid tripping over and pitching forward down the slope. Robert let go of him and with both arms free to balance was able to pick up speed, dislodging stones and sand as he broke into a shuffling run. Ravi followed close behind, using Robert's footprints to give himself some sort of purchase on the slope. Hardly daring to look up, he risked a glance over his shoulder and was shocked to see the creature closing in, its wings spread out wide and its eyes focused on him.

"Faster, Robert! Faster!" he cried, though in his heart he knew it was too late. He just hoped that his friend would make it clear. And that was when he tripped. In his rising panic, he failed to lift his foot high enough over a rocky outcrop and, stubbing his toe, pitched forward, landing face first in the red sand. Instinctively, he thrust his hand out and managed to grab onto a rock to stop himself rolling down the slope.

"Ravi!" Robert yelled, sliding to a stop some fifteen feet ahead of him and turning back to look.

Ravi looked over his shoulder and saw the creature home in on him, swinging its lower body up to reveal two long, scaly legs and feet with wicked black talons at their tips.

"Oh, my…!" was all he could say before a dark shape plummeted through the air and slammed into the creature in an explosion of grey feathers. The two bodies slammed into the slope a few feet below Ravi, throwing up a cloud of red dust. Dreadful screeching noises pierced the air, followed by horrific tearing and rending noises as the two creatures rolled down the slope, bouncing off rockfalls while battering and clawing at each other.

"Ravi! Come on!" yelled Robert.

Ravi tore his eyes away from the conflict and scrambled to his feet, his face, arms and clothes smeared with red dust. He stumbled forward into a run as Robert turned and, arms pumping, sprinted towards the fissure some fifty yards ahead of them. Overhead, other creatures circled around, each careful to stay within the shadow of the cliff, but seemingly more interested in the desperate battle going on at the bottom of the slope than the two fleeing humans. Ravi ran on, glancing nervously around, expecting an attack at any moment. Miraculously, none came. Then he heard a terrible screech that seemed to reverberate across the valley and stopped Ravi in his tracks. It was answered by excited caws from the other creatures, and Ravi turned to see them all descending like flies on the dark shape lying prostrate on the ridge below him. The beasts tore into the prone form with their claws extended and another conflict erupted as each one sought to drive off the others, frantically flapping their wings and contorting their faces in bestial snarls to intimidate their rivals.

As Ravi watched, hands on knees, he noticed there was one creature that stood to the side of this melee, its feathers ruffled, and in some places torn. It observed the fight for a few moments, showing no interest in joining the fray. Instead, it shook its wings free of the dust that covered them and looked up the slope in his direction. Two yellow eyes bore into his and Ravi felt fear grip his heart.

"Ravi, are you coming or what?" yelled Robert.

Ravi just gaped as the creature launched itself into the air.

"Ravi, quick! While there's still time!"

Ravi didn't hesitate any longer. He turned and ran towards his friend, who was already standing in the mouth of the fissure in the cliff wall. Ravi sprinted the last few yards and almost fell into Robert's arms.

Ravi turned and saw the creature flapping its mighty wings, churning up clouds of dust as it climbed towards them. But something about the slope made Ravi stop and pause a minute, his brow furrowed in confusion.

"Robert...?" he began, and he pointed at the footsteps, leading away from the entrance.

But his friend grabbed him by the shoulders and thrust him into the tunnel.

"No time for that now! It's almost here! Come on!"

Robert began pushing him from behind and Ravi stumbled into a run, his mind reeling. But before he could make sense of his thoughts, the tunnel mouth went dark as something huge landed outside the entrance to the cave. The screech ripped through Ravi's senses and drove everything from his mind. He didn't look back at what was coming because the terror he felt told him all he needed to know. Instead, he fled for the stars.

*****

The knock on his study door made Ravi jump. It took him a few seconds to realise that the darkness now surrounding him was no dark tunnel, but the unlit haven of his college room, high up in the corner of Second Court. He leant back in his chair, exhaling slowly and stared up at the ceiling above his head, mercifully free of suns, stars or other more predatory celestial bodies. The memory had been so real – too real, perhaps. His shirt felt clammy, and Ravi reached into his pocket for a handkerchief, which he used to wipe beads of sweat from his forehead. Wondering what the time was, he stretched out a shaking hand and turned on the desk lamp. The shaded light illuminated stacks of papers that covered the leather-bound surface of his desk, bringing a reassuring measure of calm to his troubled thoughts. Glancing at his watch, he saw it was past eleven already.

The knock came again, firmer this time.

"Go away," he mumbled, more to himself than the caller.

A familiar and respectful voice called out, "Professor Gupta, sir."

Ravi sighed. For him, on this day, there could be no peace, it seemed.

"Just a minute, Bert," he said, relenting.

He eased himself up from his desk and crossed over to the door. There he paused, composing himself. Conscious of his crumpled suit, its knees still stained from the flower bed, he took a deep breath and opened the door.

The old porter stood there, his usually cheerful face anxious.

"Sorry to disturb you, Professor. I know this must be a difficult time. Only I needed to speak with you."

Ravi nodded. "Come in, Bert," he said, leaving the door ajar and heading back towards his desk. The porter followed him inside and closed the door behind him.

"I'm sorry about Professor Mackenzie," he said. "I know you were close."

Close? Is that what it was? Could such a simple word describe the depth of the relationship he and Robert had formed over the years? A connection that had been forged so long ago and had survived so much but was now severed forever.

"Thank you, Bert," said Ravi, reaching the desk and sitting down wearily in his chair. "What can I do for you?"

"I just thought you'd like to know that Miss Hamilton is out of the hospital. She wanted me to pass the message on. Her grandmother is staying another night as it was too late to organise a train home this evening."

"Thank you, Bert. That is good news," said Ravi with an effort. "I'm pleased she is feeling better." That reminded him of something else he had meant to do that day. "Tell me, Bert, did Brett Davis' mother arrive?"

"Yes, Professor, I saw her earlier this afternoon," said the porter. "I explained why you were not able to see her, and she was very understanding. She asked me to pass on her thanks for looking after her son."

Ravi nodded.

"I've put her in Corfield Court, same as Mrs Hamilton."

"Thank you."

Ravi hoped the porter would leave him now, but was disappointed to see him standing there, looking awkward.

"Is there anything else?"

The porter approached the desk carrying an envelope.

"There was this," he said, placing the envelope on the folded scarf.

Ravi stared at it. It was addressed to him, and the

handwriting was unmistakable. It was Robert's.

"When did you receive this?" he asked, looking up at the porter in confusion.

"I think it must have been some time yesterday, Professor. It was in your pigeonhole, but of course, you hadn't been in all day. I was knocking off this evening, so thought I'd check to see if you'd had any mail. Just in case there was something urgent. That's when I saw it."

Ravi stared at the handwriting.

"Have you told anyone about this?" he asked.

"No, Professor," said Bert.

Ravi looked at him.

"We look after our own," said the porter quietly.

Ravi did not know what to say but felt a stinging sensation grow behind his eyes.

"Anyway, best be on my way," said Bert, nodding and turning to leave. "Goodnight, Professor."

"Goodnight, Bert. And thank you."

Ravi heard him shut both doors to the study, ensuring he would not be disturbed. He looked again at the envelope and then reached for his old metal ruler. He found his hands trembling as he slit it open and held the parchment paper under the desk light.

Dear Ravi,

The deed is done. I have told Julian that I am withdrawing from the programme. He didn't like it. The angrier he got, the easier it was to say no. Not a very nice man in the end. There again, I'm sure you are not surprised. Thank you for looking out for me, once again. Anyway, thought you should know.

There are a few loose ends to tie up, and I may need your help with those. Perhaps we can discuss things tomorrow when you are free. You'll be glad to know I have acquired some Earl Grey tea. I'd forgotten your fondness for the stuff. Must be old age.

Your good friend,

Robert

Ravi re-read the letter, his gaze lingering on the last four words. As his eyes absorbed the full meaning of those characters, the debilitating guilt that had weighed down on him all day began to dissipate, and with it, a sense of hope returned to his grief-burdened mind. Not only had Robert listened to and taken his advice, but it also seemed he had forgiven Ravi for the harsh words he had uttered at their parting. Feelings of relief and gratitude washed over him, and Ravi closed his eyes and sat there in silence, revelling in their restorative powers.

Some minutes passed and, as his sense of equilibrium returned, another thought began to emerge. One that started like a pinprick of doubt and grew into a sharp and twisting stab of fear and alarm. If Robert's death was not suicide, then what had caused him to fall from his room to his death?

Ravi opened his eyes and looked again at the letter. There was no date or time. But if Bert was right, at some point between Robert's confrontation with Julian and his fall from the window, he had written this note and put it in the big red post box for internal mail that sat in the corner of New Court. That was why no one had found it in the Dean's office, and with Ravi busy at the hospital, it had remained there undetected until Bert's thoughtful action this evening.

Ravi knew he should tell the police about the note. He checked his watch. It was well after midnight. Too late to call them now, and besides, something was nagging at the back of his mind, which he wanted to resolve before he shared the note with anyone. What had Robert meant by "tying up loose ends"? And why did he need Ravi's help? This would be the first thing the police would want to know, and Ravi needed time to think about what his response would be. Ravi was certainly not going to share with the police, or anyone else for that matter, what he and Robert had spent half a century trying to keep secret. Not now that Ravi was the only one who knew about their world-changing discovery. Or was he? Had someone else uncovered the truth and found out about their secret? Or worse, *his* secret?

Ravi frowned. It was no good speculating. He needed to get home and sleep on it. The walk and a stiff gin and tonic would allow his mind to process things overnight. In his experience, the solution to his problems always became clear by the morning. Picking up his satchel, Ravi slid Robert's letter and envelope inside, before turning off the desk lamp and leaving his room.

At the bottom of the stairwell, he saw that his nameplate had already been moved to OUT. Ravi thought of the porter and smiled as he started out over the cobbles and turned into Third Court. Walking between the two immaculate squares of grass, he began climbing the ramp onto the Bridge of Sighs and paused when he reached the top to look out through its arched window towards the Kitchen Bridge.

Images leapt into his mind of sunny days spent lounging there with Robert and his friends. He remembered the occasion when Robert had reached over the balustrade and caught a rising punt pole from an unsuspecting punter, followed by their cheers and laughter as he held the pole triumphantly in the air, while the punt drifted helplessly downstream.

His thoughts were broken by the sound of voices behind him. He turned and saw two familiar figures walking onto the Bridge of Sighs from Third Court.

"Evening, Professor."

"Annabel?" he said, surprised, and then recognised the tall figure next to her. "And Nick?"

"Professor," said the boy.

"It's good to have you back, Annabel, though I'm surprised to see you out and about this late. Shouldn't you be resting?"

"We took Gran out for dinner," she said. "Thought it was the least we could do after the fright I gave her."

"That was good of you."

He was about to ask about Mrs Hamilton but was interrupted by a noise above them. The others had heard it too. It sounded like someone calling for dinner. Ravi looked out towards the Kitchen Bridge and for a moment imagined he could see Robert capering about with the punt pole held triumphantly above his head. Only the figure was moving towards them. And as it grew in the window frame, he realised it was not Robert, but another figure from his past. One that screeched like a banshee as it came for him.

Chapter 23

Giles had been standing for about a minute, his arms raised above his head, when he heard familiar voices on the bridge below him. He froze and looked over to the Kitchen Bridge, where Ying and Trevor were standing up and no longer filming. Instead, they seemed to be waving at him to get down. They must have spotted the people on the bridge too.

And that was when Giles saw movement above them. At first, he was not sure what it was, just a deeper blackness against the night sky, but as he watched, it grew bigger and began to take shape, framed against the windows of Trinity's Wren Library. A pair of enormous wings sweeping towards him.

"There you are," he breathed.

His words were drowned by an ear-splitting screech that shocked him into action. Instinctively, Giles leapt to one side and flung himself flat behind the bridge's parapet. Moments later a gust of wind swept over him, ruffling his hair as he pressed his face against the leaded roof. He lay there for a moment, his heart racing with fear and excitement. It was back!

Giles pushed himself up from the roof and looked downstream towards the Master's Lodge. He saw the creature's wings flapping as it gained height above the trees on the lawn. Then it banked around in a tight circle before sweeping back towards the bridge, accelerating towards him in a steep dive. Giles saw the two yellow eyes boring into him and beneath them, two vicious-looking claws swinging forward, extending enormous talons.

"Oh, crap!" he said, any sense of bravado evaporating as it closed in for the kill.

At the last moment, Giles tore his eyes away from the terrifying sight and flung himself down below the parapet.

There was a bone-jarring crash as the creature hammered into the bridge. Giles felt the stonework shake with the force of the blow. All he could hear was a blood-chilling scream.

*****

Annabel was flung sideways by the impact, screaming as she and Nick slammed into the far wall of the bridge. Dazed, she looked up from the floor and could not believe what she saw. Two huge claws had reached through the bars of the window and gripped the professor's satchel, still held by a strap to his shoulder. The old man was struggling in vain as the talons dragged him and the bag hard against the bars of the window. Annabel screamed.

"No! Professor!"

Then Nick was there, standing above her. He grabbed the professor by his shoulders and, bracing his feet against the bridge's stonework, hauled the old man back. For a moment, she thought he was winning in this dreadful tug of war, but then the bag was yanked through the window with tremendous force, dragging the professor and Nick into the bars. The old man hit them with a sickening thud, his face screwed up in pain as the breath was knocked from him.

"Nick, the strap!" screamed Annabel. "The strap!"

Scrambling to her feet, she rushed towards the two struggling men. Nick was grunting with effort as he fought to prevent the professor from being pulled through the bars. Annabel grabbed the satchel strap and tried to prise it off his trapped shoulder. Risking a glance out of the window, she gasped. Two baleful yellow eyes glared back at her, and for a moment her resolve faltered.

A piercing screech of frustration split the air and Annabel closed her eyes as a blast of breath hit her in the face, its rank smell reeking of death and decay. She gagged and felt Nick sag beside her.

"Heaven help us!" she screamed, as the strap began to slip from her grasp.

*****

Giles picked himself up from the roof of the bridge and staggered towards the parapet. He leant over and saw the vast wings flapping some ten feet below him. The creature was reaching through the bars of the window, trying to drag something free of the bridge. It was impossible to see what it had in its claws, but whoever was holding onto the other end was putting up a tremendous struggle. The creature was beating its wings frantically, screeching in frustration. That was when he heard the girl's scream for help.

Giles knew he had to do something. He looked around the roof of the bridge and saw the two ice axes lying where he had dropped them after the first pass. Stooping down, he grabbed one in each hand, glancing back towards the Kitchen Bridge, where he could just make out the shape of Ying and Trevor in the distance, both staring over towards him. Neither would be able to see the creature, which was on the other side of the Bridge of Sighs, shielded from view by its superstructure.

"Bloody typical!" he growled, realising there was no way that what he was about to do could be caught on either camera. Still, there was nothing for it. Gripping the axes firmly in each hand, Giles stood on the parapet, poised above the flapping wings below him. He thought he might have heard Ying call out his name, but he ignored her. No doubt she thought Giles had gone insane. There again, maybe he had. An image flashed into his mind, and a wild, maniacal grin spread across his face as he raised both axes. Giles leapt into the dark, yelling at the top of his lungs.

"Here's Johnny!"

For a few exhilarating seconds, the wind rushed past him as he twisted in the air to face the bridge. In that instant, he saw the faces of the two freshers and the professor staring wide-eyed up at him, before his feet slammed into the creature's back with a bone-jarring impact. It was like hitting solid rock, and Giles grunted as his knees buckled beneath him, almost pitching him into the river. Instinctively he swung the axes down between the creature's heaving shoulder blades, feeling the serrated edges bite deep into the densely packed plumage.

The creature screeched and convulsed in pain, bucking like a bull in a rodeo. Giles bounced down its back, his ice axes ripping through its leathery hide as gravity dragged him down towards its tail. Its wings beating furiously, the creature sprang back from the bridge, slamming into Giles' ribcage.

"Oof!" he gasped as all the air was driven from his lungs.

Before he could react, the creature had bucked again, and Giles heard the metallic twang of an axe tip snapping as, with another tremendous lurch, he was thrown clear of the heaving back.

For several seconds he found himself flying through the air like a rag doll, arms and legs flailing helplessly. He hit the river with shocking force, its dark waters covering his face and muffling his cry as he sank below the surface.

Looking up through the cascade of bubbles from his nose and mouth, Giles saw the moon shimmering above him, looking strangely beautiful, as he drifted down in silence. Years of white-water rafting had prepared Giles for moments like this. Instead of panicking, he allowed his body to stay relaxed until the remaining air in his lungs gave him some buoyancy. When this happened, he gently struck out for the moonlight above him, exhaling slowly as he rose. Within seconds, his head broke the surface, and he took a deep breath of cold night air.

Giles looked over at the Bridge of Sighs. The creature was nowhere to be seen. He craned his neck around, looking first at the sky and then at the leaded windows of the Old Library rising above him. He realised he had been thrown some twenty yards, almost as far as the Master's Garden.

Turning, he began to swim with slow, easy strokes downstream towards Lower River Court, the lawn that lay between New Court and Cripps. The wall of the Master's Garden ran along the river on his right-hand side, and he was glad of the cover provided by the branches of the huge plane tree, spreading out over the river, shielding him from the heavens and whatever might be circling there. He still had the broken ice axe hanging by a strap from his wrist. Where the other one was, he had no idea – probably at the bottom of the river somewhere. Even if he had it still, he knew he was in no shape to deal with the creature if it decided to come back for him. But he hoped that, like him, it had had enough excitement for one night.

Giles paddled over to the grassy bank by Cripps and rested there for a moment while he adjusted the axe in his grip. Mustering the last of his strength, he levered himself up with one arm and swung the other over his shoulder to bury the broken axe point into the soft lawn. Using it as an anchor point, he dragged the rest of his body out of the river, crawling a couple of feet before rolling over onto his back to stare breathlessly at the heavens.

"Wow!" he said, a weary grin spreading across his face. "That was truly insane."

"Insane? I'll give you bloody insane!"

He turned his head and saw Ying and Trevor running towards him.

"Oh? Hi guys."

"What the hell do you think you were doing!" yelled Ying. "I thought you said you weren't going to do anything stupid."

"What do you mean?" he said, getting slowly to his feet. "Didn't you see what happened?"

"What? You jumping off the Bridge of Sighs, you mean? Oh, yes, we saw that all right! What did you go and do that for? Have you got some sort of death wish or something?"

"Now, hold on..." Giles began, but to his astonishment, Ying shoved him in the chest.

"No, don't you try to justify it! Don't you dare!" Her voice was choked with emotion as she continued. "In case you didn't realise it, Trevor and I actually care about you. And all you can do is throw that back in our faces. Have you ever thought what would happen if you actually did manage to kill yourself for once? Eh? Have you?"

Giles was so shocked at her reaction, he didn't know what to say.

"You don't understand..."

"No, *you* don't understand, Giles! We only agreed to go along with this crazy night climbing thing to keep an eye on you. To stop you from doing something idiotic. You think we want to see you throw your life away in some attention-seeking prank?"

"That's a bit harsh..."

"Harsh? You want harsh? Fine! Giles, you need to face up to the fact that you need help. Professional help. Because we can't do it anymore. Your parents don't give a shit about you, well boo-bloody-hoo! Deal with it. But don't go hurting the people who do care about you in the process.

Giles stood there, stunned. Trevor shifted uncomfortably behind Ying, whose tear-filled eyes looked shocked at what she had said, but still angry.

A light came on in one of the Cripps rooms above them, and a head appeared in the open window.

"Oy! Will you lot shut it! Some of us are trying to get some sleep!"

None of them spoke. Eventually, the light went out again, leaving them in the darkness, staring at each other. In that uncomfortable silence, Giles was even more conscious of the gap that had begun to open up between him and his friends.

"Fair enough," he said, his voice resigned.

"Listen," said Trevor. "Maybe we should call it a night and talk about this tomorrow."

"Probably wise," said Giles.

Ying just stared at him. He wasn't sure if she was going to burst into tears or take a swing at him.

"Come on, Ying, let's go and get the equipment," said Trevor.

Ying glared at Giles for a few seconds more, then turned on her heel and strode off across the lawn. Trevor looked at Giles. "Will you get the ropes and other gear?"

"No problem," said Giles, staring after the retreating figure.

Trevor nodded. "OK, well, goodnight, then."

"Yeah, goodnight."

Trevor paused a moment before turning and walking after Ying.

Giles stood alone, feeling a chill that had nothing to do with his sodden clothes.

*****

Annabel crouched over the crumpled body of Professor Gupta, lying motionless where he had fallen against the far wall of the Bridge of Sighs. There were rips down his suit, and one sleeve was missing where the satchel strap had been torn away.

"Is he dead?" asked Nick, who squatted opposite her, his breathing still laboured after the struggle with the creature.

"I'm not sure," she said, reaching forward and gently lifting the remains of his suit. Beneath its tattered folds, she could see his brown skin moving up and down through the ripped shirt. A bony hand gripped her wrist, and she jumped.

"Oh! Professor! You startled me!"

"Has it gone?" he asked, looking up at her, his eyes glassy.

"What? Oh, yes. I think so."

Annabel looked at Nick, who nodded.

The old man blinked and sagged back against the wall, his face looking ashen even in the moonlight.

"Professor, I thought we were going to lose you back there," she said.

"Not just yet, my dear," he sighed. "It seems I will live to fight another day."

"What was that thing?" asked Nick.

"I believe we both know the answer to that, don't we, Nick?" said the professor with a rueful smile.

"What do you mean?" asked Annabel.

"It was Nick's statue."

"Statue?" asked Annabel, remembering those cold yellow eyes.

"Of sorts," said the professor. "You couldn't help me up, could you? I think I have recovered my breath now."

"Are you sure?" asked Annabel.

"Quite sure," said the professor, making to get up.

Annabel took one hand while Nick reached under his arm and lifted him to his feet. The old man winced.

"Sorry, Professor," said Nick. "I hope nothing's broken. You took one hell of a pounding."

"Just bruised, I think," said the professor as he flexed his shoulder gingerly. "I thought my satchel had done for me back there. Just goes to show, you should never take work home."

"I'm afraid its contents are spread all over the river," said Annabel. "I hope there wasn't anything important?"

"Not anymore," said the professor, sadly.

Annabel was not sure what he meant by that. Then she heard footsteps. They all turned to see a figure approaching them from New Court.

"Giles!" Annabel cried, letting go of the professor and running towards him. Before Giles could protest, she threw her arms around his soaking wet body.

"Thank you!" she said, before releasing him and looking into his face. "You were amazing!"

He gave her a half-hearted smile.

"Are you guys all right?" he asked as they joined the others.

"A bit bruised, perhaps," said the professor.

"Still, you put up quite a fight."

"I had some help," said the old man, indicating Nick and Annabel.

"How are *you* doing?" Nick asked Giles. "That was quite something."

"I'll live."

Annabel heard the sadness in his voice.

"Did any of you see what happened to the angel?" Giles asked.

"The angel?" said Annabel, startled. "Is that what it was?"

"A demon, more like," said Nick.

"It was neither, really," said the professor.

"You know what it is, then?" asked Annabel.

"I'm afraid so," he said, and at that moment, Annabel thought he looked very old indeed. "But that will have to wait until the morning. I don't think I'm up to explaining everything just now. And after tonight, I feel you all deserve an explanation. Perhaps we can meet at my study at ten a.m.?"

They exchanged looks. Annabel wasn't sure she could wait that long, but there again, the professor looked so worn out, she didn't feel she could ask anything more of him tonight. The others must have been thinking the same, because they all nodded.

"Good. In that case, perhaps, Giles, you will be good

enough to escort me to the Forecourt Lodge, so I can order a taxi?"

"No problem," said Giles, taking his arm.

"But, before we go," said the professor, his voice recovering much of its authority, "can I ask that each of you keep what has happened here tonight quiet?" He fixed each of them with a look. "What you have seen tonight is not something you can talk about to anyone else. Friends, family or Facebook. Is that agreed?"

They all nodded.

"Good," the professor said. "Until tomorrow, then."

He turned and allowed Giles to guide him away into Third Court.

Annabel found herself alone with Nick on the bridge. The professor was right – Nick had been incredible tonight. And here he was with her now. Just the two of them. Annabel looked up at him, and their eyes met.

"Annabel?" he said, hesitantly.

"Yes, Nick?" she said, her heart beginning to beat a bit faster.

"Can we get off this bridge? Only I'm feeling a bit exposed here now." He glanced uneasily through the bars towards the Master's Garden.

"Oh!" she said, disappointed, but recovering quickly. "Yes, of course, good idea!"

He led her in the direction of New Court. As he did so, her hand brushed against his, and she felt a warm glow radiate up her arm. She looked up at him but found he was looking elsewhere, his eyes scanning the passageways and rooftops as they passed through the Wedding Cake and across the open ground towards Cripps. When they reached the bottom of A Staircase, she turned to speak with him, but he interrupted her.

"Not here. It isn't safe."

"Not safe?" she asked, confused.

Nick ushered her up the stairs and didn't speak until they made it to the landing outside his room.

"I never told you, but that creature tried to get me once before at the bottom of these stairs."

Annabel stared at him in disbelief.

"Nick, why didn't you tell me?"

He shrugged. "I didn't want you to think I was some sort of idiot."

She knew he had a point, but it still hurt her feelings that he hadn't felt comfortable confiding in her. In fact, the more she thought about it, Nick hadn't spoken much about himself at all. His hometown, his family or friends. Why was that? There again, why hadn't she talked about her own family to him? Did she trust him enough yet with something like that?

"No, I don't," she said.

"Sorry?" he asked.

"Think you're stupid."

"Oh," he said, sighing. "That's good to know."

"I'll see you in the morning," she said.

He nodded. "See you then."

They both stood there for a few seconds, saying nothing. To Annabel it felt like Nick was leaving it to her to make the first move and she knew she wasn't ready. Closing her eyes, Annabel turned on her heel and headed up the stairs. As she climbed, she didn't look back, worried that he might call after her. Instead, she continued to climb in silence, until she finally heard the sound of his key turning in its lock, followed a few seconds later by the clunk of a door closing. Annabel paused and breathed out slowly, realising how close she had come to doing something she wasn't yet ready for. She took a steadying breath and carried on up the stairs, trying to ignore the sense of sadness growing inside her with every step. By the time she reached her own landing, Annabel had never felt more alone.

Chapter 24

The next morning, Ravi opened the front door of his terraced home in Newnham and stepped outside with great care. It had been a slow process getting dressed that morning. His body ached from the battering it had received the night before on the Bridge of Sighs. An ugly lattice of bruises ran across his chest from where he had been crushed against the window bars, and he had difficulty raising his left arm. His clumsy attempt at shaving had left him with a painful nick on his chin, and after a futile attempt at putting on a tie, he had gone without. Besides, his suit lay in tatters in the dustbin, and he had opted instead for a pair of faded cords and tweed jacket.

"It won't matter, I suppose," he told himself. "It is the weekend."

It also felt strange to be without his satchel, which was no doubt somewhere at the bottom of the river. Though that did leave his good arm free to lean on a stout walking stick, which he used to good effect as he began heading down Grantchester Street towards Newnham Road.

It was still early, and his neck felt bare without the faded college scarf that lay on his desk in Second Court. The one Robert had given him all those years ago. That thought brought back the image of his friend's body lying broken in the New Court shrubbery. Ravi doubted he would ever feel comfortable wearing that scarf again.

Ravi took a deep breath and found the fresh air helped to sweep away his grim mood. Gripping the walking stick a little firmer, he resolved that today would be different. It was time to put matters right. He owed that to Robert and to the college. He gritted his teeth and picked up the pace again.

A jogger overtook him on the pavement, her breath misting the air as she ran past. A group of bicycles approached him on the road, their Lycra-clad riders chatting as they headed out of town on their weekend ride. There were few cars about at this time of the morning, apart from a white van that had pulled up at the side of the road, its driver speaking on a mobile phone.

Skirting the edge of the park, Ravi crossed the Fen Causeway and continued down Newnham Lane. Here the road narrowed between the rows of shops, but the pavement was deserted apart from a man in a hoodie slouching in a doorway up ahead. The figure glanced up in his direction, and though Ravi couldn't see his face, he felt there was something familiar about him. But his attention was distracted by the sound of the engine behind him.

At first, he assumed the vehicle was merely accelerating away from the roundabout, but the engine's roar grew to such an intensity that it made him turn. The white van was speeding down the road at such ridiculous speed that he thought the driver either reckless or stupid. When it veered towards him with a screech of tyres, and he saw the ruthless expression of the man hunched over the wheel, he realised he was neither.

The van mounted the curve and, stiff leg or not, Ravi knew there was nothing he could do. The vehicle was going to crush him.

At that moment something slammed into his body and knocked him aside. He fell into the alleyway between two shops and crashed into a line of wheelie bins. Moments later, the white van smashed into the shopfront inches from where Ravi had been standing. The vehicle glanced off the wall and careered down the pavement, its bodywork screeching horribly as it scraped along the shopfronts.

Ravi turned and saw the hoodie jump to his feet and rush to the entrance of the alleyway where he pulled something from the pocket of his hoodie and pointed it down the street. There was a screech of tyres, the van's engine roared again as it sped off, the noise finally fading to leave the alleyway silent, save for Ravi's rapid breathing.

The stranger remained at the corner of the alleyway for a moment longer, before putting the object back in his pocket. Then he bent down to retrieve something from behind an upturned bin and approached where Ravi lay.

"I believe this is yours, Professor?"

Ravi stared at the wooden handle of his walking stick and then up at a pair of familiar grey eyes staring back at him.

"Cummings?" he said in disbelief.

With a smile, the big man removed his hood and

extended a hand. Without thinking, Ravi took it and allowed himself to be helped to his feet. Leaning on his walking stick, he stood there gathering his bewildered thoughts, trying to understand what had just happened. He stared around at the upended bins, then at the chipped brickwork of the alleyway entrance.

"The van?" he asked.

"Someone trying to tie up loose ends," said Cummings.

Ravi stared at him in confusion.

"Sorry?"

"Not now, Professor. Time to move. Are you OK to walk?"

Ravi flexed his leg. Though stiff and sore, he suspected this was still from the previous night's struggle on the bridge. He tried a few tentative steps.

"Yes, I think so," he said.

"Good. We need to get you somewhere safe."

"Where is safe, exactly?"

"The Master's Lodge," said Cummings.

"The Master's Lodge?"

"It'll be secure," said Cummings.

"What do you mean?" asked Ravi.

"I'm not working on my own, Professor," said Cummings.

Ravi was too stunned to speak.

"We can talk more about that when we're back in college. First, we need to get you there. Are you ready?"

Ravi was not sure, but he nodded. They walked to the end of the alleyway and Cummings peered down the street.

"All clear. Let's go."

Cummings led Ravi out onto Newnham Lane in the direction of the Backs, all the while keeping one hand in his hoodie pocket, the other supporting Ravi's arm. At the Mill Pond, they turned right.

"Why this way?" he asked.

"We can't use your normal route," explained Cummings. "Those characters in the white van will be looking for us."

They hurried past the neatly arranged punts moored on the water, damp and dreary, and crossed a narrow footbridge, which led to a path across the low-lying fen towards the embankment of the upper river.

"You know your way around, Mr Cummings," said Ravi.

"I used to be at Jesus College," said Cummings.

"Were you a porter there?"

The big man smiled.

"A student. I read History."

Ravi felt his face flush in embarrassment.

"I'm sorry," he said, "I didn't mean…"

But he didn't finish. He didn't know what he meant. In the last twenty-four hours his normal, ordered life had been turned upside down in such a way that he didn't trust himself to say anything sensible.

"Don't worry. It wasn't my first degree, but work brought me here."

"Work?"

"SO14, Royalty Protection."

Ravi stared at him, then he remembered.

"Prince Edward was at Jesus."

Cummings smiled. "Seemed a shame to sit in lectures

and not study at the same time."

"How did you do?"

"All right, I suppose."

Ravi looked at the man who had just saved his life.

"You got a First, didn't you?"

Cummings just smiled. They had reached the river and were walking along the towpath towards the weir that linked the upper river with the lower river. Ravi could see the familiar outline of The Mill pub on the far bank. In these tranquil surroundings, Ravi found it hard to believe that he had just escaped an attempt on his life. He decided to ask the question he had wanted to ask in the alleyway.

"Cummings, who were those people in the white van?"

"I believe they were employed by Julian Schiller."

Ravi stopped. "Schiller? What does he want from me?"

They had reached the Weir Bridge in front of the pub, and Cummings scanned up the lane towards Trumpington Street.

"I'd rather we kept moving, Professor."

"I'd rather you answered my question," said Ravi.

Cummings looked at him.

"With Mackenzie dead, I think that Schiller wanted to find out what you know."

"About what?" asked Ravi.

"I was hoping that was something you would be able to tell me," said Cummings.

That shut Ravi up.

"Listen, Professor, we need to keep moving. If they tried to get you once, they... shit!"

Ravi followed the big man's gaze. A hundred yards away, a white van had turned into Mill Lane. One of its headlights was broken.

"Move!" said Cummings, grabbing Ravi's arm and dragging him into a narrow passageway known as Laundress Lane. They ran between tall buildings, Ravi stumbling now, only kept upright by the larger man's firm grip on his arm. Ravi heard the van screech to a halt behind them and risked a look over his shoulder. A shaven-headed man and a red-headed woman jumped from the vehicle and chased up the lane after them. Panting, they reached the end of the passageway and turned right into Silver Street.

"This way!" said Cummings, dragging Ravi across to the far side of the street before turning left into Queens' Lane. Ravi was breathing hard and felt a pain in his chest as they hurried past the ancient gates of Queens' College and continued up the lane towards a closed set of arched doors in the distance.

"That's the side entrance to King's up ahead," yelled Cummings. "Will your university pass let you through?"

"I'm not sure," said Ravi.

"Well, I guess we're going to find out!"

Behind them, Ravi heard a shout.

"*Tam oni!*"

He looked over his shoulder and saw the woman sprinting after them, her partner a little way behind.

"*Speshi!*" the man yelled, his face contorted with rage.

Ravi stumbled at that point, and it was only Cummings' vice-like grip that prevented him from falling flat on his face.

"Keep moving, Professor," he said. "We're almost there."

Gasping, they neared the sizeable wood-panelled door, and Ravi spotted the wicket gate set into it. Cummings pushed Ravi ahead of him and positioned himself between the professor and their pursuers.

"Try the door," said Cummings.

Gasping for air, Ravi frantically reached into his pocket and found his university pass. Pulling it out with shaking hands, he swiped the card over the door sensor. Nothing happened. Ravi leant against the door and shoved. It didn't move.

"Professor?" asked Cummings, his voice strained.

"Locked…" he cried.

"Shit!"

Then Ravi heard movement on the other side of the door. With a click, it swung open, and Ravi stared into the surprised face of a young student in a thick duffle coat, a purple scarf wrapped around her neck.

"Go, Professor! Go!" said Cummings and shoved him from behind. Ravi stumbled through the doorway and into the girl, who yelped and backed inside. Cummings followed him through and slammed the wicket gate shut. Ravi heard the sound of footsteps running up to the door and something heavy thumping into it. The door shook but didn't budge. There came another thump, followed by a muffled grunt of "*Govno!*"

The student looked at Ravi and then at the door, her eyes wide.

"Muggers!" said Cummings. "Tried to get the professor. Alert the porters. Quick!"

There was more hammering, followed by *"Svolochi!"*

The student stared at the door then said, "Right," before turning and rushing off for the lodge. Cummings didn't wait. He took Ravi by the arm and hauled him into a cloistered courtyard.

"They'll probably head round to the front gate of King's," he said as they hurried along. "So, we'll take the exit by the chapel, leading into Trinity Lane. There's an entrance there into Trinity College."

They strode across the back of King's College, keeping behind the Gibbs Building, which faced onto the river to their left. Ravi's chest was burning, but he dared not stop. Cummings was breathing hard, scanning the area for signs of other pursuers. There were a few early morning tourists about, though none of them seemed interested in the strange pair striding along, ignoring the beautiful setting.

They came out at the west end of King's College Chapel, its magnificent Gothic facade rising high above them. Neither paid it any heed. Instead, Cummings headed for the massive wrought-iron gates that marked the northern perimeter of the college. Ravi managed to dig out his university pass again, and the porter, resplendent in a full-length gown with a broad purple sash, nodded as the two departing guests hurried through.

"Stay alert," said Cummings as they passed the entrance to Clare College and skirted behind the Old Schools building. Ravi could only wheeze in reply. Cummings pointed ahead of them.

"Trinity's side entrance is just around that corner up

ahead," he said. "Once there, we're almost home."

They headed past Trinity Hall and approached the junction with Hostel Lane, which led towards the river. Cummings put himself between the professor and the entrance to the lane, and as he did so, the shaven-headed man Ravi recognised from the van came running around the corner, his eyes widening in surprise.

Cummings did not hesitate. He rammed the palm of his left hand straight into the bridge of the man's nose. Ravi heard a sickening crunch and watched as the man's legs flipped up in the air and he fell flat on his back onto the cobbled street. His female partner appeared a moment later, only a few steps behind. Ravi saw her eyes widen in shock, and her hand reach for the pocket of her jacket. Cummings punched her full in the face and the woman crumpled in a heap on the floor. He turned to Ravi.

"Come on, Professor! Let's go!"

Ravi did as he was told. He raced up the lane and turned the corner. Ahead he saw an arched wooden door, studded with iron bolts and a small wicket gate. Ravi made straight for it and collapsed against it. Reaching with trembling hands for his pass, he swiped it against the sensor set in the woodwork. There was an answering click and Ravi stumbled through the gate, pitching forward onto his hands and knees, dropping his walking stick in the process. Cummings ducked through after him and swung the door closed.

Gasping for air, Ravi crawled over to the wall and slumped against it, his chest heaving and sweat running down his brow. He sat there for a while, sucking in air, his hands shaking as he stared across the serene setting of Trinity Great Court.

"How are you doing, Professor?" asked Cummings, who had been standing there looking down at him.

Ravi was not sure how he was doing, so he just sat there, not bothering to answer, focusing all his efforts on getting air into his protesting lungs.

"Sorry, Professor. That'll have to do for now. We need to keep moving," said Cummings.

Ravi lifted his head and saw the man had picked up his walking stick and was offering it to him. He noticed the grazed knuckles and thought back to the brief and brutal skirmish in Trinity Lane. Cummings had been unstoppable.

Taking the walking stick, Ravi pushed himself up from the floor and stood there gathering himself for one more effort. In the distance, the clock tower showed quarter to ten.

"Who are you, exactly?" he asked.

"If I told you that, I'd have to kill you," said Cummings.

Ravi looked into those grey eyes.

"A joke, Professor."

Ravi was not sure he entirely believed that.

"Come on, we can talk as we move," said Cummings, leading Ravi out of the archway into Great Court. His minder continued to look around at the few people who were out and about, but none caused him any alarm, and for the moment it felt as if they were safe.

"I'm part of a surveillance team that has been monitoring Schiller and his organisation for some time," began Cummings, his voice low. "Schiller trades in arms. It used to be hardware.

Drones, robotics, weapon systems. Then he branched out into cyber warfare. It's the new frontier in the arms trade, and he was smart enough to spot it early. He's been investing in high-tech start-ups in and around major research universities like Cambridge. Recruiting the best talent, offering them highly paid jobs where they can pursue their research without having to worry about funding. It's taken over from investment banking as the most coveted posting going. Instead of using algorithms to run share trading systems, the latest batch of graduates is now writing code to bring down operating systems or change governments."

Ravi listened in appalled silence.

"When Schiller started cultivating a relationship with Professor Mackenzie, we decided to deploy someone to John's to keep an eye on things. In the last eighteen months, Schiller began spending more and more time with Mackenzie. From what we could judge, the project seemed to be coming to some sort of critical stage. And that's when Vidal went missing."

"Alfonso Vidal?" said Ravi.

Cummings nodded.

"I was following Vidal that evening. He'd got mixed up with some unsavoury people while studying in Barcelona. An extremist Catalan independence group. With the demise of ETA, it looked like they were going to pick up the baton of breaking up the Spanish State. Our colleagues in Madrid weren't sure if his purpose here was personal or cause-related. But his proximity to Schiller seemed too much of a coincidence."

"And was it?"

"We'll probably never know," said Cummings. "I was about to make contact with him when he disappeared."

Ravi stopped short. "You were there? That night?"

"Yes, Professor. I was."

Ravi could hardly believe it. "So, what happened?"

For the first time since Ravi had met him, Cummings seemed hesitant.

"I had been waiting for him outside the college that night. He seemed very jumpy. I felt it too. There was something not right. Anyway, I followed him into Portugal Street, and that's when it happened. Vidal turned and saw something behind me. I ducked and the next thing I knew, it had grabbed him and was dragging him into the air."

He stared past Ravi, his eyes unfocused as he thought back to that night, reliving that moment.

"I ran after them, Professor. I chased them down the street, but the downdraft from its wings in that narrow gap was like a gale. I could barely see them, it was so strong. In the end, it was no use. By the time I reached the end of Portugal Street, they had gone."

Cummings looked at the professor, his usually placid face troubled.

"What was it, Professor? Where did it come from?"

Ravi considered him. Cummings had probably saved his life on two occasions today. He had also seen the creature and what it could do. This man deserved to know the truth. Ravi sighed. Standing in Trinity's Great Court, the old professor finally revealed a secret he had kept for half a century.

"It's from a parallel universe," he said.

Cummings stared at him. Ravi could not tell what the man was thinking. His grey eyes were unflinching.

"So, it's an alien, Professor."

It was a statement, not a question. No protest, no disbelief, no doubt. The man simply accepted the professor's answer. Ravi felt a wave of relief wash over him.

"Yes, it's not from this world," said Ravi.

Cummings looked hard at him.

"Have you seen this other world?" he asked.

"Briefly, a long time ago. Before we closed the portal."

"You and Mackenzie."

"Yes, Robert and I."

"So, Schiller got him to open this portal again."

Once more, it was a statement from Cummings, not a question. Ravi looked at the big man, marvelling at the matter-of-fact way he was dealing with what, to most people, would have been unimaginable.

"I believe so."

Cummings nodded. He paused and took a deep breath, looking out across the court at the ornate fountain in the middle of the square. When he spoke, the hard edge in his voice came as a shock to Ravi.

"Is the portal still open?"

"No. I believe Robert shut it again."

"How do you know?"

"He wrote me a note."

"Do you have the note?"

"I'm afraid I lost it last night. When the creature attacked me."

"You saw it, last night?"

"Yes, it only comes out at night."

"How do you know?"

Ravi looked at Cummings. He was not sure he wanted to say any more. But he knew an explanation was needed.

"When Robert and I looked through that portal, the world we looked at was an alien one. But some aspects were familiar, at least at first. The landscape was jagged and mountainous, a chaotic mix of stone and rock."

Ravi thought back to that time. He and Robert staring through the vortex, their eyes wide in amazement and wonder.

"At first, we thought it was just jagged rock, but as we looked closer, we spotted shapes in the formation. Growths. At first, I thought it was some sort of plant, lichen, perhaps."

Cummings stared at him unblinking.

"Of course, that was during daylight hours." He swallowed. "As darkness spread across the land and shadows stretched from the horizon, the growths... They came to life."

"They came to life?" said Cummings.

"Yes," said Ravi, looking up at the big man. "During daylight, they were dormant, a sort of suspended state where their bodies calcified. To preserve energy, perhaps – I don't know. But then, at night, they awoke. Their bodies transformed. Stone became flesh, scales, feathers and eyes. Eyes that glowed yellow in the dark. Searching..."

Ravi closed his eyes as he remembered seeing the creatures circling overhead.

"Searching for what, Professor?"

Ravi opened his eyes and looked at Cummings.

"Prey," he said. "They were searching for prey."

The Trinity Clock struck the hour.

Cummings stared at the professor for a few moments longer, then glanced down at his watch. "We need to move. I need to get you somewhere safe!"

He led Ravi towards the main gatehouse, where the Trinity porters were already busy processing a long queue of tourists. Cummings peered over the crowd to the cobbled forecourt that led from the entrance to Trinity Street.

"Do you see anyone?" asked Ravi.

"I'm not sure. There may be more watching the Main Gate at John's."

Cummings looked around and indicated a group of students loitering around a noticeboard in the archway. They wore tops printed with the words FIRST AND THIRD TRINITY BOAT CLUB.

"Ever fancied rowing, Professor?"

"Not up to now," said Ravi.

"Looks like this might be the time to try," said Cummings as the group started edging towards the front gate. "If they're heading for the river, they'll go past John's."

Pulling his hoodie over his head, the big man took hold of Ravi's arm, and they joined the back of the group as it filed out of the members' gate. The students were in high spirits as they crossed the cobbled forecourt. A couple of the girls looked back at Ravi, but he smiled back at them, and they kept walking.

"Keep your head down, Professor," said Cummings. "It's you they're looking for."

The group turned left and headed down Trinity Street, just as Cummings had predicted they would.

"Almost there, Professor," said Cummings.

"Come on, folks, training begins now!" said one of the students. There were a few good-natured groans, and to Ravi's horror, the entire group started jogging.

"Quick, Professor!" said Cummings, pulling Ravi towards the entrance to John's. Just then a large party of tourists emerged from the gatehouse, chatting excitedly and holding up selfie-sticks to take pictures in front of the gates. There must have been more than forty of them, jostling and posing for photos, blocking the archway completely. Cummings looked exasperated.

"We'll go to the Forecourt entrance instead," he said.

"*Niet!*" came a female voice behind them and Ravi felt a hard object dig into his back. Cummings began turning but stopped when the man, his broken nose still swollen, stepped in behind him and thrust a long, metallic object into his ribs. Ravi looked at Cummings, who gave him a quick shake of his head.

"Good. Now, this way," said the woman, in a clipped accent.

Ravi turned and saw the bruised face of the redhead standing behind him. He felt something dig into his kidneys and glanced down at the gun with the stubby-looking silencer wedged between them. She nodded towards the passageway opposite the Great Gate and her partner shoved

Cummings towards it, a murderous look on his battered face. Ravi felt an increase in the pressure of the barrel in his side and had no choice but to follow the others across the street towards the relative quiet of All Saints Passage. Behind them, the tourists continued to mill around in excitement, providing the perfect diversion for their abductors.

"Cummings…?" Ravi began, but was rewarded with a jab in the ribs.

"Quiet!" hissed the woman.

The noise of St John's Street receded as they entered the alleyway and were ushered past the entrance to the Old Divinity School, towards the shadowy recesses at the far end of the little square.

"Why, Professor Gupta, how nice to see you!" came a familiar female voice. "Did you come to see me off?"

Ravi looked up, and there was Mrs Hamilton. She was wheeling an overnight bag between the iron gates of Corfield Court. He felt the woman behind him tense and up ahead her partner hesitated, turning towards the old lady in surprise. This was all Cummings needed. Snapping his elbow back into the man's face for the second time that morning and gripping him by his throat, he slammed his captor into the railings. The man raised his gun, but Cummings grabbed its silencer with one hand and yanked it upwards as it repeatedly coughed, bullets chipping off the brickwork opposite. Then he headbutted his pinned opponent, and the man slumped, his lifeless finger slipping from the trigger.

Suddenly Ravi felt a vicious shove in his back, and he

pitched forward, hitting the paving stones with a painful jolt before rolling onto his side and staring back up at his assailant. He expected to see the gun aimed down at him. Instead, he saw the redhead raise it in both hands and, aiming it directly at Cummings, pull the trigger. Its stubby silencer barked twice.

Then from nowhere came a terrible buzzing sound and the redhead screamed. Her whole body convulsed, and the gun fell from her hands as her arms jerked up and down like some sort of grotesque marionette. The buzzing sound continued, and the woman fell to her knees, her eyes rolling up into their sockets. She fell forwards, hitting the flagstones at Ravi's feet with a sickening sound. The buzzing stopped, and Ravi stared at her still-spasming body in disbelief. Then he looked up at Mrs Hamilton, who was standing there with her handbag in one hand, an electronic taser in the other.

A groan behind him brought him to his senses. He turned and saw Cummings lying slumped against the gates of Corfield Court, blood pooling on the paving stones beside him.

"Cummings!" Ravi cried, crawling over to kneel by him.

The man looked up at Ravi, a bemused expression on his face, then down at the front of his hoodie. It was stained dark with blood.

"Bit of a mess," he said. "What about the other two?"

Mrs Hamilton moved over to the prone form of the attacker next to the railings and checked for a pulse.

"Alive," she said. "So is the woman." She came over to Cummings and knelt next to him.

"Mrs Hamilton, I presume," he said. A trickle of blood came from the corner of his mouth.

"I need to see to those wounds," she said in a professional tone.

Cummings looked up at her then nodded. She lifted the front of his hoodie and peeled away his blood-soaked T-shirt. Ravi could see two dark red holes in the pale skin, blood oozing from both.

"Abdominal gunshot wound. We'll need to stem the bleeding," said Mrs Hamilton. "Professor Gupta, my suitcase!"

Ravi stared at her.

"Quickly now, Professor! The suitcase, if you please!"

Ravi struggled to his feet and limped over to the bag, which stood in the alleyway next to the other body. He grabbed its extended handle and dragged it over to her, its wheels drawing red lines through the expanding pool of blood. Mrs Hamilton undid the zip, reached inside and removed a pink towelling dressing gown. She removed the drawstring from the robe, which she then folded into a long compress.

"Professor Gupta, help me here," she said. "I need you to press this dressing gown against the entry wound."

Ravi looked down at the tightly folded robe and the bloody puncture wound in Cummings' chest.

"Now, please!" demanded Mrs Hamilton.

He did as he was told, taking the pink towelling robe and pressing it firmly against Cummings' chest. Mrs Hamilton looped the drawstring around the man's back and began to tighten it against the compress.

"This may hurt, Mr Cummings, but you look like you can handle it," she said.

"Do it…" he said.

Mrs Hamilton pulled the drawstring tight. Cummings winced, and perspiration gathered on his forehead, which was still red from the headbutt he had given his attacker. Mrs Hamilton tied a knot in the drawstring and patted him on the shoulder.

"That's better," she said.

Cummings looked up at her.

"Were you a medic, Mrs Hamilton?" he asked.

"Nurse, RAF, Dhofar," said the old lady. "Plenty of practice with these sorts of wounds during the uprising."

Ravi heard the sound of footsteps and turned to see Bert stepping over the prone bodies in the alleyway.

"My lord!" he said. "Professor? Mrs Hamilton? What happened? Are you all right?"

"We're fine," said Mrs Hamilton.

Ravi was not so sure he was OK, but decided that if Mrs Hamilton said so, then he must be.

"Bert. We need an ambulance for Mr Cummings here," said the old woman. "Tell them he's been shot and has lost a lot of blood."

"Shot?"

"Yes, Bert, you heard me. Gunshot wounds," said Mrs Hamilton. "Have you got that?"

"Yes."

"Well, go on then, man!" said Mrs Hamilton.

"Right. Ambulance," said Bert, turning and rushing back down the alleyway.

Cummings coughed, and more blood bubbled from his mouth.

"Mr Cummings, the ambulance is on its way," said Mrs Hamilton. "I need you to stay as still as possible. They'll be here soon."

"Not soon enough…" he wheezed, looking up at her. He seemed to be having trouble focusing. Ravi glanced at Mrs Hamilton, and the look of concern on her features told him all he needed to know. The man was fading fast.

Cummings lifted his hand and managed to grip Ravi's sleeve.

"Professor…" he wheezed, his eyes blinking away the sweat that was pouring down his forehead now.

"I'm here," said Ravi, leaning in closer.

"That thing… we talked about earlier… That creature."

"Yes," said Ravi, quietly.

"It doesn't… It doesn't belong… here."

Cummings' voice was barely a whisper.

"No, it doesn't," said Ravi, feeling the grip tighten on his sleeve.

"So… Professor… Do me a favour… Will you?"

Ravi leant in close and felt the man's hot, wet breath against his ear.

"Of course, Cummings. You know I will."

Straining, Ravi heard him murmur two words.

"Finish it."

Chapter 25

Giles emerged from his staircase and stood at the foot of the steps, looking across Second Court. Sucking in the crisp morning air, he exhaled slowly, willing his escaping breath to take away the troubling thoughts that had greeted him when he woke that morning.

Lying in bed, Giles had replayed the previous night's encounters in his mind, and he wasn't sure which was the more bruising: the physical battering he had received from the creature or the emotional beating he had suffered from Ying. While the creature's retaliation had been brutal, the damage done by Ying's words had hurt him more. She had opened a wound that had never fully healed since he had first become aware of his parents' indifference to him. Despite all his awards and achievements at school and now here, he had never been anything more than an inconvenience, a mistake, a discrepancy in the accounts of their careers. His parents had never said it to his face, but he knew it to be true. At every opportunity, they had passed him on to others or sent him away. Their actions spoke louder than words.

Ying was no fool, nor Trevor. They had worked it out

too. But neither had ever confronted him about it before. Last night was the first time one of them had voiced it aloud. And he hadn't been ready. Not after the adrenaline rush of the fight with the creature. Ying had caught him with his guard down, and it had hurt. More than he wanted to admit to them or to himself.

His thoughts were disturbed by the sight of Nick and Annabel emerging from Third Court. Nick had his hands in his jean pockets, and Annabel's head was down. They weren't holding hands, he noticed. Annabel glanced up and waved.

Giles took a deep breath and began to saunter across the court. "Hello, lovebirds!" he called out.

As he did so, he noticed a woman emerge from the passageway to Chapel Court. She wore a tan coat and dark glasses, and her long black hair cascaded in waves over her shoulders.

"Raquel!" he called out, heading towards her.

Her face broke into a smile. "Good morning, Giles."

"What brings you into college this morning?"

"I'm here to see Professor Gupta."

"Just heading there myself," he said, smiling. Raquel's expression was hard to read behind her glasses, but by the angle of her head, he wasn't sure how pleased she was by this news.

"He told us last night you might be coming along," he explained, indicating the entrance to the stairwell in the corner of the court, where Nick and Annabel were standing.

"Nick!" Raquel cried, letting go of Giles' hand and

running over to the others. Giles watched as she ran up to the fresher, taking his face in her hands and kissing him on both cheeks. If Nick looked surprised by this, that was nothing compared to the look on Annabel's face.

"You're going to be in trouble now, Nick, my friend," Giles said to himself.

*****

Annabel felt her mouth drop open as the raven-haired beauty kissed Nick.

"I have thought of you," the woman said, "after the other night. I did not thank you enough." Reaching up, she touched Nick's swollen eyebrow. "Your eye, it is better?"

Nick flinched away. "It's fine. Listen, Raquel, this is Annabel."

The woman turned to face Annabel and, removing her dark glasses, offered her hand.

"Hello, Annabel."

"Hello," Annabel replied, taking her hand. Raquel's grip was firm, and Annabel did her best to match it while staring at the bruising around the woman's nose and then at Nick's own battered face. "I'm sorry, I must have missed something. How is it you know Nick, exactly?"

"We were in a fight, the other night," said Raquel. "He did not tell you about us?"

"A fight?" Annabel said, turning on Nick.

"Ah, no," said Raquel, quickly. "I say it wrong. Nick fought for me."

"He did what?" said Annabel.

"With, how you say, not nice men? He was helping me."

Annabel stared at Nick.

"They were drunk," he mumbled.

"You didn't mention it."

"It didn't seem that important," he said.

"Well, glad that's all cleared up," said Giles, who had just joined them. "So, shall we see if Professor Gupta's in?" He indicated the stairwell in the corner of the court.

There was an awkward moment when Raquel looked at Nick, who suddenly seemed very interested in the cobblestones, before she turned to Giles and said, "*Sí*, we go now."

The four of them set off, Giles alongside Raquel, with Nick and Annabel following behind in silence. When they reached the entrance to the stairwell, the sign read E5, Professor R. Gupta, OUT.

Giles turned to Annabel. "He's your tutor, Annabel. What do you think?"

"I sometimes forget to switch mine," she said. "The professor was a bit shaken up yesterday. Let's give it a go."

Annabel had been to his rooms before, so she led them up the broad stairwell and past the entrance to the Old Library.

"Professor Gupta's on the next one up," she said.

"He's really in the rafters," said Nick.

"Nepalese," said Giles. "Loves climbing things."

They made their way up the final twisting staircase.

"There you go," said Annabel, pointing at a door at the end of the landing. "Looks like he's in after all."

The outer door of Professor Gupta's study was open. Annabel walked up to it and knocked.

"Morning, Professor," she called.

No response. Annabel looked back at the others.

"He might be in his kitchen," suggested Nick.

"Or having a crap," offered Giles. He seemed to be enjoying himself.

"Do they have toilets in Second Court?" Annabel asked.

"No, but they have washbasins," whispered Giles, tapping his nose.

"Really?" said Annabel, looking disgusted. "Who would do that?"

Giles pointed at Nick behind his back.

Annabel rolled her eyes and turned back to the door.

"Professor Gupta? It's Annabel," she said, turning the handle and opening the door. "You said ten o'clock?"

Annabel stepped into the room and gasped.

*****

Giles peered over Annabel's shoulder and saw a man standing behind the old mahogany desk. He had slicked-back hair and was wearing jeans with a crisp white shirt under a dark blazer. He closed the laptop he had evidently been looking at on the desk and stood up.

"Good morning, everyone. Have you come looking for the professor?"

"Who are you?" asked Annabel.

"I'm one of his former students," said the man. "I was in Cambridge this weekend and came to visit him. He's just popped out for a moment. I'm sure he'll be back shortly."

"Really?" said Annabel. "Only we didn't see the professor come downstairs."

The man just smiled and indicated the sofas away from the door.

"Please take a seat," he said. "I'm sure the professor will be along shortly."

Annabel hesitated, but then began to move towards the sofa, and the others followed. Something did not feel right to Giles, who had been in trouble so many times over the years that he could spot bullshit a mile away.

The man smiled and began heading for the door. "I'll leave you to the professor. Enjoy your Astronomy tutorial."

Alarm bells rang in Giles' head, and before he knew what he was doing, he had stepped over to the door and closed it. He turned to face the stranger, who had stopped a few feet from him. The man's smile faltered for a moment.

Giles beamed. "I don't think I caught your name?"

"My name is Julian," he said.

Giles was conscious of the others over by the chairs, staring back at the pair of them.

"You see, Julian," said Giles, "what I don't understand is why a former student of Professor Gupta would think we were here for an Astronomy tutorial. Supervision, yes, but not a tutorial. A tutor looks after your emotional needs, not your academic ones, as any genuine Cambridge student would know."

There was a flicker of anger in the man's expression before he smiled again and held up his hand in a sign of apology.

"Of course. I was thinking of my time at Oxford. Enjoy your meeting with the professor. I must be going."

He took a step forward, but another figure moved across the room to stand alongside Giles at the door. It was Nick, his black eye adding an intimidating edge to the glare he was giving the stranger.

Julian stared back at them. He was not smiling anymore. That was when Giles remembered where he had seen that slicked-back hair before, illuminated that time by the flame of a match.

"Besides," said Giles. "Now that I think about it, I think I've seen you around college before. You and the Dean were arguing in New Court, not long before he was found…"

Giles didn't finish. The idea of something genuinely monstrous had begun to form in his brain, but his thoughts were interrupted by a sudden movement. Without warning, Julian leapt across the room and grabbed Raquel by the hair. She screamed in agony as he yanked her against him and backed towards the desk. Nick started forward, but Annabel cried out, "Nick, stop!"

Nick froze, and Giles saw what Annabel had seen. Julian was holding some sort of knife to Raquel's neck. As he backed away, he pressed it harder against her skin. Raquel stopped struggling, her eyes wide with fear.

"I'd like everyone to stay calm," said the man, "and this young lady will walk away from this unfortunate incident unharmed."

There was an edge to his voice that was every bit as hard and unyielding as that blade.

"Now it really is time for me to go, so I'm going to ask you to kindly move to one side and allow this young lady and me to leave."

Nick stood his ground like a bull, looking ready to charge at any minute.

"Steady, Nick," said Giles. "Not the time for heroics just yet."

Nick remained motionless for a moment longer, then reluctantly stepped back.

"Very sensible," said Julian, the blade still pressing against Raquel's neck. "Now please go and sit down over there on the sofas." He nodded towards the seats surrounding the coffee table.

"Nick?" said Annabel, who sat down on the edge of the sofa, her face drained of colour like she was going to be sick.

Giles saw Nick begin to move off towards her, his eyes still locked on Julian. Giles knew he had no choice but to follow. As he began to edge sideways away from the door, he racked his brain for a means of preventing Julian escaping with Raquel.

"So that night, what exactly were you and the Dean arguing about?" he asked.

"As if I am going to share that with you," said Julian.

"So, you *were* there, and you *were* arguing."

"A lawyer, I see," said Julian as he pushed Raquel towards the door.

"Wrong again," said Giles. "You seem to be making lots of mistakes, Julian. Is that why you were arguing with the Dean? Things weren't going your way?"

"That is for you to wonder and me to know," said Julian as he and Raquel moved closer to the door.

"Unless it was that research Mackenzie and Gupta had been working on."

Julian stopped. It had been a wild guess by Giles, but why else would the man be going through the professor's computer?

"What research would that be?" asked Julian. His voice was level, but there was no doubting his interest.

In for a penny, in for a pound, Giles thought, and went for it.

"Something he was planning to share with us this morning," said Giles.

"Concerning what, exactly?"

"That research paper you were looking for in this room."

"You'll have to do better than that, my friend."

Giles knew he would have to. But then, just when he needed it most, his mind went blank. His mouth opened, but nothing came out. *Come on, Giles*, he thought, but all he could see were Raquel's eyes pleading with him as Julian pressed the knife against her throat. The intruder must have sensed that Giles was bluffing and began to move again.

"Well, much as I've enjoyed our little discussion…"

"Eagles," Giles blurted out.

Julian froze, and Giles realised he had struck gold.

"Yes…" he continued, his mind clearing, "Professor Gupta is something of an authority on them."

He was not sure what he was hoping for. He just knew that if he could engage Julian's interest, he might be able to keep him here longer. Or, if Professor Gupta would shortly be returning to his room, warn the old man that someone was waiting for him.

"Oh yes, he's obsessed with them," said Giles, warming to the subject. "Mountains, you see. Great place for eagles. Build their eyries there. High up. Safe from other predators but good for seeing prey."

"Eyries?" said Julian, his eyes locked on Giles.

"Yes, eyries," said Giles. "Where the professor comes from, they worship them, you know. Eagles, I mean. Use them for hunting."

Giles did not have a clue whether the Nepalese hunted with eagles. But when it came to bullshit, he was a master.

"Hunting?" said Julian.

Giles thought he heard the sound of footsteps on the stairwell.

"Oh yes, rodents mainly. There's loads of *vermin* in the Himalayas," he said.

Julian tensed. Had he heard footsteps too? Giles continued, louder this time.

"Horrible, nasty little creatures. Not native to Nepal at all – *intruders*, really," he said, putting as much emphasis as he could on "intruders."

He could definitely hear footsteps now, moving carefully up the stairs.

"The trouble with these nasty little *rats*," he continued, "is that they are *dangerous* little buggers. *Deadly*, in fact." The words "dangerous" and "deadly" were as loud as he could make them without shouting.

It was no good. A floorboard creaked, and Julian gripped Raquel's hair tightly, causing her to gasp. Nick started forward, but Annabel shot out a restraining hand.

"Nick, no!"

They all stood there frozen, staring at each other. Giles could feel his heart thumping in his chest. Then a familiar voice from the landing broke the silence.

"Professor Gupta, are you in there? Your tea's here!"

It's Jane, the waitress, thought Giles.

"Professor? Could you get the door, please? Only this tray ain't half heavy!"

Julian stared at the door, his face a picture of concentration as he decided what to do. Everyone in the room remained motionless. Then, the knife still pressed to Raquel's throat, he moved himself and his hostage behind the door, placing his back against its wood-panelled surface.

"Professor Gupta?" called Jane again. "Are you in there?"

"Get rid of her!" he hissed at Giles.

Giles looked at Julian. The man stared back at him, his eyes cold and unflinching. Giles realised he had no choice.

"It's me, Jane. Giles Chamberlain. Professor Gupta's gone to pick up a parcel at the Porter's Lodge. We're just waiting for him now."

Julian's eyes never left his.

"Well, do you want this tray or not, Giles? Only me arms are killing me."

"Hang on a second," he said and waited for a sign from Julian as to what to do next. The man pressed the knife closer into Raquel's neck, and she gasped, tears rolling down her pale cheeks.

"Why not leave it with me?" said Giles, as much to Julian as to the waitress standing out on the landing. Julian looked hard at him, then nodded slowly and edged to one side of the door.

"Well, hurry up then," said Jane. "I can't stand here all day, or the tea will get cold."

Giles glanced at the knife held against Raquel's neck. He'd risk himself, but not Raquel. Reaching with a shaking hand for the doorknob, he slowly opened the door.

Jane stood outside, a large tray in front of her.

"Finally!" said Jane. "You took your time, didn't you?"

"Thank you, Jane," he said lamely as she handed him the tray.

"There you go," she said. "Be careful, mind. I don't want you spilling it."

"Don't worry. I've got it."

"Oh, and Giles," she said, "I have a message from your Latin supervisor."

"My Latin supervisor?" he said.

"Yes," she said, looking him in the eye. "He asked, *ipse post ostium?*"

"*Ipse post ostium?*" he repeated, staring at her in surprise.

"Seemed pretty important," she said, holding his gaze.

"Oh, yes," he replied, slowly, eyes widening in understanding, "yes, of course."

She nodded. "Well, that's good to know. Mind that teapot, it's scorching."

Giles backed into the room, holding the heavy tray. Jane

reached for the door handle and began to pull it towards her. Julian, his eyes fixed on Giles, edged across in front of the door, a look of grim satisfaction on his face. And that was when Jane slammed the door into the back of his head.

Wham!

Julian staggered, thrusting Raquel in front of him as he tried to regain his balance. Raquel yelled in alarm as she stumbled, the knife nicking her throat as she fell. Giles didn't hesitate. He leapt forward and tipped the tray of steaming tea over Julian. The man screamed and raised his hands to his scalded face as the crockery flew in the air and crashed to the floor. Giles grabbed Raquel and pulled her clear, flinging her towards the nearest sofa.

Before Giles could turn to face Julian, Jane was through the door and driving her foot into the back of the screaming man's knee. There was a popping sound and Julian crumpled to the floor, writhing in agony. Jane was on him in an instant. She grabbed his knife arm, twisting it backwards and jamming her forearm against the elbow. There was a snap, and Julian screamed again. Giles saw the blade clatter to the floor. Using her full weight, Jane drove her opponent's face onto the floorboards with a fleshy thump that muffled his cries.

With her victim pinned to the floor, the waitress looked up at Giles.

"Check the others," she said.

Giles looked across the room. Nick had been halfway across the room but had stopped and was now staring in disbelief at the writhing figure on the floor. Annabel had jumped to her feet and was squatting next to Raquel, who lay sprawled on the sofa, her hand clutching her throat. Giles thought he could see a trickle of blood through her fingers.

"Annabel! How is she?" he asked.

Annabel gently but firmly prised Raquel's hands away and inspected her neck.

"She's good, I think," she said. "It's just a scratch."

She reached in her pocket and pulled out a handkerchief, which she applied to the cut. She placed Raquel's hand back on it, smiling reassuringly at the pale woman.

Giles looked around for the discarded weapon and saw it lying amidst the broken crockery and spilt tea. Bending down, he picked it up. It was an old school ruler, worn to a thin point at one end.

"Is everyone OK?" came a surprisingly cultured voice behind him. He turned, expecting to find someone else had entered the room, but it was Jane, her knee pressed into Julian's back. She had retrieved a plastic cable tie from somewhere and was binding the man's wrists, none too gently.

"I said, is everyone OK?" she repeated, looking hard at him.

"Yes, yes, I think so. We're fine."

Jane nodded and pulled a mobile phone from her waistcoat pocket. She thumbed a code and held it to her ear.

"All clear here. No casualties." She looked over at the others. "Wood, Hamilton, Chamberlain."

Giles stared at her.

"Understood. I'll send them over now." She stuffed the mobile into her pocket.

"OK, you need to head over to the Master's Lodge. I have to wait here for backup."

Giles just stared at her.

"Who are you?" asked Nick from behind him, echoing the question in Giles' head.

"No time for that," said Jane, indicating Julian pinned beneath her. "You need to get over to the Master's Lodge. He's waiting for you."

"The Master?" asked Annabel. "What about the professor?"

"We're still trying to find him. First, we need to get you somewhere safe while I deal with this situation here." She applied pressure to Julian's back, and he whimpered. "Is that understood!"

It was not a question. It was a command.

"Understood," said Giles. He turned to the others. "You heard her, let's go."

Annabel helped Raquel to her feet and led her towards the door. Nick followed.

"Are you sure you don't need a hand with him?" he asked Jane.

"No thanks, Psycho, I think I can handle him."

"Well, you know where we are," said Nick.

"I do," she said.

Giles stepped over the shattered crockery and onto the landing. He was halfway towards the stairs when a thought struck him. He turned and looked back at the waitress.

"Jane, where did you learn Latin?"

She looked up at him and grinned.

"At the Other Place."

"Right," he said, "of course."

When he reached the bottom of the stairs, Giles found the others waiting for him. Raquel had the handkerchief pressed to her neck and was leaning on Annabel. Nick was standing protectively behind, his head turned, scanning the court.

"Giles," asked Annabel, "what was all that stuff in Latin?"

"What? *Ipse post ostium,* you mean?"

"Yeah, that."

"Well, if a waitress knew you were a Latin scholar," said Giles, "she'd expect you'd know what it meant."

"Which is?" asked Annabel.

"Roughly translated: 'Is he behind the door?'"

The others just stared at him.

"Shall we?" he said, indicating the passageway leading to Chapel Court. "Only, I think we have a meeting with the Master."

Chapter 26

Giles led them through Chapel Court and past the entrance to the library, Raquel giving the library door a wide berth. In the far corner, they entered a short passageway and followed the path past the Master's Garden to the courtyard in front of the lodge itself. The Victorian manor house was set back from Bridge Street, behind a high brick wall with intimidating iron gates. The extended limbs of an old chestnut tree hung over the driveway, providing shade for an ancient Morris Minor Traveller parked next to a row of black Land Rovers.

"Which do you think is the Master's?" asked Giles.

"I think you'll find it is the Moggie," came a voice behind them.

Giles turned to see the rotund figure of the Master filling the entrance to the lodge.

"My children used to call him Bilbo, in honour of another famous traveller," he said. "We would squeeze the whole family inside for our summer holidays in Cornwall and, true to his namesake, the little chap always got us there and back again."

Giles smiled at the Tolkien reference, though none of the others did.

"Yes, well," said the Master, catching his eye, "here I am, letting you stand on the doorstep when I should be inviting you in for tea and seed cake. Come in, come in."

They filed up the steps and through the ornate Gothic doorway. Giles found himself in an entrance lobby filled with hooks that were covered in an assortment of coats and gowns. Opposite the front door itself, a portrait of Lady Margaret stared down at them from her gilt picture frame.

"Let us start with introductions," said the Master, closing the heavy oak door behind them. "I don't believe we have met, young lady?" He held out a pudgy hand, and Raquel took it.

"Hello, sir. My name is Raquel."

"Ah yes, the sister of Alfonso Vidal," he said, a look of genuine concern on his face. "I very much hope we can get to the bottom of what has happened to your brother. I realise how worried you must be."

Raquel nodded and the Master patted her hand before turning to Giles.

"And Giles. Glad to see you have been working on your Latin over the holidays. I enjoyed your performance in Hall the other night."

"Oh, that? Well, it had to be done," said Giles.

"Of course, in my day we all knew the College Grace by heart. Not because we were all Latin scholars, mind you. No, in those days, if your friends spotted a mistake in the Grace, they were entitled to claim a free pint from you in the

College Bar! Even the rugger buggers were silent and hanging on every word." He smiled at the memory, then stopped himself when he saw Nick with his black eye. "Oh, yes. I believe you play a bit, Mr Wood?"

"Now and again, Master," said Nick.

"Well, believe it or not, Nick, I used to turn out for the Redboys in my day."

"Really? What position?"

"Hooker," he said with a smile. "In those days, I used to like a good scrap. There again, don't we all?"

The Master gave Nick a wink and Giles saw the fresher's ears burn red. But before Nick could say anything, their host had moved onto his last guest.

"Nice to meet you, Annabel."

"And you, Master," said Annabel, smiling self-consciously.

"It seems that you have been having quite an eventful term. I hear that Brett Davis is on the mend."

"Oh, you know about that?"

"Accidents happen. I hope it hasn't put you off rowing. LMBC could do with some new blood. We are hoping the women can go to Head of the River in the next few years."

"Right," said Annabel.

"Anyway, come through to the living room, while I organise some refreshments. Have you had any coffee this morning?" He led them through a grand hallway, its walls hung with portraits.

"No, Master," said Giles, "I'm afraid I dropped a tray earlier."

"And I thought you had good hands, Giles, with all that climbing you and your friends do. You are still climbing, aren't you?"

"When I have time."

"Indeed." The Master stood to one side of a doorway, indicating that they should enter. "I'm always amazed at how much you pack into your days. And nights, of course," he said, giving Giles an appraising look.

Oh, crap, he thought. *He knows about R&R.*

"Make yourself comfortable," said the Master, "and then you can tell me everything you have been up to."

Comfortable was the last thing that Giles felt at that moment.

*****

Annabel entered the living room and flinched in the glare of the sunlight streaming in through the enormous south-facing windows. She shielded her eyes and, as they adjusted, found herself looking out onto the Master's Garden stretching out in front of her. The lawn was bordered by buildings, including the library, on one side and by the river on the other. In the distance stood the Bridge of Sighs, providing the lodge's occupants with one of the most breathtaking views in college.

She turned and found that the others had already headed over to a set of sofas either side of the large fireplace in the centre of the room. Its white marble surrounds contrasted with the oxblood-red of the walls and the dark-timbered ceiling, hung with a large brass candelabra. Annabel headed over to join them, glancing around at the portraits she assumed were former Masters, staring down at her from their gilt frames.

By pausing to admire the view, Annabel found that she was now the last to sit down. To her annoyance, Raquel had already taken the space next to Nick, so Annabel joined Giles on the nearest sofa. He gave her a brief grin, but looked distracted for once, his eyes following the Master as the portly figure walked over to the fireplace and tugged on a woven bell pull. A few moments later, a familiar-looking waitress appeared in the archway of the adjacent dining room.

"Ah, Aurelia, my dear. Would you bring us some coffee and tea? And cake, too, if we have any? We'll need plenty of sustenance for what we are about to discuss. Many thanks."

Aurelia swept out of the room, and their host turned back to face them.

"Before we begin, I have something to return," he said, walking over to a desk by the window and picking up a Ryder and Amies bag. He handed it to Nick.

"A new gown. I'm afraid the last one couldn't be repaired."

Nick stared at the contents of the bag and then up at the Master.

"How did…?"

"A friend of mine overheard you talking with Gareth Evans by the Corpus Clock. We've been following up on all sightings in the past few weeks."

"Sightings?" asked Annabel.

"You are not the only ones to have witnessed strange goings-on, my dear. Imagine my surprise one afternoon, to look out of these windows and see a winged statue in the middle of my lawn, and a few seconds later to find it gone."

Annabel looked across at Nick, who was watching her. He was silent, but his eyes said it all.

"Since then we have been looking for further evidence of the creature," the Master continued.

"When you say *we*, who do you mean, exactly?" asked Giles.

"An old student of mine, Jack Cummings. I was one of his supervisors when he read History here before he went on to do… other things. He's been in and around college for the last few weeks. You might have seen him around, as I asked him to keep an eye on you." He glanced at Annabel. "He sometimes wears a hoodie."

Annabel thought back to the man on the bridge who had pulled her and Brett from the water.

"That was Cummings?" she said, her mind reeling.

The Master nodded.

"I think I saw him at the hospital," said Nick.

Annabel turned to him.

"Outside your ward," Nick explained. "He left when I arrived."

Annabel stared at him as she tried to process all this. Her thoughts were interrupted by the doorbell.

"If I am not mistaken," said the Master, "that will be Jack with Professor Gupta."

He rose and left the room, his footsteps echoing from the

hallway. Annabel looked down at her hands, which were clenched tightly together as she thought back to that dreadful moment at the river. Later, in hospital, as she had been drifting back to consciousness, she had felt as if there had been some guardian angel watching over her. In some strange and mystical sense, Annabel had half hoped it had been her sister or parents reaching out to her. But now she knew the truth, that half-formed hope had died. The forces that had saved her were not from some other supernatural world. They were far more human and tangible. Genuine flesh and blood. And she was going to come face to face with him now.

"Annabel, are you OK?" Nick asked.

Annabel looked up and nodded, though in her heart she knew she was not. The deep, dark hole of loss was opening up within her again and she felt herself teetering on its edge. She tried not to look down into it, but she felt its inevitable pull, dragging her from the reality of the room in which she sat.

What would have happened, she never found out. At that moment there came a muffled exchange from the hallway and the sound of footsteps striding across the hallway floor. Annabel looked up and saw the others all turned towards the door. She spun around and saw the Master stride into the room.

"It seems I have misled you, Annabel," he said, his face grave. Behind him Professor Gupta limped stiffly into view, leaning on a walking stick and looking more hunched than usual.

"Professor?" cried Annabel, rising with the others at the sight of him.

The old man looked ashen-faced, and his shirt was covered in dried blood. He smiled briefly and swayed on his feet. Giles spotted the danger and was the first to react. He sprang across the room and grabbed the professor's arm, preventing him from toppling over and allowing him time to recover his balance.

"Thank you, Giles, that was good of you," said the old tutor.

"Here," said the Master, indicating a high-backed armchair by the fireplace. "Set him down in this, before he does himself an injury."

"Professor, are you hurt?" asked Annabel, going over to join him as Giles showed the professor to the chair. "Only your shirt…"

"What?" he said, looking down. "Oh, that. Don't worry, my dear, it is not mine. I am fine, thank you."

"You don't look fine," she said. "Can I get you something?"

"There's tea on the way," said the Master.

"Perfect, Master. Thank you."

The old man settled into the chair, which seemed far too big for his crumpled frame, and stared up at the others. "Please don't stand on my account. I'm fine. Honestly."

Annabel looked at Nick, who frowned but resumed his seat, Raquel following. She returned to the sofa with Giles while the Master sat in an armchair furthest away from the fireplace. She looked at Professor Gupta, who was staring around the room, taking in the others.

"You know everyone here, I take it, Professor?" said the Master.

"Yes," said the professor, smiling briefly at each of them. "I'm so sorry that I missed you this morning, but I was unavoidably delayed."

"I was just telling the others that I was expecting you and Mr Cummings to arrive together," said the Master. "I'm surprised he's not with you."

"I'm afraid Mr Cummings won't be coming, Master," said the professor.

"Why not? I sent him to fetch you personally."

The professor looked at the Master and said, "Mr Cummings won't be coming today because he's been shot."

*****

Nick heard Annabel stifle a sob when the professor dropped his bombshell. But what startled him most was the change in the Master. The genial host was gone, replaced by an assertive inquisitor.

"Shot? Where? When?"

"In All Saint's Passage, opposite the Main Gate," replied the professor. "It must have been around ten o'clock."

"Who shot him?"

"A man and a woman. I believe they were working as a team."

"How is he?" asked the Master, and Nick thought he detected genuine concern in his voice.

"He's lost a lot of blood. Annabel's grandmother

managed to stem the bleeding."

"Gran?" cried Annabel, her eyes growing wider still.

"She's fine, Annabel," said the professor, turning to her. "She came to our rescue and administered first aid. I don't know what we would have done without her."

"But where is she now?" asked Annabel, panic in her voice. "Why isn't she here?"

"She insisted on accompanying Mr Cummings to hospital. Neither the medics nor the police could persuade her to do otherwise," said the professor. "She is a remarkable lady, your grandmother."

Nick could picture Mrs Hamilton squaring up to a police officer and knew who his money would be on. He glanced over at Annabel and gave her a reassuring smile, which she returned, though her face looked almost as pale as the professor's. If ever she looked like she needed a hug, it was now. But his thoughts were interrupted by the Master, who spoke in such a deep, authoritative tone that everyone in the room turned to face him.

"Given this serious news, I think it is time that one of you explained to the professor and me what transpired in his room this morning."

"My room?" said Professor Gupta, confused. "What do you mean?" He looked at each of them, and his eyes rested on Nick.

"We had a run-in with some bloke called Julian."

"Julian Schiller?" said the professor.

"That's him," said Nick. "A complete git."

"Nick!" said Annabel.

"Yeah, well, he was," said Nick.

"Go on, Nick," said the Master.

For the next twenty minutes, Nick described their encounter in Professor Gupta's room. The others were mostly quiet, even Giles, who looked down at his shoes, his blond hair covering what appeared to be a slight glow in his cheeks when Nick described the role he played in overpowering Julian. It was only when Nick finished that Giles spoke up.

"Master, who is Jane, exactly?"

"I'm not at liberty to divulge that information," said the Master, his face a mask. "Let's just say that she has been on secondment to St John's to investigate Mr Schiller."

Giles considered this before replying. "Well, you might want to pass onto her that I saw Julian go with Professor Mackenzie to his room in New Court the night before he died."

Professor Gupta looked up sharply at that. "What?"

"When exactly was that?" the Master asked.

"Wednesday night," said Giles.

The two older men exchanged grim looks.

"If you'll excuse me, I need to make a phone call," the Master said, rising from his chair and striding across the room. When he reached the doorway, he turned. "And when I get back, Professor, I think it is time that you share with us everything you know about this affair. And I mean everything."

Chapter 27

Ravi watched as Aurelia brought in the tray and laid it on the coffee table. She smiled at him, but for once he found it hard to respond. The others were subdued as well. The atmosphere felt oppressive, despite the sun streaming through the windows.

Ravi felt dreadful. Had his friend been murdered? After what Julian and his people had done to him and Cummings this morning, Ravi had little doubt that the man was capable of anything. He was so lost in his thoughts that he started when the Master came back into the room.

"Thank you, Aurelia. You can go now. I have some matters I wish to discuss with the others."

Aurelia nodded and left the room, closing the door behind her. Ravi suddenly felt very alone.

"I've been speaking to Jane, who informs me that Julian is in custody, as are several of his staff. They are being charged with burglary, kidnap, assault and attempted murder. I think it is fair to say that they won't be bothering this college anymore."

His look of grim satisfaction was of little consolation to Ravi.

"How is Mr Cummings?" asked Annabel.

"Jane has been speaking with the hospital and tells me that Cummings' condition is critical," said the Master. "Mrs Hamilton is still with him."

Ravi closed his eyes and let out a long breath.

"So, I think, Professor," continued the Master, his tone brooking no argument, "the time has come to explain your part in all this."

They were all watching him, the Master, Giles, Raquel, Nick and Annabel. Each of them a witness to the horror that he and Robert had unleashed. Like Cummings, who now lay critically injured in intensive care, he knew that each of them had earned the right to hear the truth. With a shaking hand, he placed the cup and saucer on the table and sat back in his chair. It was time.

*****

"This all goes back to a time in the 1960s," began Ravi. "Robert, the Dean that is, and I were undergraduates. We were both reading Mathematics but I, like many at that time, was obsessed by the prospect of mankind travelling beyond our planet. The Cold War between Russia and the West was approaching its zenith, and the space race was well and truly on. Cambridge was in the thick of it. The Russian spies, Burgess, Blunt and Maclean, were only the tip of the iceberg. People were being approached left, right and centre and invited, persuaded or blackmailed to take sides in that titanic battle of ideologies."

Ravi looked up and found the Master studying him, his

brow furrowed. The others sat there waiting, their expressions a mix of excitement and curiosity.

"For some of you, it will be hard to imagine. There was a pervasive fear of war, one in which nuclear weapons would signal the opening salvo, not the final act. After the Cuban Missile Crisis, President Kennedy was keen to demonstrate the West's technological superiority over the Soviet Union by beating them in a race to the moon. They were like two street fighters trying to intimidate each other, flexing their muscles in public. The sense of imminent peril was palpable. Everyone was talking about it across the university, in common rooms, bars and halls."

He paused as he remembered some of the heated debates in smoke-filled bedsits. Friendships strained or sundered, otherwise rational people advocating extreme positions that only heightened the likelihood of global warfare.

"Madness," he said aloud, and the sound of his voice brought him back to the present.

"Anyway, Robert and I considered ourselves thinkers rather than idealists. As such, we refused to let ourselves be drawn into taking sides and preferred to tackle the problem with calm, logical thought. When we both graduated, we decided to stay on to study Astrophysics, and each of us retreated to our own areas of study, Robert to the physics lab, myself to the observatory.

"It was at this time that Robert started getting excited by some of the latest theories in quantum mechanics. In particular, something that had been written by an American academic at Princeton: a science fiction devotee called Hugh

Everett. Everett's field was quantum physics, and he had published a paper in 1957 on what he called 'MWI', or the Many Worlds Interpretation. In his paper, Everett argued for the existence of multiple universes that are parallel to our own. It was ridiculed by all the leading academics. I remember one of our heroes, Niels Bohr of the Copenhagen school, being particularly dismissive. It's funny how opinions change over time. In recent years Stephen Hawking has revisited Everett's work when developing his M-theory. As a result, Everett's ideas are no longer regarded with the derision with which they were received in the 1960s."

"Professor?" asked Annabel. "What has this got to do with the creature?"

"Forgive me, Annabel, I was drifting. In the 1960s, Robert wanted to investigate Everett's theory of multiple universes, but no one else in the Physics faculty was interested. They were obsessed with weapons systems and were getting huge levels of funding from the military to pursue that line of research instead. Destroy rather than discover."

He shook his head.

"Anyway, Robert sought me out at the Cavendish, probably just to get away from the claustrophobic atmosphere of his own faculty. But after a while, our conversations became more serious. And it was while we sat there gazing at the stars that we began talking about the possibility, the unimaginable possibility, that Everett was right. That there were indeed parallel universes. Apparently unconnected worlds that could be linked with ours in some way. Where we could travel from one to the other, without the need for ever more powerful rockets as delivery systems and all the risks that these brought."

"Of course, at that stage, at the Astronomy Institute, we were just beginning to understand the vastness of space. The mathematical probability that in the billions of galaxies and solar systems we had started to discover, there would be intelligent life. Sentient beings like us, sitting in a room like this, having a conversation, quite possibly drinking cups of tea. However improbable that may sound, the size of the universe made it a mathematical inevitability."

Looking up to gauge their reaction, Ravi found the same expressions of scepticism that he remembered from his former colleagues. Even from the Master, who was eyeing him with a look of concern. He sensed that the young people wanted to believe him, but he knew he was asking a lot, so he decided to take a different tack.

"Which famous physicist once said, 'Logic will get you from A to B, but imagination will take you everywhere'?"

"Einstein," said Giles.

"Excellent, Giles," said Ravi, nodding. "It was indeed Albert Einstein. We were inspired by his liberal philosophy. And that is why we started to look for it."

"Look for what?" asked Giles.

"A portal," said Ravi.

"A portal?" asked Raquel, looking confused.

"Yes, a portal. A door or gate," he explained, smiling.

"Oh, *sí*," she said.

"I don't understand, Professor," said Annabel. "A portal to where, exactly?"

"Why, a parallel universe, of course."

The room went very quiet, and Ravi lowered his eyes to stare at his hands. He was too afraid to look at the expressions of the people in that circle now. No doubt they would either think him a liar, or worse, insane. Instead, he merely waited, like a condemned man waiting to hear what his sentence would be.

"When did you find it, Professor?"

Ravi looked up in surprise at the person who had asked the question. Nick sat on the sofa a few feet from him, his expression open, interested even. *It's always the quiet ones*, he thought.

"We discovered it in 1969."

"Are you saying that you and Professor Mackenzie found a portal into a parallel universe in 1969?" asked Giles.

"Yes, Giles, we did."

Giles studied the professor. Then his face broke into a smile.

"Professor Gupta. That is seriously cool."

Ravi felt the knot in his stomach ease a fraction, and he found breathing a little easier.

"So how come we have never heard of it, Professor?" asked Annabel. She glanced around at the others. "I don't mean to sound disrespectful, really, I don't. It's just – something like that. It's not the sort of thing that people keep quiet about."

Ravi noticed Nick shift in his seat, apparently frustrated at her doubts, and decided to address her concern, which was perfectly valid.

"You make a good point, Annabel," he said before Nick could say anything. "When we set out on our quest, Robert and I wanted to shake everyone out of their obsession with the Cold War. People were being bent out of shape by fear. It was polarising. And as people became more and more frightened by each other, Robert and I felt that this would inevitably lead to someone making a terrible mistake."

He glanced at the Master, whose face was unreadable.

"We hoped that by finding a parallel universe we could put our own world's ideological posturing into some sort of perspective. We hoped to show that there were more important and more exciting opportunities for mankind than devising larger and more sophisticated ways of destroying ourselves."

"So why didn't you say anything?" asked Annabel.

Ravi smiled.

"Something happened in 1969 that made our research moot."

Ravi stopped and waited for one of them to work out the solution. It was Raquel who spoke first.

"We landed on the moon."

Ravi nodded.

"Thank you, Raquel. On 20th July 1969, Apollo 11 landed on the moon. A day later Neil Armstrong stepped off the ladder of the lunar module. One small step for man became one giant leap for mankind. And two days after that, while the crew of Apollo 11 was still travelling back to Earth, Robert and I discovered a portal to a parallel universe."

Ravi looked down at his hands, remembering his skin

caked in red dust, his nails bloody and torn. Robert and him sitting in their room, sunburnt and exhausted, their clothes ruined.

"That night, Robert and I went to The Eagle pub, in the footsteps of Watson and Crick. Their visit there in 1953 had been one of celebration for their discovery of DNA. For us, it was more of a funeral wake. We knew, of course, that following the moon landings, the whole purpose of our research had become redundant. NASA had provided the solution to the problem we were seeking to solve. By winning the space race, the prospect of the Russians taking on the Americans militarily had receded. The whole world began to look to space as the next challenge for mankind, not a turf war between nuclear powers. Once again, minds began to open themselves up to exciting scientific possibilities, and tensions over ideological differences could ease as everyone looked to the potential for mankind offered by the stars."

He smiled grimly.

"Robert and I realised that our research had become pointless in the end. It was strange, really. We had made one of the greatest discoveries in the history of science, only to find that there was something more important to do. Which was to bury it."

"But why, Professor?" asked Giles. "Your discovery would have made the moon landing look like a school outing!"

Ravi shook his head. He could not help the edge of bitterness creeping into his voice.

"The moon landing was a remarkable achievement. One that had given the West a technological and psychological upper hand. Revealing the existence of the portal here on earth would only have provided both sides with another arena over which to battle. Cambridge would become the focal point for forces that the college was ill-prepared to deal with. Governments and other nefarious forces would have crawled all over its lawns looking for some means of exploiting our discovery for strategic gain. The role of St John's as a beacon of education and learning would have been the first casualty."

There was silence in the room. It was a long time before anyone spoke. In the end, it was Annabel, her voice quiet.

"Professor, what did you find at the end of the portal?"

Ravi grimaced.

"Entities or creatures that couldn't be. That shouldn't be, at least not in our world."

He stared around at his circle of listeners, aware that most of them already knew what he was talking about.

"The creature that we saw yesterday was one of many I had seen from the world on the other side of that portal. They are natural hunters. And they do so in darkness."

"At night, you mean?" asked Nick, sitting forward on the sofa. He was more animated now than the professor had ever seen him.

"It has been mainly at night here, but in their world, I have seen these creatures use the shadow of a cliff face or the depths of a stream. Anywhere out of direct sunlight."

"Why is that?" asked Giles.

Ravi reached into his pocket and removed a curved grey object, the length of a finger. He held it up for them to see. "This is the tip of a talon that was torn from the creature last night. I found it snagged in my jacket when I got home."

He tossed the object on the coffee table and it rattled across the mahogany surface, coming to rest in front of Giles. He reached forward and took it, cradling it in his hands.

"It's quite heavy. Almost as if it's made of stone."

"Today it is inanimate stone, but I'm sure you will agree that last night it was very much alive. I have no idea why or how this transformation happens. In the dark they are as real and lifelike as you or me, but exposed to direct sunlight, the creatures become dormant, fixing limpet-like to a surface until the shadows return. When I first saw them, I mistook them for huge clumps of lichen, growing against cliff faces, or boulders clustered at the bottom of riverbeds. But once the shadows lengthened and covered their bodies, they stirred into life. And that is when I discovered a significant problem with conducting any further research. An obvious one, really."

Ravi looked around the room for suggestions. This time there were no takers, so he continued.

"While I was fascinated with the amazing world we had discovered and the creatures that inhabited it, I was unable to remove any specimens to bring back. You see, the portal emerged into their world from a fissure in a cliff face. And the passageway itself, or 'wormhole', as I like to call it, lies in darkness."

"So, if you tried to remove any specimens, they would be reanimated," said Giles.

"Precisely. Something these creatures wouldn't take kindly to, as I am sure you can imagine. In fact, using the passageway itself became enormously hazardous. The first time we ventured through the portal, one of the creatures tried to follow us. It was Robert who saved me. He managed to hold the passageway against it until I could close our end. After that, we feared to return that way, aware that it could be lurking somewhere in the darkness, lying in wait for us. If it had taken us before we had managed to seal the portal, I shudder to think what would have happened."

The room was still. It was as if no one dared breathe.

"So, if you didn't bring it, Professor," asked Nick, "how did the creature we saw get to be in our world?"

Ravi looked at the Master, who held his gaze. But before he could respond, Raquel spoke.

"I am sorry, but this creature," she said, frowning. "It is here in Cambridge?"

Ravi looked at her. "Yes, I believe it is."

"So, I am the only one not seeing it?" she asked, looking around at the others, who nodded.

"So why you are telling me this secret, Professor? Did Alfonso see this thing?"

The room was deathly quiet, and Ravi felt a weight settle in the pit of his stomach.

"Yes, Raquel, I believe he did," he said, thinking back to what Cummings had told him of that night in Portugal Street. "I now know that it was the creature who took your brother."

*****

Giles looked at Professor Gupta. The old man sat hunched in his chair, his hands clasped in his lap, his face a mask of remorse. It had cost him a lot to say those words.

Opposite him on the other sofa, Raquel sat frozen, staring at the old man. The rest of them sat in stunned silence.

"No, you are crazy!" Raquel yelled at the professor, jumping to her feet.

The old man did not flinch. Raquel rounded on the others.

"You are all crazy!"

Giles did not know what to say. He could not imagine what it would be like to hear something like this for the first time. Trevor and Ying had not believed him on the Wedding Cake, not even after the Bridge of Sighs, and they were friends. How could they expect Raquel to accept the word of virtual strangers?

"You say there are monsters!" she continued, her voice becoming more strident. "Here in Cambridge? That a monster killed my brother?"

Annabel tried to reason with her.

"Raquel, please listen. I know it's hard to believe, but we saw the creature attack the professor last night."

"No, this is crazy. You are crazy. All of you!"

She turned away from the sofas, skirted past the armchair by the window where the Master sat, and headed for the living room door.

"Miss Vidal, please," said the Master, rising.

But Raquel was beyond listening. She reached the door

and yanked it open, disappearing into the hallway.

The Master hurried after her, but Giles knew he wouldn't be able to intercept her in time. He sprang to his feet.

"Master," he said. "Leave it to me. I'll fetch her."

As he passed the Master, the older man placed a hand on his arm.

"Be quick, Giles. She must not speak of this to anyone."

Giles nodded and headed out into the hallway just in time to see Raquel disappearing through the front door, slamming it behind her. He rushed through the hall and yanked the heavy door open.

Outside he turned right and took the sandy pathway that led back into college, breaking into a run. A few seconds later he emerged from the passageway into Chapel Court. Looking around he saw Raquel running towards the entrance to Second Court.

"Raquel!" he called, but she ignored him.

Students leaving the library stepped back and stared as Raquel ran blindly on. Giles chased after her, cutting diagonally across the hallowed grass and ignoring the "Don't walk on the grass" sign.

Raquel disappeared into the passageway, and he bounded after her, narrowly avoiding an elderly couple who pressed themselves against the wall to allow him to pass. Emerging into Second Court, he saw her reach the crossroads at its centre and stop, unsure of which way to turn.

"Raquel!"

She turned, and the transformation of her face brought

him up short. The eyes that had been so proud and strong before were like those of a young girl, lost and afraid. Her flushed cheeks were wet with tears and her mouth quivered with emotion. She stared miserably at him as he walked towards her.

"Raquel," he said, softer now, holding his hands out wide to show he meant her no harm.

Raquel's shoulders sagged, and she bent forward, arms hugging her stomach as her face finally gave in to grief. In a few strides, Giles was there, wrapping his arms around her shaking shoulders and drawing her unresisting body against him.

Giles held her there as deep, wracking sobs reverberated from her ribs to his, her soft hair resting against his stubbly chin. He said nothing, mainly because he didn't know what to say. Giles had no siblings and barely had a family to speak of. How could he possibly express anything that would be of help? The best he could do right now was to wrap her in his arms and hold her close, safe in the heart of this timeless college.

How long they stood there, Giles never knew. He was vaguely aware of the people walking past, their hushed voices and the sound of the wind swirling around the courtyard. But these were as nothing compared to the sensation of this living, breathing soul who clung to him, trusting herself to his protection at this, her most vulnerable moment. It was something he had never experienced before, and he was affected by it in a way that was both surprising and disarming.

Giles had found patience he had not known he had. It

was a revelation to him that his role now was to wait, understanding it was for her to tell him when she was ready.

When Raquel did eventually stir, it felt to Giles like they were both waking from a dream. Her head leant back, and her face stared up at him. The tears had gone, replaced by dark smudges of eyeliner under watery eyes that stared into his. She opened her mouth to speak, and he smelt her breath for the first time.

"Thank you," she said.

Looking down, Giles noticed that grief had removed the proud mask Raquel had worn since he had first encountered her. With that gone, he saw a softness in her features that he hadn't seen before, and this only made her all the more beautiful in his eyes. As a consequence, Giles didn't dare open his mouth for fear of mumbling something incomprehensible. Instead, he remained silent and hoped that his eyes could communicate something of how he felt towards her at that moment.

Raquel let go of him to wipe her eyes, sniffling at the smear of mascara on the back of her hand.

"I am a mess, yes?"

"I've seen worse," he said, reaching forward and gently wiping away a smudge from one cheek. Raquel didn't resist.

"Listen," he said gently, "I think we need to head back and find the others. They'll probably be worrying about us. What do you think?"

"Is no need. See? They are coming."

Giles turned and saw the professor striding across the court towards them, Nick and Annabel following close behind.

Chapter 28

When he saw the couple standing in the middle of Second Court, Ravi felt a massive sense of relief. He had been worried that Raquel might have given Giles the slip or run into more members of Julian's team. Either way, he had been pleased when Nick, who was clearly frustrated at not being able to do something, spoke up.

"Master, would you like me to see if I can find them?"

The Master, who had been pacing up and down the room, looked at the clock on the mantelpiece.

"They do seem to be taking a long time," he said. "All right, Mr Wood. But I don't want you looking alone. Annabel, you go with him. But when you have found them, I want you all to return to the lodge."

"Of course, Master," said Annabel.

"And the creature?" asked Nick.

"No one is to do anything about the creature until we have come up with an agreed course of action," said the Master, looking at each of them. "There are forces at work that we do not fully understand, and as a college, our primary duty of care is to keep you all safe. Do you agree with me, Professor Gupta?"

"Absolutely. We shouldn't do anything until we have an agreed plan."

Ravi remembered how unhappy Nick had looked at this, and for a moment he thought the student might argue, but after a moment's hesitation, Nick nodded.

"In that case, Master," Ravi had said, rising from his seat, "I should like to return briefly to my room. If Julian Schiller has been searching my desk, I want to ensure he hasn't removed anything that could prove damaging to the college's reputation."

"What do you mean, Ravi? *Was* there anything?"

"I'm afraid so, Master. Though it may also prove useful in formulating our plan going forward."

"Then you had better hurry. In the meantime, I'll call Jane to find out whether Schiller has said anything. We are going to have to keep a lid on this thing or the press are going to have a field day!"

Ravi remembered the look on the Master's face as he let them out of the lodge. It was a mixture of anger and fear. They both knew how high the stakes were. Now, as he walked across Second Court towards the others, he wondered if the Master would ever forgive him. Not for his role in keeping the existence of the portal secret for all these years. On that score, Ravi felt he had nothing to be forgiven for. He had, after all, been acting in the best interests of the college. No, he hoped that one day the Master would forgive him for what he was about to do next.

As he approached Raquel, he noticed the protective way

Giles stood behind her. That was good. Perhaps the boy was finally beginning to grow up. If so, it wasn't before time. As for Raquel, he could tell from the blotchy complexion of her face that she had been crying.

"Raquel, I am so sorry…" he began.

"Is OK, Professor," she said, interrupting him. "You speak the truth. I know now."

She offered her hand. "We are good, you and me."

"Thank you, Raquel," he said, taking it. "That means a great deal to me."

"So, Professor, what now?" asked Giles.

Ravi thought back to the promise he had made to Cummings as he lay bleeding in the alleyway.

"We finish it."

"Yes!" said Nick, punching the air.

"But Professor," said Annabel. "You heard the Master. He specifically told us to take no action, and you agreed."

"Actually, Annabel, what I agreed with the Master was that I wouldn't do anything until we had a plan."

"But we don't have one yet, do we?"

"On the contrary, I do have a plan," said Ravi, tapping his temple. "The only question is whether we are all agreed on it."

"So, what's the plan, Professor?" asked Giles, with a grin.

"Let me be clear: I will only share this with you on the basis that you are under no compulsion to go along with it. There will be risks, and I quite understand if anyone decides they want no part of it. In which case, you are perfectly at liberty to return to the Master's Lodge, and I only ask that you keep its contents confidential until midnight. That said, any who do decide to take part will do so safe in the knowledge that I will take full responsibility for any consequences."

"Fair enough," said Nick, looking at Annabel. "It can't harm to hear the professor out, can it?"

"I suppose not," she agreed.

"Good. Well, then, the creature hasn't eaten for some time," Ravi said, careful to avoid looking at Raquel, aware of what the creature's last meal had most likely been. "So, we need to find its nest before it hunts again." He checked his watch. It had gone five o'clock. "It will be dark in an hour, so we don't have long."

"So, you don't think it has left for this other world?" asked Annabel.

"No. Professor Mackenzie wrote to me before he died and indicated he had closed the portal. I think, therefore, that the creature is still trapped in this one."

"Then we can hunt it here, yes?" asked Raquel.

"Yes, Raquel," said Ravi. "I believe we can."

Nick and Giles exchanged looks, and he knew they were on board, so continued.

"Let's start with the various sightings of the creature and see if we can see some sort of pattern. We could do with a map."

Giles reached into the back pocket of his jeans and pulled out a dog-eared book.

"Will this do? There's a plan of St John's inside."

Ravi took *The Roof-Climber's Guide to St John's* and

turned to the map in the Foreword as the others gathered around.

"There have been sightings in Portugal Place, the Master's Garden, New Court and on the Bridge of Sighs." He pointed to each location on the plan.

"It also tried to get me in Cripps," said Nick.

"And Jane said she saw it attack the Corpus Clock – that's over to the south," said Giles.

They looked at the different locations, which covered all points of the compass in and around the college.

"That means we are looking for somewhere high up, where the creature can hide during the day, and hunt from at night."

"Like that, you mean?" said Annabel.

Ravi looked at her and saw that she was pointing over his shoulder. He turned and saw the massive bulk of the Chapel Tower looming high above them.

"Yes, Annabel," said the professor. "Just like that."

"So, the creature could be up there right now?" asked Giles.

"Quite possibly," said Ravi, wondering why he hadn't thought of it before.

"In a dormant state, because it's still light?" said Nick.

"In all likelihood, yes."

"So, we go hunt it now," said Raquel.

"That would be my suggestion," said Ravi, turning to look at the one person who was silent.

Annabel was staring up at the tower.

"How exactly do we get up there?" she asked.

"There is a stairwell," said Ravi. "The choir uses it to gain access to the roof to sing on Ascension Day each year."

"The choir sings from up there?" asked Annabel.

"For over a hundred years," said Ravi.

"It's true," said Giles. "Started over a wager, apparently." Annabel looked at him, and he shrugged. "Scout's honour."

"What if the creature's not there?" she asked.

"Then," said Ravi, "we will have ruled out the most likely location in the college, which is something I'm sure the Master will be relieved to hear."

"And if it is, what then?"

"If Giles is happy to lend us his climbing ropes, we will tie it down and report back to the Master. He can then deploy whatever resources he has at his disposal to deal with it."

Ravi was thinking about the row of black Land Rovers outside the Master's Lodge. He had little doubt that Jane and her colleagues had more than Hunter wellies in the back of them.

Annabel remained quiet while the others watched and waited. She apparently had misgivings, and he supposed it came down to whether she trusted him or not. After what seemed an age, she turned to him and gave him a determined look that reminded Ravi of her grandmother.

"In that case, Professor, I agree. We have a plan."

"I knew it!" said Nick, wrapping an arm around Annabel's shoulders and squeezing her against him.

"Ow!" she said, smiling. "Don't go injuring me just yet. I've got a tower to climb."

"Thank you, Annabel," said Ravi, relieved. Overhead, storm clouds were building up, and the sky appeared noticeably darker already. "Giles, take Raquel and get your climbing equipment, please. The rest of us will collect the tower key from the Porter's Lodge. We'll meet you at the main entrance to the Chapel in First Court."

"Right you are," said Giles.

The two of them ran off towards his stairwell, while Ravi led Nick and Annabel to the Porter's Lodge. There they found Bert, watching the clean-up operation in All Saints Passage on the CCTV cameras.

"Terrible business, Professor," said the porter, indicating the cameras. "Helluva mess."

"Bert, could I trouble you for the key to the College Tower?"

"It's a bit late to be climbing the tower, Professor. It'll be dark soon. Not sure what sort of view you'll get now."

"All the more reason to hurry, while there is still light," said Ravi.

Bert looked at him and then the others, both of whom were freshers and wouldn't have been up before. He went over to a rack on the back wall and removed a large key with a red tag on it.

"There you go. There's a light switch on the left as soon as you enter. But you might want to take this as well." Reaching under the counter, Bert took out the torch he carried with him on his rounds. "Might come in handy."

"Thank you, Bert," said Ravi. "I will return both when we are finished."

"Right you are," said the porter.

Ravi led the others back to First Court, where they found Giles and Raquel waiting for them. Giles had a rucksack over one shoulder with the broken ice axe strapped to it.

Giles saw him looking at the axe. "You never know, Professor. Could come in handy."

Ravi led them towards the Chapel's main entrance, where he stopped by a small arched doorway set back in the wall. Its weathered wooden door had a rusty keyhole. He inserted the key and twisted until he heard a loud click. With a shove, the door swung inwards on rusty hinges to reveal a narrow spiral staircase twisting up out of sight in a clockwise direction. Ravi caught a stale, musty smell that suggested the stairwell hadn't been used for a while. Fumbling inside the doorway, he found the light switch that illuminated the stone steps with a dim orange light.

Ravi turned to the others, who were gathered around the entrance.

"Now remember. We have no idea what we will find up there. There may be nothing, of course. But if the creature has been nesting there, we may find all sorts of remains."

He looked at Raquel, who caught his meaning. Her face went pale, but her expression was resolute.

"*Sí*, I understand," she said. "I am ready."

"I'm with Raquel," said Giles.

"And me," said Annabel.

"Let's finish this," said Nick.

Ravi smiled at them all. "Very well," he said. "It will be getting dark soon, so we don't have much time."

Giles nodded and, reaching into his backpack, retrieved a headtorch, which he pulled over his blond hair.

"The first stairwell is quite wide until we get to the Chapel roof," continued Ravi. "From the roof, we have to cross over to the main tower itself. Leave a sufficient gap between you, as it is easy to stumble on the steps. As you have the backpack, Giles, I suggest you and Raquel bring up the rear. Nick and Annabel, you follow me. Ready?"

They nodded in unison.

"Very well then."

Ravi ducked under the low doorway and began to climb.

Chapter 29

Annabel followed the professor into the stairwell, aware of Nick's reassuring presence behind her. The professor led at a steady pace. He did not turn his torch on as there was sufficient light from the lamps set at regular intervals in the wall. The stone steps were broad and well maintained. Every couple of turns there was a window, reminiscent of the defensive slits in castle keeps. In the gathering gloom, it was still possible to see the green lawn of First Court below them, the foundation stones of the former Chapel clearly visible in the turf.

Annabel tried not to think about what they would find when they reached the top of the tower. If the professor was right, and this was where the creature had been hiding throughout the day, she hoped he was also right that it would still be in its dormant state. How they would secure it there, Annabel had no idea, but the others seemed set on doing something, so best to go along. But in her heart of hearts, she hoped they were all wrong, and there would be no trace of the creature, its nest or any other remains in the tower so they could return to the Master's Lodge and leave it to someone else to sort out. Either way, she wanted to get up and down as quickly as possible, even if it meant disappointing Nick and the others. Wherever the creature was, standing exposed on the tower as darkness fell would be asking for trouble.

She was so immersed in these thoughts that when the professor stopped climbing, she almost bumped into the back of his legs. Behind her, Nick's head butted against her calves, and he murmured an apology. The others stopped climbing too, and the stairwell fell silent.

Looking past the professor, Annabel could see they had arrived at a small circular landing at the top of the stairwell, illuminated by the dim light shining through a pair of viewing slits cut into the wall. These framed a large wooden door, which was bolted from the inside. But that couldn't prevent the rank smell of decay seeping into the confined space from somewhere outside.

"Professor?" she whispered, wrinkling her nose. "What is that?"

"I'm not sure, but it's coming from the other side of the door," he whispered back.

The professor stepped onto the landing and motioned for her to join him. There wasn't a lot of room, but she did so and turned to see Nick's head appear in the stairwell behind her.

"I'm going to open the door to check outside," said the professor. "Don't follow me just yet. I may need space to duck back inside. Is that understood?"

Annabel looked back down at Nick, and they both

nodded. As the professor began to unbolt the door, Annabel positioned herself behind him, making sure he had enough space to swing it open. Holding his large torch in one hand, the professor gave her one last look and pulled the door open.

The stench wafted into the stairwell, and Annabel gagged as she tried to cover her nose and mouth with her hand. The professor grimaced but kept shining his torch out of the doorway towards the roof space beyond. After a few seconds, he took a step forward and disappeared from view. Annabel heard Nick shift on the stairs, but she held out a restraining hand, mindful of the professor's instructions.

"It's all right," said the professor. "You can join me now."

Still holding her hand over her face, Annabel peered around the doorway and saw the professor standing on a walkway of plastic duckboards that lay between the steep tiled roof of the antechapel to her left and a stone balustrade looking over First Court to her right. The professor stood a few strides further along the walkway, looking up at the Chapel Tower rising above him, then down at a dark object lying at his feet.

"What's that the professor's looking at?" whispered Nick, who had joined Annabel on the landing and was peering over her shoulder through the doorway.

"It's a dead squirrel," said the professor. "One of many, it would seem."

Annabel edged forward and stepped carefully along the walkway, using the parapet on her right as a handhold. She followed the beam of the professor's torch and gasped into

389

her hand when she saw what lay there.

The circle of light revealed a collection of half-eaten torsos that had collected in the walkway like discarded leaves in a gutter. While the poor creatures were apparently dead, Annabel could still see movement from the bodies. Peering closer, she almost retched when she spotted the pulsating mass of maggots writhing in their entrails. They had found the source of the foul smell.

"That's rank," said Nick.

They heard a gasp from behind them and saw that Raquel had emerged onto the roof and was staring wide-eyed at pile at their feet, her hand over her mouth.

"Dead animals," said Annabel quickly, realising that Raquel may have thought it was something else. A look of relief and revulsion spread over the young woman's face.

"Up here, so high?" she said.

The professor looked up at the tower rising above them and then at the steep roof to their left.

"I think they may have fallen from up there," he said, indicating the tower and then the dark stains running down the tiles with his torch. Annabel looked up and saw a monstrous face leering down at her. She had a sharp intake of breath and would have screamed but for Nick's timely intervention.

"Using that gargoyle as a perch, do you think?" asked Nick.

"Probably," said Giles, who had now joined them on the walkway.

Annabel stared at one of the four stone gargoyles jutting

out into the early evening sky from the corner of the tower roof. Her heart rate, which had peaked seconds earlier, eased slightly as she saw the figure for what it was. Relieved that she hadn't given herself away in front of them all, she managed to cover her shock by commenting on the pile of carcasses that littered this section of the roof.

"Ugh! This is disgusting."

Nick placed a reassuring hand on her shoulder, and she was surprised how much strength that gave her.

"We need to hurry," said the professor. "It's getting dark, and given the evidence here," he indicated the mutilated bodies, "I think there's a good chance that the creature's eyrie is indeed on the tower."

He looked at Giles. "We'll need to empty that backpack here, Giles. The stairs on the next stretch are very narrow. We will have to carry the equipment between us."

Giles opened the backpack and removed the ropes, looping one over his shoulder like a bandolier and passing the other to Nick, who did the same. He then divided the slings and carabiners between them and unclipped the ice axe, which he looped around his wrist. Looking up, he caught Annabel's eye and gave her a wink.

He's actually enjoying this, she thought.

"Good," said the professor, looking up at the sky. "There is still enough light, but we will have to move fast. If the creature is still dormant, we will need to get those ropes around it and tied to the roof as quickly as possible."

Annabel looked across at Raquel, who had a haunted look on her face and didn't appear to be paying the professor much attention. Annabel suspected that the prospect of finding whatever remained of her brother up there was weighing heavily on her mind.

"I'll go with Raquel," she said, and the young woman looked at her. "We girls have to stick together," she added.

"You and me then, Nick," said Giles.

"Got it," said Nick.

"Good," continued the professor. "I shall help out where needed. Now, remember, all of you. As soon as the creature is tied down, we head back down the stairwell. No hanging around. No trophy hunting. No selfies," he said, staring at one person in particular.

"What are you looking at me for?" asked Giles in a mock tone of innocence, making them all smile, breaking the tension.

"And if it is awake?" asked Nick.

The professor frowned.

"Then we return down the stairwell and report to the Master. There is nothing else we can do. Is that understood?"

The professor was looking at Nick now, who returned his stare.

"Understood," he said.

"In that case, let's get going," said the professor, turning and heading for a small arched doorway at the far end of the walkway. Nick and Giles followed while Annabel waited for Raquel.

Just before she ducked through the doorway, Annabel glanced up one more time at the tower. As she did so, the glow of the dipping sun in the west turned a darker shade and Annabel shuddered as the sandstone surface of the Chapel was transformed into a crimson column, rising high above the college.

Chapter 30

Giles stayed focused on the professor's shoes moving a few feet above him, lit by the light from his headtorch. Every now and then the blade of his axe would catch the rough sandstone wall and make a ringing sound. His shoulders brushed the sides of the stairwell, and he wondered how someone as broad as Nick was managing behind him.

Above him, the professor's feet kept up their steady pace, but Giles could hear the old man's breathing becoming more laboured. He also became aware of something else. It was an aroma, sickly sweet and more pungent than the one they had experienced earlier, strengthening with every step they climbed.

"Giles, can you smell that?" came Nick's voice.

"It wasn't me," he replied, but Nick didn't laugh.

Giles tried not to think about what might have caused the smell. He had never seen a dead body before, though he suspected that was about to change. His thoughts turned to Raquel and how fragile she seemed. He hoped that whatever they found on the tower, she could hold it together until they had dealt with the creature.

Ahead of him, the scrape of the professor's shoes began to slow, and finally, they stopped moving altogether as he paused on the step above Giles. Giles looked up, his headlamp illuminating the bottom of a wooden door. The professor was staring down at him, his face calm, but his eyes bright in the dark. He held a finger to his lips. Giles nodded and, twisting to look down at Nick a few steps below him, he made a similar gesture. Nick nodded and followed suit.

Giles turned back to the professor and gave him a thumbs-up.

The old man held up three fingers. Giles understood.

He turned to Nick.

"We go on three," he whispered. Nick nodded.

Giles turned back to the professor. The old man closed one finger.

"One," whispered Giles.

A second finger closed.

"Two,"

Then the third.

"Three!"

The professor pulled open the door, and crimson light flooded the stairwell. This was followed by a stench so foul that Giles had to cover his mouth to prevent himself from gagging. Squinting against the glare, he watched as the professor stood there for a moment, his hunched body framed in the doorway. Then he took a step forward and disappeared from view. Giles didn't hesitate. He leapt up the last steps and sprang out through the door, axe in hand. Half blinded by the glow from the setting sun, he almost bumped into the professor standing only a few feet from the opening, his diminutive frame rooted to the spot. Moments later, Nick and the others emerged from the stairwell and fanned out either side of them. They, like the professor, just stood there in stunned silence, taking in the enormity of the entity in front of them.

"*Maré de Dieu*," breathed Raquel.

Squatting motionless between the pinnacles and balustrades of the Chapel Tower was a massive stone statue filling the space. Its back was towards them, shoulders bunched between enormous wings that were spread out flat across the broad expanse of the roof. Somewhere, buried beneath its body, were its head and neck, tucked out of sight, hidden from view.

If this was the same animated creature they had grappled with the night before, the transformation was astonishing. Plumage that had flexed and shifted to propel it through the air was now as stiff and unyielding as fossilised stone. The glossy black feathers that had cushioned Giles' fall from the bridge were now a dull grey granite, their colour matching that of the lead-lined roof. But the chameleon-like blending into its background could not disguise the sheer bulk of the creature before him. It had seemed monstrous when he had encountered it flying above the college buildings, but here in this confined space, its scale was genuinely terrifying.

"I believe we have found your statue, Nick," said the professor.

"Yeah, that's the one," Nick replied.

"I'm so sorry, Nick," whispered Annabel. "I had no idea."

The sound of the others' voices broke the spell that had rendered Giles motionless since he had run out of the stairwell. He dragged his eyes away from the statue and looked down at the surface of the roof and the vast amount of debris that seemed to be scattered everywhere.

"Professor?" he said, reaching up for his headlamp. "Is this a nest we're standing in?"

The beam of white light illuminated the tangled structure that lay around their feet, which until then had been hidden in the shadows cast by the tower's balustrade. When Giles saw what it was made of, his stomach churned.

"Oh, no…" he said, revolted.

Instead of twigs and branches, the nest was made of bones. Carcasses of all types of creature had been strewn across the surface of the roof and piled up around the statue. Most were small: rodents, rabbits, ducks and cats mainly. But there were larger ones too. Giles could make out geese, dogs and even deer. The stench of rotting flesh was overpowering, and he could see flaps of tissue and fur wedged between the bones, staining the structure with dark, dried blood.

Giles looked at the others, who, like him, were staring at the ground with a mixture of horror and revulsion. All except Raquel, who was no longer there.

Panicking, Giles looked back at the empty doorway and was about to run after her when he heard an anguished moan from the far side of the roof. He spun around and spotted a slender figure kneeling next to the spire on the far corner of the tower. It was Raquel. And she was staring at an object on the ground.

"Oh no," he said, breaking into a run.

Raquel reached forward, and with deliberate care, picked the object up. In the shadow of the spire Giles couldn't make it out at first, but as he grew near, the glow from his headtorch briefly illuminated the tattered bundle she held out in front of her.

"Oh, Raquel," he said.

It was a leather jacket. Or had been. Now it was shredded, its material in tatters. Giles could see the jagged rips running down the front and back. Raquel reached into the pocket, removed a shattered Nokia phone and just stared at it.

"It is his," she said, her voice dull, almost matter-of-fact. "I bought it for him. In Palma. Before he leaves."

"Raquel, I'm so sorry," he said.

Giles heard someone approaching. It was Annabel. She touched him lightly on the arm as she passed.

"Giles, I've got this. You are needed with the others."

Annabel squatted down next to Raquel, putting her arm around the woman's shoulders. Giles saw Raquel's body begin to shake as she bent forward and buried her head in the bundle of torn leather. Annabel turned to him.

"Go!" she mouthed silently.

Giles glanced back towards the stairwell and saw Nick and the professor uncoiling one of the ropes. He took one more look at Raquel, lost in her grief, her muffled sobbing painful to hear. Annabel was right. There was nothing he could do here. Nodding, he turned and ran back to the others.

"Giles, good," said the professor. "We need your help in securing the ropes. We haven't got long."

Giles looked over the hunched shoulders of the creature at the western sky. There was a thick canopy of storm clouds overhead, and in the distance, he could see the darkening sun dipping behind the distant University Library, its massive square tower casting a long, dark shadow towards them.

"Right," he said, slipping the coil of rope he had been carrying from his shoulder and shifting his focus back to the task at hand. Giles looked at the statue, its wings splayed out across the nest, its head buried out of sight.

"We'll need to loop a rope around its neck and wings to make a yoke," he said, "then we need to fix it to something to stop it getting airborne."

He scanned around the tower for something that could act as an anchor point, but the leaded roof was smooth and free of anything that he could attach it to. That only left the stone balustrade. It was five feet high and had narrow arches supporting the top railing. This had a metal cover running along its length from which stainless-steel rods ran diagonally inside to fixing points in the roof, preventing the balustrades from toppling down into the courts below. These were as good as they were going to get.

"If we can make run lines from the yoke to the balustrade and pull them tight, we can keep the creature flat to the roof, and it won't be able to generate enough lift with its wings."

The professor nodded. "Agreed."

Nick had his rope ready. "Fine. Where do we start?"

Giles had half hoped that one of them would have protested and come up with a better plan. He wasn't entirely convinced that this one would work. Still, there was nothing for it now.

"Give me that rope, Nick. I'll make it fast to the statue first, while there's still time."

"Hurry," said the professor, looking towards the west. "The light will be gone soon."

Giles took the rope in one hand, and with the ice axe in the other, approached the creature from behind. Ignoring the sickening sound of what he hoped were animal bones crunching under his shoes, he kept his eyes fixed on the gap between its shoulders, waiting for the head to appear or for any other indication that the creature was about to stir.

When he reached the wing, he placed his hand on top of the plumage to lever himself up.

"Ouch!"

"What is it?" asked the professor, alarmed.

Giles looked down and saw that one of his fingers was bleeding. The serrated edge of the feathers had cut through his skin like a bread knife.

"It's nothing," he said, sucking his finger. "Just a bit clumsy, that's all."

Looking down at the edge of the wing, he also noticed that his blood had been absorbed by the surface like a sponge.

"Probably not a good sign," he said to himself and glanced at the shoulders again. Nothing moved.

Carefully, he lifted a foot and placed it on top of the

wing. It felt solid enough. Trying to imagine this was no more than a stone boulder, Giles eased himself up and placed his other foot alongside the first. He hardly dared breathe. At any moment, he expected the creature to explode into motion, throwing him over the nearby balustrade to fall to his death on the cobbled courtyard hundreds of feet below. But nothing happened. The wing didn't so much as twitch.

Trying to control the urge to leap clear and head for the stairwell, Giles took another tentative step, and then another, until he was standing at the apex of its hunched shoulders. There he squatted down, noticing with grim satisfaction a ragged pattern between the feathers, testament to the damage done by his axe the night before. Taking a firm grip on its handle once again, Giles breathed out slowly, before peering over the shoulders. There, at the end of the arched neck, he finally saw the creature's head. To his immense relief, this was pointing away from him, down at the nest, its hideous features hidden and as still as the rest of its body.

Giles needed both hands free now, so with some reluctance, he clipped the axe to a carabiner on his belt and began making a bowline with the rope. He carefully dropped the noose over the motionless head and pulled so that it was tight against the thick neck. Then he edged back down the damaged spine, ensuring that he kept the rope tight.

"Nick," he called out. "I need you to take this and run it under the wing and back to its head."

Nick came forward and took the coil of rope.

"And mind those feathers. They're razor-sharp."

Nick nodded and did as he was told, working his way around the wing, looping the rope underneath it as he did so. Giles moved back to the top of the shoulders and took the line from him, noticing Nick staring at the bowed head of the creature with suspicion. Giles tied the cable to the bowline around its neck, seeing as he did so a slight give in some of the feathers when he pulled the knot tight.

"Now the other side," he said, trying to remain calm and prevent his growing sense of unease creeping into his voice. Nick skirted back around the wing and tail of the creature as Giles hurried down its back and handed the rope to him. This time Nick ran the cord under the other side and returned it to Giles, who made it fast to the bowline, ensuring that they now had a yoke around its neck and torso.

"Right, that should do it," he said. "Now to attach it to the roof!"

He took the rest of the rope with him as he retreated down its back, where he and Nick joined the professor.

"Professor, we'll need your help for the next bit."

"I am yours to command."

They headed for the balustrade overlooking Chapel Court, where Giles briefed them on what they were going to do.

"I'm going to put a sling around this balustrade, and I need you to run the rope through it until it is tight and hold it fast. Then the other one is going to take the line to the far side of the tower and do the same thing there, before bringing the end back to the creature, where I will attach it to the yoke. That way it will be secured between the two balustrades. If we have time, we can then use the other rope to do the same thing again as a safety. Understood?"

"Understood," they said.

Giles looped a sling off his neck, hung it around the balustrade and attached it with a carabiner. The professor fed the rope through the metal fastening and pulled it tight so that it was taut from the yoke to the balustrade. Then Nick took the line and ran with Giles to the other side of the roof, where he attached a similar sling to the balustrade there. Nick pulled it tight, taking up the slack from the professor on the other side of the tower, who stepped clear of the taut line.

"OK, I'll take the remainder and tie it to the yoke," said Giles. "That should hold our feathered friend flat against the roof. When we've done that, we can get the other rope on as a safety."

"Got it," said Nick, leaning back to maintain the tension against the sling.

Giles picked up the final length of rope and ran back to the creature, ignoring the crunching underfoot as he leapt for the wing. But when his feet hit the surface, he felt something give and, with a fearful CRACK, he pitched forward and fell.

"Giles!" cried the professor, running from the other side of the roof towards him, while Nick held the rope tight.

Giles pushed himself up from the creature's back, expecting to find himself lacerated by the sharp-edged plumage. To his amazement, his clothes and skin were scuffed in places but mostly unscathed. That could not be said for the wing he had leapt on a few seconds before. A section of feathers almost a metre in length had snapped off, leaving a ragged V in the wing structure. As he got to his feet, he noticed the missing section lying forlornly in the broken bones of the nest. Even as he watched, the granite-like feathers grew paler and lost their previous definition, their surface becoming calcified and flaky before crumbling into dust.

"Giles!" said the professor. "Are you all right?"

"I'm OK, Professor," he said, pointing at the gap and the pile of dust underneath. "But the wing isn't. Look!"

The professor stared down at the damaged wing. Shadow was spreading like an ink stain across the feathers, some of which were beginning to stir and flutter in the evening breeze.

"Professor, I think it's time to get the others off the roof," said Giles, looking over his shoulder towards the horizon, marked only by a thin red line as darkness descended. "Nick will hold the line tight while I make this end fast."

"Yes… Right," said the professor, backing away.

Giles turned and ran up the creature's back. He knelt down, his knees sinking into the yielding plumage as he fumbled for the yoke. His hands brushed the exposed hide through the rent in its feathers. The leathery surface was warm.

"Oh, crap," he said.

As if alerted by his touch, a shudder ran through the creature's body as muscles flexed across its massive back. Inch by inch, the neck in front of him uncurled from its resting state, and the monstrous head that had remained hidden until now extended itself upwards towards the storm-darkened sky.

"Oh, crappity-crap," breathed Giles.

They had run out of time.

Chapter 31

Nick was still holding the rope when he heard Giles swear. Glancing over his shoulder, he watched in horror as the creature's neck began to unfurl with Giles still squatting transfixed on its back.

"Giles! Get out of there!" he yelled.

This seemed to wake Giles from his trance.

"Right," he said, looking down at the rope in his hands. "Just one more knot..." he mumbled and began fumbling again with the yoke.

Nick saw the creature's head begin to turn and was about to let go of the rope and run to help his friend, when he saw a movement out of the corner of his eye that stopped him in his tracks.

The professor was striding around the far side of the tower, past the outstretched wing and into the creature's forward arc. If that wasn't startling enough, he was also waving his arms in the air in an uncoordinated windmill motion. The beast must have noticed him too, because its head stopped turning towards Giles and instead swung round to follow the old man's bizarre-looking antics. The professor continued until he was standing right in front of the creature, where he began to shuffle from foot to foot, his fists raised, like some sort of boxer.

"You've got to be kidding," Nick moaned, bracing himself against the rope, expecting the creature to lunge forward at any moment. But for some strange reason, it seemed mesmerised by the diminutive figure cavorting before it. Nick felt a tug on the rope and realised that Giles had managed to get a half hitch on the yoke and was desperately trying to complete the knot while his mount was distracted. With a surge of hope, Nick thought they might just do it, after all. And that was when disaster struck.

Whether the professor was finally beginning to tire, or his luck had merely run out, the old man chose that precise moment to miss his footing. With a yell of surprise, he pitched backwards, kicking up a cloud of bones and landed with a painful bump. There he sat for a few seconds, looking up at the monster, which stared down at him, perhaps as surprised as he was, before its predatory instincts took over. Bending its head low towards the prone figure, it let out a deep, ominous growl. The colour seemed to drain out of the professor's face as, feet scrabbling for purchase on the slippery surface, he began shuffling backwards across the roof, while at the same time reaching for something in his jacket pocket.

Nick felt helpless, his hands still gripping tightly to the rope.

"Giles!" he yelled. "Now would be good!"

"Almost done…" groaned Giles, desperately trying to secure the knot.

The monster flinched, registering perhaps for the first time that it was carrying a passenger. At the same moment, the professor finally managed to extract from his pocket the large torch Bert had given him and, pointing it up into the creature's distracted face, depressed the switch.

The beam of light was dazzling against the blackness of the night sky, but its impact on the creature was nothing short of blinding. Its head recoiled as if it had been hit with a hammer, slamming into Giles and knocking him from its back like a rag doll. Carabiners, slings and ice axe went flying into the air as he landed heavily on the roof and skidded across its surface, throwing up a bow wave of bones.

The creature reared against the tension in the rope, and the knot Giles had just been working on came loose, its end whipping back towards Nick and missing him by inches. The line on the far balustrade still held and as the monster tried to rise it was jerked sideways, causing it to overbalance and crash into one of the spires, screeching in frustration and alarm. To his amazement, Nick saw the professor continue to advance on the creature with his torch held in front of him, focusing the beam on its eyes. The beast screeched again, louder now, as it regained its footing and thrust up with its sturdy legs, straining against the yoke to launch itself into the air.

Nick looked on in awe as the crumpled old academic, looking so small and fragile compared to the monster towering over him, continued to advance towards it. And then, for some unknown reason, the professor hesitated, distracted by something in the nest. As Nick watched in horror, the old man lowered the beam of the torch onto a spherical object lying amongst the heaped circle of bones.

"What the...? No, Professor!" he yelled. "Get out of there!"

But the old man just stood there transfixed, and the creature's eyes, no longer blinded by the powerful torchlight, turned back to its tormentor, now only a few feet away.

Nick looked down at his feet and saw the frayed end of the climbing rope lying there, still looped through the sling on the balustrade. Reaching down, he grabbed it and sprinted towards the eagle, hauling the rope with him. The line straightened, stretched and then twanged like a bowstring from one balustrade to the other before biting against the yoke attached to the raptor's back. Rather than pouncing on the professor, Nick saw the eagle stagger backwards on unsteady legs, slip on the leaded roof and crash once more in a cloud of feathers. Nick leant into the rope, using it as a pulley to pin the eagle against the ground. He hoped he could hold it there while the professor made his escape. But the old man just stood there, looking at the nest.

"Professor!" he shouted.

Then Annabel was next to him, hauling on the rope as well.

"I'm with you, Nick!" she said, gasping.

Nick heard footsteps behind him and there was Giles, blood streaming from what looked like a broken nose, grabbing the rope and heaving alongside them. With three of them pulling, the creature was yanked back once more, staggering against the far balustrade.

"Professor!" yelled Nick again. "Get out of there!"

But instead of fleeing for his life, to Nick's disbelief, the professor stepped into the nest.

"What are you doing?" he yelled in frustration.

The creature, too, was staring at the old man and screeching in rage. The professor ignored them both and reached down. When he rose, he had something cradled in his arms. Nick could hardly believe what he was seeing. It was a spherical object, its surface marbled in black and grey.

"Nick!" said Annabel, straining beside him. "I think that's an egg!"

"Oh, shit!" he replied.

"Mum's not going to be happy about that," added Giles.

With a screech that could have woken half the college, the monster leapt at the professor. Nick felt the rope lurch, and he almost lost his footing as he and the others were tugged towards the restraining sling. Nick wedged his trainers against a ridge in the leaded roof and hauled back on the rope like the anchorman in a tug of war competition. The line tore at his palms, and he grunted with pain and effort. The strain was incredible, and he knew they wouldn't be able to hold on much longer, but before he could yell a warning to the professor, he heard Giles cry out.

"Raquel, no!"

Risking a glance over his shoulder, Nick saw Raquel retrieve something shiny from the floor of the roof. It glinted in the light of Giles' headtorch, and he realised it was the ice axe, which had been lying forgotten after Giles had been thrown from the creature's back. Nick saw the look on

Raquel's face as she stood, axe in hand, glaring at her brother's killer, straining against its restraint.

"*Puta!*" Raquel yelled and charged.

Nick could only watch in disbelief as the girl leapt over bones and closed on the creature. Had it seen her coming she would have had no chance, but it was so fixated on the professor holding its egg that it did not notice her until the last moment. By the time it did, Raquel had raised the axe above her head and, with a scream of pure hatred, buried the blade in the monster's neck.

The creature screeched in anger and pain, drowning out Raquel's yell of fury. But as she tugged at the axe to free it for another blow, the monster swung its head round in a devastating arc and slammed it into her chest. Raquel was flung back, axe in hand, dark blood spraying from the blade as she crashed into the floor.

"Raquel!" cried Giles.

At that moment, there was a terrible cracking sound and the sling attached to the far balustrade tore the steel restraining rod from its mountings in a shower of sandstone and dust. In an instant, the rope went slack, and Nick stumbled backwards, tripping on Annabel's outstretched foot. She yelled in pain as all three of them fell to the ground. As they disentangled themselves from each other, Nick looked across at the creature. Like them, it had stumbled when the balustrade collapsed, but now it was rising to its feet, arching its back and standing fully upright for the first time. It was huge. It spread its wings in a show of aggression and menace that was genuinely terrifying, and advanced on the diminutive figure of the professor, who was, unbelievably, still standing in the middle of the nest.

"Why the hell doesn't he run?" Nick exclaimed, his anger rising.

"Look!" said Annabel, pointing at the creature. "Its wing!"

"What about it?" said Giles, his voice sounding nasal as blood continued to run from his broken nose.

"It's crippled," she said. "Those are flight feathers it's missing! See?"

Nick stared at the outstretched wings and saw that one of them now had whole sections missing. He turned to look at Annabel, then at Giles, who grinned back through bloody teeth.

"Fancy a game of chicken, Nick?"

"Hell yeah!"

*****

Ravi was holding the egg in his arms as the monster loomed above him. Its baleful yellow eyes stared down, feline pupils narrowed in malice. The professor stood rooted to the spot, unable to move, both from wonder and fear. He hadn't expected this. The creature had been breeding. But how was that possible? Unless…

"I've got it, Professor!" yelled Giles.

Ravi turned in time to see the blond figure, rope in hand, sprint past him and duck under the outstretched wing of the startled creature. Ravi caught a glimpse of the headlamp beam bobbing up and down behind the tattered plumage as

Giles, picking up speed, raced for the gap in the balustrade and threw himself from the tower.

"No!" Ravi cried, unable to believe what he had just seen.

There was a moment's silence before the monster was yanked back by the yoke still tied around its neck. It emitted a strangled shriek and Ravi watched in horrid fascination as, claws scratching deep grooves in the leaded roof, the creature was dragged towards the gap where Giles had disappeared seconds before. With a surge of hope, Ravi thought that it too might disappear from view, but then the outstretched wings collided with the buckled steel restraining rods either side of the breach and the monster's momentum ceased. For a few heart-stopping moments, it tottered on the edge of the tower, before its claws finally gained some purchase and it managed to drag itself away from the danger.

Almost immediately, its focus returned to him and what lay in his arms. Ravi knew he had only seconds to act if he was to make it to the stairwell before the creature could drag what he feared was Giles' deadweight after him. Turning, he was about to run across the few treacherous yards of roof space that separated him from the doorway, when he found himself confronted by Annabel and Nick, who stood barring his escape.

"I don't think so, Professor," said Annabel.

"What? I... I don't understand," he stammered, confused.

Nick stepped forward and raised his fist. Ravi flinched, thinking the boy was going to punch him. Instead, Nick drove his fist down between the professor's arms and expertly ripped the egg from his grip. Before Ravi could stop him, Nick had circled the nest and was striding towards the creature.

"You want this?" he asked. "Eh? Do you?"

The creature screeched at him, acknowledging his challenge.

"Fine!" said Nick, not breaking stride. "Then go get it!"

With that, the Redboy winger drew back his arms and threw the egg in a long spiral pass out over Chapel Court. With a deafening screech of panic and distress, the monster pivoted, crouched and leapt from the tower.

There was a long, keening shriek that echoed around the courtyard as the creature dived. The cry rose in pitch as the creature fell, until it was cut short by a thunderous crash far below.

Ravi hurried across to the broken balustrade, stumbling over scattered bones and broken stonework in his haste. Arriving at the gap in the structure, he used a twisted metal rod as support and peered over the edge. He was joined moments later by Nick and Annabel, and the three of them gazed down into the court below. The lights from the library illuminated the little square in front of the entrance, where the remains of a magnificent winged statue lay shattered in its centre.

Ravi looked at the wreckage in disbelief. "It crashed? Why did it not pull up?"

"It was crippled," said Annabel. "Giles broke its flight feathers when fixing the yoke."

Ravi nodded. "Of course, your zoology studies."

"That's why I threw the egg," said Nick. "I thought the mother would try to save it."

"Indeed," said Ravi, studying him. "Ruthless, but effective."

There was a noise behind them, and Ravi turned to see Raquel getting to her feet.

"Giles?" she said, shakily. "Giles?"

Ravi remembered the figure running past him with the rope and leaping from the tower. His stomach lurched as he turned and peered down into the courtyard at the shattered remains of the statue. Tiny figures were converging on the wreckage, some of them pointing at the tangle of ropes still wrapped around the broken torso. And there, lying amidst the stone debris, Ravi saw the flickering beam of a headtorch.

"No," he murmured in disbelief.

"What?"

Ravi turned to see Raquel, pale-faced, stumbling towards him. "It is Giles? Can you see him?"

Annabel moved to intercept her.

"Raquel, please," she said. "You mustn't go there. It's…"

"No!" Raquel moaned. "Not Giles… Not him…"

Tears welled up in her eyes as Annabel reached out and wrapped her in her arms. Raquel began to sob as Ravi stood there helpless, unable to express his feelings of misery and guilt. He felt Nick's arm go around his shoulder, his tall, silent presence an unexpected rock in the storm of emotions he was experiencing.

And then, from somewhere far off, Ravi heard a familiar voice.

"Once more unto the breach, dear friends, once more;
Or close the wall up with our English dead!"

"Giles?" said Nick, releasing Ravi and turning back towards the balustrade. Ravi turned to see him peering down at the tower wall. "Professor, do you have that torch?"

Ravi fumbled in his pocket and retrieved Bert's torch. Drawing alongside Nick, he switched it on and pointed the beam down the side of the tower. Some twenty feet below he caught sight of movement and shone the beam over towards a corner section. There, set into a cornice in the tower wall, was the statue of Lady Margaret, staring out over the court. And clinging to her neck was a familiar figure with a mop of blond hair.

"Professor," said Giles, his battered and bloody face squinting up at them through the bright beam of the torch. "You couldn't pass me down another rope, could you? I seem to have dropped the other one."

Chapter 32

The morning sun shone through a gap in the curtains, tracing a bright line across the floor of the room to the bed where Annabel lay, enjoying its warmth on her face. Her phone beeped from the top of her bedside drawers, and she reached over to peer at the screen. It was six-thirty a.m., the time Annabel usually woke for her morning run with Nick. She wondered whether he would be up for that today. After the events of the previous day, she thought he might want to give it a miss for once. Though with Nick, she never quite knew what he was thinking.

Last night there was a moment on the roof when he looked like he was going to strike the professor, before surprising the old man by ripping the egg from his arms. Then Annabel had watched in disbelief as Nick had hurled it from the roof, tricking the beast into diving to its death and saving them all. She remembered staring at him, standing there amidst the carnage of the Chapel Tower, his face set and his chest heaving. The memory sent a shiver through her and Annabel realised something about Nick that she hadn't appreciated before. However grim things looked, however bad it was, Nick would not yield, whatever the odds.

Annabel swung her legs out of bed and looked across at the photo on her desk. The one that contained the three people who she had cared most about in the world. The ones who had been there for her throughout her life, had supported and cared for her, had shared her moments of joy and laughter, had loved her. Annabel had never imagined them not being there. They had seemed ever-present, indestructible, even. Not so, as it turned out.

All Annabel had now was Gran, and tough as the old woman was, Annabel knew she was not going to be there forever. The last twelve months had been as hard on her grandmother as they had been on her, and Annabel had noticed how much she had aged over that time. The care lines in her skin had become more ingrained, the grey hair whiter, the shoulders more stooped. Annabel didn't want to be a burden to her any more.

Rising from the bed, Annabel washed and dressed quickly, before dragging a brush through her hair and checking herself in the mirror. The young woman who looked back at her was different from the one she had seen reflected in a train window just over a week before. Not whole yet, but not broken either. What did they say about broken bones? Sometimes they grew back stronger?

"We will see," she said.

Annabel left her room and went down the stairwell to Nick's landing. When she reached his door, she paused to take a breath, before knocking three times. Annabel waited in silence but heard no noise coming from the room. A flicker of doubt crossed her mind. Perhaps he had left already for his jog without her?

Frowning, she knocked three times again, her rhythm slow and firm.

"Coming!" came a voice from inside.

Surprised, Annabel stepped away from the door, feeling her heartbeat quicken as she heard the sound of feet padding across the parquet floor. The bolt began turning in the lock, giving her just enough time to pull her shoulders back and compose herself.

The door swung open, and there was Nick, standing in the doorway, naked but for a pair of boxer shorts. Annabel had a moment to register the SpongeBob SquarePants design before dragging her gaze up to his face. Nick's hair stood up at a strange angle, and his half-closed eyes blinked away sleep as they tried to focus on her.

"Hi," he said.

"Hi."

He shifted on his feet. "Sorry, I thought you must be a porter. You know, a fire drill or something."

"No, it's just me."

"Did… did you want to go for a run or something? Only, I thought I might give it a miss this morning."

"Yeah, me too."

He stared at her, confused.

"So," he said, "do you… Do you want to come in?"

"If that's OK?"

"Well, yeah… Yeah, I suppose so."

Nick turned around and padded back into his room. She

noticed the bruising around his shoulder, and the rope burns down his back, some so deep they had drawn blood. Annabel waited a couple of seconds, took a calming breath and followed him in.

The room was dark, but she could make out Nick's pale body as he headed over to the window and drew the curtains back. Light streamed into the room, revealing the unmade bed with its duvet thrown back and crumpled pillow, where he had been sleeping moments before.

"Sorry for the mess," he said, shuffling over to retrieve from the floor the discarded clothes he had been wearing the day before. Annabel moved out of his way and headed over towards his desk, noting the collection of dried rugby socks hanging over the radiator. By the desk lamp there was a stack of law books from the library, next to a photo of a chubby little boy in a school uniform, staring at her with a cheeky grin. From the likeness in the eyes, she guessed it was Nick's brother, though she had never asked him about his family. It wasn't a topic of conversation she had felt comfortable talking about before. With anyone.

"Sorry about that," said Nick.

Annabel looked up from the desk to see him standing over by the wardrobe. Though still barefoot, he now wore a pair of jeans and a T-shirt. Nick had tried to flatten his hair, but it still stood up at a funny angle. It made her smile.

"You wanted to see me?" he asked.

Annabel looked into those open, blue eyes, and for the first time since her family's accident, she felt she had found the person she could trust with her past.

"Nick," she began, "there's something you need to know about me…"

*****

Giles left the Buttery carrying a carton of milk and a paper bag filled with croissants. As he strode across Second Court, the morning breeze tugging at his dressing gown, he glanced up at the Chapel Tower, noting the red-and-white hazard tape that had been strung across the gap in the balustrade.

That's going to take some explaining, he thought to himself as he made his way over the cobbles towards his staircase in the corner. What would Ying and Trevor make of it when they saw the Chapel? Would they suspect he had something to do with it? Not that he could tell them, of course. The professor had sworn each of them to secrecy. Besides, Giles didn't think Ying would believe him without hard evidence. He glanced up again at the tower and remembered the rush as he leapt out into the night sky.

Next time, I'll just have to wear my GoPro, he thought with a grin.

An excited yell came from the direction of Hall. Looking up, Giles saw a large crowd of people spilling out of the passageway wearing yellow tops and red baseball caps. They were led by a tour guide holding up a matching umbrella.

"Well, well," he said, recognising his old friends from Fitzbillies. One or two of the tourists spotted him and began gesticulating enthusiastically. Giles waved back.

"Welcome!" he called out, opening his arms wide. "So good of you to come!"

A gust of wind whipped beneath his dressing gown, causing a mild stir amongst the visitors, followed by the staccato clicking of cameras as the crowd surged towards him. Within seconds he was surrounded by his selfie-seeking mob of admirers.

"Lovely to see you all again!" he said, smiling. "Hope you are enjoying your time in Cambridge. Any sightings of the Duke and Duchess yet? No? A shame…"

Some of the women pointed at his bruised and swollen nose, making "Oh" and "Ah" noises.

"What? This? Oh, girl trouble, I'm afraid." He shook his head sadly. "Was never going to last. She dumped me last night."

More "Oh" and "Ah" noises followed, as his comments were translated by the guide.

"Still, can't be helped, these things happen. The lovely lady was pretty cut up about it in the end. I don't think we'll be seeing each other again."

More sympathetic noises followed, and Giles felt the pressure build as the crowd closed in, many of the women trying to pat him consolingly. Realising he had perhaps overdone this one, he attempted to edge his way closer to his stairwell, but was blocked by the tightly packed rows of well-wishers commiserating and offering advice in a language he couldn't understand.

"Sorry, must be leaving now," he tried. "Important meeting. Thank you for your concern…"

By the time he reached the first step of his staircase, with no let-up in their persistence, it had dawned on him that the crowd might be under the impression that he would be leading them on a tour of his room. By the expectant look of their upturned faces, they seemed eager to experience this unique behind-the-scenes insight into student life.

That was when he spotted the distant figures of Nick and Annabel arriving in Second Court from the Bridge of Sighs heading towards the Buttery.

"Perfect timing," he said to himself with a grin.

Standing on tiptoes, he pointed above the throng of heads at the two freshers on the far side of the court, his eyes wide.

"I can't believe it! You're in luck! Guess who's just popped into college?"

A few heads turned. Giles began to wave.

"Yoo-hoo!"

Nick spotted him and nudged Annabel, who looked over in his direction. Giles waved again as more of the crowd began turning their heads to look at the tall blond boy with the dark-haired girl at his side. Giles muttered under his breath.

"Come on, you two, come on…"

He gave one more enthusiastic wave, and just as he thought they might let him down, Annabel gave a self-conscious wave back. Giles beamed.

"Yes, yes! It's them!" he said excitedly. "Fancy that. William and Kate! What a surprise!"

A few faces still looked up at him, confused, but the rest were craning their necks as they looked at the young couple across the court.

"There they are," Giles announced, trying to keep a straight face. "The Duke and Duchess of Cambridge, here to visit his old college!"

The last heads turned, and a murmur grew amongst the crowd. It started as a low rumble and built in intensity, becoming louder and more animated as the excitement grew. Giles stood behind them, waving his hands like a conductor, building his orchestra to a crescendo until finally they broke like a tsunami and began streaming across the courtyard towards the open-mouthed couple.

"Brilliant!" laughed Giles, springing up another couple of steps for a better view. He saw Nick ushering Annabel protectively towards the Buttery entrance as she looked over the heads of the approaching mob in his direction. Giles bowed like a royal courtier and was rewarded with a scowl that made him laugh even more before she and Nick disappeared through the opening with the crowd hot on their heels.

Chuckling to himself, Giles took the steps two at a time until he reached his landing, where he tucked the milk carton under one arm while he ran fingers through his hair. Then he opened the inner door and crept into his room.

"Giles?" came Raquel's sleepy voice. "Is that you?"

"*Sí, el meu amor*," he replied and closed the door behind him.

*****

The figure sitting at the top of the stairwell was wrapped in a thick North Face parka. She watched Giles shut the door and sat there quietly, listening to the sound of his bare feet padding down the slight incline in his room towards the corner bed. She remained motionless for some time, staring at the door. Then the woman rose to her feet and, stepping silently across the landing, gently shut the outer door to Giles' room with her pink mittens. She paused to make sure she had not been heard, before descending the stairwell, expertly avoiding any creaky boards.

At the same time, on the other side of Second Court, Ravi sat in his study, looking at an assortment of items spread out on his desk. He had left the Master's Lodge early that morning after some of the most uncomfortable hours of his life. The Master had been livid that Ravi had defied his express instructions and tackled the creature on his own, endangering the lives of the others as well. When Ravi had described the discovery of an egg and its subsequent destruction along with the mother, he saw the Master's flushed face lose all of its colour.

"It laid an egg?"

"Apparently, yes."

"And you destroyed it?"

"We did, Master."

Then the Master had said something that had chilled Ravi to his core.

"So, there is no way of reconstructing it? From the remains, I mean?"

"No, Master. There is not. Once they lose their life force, their bodies crumble to dust."

It was true. Overnight, the shattered remains of the

creature and its offspring had already begun to disintegrate, the fragments scattered in a light grey cloud by the squall that swirled around Chapel Court before the storm clouds finally broke. In the subsequent deluge, any lingering traces were washed away into the drains and sewers that ran beneath the college.

The Master studied him for a long while, but Ravi returned his gaze, unmoved. He now knew that the Master would have sought to recover the egg rather than destroy it. For that, Ravi had Nick to thank. It was the boy who had snatched the egg from his grasp and used it to trick the creature into diving to its death. Part of Ravi could still not understand why he had not done so himself. Why, on seeing the egg, he had felt compelled to rescue rather than destroy it. That worried him. Worried him deeply. Robert had fallen under the spell of this other world and, for a second time, so too had Ravi.

"Some things are best left buried," he said, as much to reassure himself as the Master.

As for covering up what had really happened that night, the well-oiled College Critical Incident Plan had been deployed. An announcement had been sent out to the Fellows and students, which, as expected, had immediately been fed through to the press. It explained that part of the Chapel Tower had collapsed before the storm. No significant damage had been done to surrounding buildings, other than an impact crater in the paving stones of Chapel Court. The college had been fortunate that no one had been walking through the courtyard when the masonry had fallen.

Thankfully, that early in the term, few students had been interested in visiting the library on a Saturday evening.

By the next morning, when the press cameras arrived, there was so little evidence left to see that there was no reason to doubt the story. The gap in the tower's balustrade, now sealed off by hazard tape, was clear for all to see from the ground. The Master was quick to reassure the journalists that a structural survey had already been commissioned by the Domestic Bursar. A more observant reporter might have noticed that the size of the impact crater suggested something more substantial had fallen, but Peter and the other gardeners had already begun work on filling it in.

The remains on the roof of the Chapel Tower had been retrieved by a special forensic team supervised by Jane, minus the jacket belonging to Alfonso Vidal, which Raquel had taken with her. After what she had seen that night, Raquel did not seem inclined to pursue the matter further. She had clung to Giles as they had descended the tower and had stayed with him after Ravi had gone to debrief the Master. Nick and Annabel had offered to accompany him to the Master's Lodge, but he had told them to return to their rooms. If statements were needed, Ravi would let them know. For the moment, he had asked them not to breathe a word to anyone, not even Annabel's grandmother, who was probably concerned enough about her as it was. They had readily agreed, Nick, in particular, seeming glad to avoid any unwanted attention.

That just left Ravi, sitting here looking at the assortment of items on his desk. These included his old metal ruler,

Bert's torch and two faded scarves, one in the college colours and the other a Cambridge Blue. He had retrieved Robert's from his room after leaving the Master's Lodge in the early hours. Ravi suspected his friend's apartment would shortly be reclassified as a crime scene. Tracing his hand over it, he felt for the torn piece of paper that had been sewn inside. There was a similar one inside his own. Julian must have seen both scarves in his search of their rooms and not suspected that what he was seeking lay within.

Using the point of the old ruler, Ravi carefully unpicked Robert's scarf and retrieved the item which had been kept safe in an oiled silk pouch, before doing the same with his own. He matched both pieces of paper together, the two halves joining seamlessly, even after all these years. Reaching into his desk, he took a sheet of writing paper and wrote a short letter, which he signed and dated. After carefully folding the note, Ravi inserted it with the reunited pieces inside a manila envelope. Sealing it, he slipped the package inside his jacket pocket. Next, Ravi picked up the ruler and studied it, turning the blade over in his hand, before sliding it into another jacket pocket. Finally, Ravi took the scarves and laid them carefully in an old Heffers bag with Bert's torch.

Pushing himself back from the desk, he picked up the bag and headed for the doorway, stepping over dried coffee and tea stains on the rug. Then he descended the winding stairwell, past the Old Library entrance to the ground floor.

As he crossed Second Court, Ravi glanced up at the Chapel Tower and the hazard tape fluttering in the breeze.

He thought about those desperate moments on the roof and felt an involuntary shudder at how close they had come to disaster. It had been a close-run thing. Too close. It was time to make sure nothing like that ever happened again.

A few minutes later he entered the Porter's Lodge and was greeted by a bleary-eyed Bert.

"Morning, Professor."

"Good morning, Bert," said Ravi. "I have something to return to you."

He reached inside the bag, retrieved the torch and handed it across the counter.

"That's very good of you, Professor," said Bert. "I hope it came in useful."

"You have no idea," said Ravi, placing the plastic bag on the counter. "I have another favour to ask of you, if I may?"

"Go right ahead, Professor. That's what we're here for."

"I'm afraid I have a couple of old scarves here where the stitching has come away." He removed them from the bag and showed Bert. "I'm rather fond of them, you see, and with winter coming on, it would be good to get them repaired."

Bert inspected the scarves and checked the labels, pausing when he saw Robert Mackenzie's name on the light blue one.

"I see," he said, glancing at Ravi. "While I would normally recommend you take them to Ryder and Amies, as a mark of respect for Professor Mackenzie, why don't I get my Sue to do it for you, Professor?"

"That would be most kind," said Ravi. "Are you sure that it's not too much trouble?"

"Not at all, Professor. I'm sure the missus would be delighted to do it for you."

"That's very kind of you. Thank you, Bert."

"Like I say, Professor. We look after our own."

Ravi left the Porter's Lodge and headed back through college for his last task that morning. He had just emerged from the passageway between the kitchens and Hall when a voice called out to him.

"Hello, Professor."

He turned sharply, his hand instinctively reaching for the ruler in his jacket pocket. A figure was standing at the bottom of Giles' staircase.

"Jane?" he said, not recognising the voice.

The former waitress walked towards him, wrapped in her long dark coat, her peroxide hair blowing in the breeze.

"I have a message for you," she said.

"From whom, exactly?" asked Ravi, keeping his hand there.

"Cummings."

A wave of relief washed over him.

"How is he?" he said. "I was hoping I might visit him today."

"That will not be possible, I'm afraid," she replied. "He's been moved to another facility."

"Is that a good thing?" he asked.

"It was necessary. Too many journalists asking too many questions," she explained, before adding, "Though, Mrs Hamilton did a pretty good job of chasing most of them away."

Ravi smiled. "I can imagine."

"Cummings asked me to say thank you," continued Jane. "Thank you? For what?"

"For finishing it." She paused. "It is finished, isn't it, Professor?"

Ravi looked at her. "It will be, Jane, yes."

"Good," she said, her eyes never leaving his.

"I won't see him again, will I?" said Ravi. "Cummings, I mean."

"No, Professor, you won't."

He nodded.

"Then please give him my best wishes. And my thanks."

"I will," she said, and held out a mittened hand. "Goodbye, Professor."

Ravi took it.

"Goodbye, Jane."

She smiled and cocked her head to one side. For a moment, he caught a glimpse of the waitress again, before she turned and clacked her way past the college kitchens for the last time.

As her footsteps receded, Ravi remembered Mrs Hamilton and wondered where the old lady was now. He turned to ask Jane if she knew, but he found that the passageway was now empty and, as far as he could tell, so was First Court.

Jane, he realised, was gone.

Ravi stood there as the wind whistled through the gap and out into the court, carrying traces of fine dust and sending a chill down his neck. Reaching for his scarf, he remembered it was no longer there, and his thoughts returned to Robert. He was gone too. And for the first time since he had been a fresher all those years ago, Ravi felt strangely alone. It was an unsettling feeling and one that he did not want to dwell on. So, with a resolve he vowed would never waver again, he focused back on the one remaining task he had to do that morning and continued on his way.

On entering Chapel Court, he found a group of students gathered around the taped-off area in its centre, peering at the crater with its cracked and damaged paving stones. Amongst them was a scruffy-looking type with a goatee and a dark pea coat, carrying a notebook and pen. He glanced up and studied the professor as he walked around the edge of the court towards the library entrance. When Ravi reached the revolving door, he looked back and saw the boy take a long drag on a cigarette before flicking it dismissively in the air.

Ravi was about to say something but decided against it. He had more important matters to attend to and didn't want to draw undue attention to himself. Pushing open the cumbersome revolving door, he stepped into the lobby, where Mr Weston greeted him from behind the reception desk.

"Good morning, Professor."

"Good morning, Mr Weston."

Then a thought occurred to him.

"Oh, Mr Weston, I just saw a student smoking outside your library entrance. You might want to remind him that we are a no-smoking college."

Mr Weston stepped around the counter.

"I certainly shall, Professor. Thank you for letting me know."

Feeling somewhat better, Ravi crossed the lobby and entered the exhibition area. From there he made his way to the basement of the Old Library, where he found the college's two archivists sitting behind their desks as always, only this time they were in deep conversation.

"Morning, ladies," he said.

"Morning, professor," they replied. "Have you heard about the Chapel Tower?"

"What about it?"

"Some masonry fell off last night in the storm. It's a wonder no one was killed."

"A wonder indeed," he said, signing himself into the register and passing through the two glass fire doors to enter the lower archive. Walking between the overflowing bookcases, he approached the oriel window overlooking the river and began climbing the wrought-iron spiral staircase to the Old Library, his shoes ringing on the intricately designed steps.

At the top, he was greeted by the marble bust of John Couch Adams, Professor of Astronomy 1858–1892, who stared impassively down at him. Next to Adams, in a glass cabinet, was the life mask of William Wordsworth, his closed eyelids giving the impression that the great man was fast asleep. Ravi nodded to each, as was his custom, and, turning left, began walking down the length of the cavernous room.

He continued along the spine of central display cabinets between the ribcage of antique bookcases, covered in parchment and leather. Sun streamed in through the south-facing windows, filtered by the heavy UV blinds that hung above their arched frames. The hessian carpet muffled the sound of his shoes as he neared the former entrance at the far end, but the old joists and floorboards that creaked under his weight gave away his position to the archivists now below him, just as he intended.

Ravi paused there for several minutes, patiently inspecting the intricately carved coat of arms of Bishop John Williams on the wall above him, before returning down the other side of the central displays, passing Hoyle's highly polished brass telescope, until he came to the last alcove on the north side. There he paused and stared out through the leaded window towards the Master's Lodge and its lush green lawn, where only a week before, a winged statue had stood in shadow, its presence announced by thunder and lightning.

With a sigh, Ravi reached inside his jacket pocket and retrieved the manila envelope. On its cover, he had written the college motto, *Souvent me souvient*, in spidery handwriting.

"Often I remember," he murmured out loud, before shaking his head. There were some things he did not want to remember. Reaching out with his hand, he traced his finger gently down the ornately carved bookcase.

Five minutes later Ravi walked back through the lobby. Mr Weston was once again behind the counter.

"Seems you have caused quite a stir, Professor," he said as Ravi walked past.

Ravi stopped and gave him a sharp look. "I'm sorry?"

"Turns out your smoker wasn't one of ours, but a student reporter from The Tab."

Ravi relaxed. "Oh? I see."

"Though he didn't take too kindly at being told not to smoke. Referred to me as a right-wing fascist defending a bastion of privilege. At least I think that's what he said as the porters escorted him out. Nice turn of phrase, mind you. Should make a good journalist."

"I'm sorry to put you to any trouble, Mr Weston."

"Sticks and stones, Professor. Sticks and stones."

After leaving the library, Ravi intended to head back to his room, but as he entered Second Court, he caught a whiff of bacon on the breeze, and his eye was drawn to the entrance to the Buttery in the opposite corner. An image of a robust and proud woman came to him, spatula in hand, and he felt his blood grow warm despite the cold. Not entirely alone, perhaps. Adjusting his jacket, Ravi limped across the court, his jaw set and a glowing ember of hope in his heart.

Epilogue

Alfonso's eyes blinked open and he saw stars twinkling above him in the dark. He lay there for a few moments, pain throbbing in his temples as he tried to recall where he was. His thoughts were fuzzy, as if he had been sleeping for some time. The last thing he remembered was heading into Portugal Street on his way home and hearing a noise behind him. Then everything had gone blank.

Alfonso remembered being alarmed, frightened even, but beyond that he could only remember the sound of the wind rushing over him. Had he passed out? Or been attacked? Was that where he was now, lying in the alleyway, staring up at the heavens? Was that why his back felt so sore?

"*Merda*," he groaned and turned his head to get his bearings.

But there were no buildings around him. Instead, all he could see were more stars, tiny pinpricks of light shining back from all around him. Alfonso craned his stiff neck and realised with a shock that the stars seemed to be beneath him as well. He closed his eyes. This couldn't be right. He was imagining it. He couldn't be suspended amongst the stars –

that wasn't possible. Not unless… Unless he was in heaven.

Tentatively, Alfonso opened his eyes again and, sure enough, the stars were still there, staring back at him as if willing him to believe the truth of what he was seeing. He thought back to that moment in the alleyway and remembered something that made him gasp out loud. The wings! Those huge, pale wings that had swept towards him, moments before he was plucked from the earth.

"*Angel de la mort!*" he cried out, as it finally dawned on him that he was no longer on earth but was genuinely amongst the stars!

Alfonso lay there, his heart racing as he tried to come to terms with this revelation. But as he did so, a doubt formed in his mind. If this was, well, heaven, why did it feel so real? The ground felt hard under his body, and as he tried to rise, he groaned as pain erupted across his back and shoulders where the angel had grabbed him.

Alfonso looked down at his legs, and he could see from the pale light of the stars that he was still wearing the black trousers of his waiter's uniform, and his white shirt, crumpled and torn in places. His leather jacket, though, was nowhere to be seen.

It was while he was looking around to see if it was lying somewhere near that Alfonso saw the light in the distance.

"Aha!" he said, beginning to understand what was going on. He wasn't in heaven at all. The reason that his aches, pains and torn clothing all felt so real was that he hadn't passed over yet! What was it they all said? Walk towards the light? And there it was, at the end of the passageway!

Ignoring the stab of pain from his back and shoulders, Alfonso pushed himself up from the floor and struggled to his feet. For a moment or two he stood there, not trusting himself to move, as the stars swirled around him. Then as his sense of balance returned, he focused his eyes on the light in the distance and began, one step at a time, to walk towards it.

Progress was slow at first, but as his muscles lost their initial stiffness, he settled into a comfortable rhythm and was able to increase his pace, feeling a sense of excitement as well as serenity growing as he neared his final destination. His thoughts drifted back to his family, their hopes and dreams and concerns about the future of Catalonia. The Catalan struggle for independence seemed so petty now when, like him, you could walk amongst the stars and see what an insignificant part mankind must play in the cosmos. Alfonso thought about his sister and wondered what she would do now that he was gone. She would come looking for him, of course, and take his body back home to be buried alongside the others in the family plot. But then what? Would she continue the armed struggle, or would she settle down and have a family of her own? A boy, perhaps, named after her brother? Either way, he hoped that Raquel would find what she wanted and, if not, would find a greater peace, as he hoped to do now.

But peace seemed to be taking quite a long time to find, Alfonso thought as he tramped down the passageway, breathing harder now. It seemed to him that the closer he came to the light, the warmer the tunnel became, and he found himself using the arm of his shirt to wipe sweat from his brow. It wasn't exactly purgatory, but he was certainly having to work for his place in the sun.

Using his hand to shield his eyes against the intense glare, Alfonso peered ahead and could just make out what he thought was the end of the passageway. The dark walls converged on a wide aperture framing the source of the light, and despite its intensity, he thought he saw a figure standing to one side of the opening, waiting for him. Alfonso felt a surge of excitement and, ignoring the fatigue in his limbs, he strode forward once again, eager to meet the guardian to the place beyond.

As his eyes adjusted to the light, Alfonso saw that the figure was bathed in sunshine, its features hidden beneath the cowl of a garment with long arms and flowing folds gathered at the waist by what appeared to be a belt of rope. The gatekeeper leant on a staff, much like a shepherd waiting for one of his flock, studying him from the depths of his hood.

"*Deu meu!*" breathed Alfonso as he approached the figure, his pace slowing to a hesitant, stumbling walk, as he realised that he was seconds away from the most important moment of his life, or death, or whatever this was. It was time for all those things he had done since birth, all the good, the bad, the worthy, the shameful, to be weighed and balanced before judgement was given. The enormity of what was about to happen almost overwhelmed Alfonso. He fell to his knees in the shadow of the passageway and bowed his head before the one person who would truly know him and decide his fate.

Alfonso waited in silence, his heart hammering in his chest. Sweat trickled from his eyebrows and down his nose before dripping with a slow, steady rhythm onto the red earth beneath his knees. He felt a breeze kiss his cheek and heard the rustle of cloth as it swirled gently around the person standing over him. Still he waited, not daring to move, to speak, to even breathe, for what did that matter now?

Finally, he heard a deep sigh and he knew in his heart that the moment had arrived.

"Ravi?"

Alfonso froze. What was that? Was it a judgement? If it was, he wasn't sure what it meant. Maybe it was another language? Hebrew, perhaps? What should he do now? Could he, should he, ask for clarification?

"Ravi? Is it you?"

The voice sounded strange. Not what he had expected at all. It was high-pitched, when he had expected something deep and sonorous. It sounded more like...

"I said, is it you, Ravi?"

Alfonso felt something rough and hard reach under his chin and lift his face up. He saw it was the shepherd's staff, held by two leathery brown hands that had appeared from under the folds of the long sleeves. Alfonso looked along the length of the gnarled and twisted shaft and found himself gazing into a face that was still partially hidden in the shadow of the cowl. But even in that light, there was no mistaking the pale blue eyes staring back at him from the darkness with an intensity that would have made him look away, but for

440

the staff forcing him to maintain eye contact.

"I am sorry," he stammered. "I do not understand."

"Shit!" said the voice, as the staff was yanked away.

Alfonso dropped his head in shock and bewilderment. That was a word he did understand, but coming as it did from this person, at this moment? It just didn't make sense to him. Mind racing, he raised his head enough to get another look at the figure standing above him. The wrinkled hands, leaning on the staff for support, suggested the person was old. The head was bowed, staring at the earth, apparently lost in thought.

"I am sorry if I have disappointed you," he said.

The head looked up and surveyed him but said nothing.

This wasn't going how Alfonso thought it should, so he tried again.

"Forgive me, but I do not know who you are?"

The figure remained motionless, staring at him, and Alfonso waited, not knowing what else to say or do. Eventually the strange voice spoke.

"My name is Mary."

"Mary?" he breathed, crossing himself. "*Mare de Deu!*"

The cackle that followed was so harsh and unexpected that Alfonso winced. The woman, for that was what she was, bent over double, leaning on her staff for support as she continued to laugh, shaking her head back and forth, braying like an old donkey. He looked on wide-eyed, unable to believe what he was witnessing, until eventually she regained control of herself and stared down at him, her head cocked to one side.

"No, you fool. I'm not *that* Mary. Heaven forbid it!" She snorted again.

"Then what is this... Ravi?" asked Alfonso.

"Not what, but who? He's the worthless piece of shit who abandoned me here. Him and that ape, Robert."

"I don't understand – abandoned you *here?*" said Alfonso, looking around at the landscape for the first time. In the distance he could see the sheer-sided red cliffs surrounding the wide valley with its giant columns jutting up from the meandering riverbed far below. It was strikingly beautiful, impressive even, but not what he had expected. "This... This is not heaven?"

"Heaven?" cried the woman, breaking into another fit of laughter that sounded harsher and more manic than before. When she finally finished, her pale eyes stared at him with unconcealed contempt.

"This isn't heaven. This is a living hell. One that I've been waiting to share with my old friends Robert and Ravi. But it looks like my messengers brought back the wrong guest."

Alfonso didn't understand. Perhaps it was his English. But before he could ask what she meant, the woman had begun tramping down the slope, leaning on her staff for support. Alfonso looked from her to the surrounding landscape, and it was only then that he noticed the second sun dipping beyond the far horizon.

"*Mon Deu!*" he breathed as long shadows stretched over the slope, covering the whole escarpment in darkness.

"He's not going to help you here, I'm afraid. I doubt he

even knows this world exists," the old woman called over her shoulder. "It's just you and me for the moment. Oh, and my children, of course. Bring him, girls!"

Alfonso heard the beating of wings overhead. Twisting, he looked up in time to see a pair of angels, swooping down from the darkening sky, their talons reaching out towards him.

GET THREE FREE
SHORT STORIES FROM
CAMBRIDGE GOTHIC

If you enjoyed *College of Shadows* and would like to learn more about the fantasy world of *Cambridge Gothic,* sign up to my mailing list, and I'll also send you three **free stories**:

1. *Come Out to Play* - a creepy encounter for Ying and Trevor from their first term as Freshers.

2. *A Late Arrival* - a chilling tale set in the Cambridge admissions week.

3. *A Poisoned Chalice* - a prequel involving Alfonso, Raquel and their family in Mallorça.

To receive your three stories **for free,** and other exclusive content, sign up to the *Cambridge Gothic* mailing list on my website www.marknwells.com

DID YOU ENJOY THIS BOOK?
LET PEOPLE KNOW

Reviews are the most effective way of building awareness of a series you have enjoyed. While I'd love to tell more people about *Cambridge Gothic*, the most effective way to do that is through a committed and loyal group of readers. Honest reviews help bring my books to the attention of other readers.

So, if you have enjoyed *College of Shadows*, I would really appreciate it if you would spend just a few minutes leaving a review (it can be as short as you like) on the book's page.

Many thanks,

Mark

CAMBRIDGE GOTHIC BOOK 2
GATE OF SHADOWS

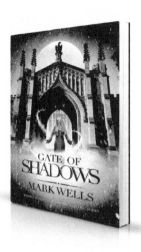

A mystic portal lies open. A chilling predator stalks the night. Can an undaunted student stop the darkness from spreading?

Giles Chamberlain returns to a snowbound Cambridge after Christmas spent with his girlfriend. Determined to prove himself to her family, he sets out to discover what became of her missing brother. But when he encounters a sinister figure prowling the college's rooftops, he suspects last semester's creature was not the only entity to cross into our world.

After the tight-lipped Professor Gupta refuses his plea for help, Giles enlists his feuding friends to locate the otherworldly passage. As hunters and hunted converge on the portal, the students discover just how far the old academic will go to keep his secret safe.

Faced with forces beyond his imagination, can Giles conjure up the key to save them all?

Gate of Shadows is the spine-tingling second book in the Cambridge Gothic fantasy trilogy. If you like resourceful heroes, nail-biting action, and atmospheric settings, then you'll love Mark Wells's page-turning tale.

Buy *Gate of Shadows* to ward off the darkness today!

ABOUT THE AUTHOR

Mark Wells read law at Cambridge University and after a career in business returned to his old college as a Bursar and Fellow. He has published short stories for Games Workshop's Black Library under the pen name Nicholas Alexander, and is currently writing two new fantasy series set in and around the UK:

- *Cambridge Gothic* follows the fortunes of Nick, Annabel, Giles and Professor Gupta as they battle dark forces converging on their beloved college. For more details visit www.marknwells.com

- *The Hidden Tales* is a series of illustrated children's books funded by the Arts Council of England where readers visit museums, solve puzzles and decipher codes to outwit the sinister Keeper and rescue the mysterious Hidden from the World of Secrets. For more details visit www.hiddentales.co.uk

Mark lives in Cambridge with his family, and can be found wandering its ancient courts and passageways. Plotting...

You can follow Mark on:

Facebook www.facebook.com/markwellsauthor/

Instagram www.instagram.com/marknwells/

Or you can email him at mark@marknwells.com

ACKNOWLEDGEMENTS

My thanks to all who have helped with the publication of this book:

To my amazing editorial team, Philippa, David and Claire, for your sound advice.

To Hugo, Daniel, Polly, Stephen, Jolanta, Claire, Melendra, Miaoyue, Sam and Carrie for your help and encouragement.

Made in the USA
Las Vegas, NV
26 April 2023

71152895R00267